ASSUMPTION OF RISK

JIM SILVER

SIMON & SCHUSTER

New York • London • Toronto • Sydney • Tokyo • Singapore

SIMON & SCHUSTER
Rockefeller Center
1230 Avenue of the Americas
New York, NY 10020

SIMON & SCHUSTER and colophon are registered trademarks
of Simon & Schuster Inc.

Designed by Irving Perkins Associates, Inc.
Manufactured in the United States of America

1   3   5   7   9   10   8   6   4   2

Library of Congress Cataloging-in-Publication Data
Silver, Jim.
Assumption of risk / Jim Silver.
p.   cm.
1. Insurance investigators—United States—Fiction.
2. Serial murders—United States—Fiction.   I. Title.
PS3569.I466A9   1996
813'.54—dc20   95-33450
CIP
ISBN 0-684-81130-8

ACKNOWLEDGMENTS

The acknowledgment to a first-time work can be dangerous. You're tasked with thanking everyone, knowing the while that you have to be forgetting someone. I apologize to those who think they are in the latter category. Any slight was sincerely unintentional, and I thank you.

There are some people who must be mentioned specifically because of the debt I owe them. A few are foremost in my mind and in my heart.

First, thanks to Lynn Thomson, a terrific writer in her own right/rite/write, who really should take this ride, too. Without her passion, cajoling, sympathy, criticism, and shared labor pains, *Assumption of Risk* would have been stillborn. She's a pushy broad who was the first ever to see the potential in what was just a story for me. She put an end to my procrastination by delivering an old battle-scarred Smith-Corona judiciously on top of my right foot, underscoring that assault with the challenge, "Now you don't have an excuse." Thanks, Lynn, for more than you know, but I suspect really do. We've shared a lot over these years. And thanks as well for the boot in the butt.

Second, I thank Kevin Parsons, Ph.D., of Armament Systems and Procedures, Inc. You meet some interesting people in the E&O racket, which is how I came to know Kevin. He volunteered invaluable time and descriptions of some technical aspects of the story, but his enthusiasm for the project was uppermost. With his permission, I gave him a cameo in the story. Both inside these pages and without, he is the only for-real person described. Indeed, he is that and more. He "knew some people in the publishing business," and he offered, early on, to send a copy of the manuscript to them. He didn't bother to mention who they were. And he delivered on his offer—in spades. Some people! Thanks, Kev, for your support, belief, and excitement through all of this. (Looks like Les Baer's come the closest, huh?)

Next, my thanks to Dave "Da Blindman" MacKnight, a pretty good blues guitar player and a PC whiz. He has saved me from my computer ineptitude more than once, and he has given of his time, expertise, and patience far beyond what any sane person, let alone any friend, ought to have. He was always there, literally day or night. Thanks, brother, but words alone won't do, not entirely. I have something else in mind that might. We've a few more tunes to play together, you and I.

Damon Cecil, ex–Cobra gunship pilot and friend, also deserves my thanks. He offered to print up the original manuscript, based on nothing more than a shared history. Like me, Damon was a silver medalist in the Southeast Asian Games a couple of decades ago. He struggled with an antiquated Wordstar program to turn out a gem of a finished product. Then he reviewed and edited some flight scenes, correcting some inaccuracies. The best part is, that dance isn't over yet. Stick around, Damon, and thank you again.

Darrell Noga, a Dallas-Ditka fan by way of Chicago, waded in with hands and feet, fine-tuning the publishing contract and clarifying all of those details until all of us were satisfied. I've dealt with lawyers for eighteen years in this business and can honestly count the ones I respect and call friend on one hand. Darrell is one of them. But the truth of our relationship is deeper. He's the only one who appreciates the nuances of ordering cheese pizza at the Plaza Hotel and driving golf balls off the roof into Central Park. Yo, Darrell! Excellent, dude!

I also thank Michael Korda, my editor at Simon & Schuster and main man. He's proof that powerball odds can strike over the telephone. He has vision few can imagine, and damn fewer still can touch. Thank you, Michael, sincerely, for the chance. And thanks to Cheryl, Chuck, Rebecca, Carol (the new kid on the block), and the rest of the family in New York.

Finally, thanks to Frank Schnorbus, my Advanced Comp teacher, and Jim Weidner, my high school sophomore English teacher. Thirty years ago they both showed me the magic in words. At least Jim will get a chance to see what I've done with that look.

DEDICATION

Dedications are traditionally personal in nature, so I submit the following:

To my wife, Ginny, who gave me the time, sometimes reluctantly but always out of love, to let me do this thing. I know it was hard, girl, but here we are. Who knew, huh? I love you, always more than yesterday, but never more than tomorrow.

To my children, Terri, Sarah, Matt, Dave, and Alex, who more than a few times asked, "Where's Dad? Oh . . . *typing* again." They may not understand the why of it for a while, but they'll sure see the result. I love you guys, always.

Next, to the unsung Mark Alexanders out there, the John and Jane Doe insurance adjusters who put in their time in the trenches handling claims. They're the ones so maligned by ambulance-chasing commercials and misrepresented almost completely by television and movie stereotypes as some sort of Banacek characters. They wish they had a nickel for every claimant who cried, "Where's my check?!," and every insured who, having never read the policy, threatened suit over something clearly excluded, or whose great, dented, rolling, rusted-out American Dream was not repaired with brand-new parts. (D'ya know how much money I put into that thing . . . ?) The hours are horrendous, the one-on-one with human tragedy and greed intense, and burnout is part of the job description. They do the job when it counts, and the public never knows what they go through. This one, in every sense, is for you guys and girls.

Luther wouldn't exist without my having gone through the PTSD outreach program at the Phoenix Vet Center. He is me, built from my experiences, and he is also the men who went back in country with me, while we all sat on couches and chairs, letting the wounds bleed, then heal. Luther came back once on the Freedom Bird, as we all did, then again years later, when he got his life back. Some of us are still making the journey. Some never came back.

To Ken and Don, who took us into the minefields one more time; to Joe, who walked point for us, and still does; and to the Group: Paul, Jack, Dave, John, Russ, Kerry, Doc, Cowboy, M.W., and Spanky; and to all still out on ops, heading back to the wire. Welcome home.

And finally . . .

To my mother, Mary C. Silver, for letting her dreamer keep his head out the window, as hard as I know it was then, because I have a few dreamers of my own now. All she's ever wanted is for us kids to be happy. Well, Mom, I am, really. This is *unreal!*

And to my father, David S. Silver, Cdr., U.S.N. (Aviation-Retired), 1919–1992. I didn't cry, did I, Dad?

PROLOGUE: FEBRUARY 1, 1990, ROUTE I-80, EAST OF SHARON, PENNSYLVANIA

Clancy Wilburn had blown out of Cape May, New Jersey, headed for Toledo, Ohio, with twenty tons of frozen bay shrimp. An owner-operator of his own rig, Clancy had leased his outfit to California/North Carolina Express. Seven miles south of Allentown, Pennsylvania, the differential on his eight-year-old Freightliner had decided without warning to self-destruct.

He'd spent a day and a half in rapidly escalating frustration as the local road warriors gutted his rig and put it back together. Now back on the road seventeen hours behind schedule, Wilburn was pounding across upper Pennsylvania, nearing the Ohio state line. He was running out of time, profits, and temper. At 78 miles an hour on I-80 at 2:00 A.M., temper was the last thing he needed to be short of.

The high for the day had been an unusual and decidedly pre-spring-like forty-six degrees. Daylight had offered clear skies while the plowed slush decorating the shoulders of the interstate melted.

This anomaly had disappeared with the sun, though, leaving behind a killer condition known as black ice, the day-long melt-off that trickled back onto the surface of the highway to freeze again when temperatures slid down the scale.

By 2:00 A.M. the ambient temperature was ten degrees, and a quarter-mile-long section of I-80 was like glass, silently waiting.

The Freightliner, burning its high beams to pave the way, hit the ice at the bottom of a 200-yard gradual rise to the left and started to float.

Clancy's fuming temper instantly cooled. The professional side of his brain told him things were bad right now. The human side threw his heart rate into overdrive as adrenaline rushed through the gates. Both sides succeeded in slowing his reactions a split second, which locked the hurtling rig into an irreversible counterclockwise slide.

In a dangerous situation, experience can sometimes save you, but it can also impart an awful knowledge. The impartial side of him factored all the possibilities even as the body started trying to change what was already going to happen. His experience kept his foot off the brake. In the final analysis, however, it didn't matter.

In less time than it took him to blink, Clancy's brain completed its calculations, recognized the inevitable, and quietly announced to the body that he was about to die. With these conditions, and at this speed, there was no other possibility.

As the sliding rig began to jackknife, the tractor cocked to the right, the trailer to the left, trying to turn the other way. The heavier mass of the trailer pushed the tractor before it, arcing diagonally across both lanes of traffic.

The left front wheels of the trailer and the left rear duals of the tractor struck the frozen shoulder of the median strip. Dirt, mud, snow, and bits of concrete exploded in a shower of debris as the rig separated at the fifth wheel. The trailer continued its momentum, swinging, then spinning to the left before flipping over, collapsing part of the aluminum-skin sidewall, spewing tons of cargo boxes across the median.

Sliding down into the middle of the median, the disintegrating mass hurtled back up and out into the oncoming lanes before grinding to a halt.

Clancy, propelled inside the cab, operated on instinct. As the horizon swept past in a blinding kaleidoscope of flashes and blackness, he felt the tractor separate from the trailer. In the same horrible instant the tractor flipped to the left and Clancy's last living sight was the ice and the dead darkened grass of the median slamming up to meet him.

The windshield blew out from the crushing force, whipping like a bent playing card into the dark. Parts of the cab broke off, smashed into the ground, and spun off across the roadway. The driver's side door was ripped from the frame, and Clancy was partially ejected.

10

He was caught by the upper sill as the mass of steel, fiberglass, and rubber thundered down.

The rolling tomb reached the other side of the freeway, rose up the embankment several yards before grinding to a stop, then toppled over and crashed to a final rest on the shoulder.

For 450 feet behind it a cruelly cutting diagonal marked the destruction trail of the rig, testimony to the awesome power that could be unleashed by a moment of stupidity. The originator of that careless disregard now lay in a jumble of flesh and fiberglass at the edge of the concrete ribbon, no longer aware that there was yet one more tragedy to be played out as a result of his error.

George Kersten approached the accident site from the other direction. Because of the rise of ground head of him he hadn't a clue that just over the gentle slope of this righthand-sweeping curve lay the remains of Clancy Wilburn and his rig.

George was a troubleshooter for Mon Valley Electric, a white-collar expert in ceramic high-voltage conductors. He was returning at that late hour from a plant near Sharon, Pennsylvania, hoping to get a few hours sleep before returning to the office in Pittsburgh to complete his report.

His company car, a Ford LTD Crown Victoria, was in the outside lane, making a prudent 56 miles an hour. Well aware of the sometimes tricky, sometimes dangerous weather this time of year, George was taking his time. He was a careful man, if nothing else, driving with his seat belt and shoulder harness on, always. He didn't push the shoulder strap behind him, as some people did. That small act and his prudent speed were enough to save him from instantly dying when he sailed over the top of the rise.

George had approximately one-fifth of a second to react to the scene his headlights illuminated. His brain flashed the warning to his feet, but the nose of the big Ford plowed into the undercarriage of the trailer before his feet began to react.

The angle at which he struck the trailer and the sound construction of the sedan contributed to George's survival. The right front of the car folded inward, puncturing and blowing the front tire. Momentum

11

carried the rear of the car clockwise, with the collapsing right corner acting as the pivot point. As the car skewed to the left, its rear end continued around sharply until the entire left side collided with the overturned trailer.

The initial impact had thrown George against the safety belts, fracturing his left collarbone as his body rolled slightly around the diagonal strap. The forward deceleration of his torso forced a section of the broken bone down and through the upper lobe of his left lung. His legs hyperextended, his right ankle breaking in three places as it tried in vain to find the brake pedal.

His head, now a weighted heavy ball on the end of his neck, accelerated forward, severely straining all the cervical vertebrae and ligaments. His upper teeth bounced against the rim of the steering wheel and bit through his lip. The wheel began to telescope inward, away from his body, as it was designed to do. But when the car's side thudded into the trailer, the sideways lateral G-force redirected George's now elastic body in a new direction. Unfortunately the laws of physics were not easily followed by a human body committed to one direction of sudden, and direct, travel.

The violent torquing effect neatly snapped George's spine low in his back. Two vertebrae shattered from the force, exploding bone shards into the spinal cord, adding additional damage as the cord itself tore through 90 percent of its thickness. In that instant George's body died from the waist down. His brain, overloaded with pain and shock, checked out in a millisecond, sending what remained of his living self into blessed unconsciousness.

George's life-support systems, minus the voluntary control of the brain, went into automatic mode in their best effort to protect and save what they could.

One half mile behind the Ford, a five-ton PennDot dump truck, carrying cinders for spreading on the isolated patches of ice, cruised along. The two-man crew, looking for new targets, had seen the taillights of the car disappear over the rise ahead. They had seen the almost simultaneously flash of white light followed by instant blackness from the other side of the hill.

Steve Brasher, driving the five-ton, knew immediately that something bad had happened. He'd put too many miles on the highways of Pennsylvania, had seen his share of nasty things and then some. He didn't need to guess about the flashes of light.

He started to say something to his partner, M. C. Malone, when Malone cut in. "Yeah, man, I saw it too. Don't look too good."

"Let's check it out," Brasher replied. "Be ready on the radio. I got a bad feelin' about this."

Brasher slowed the truck as they neared the crest, gearing down until the nose of the five-ton eased over the rise. Their headlights started to pick up the devastation before them.

"Turn on the overhead bar, M.C.," Brasher said, as he slowed the truck to a halt. Malone hit the toggle switch, and six large halogen floodlights sprayed on above the cab.

"Sweet Jesus," Malone muttered, already in motion as he reached for the door handle.

"Oh, man," Brasher chorused, reaching for the CB mike. "Breaker, breaker—Central, this is two nine at milepost"—he strained to read the closest marker staff at the side of the road—"at milepost seventeen. We got a real bad one. Looks like one passenger car and a semi. Do you copy?"

"Two-nine, this is Central," the quiet female voice answered. "We copy that last. Give us a readout soonest. We'll get the state boys rolling now."

It didn't take long. The two men encountered George Kersten's inert form first and immediately did what they could to keep him warm and protected.

While Malone set out flares, Brasher took a long-handled flashlight from their truck and went in search of the other driver. The search did not take long, although finding all of him might take some hunting, Brasher realized, fighting the sudden revulsion at the sight.

I've seen worse, he said to himself, and in almost the same thought, Yeah, but it's been a long, long time since the last one. Then in a loud voice directed to Malone, "Got the driver here, M.C. He's had it. Call it in to Central. One breathin', one KIA."

Malone's shouted reply confirmed he'd heard the message. There was no need to ask if there were any more casualties.

13

And so the cataloging and accounting of tragedy began. As a matter of general interest, this small play of destruction remained a local event, of real and immediate concern only to those participants who, because of their occupations, dealt with this sort of thing on an all too regular basis. The first state trooper units were quickly joined by a dozen others until the night was lit by the stark glare of halogen spotlights. Roadside flares made dancing shadows of silhouetted men while the stroboscopic pulse of blue and red lights splintered over the wreckage.

In the remains of both vehicles, phone numbers were identified, and one trooper began the calls, sending the rude messages out on 1-800 numbers. The trooper's bad news triggered other calls that echoed throughout the early morning hours. The first went to the survivor's company, informing the emergency operator that one of their executives had been involved in a serious accident.

The second went to the trucking company, California/North Carolina Express, based in Raleigh, North Carolina. The fleet manager, responding to the trooper's dispassionate report, passed on the information to the company's commercial liability insurance carrier, Trans Patriot Insurance. The call went to the closest field office to the accident, which happened to be in Pittsburgh.

Trans Patriot's contact took the information down on one of its company forms, called after-hours call reports, or AHCs, known as "aches" by the field adjusters. TPI's night operator rang up the twenty-four-hour duty adjuster, Mark Alexander, an hour before dawn.

Fifty-seven minutes later Mark was on the road, leaving behind a snug bed and an understanding wife who, after three years of marriage, was used to pre-dawn interruptions.

The sun crept up into a clear sub-zero morning, beginning what for Mark Alexander would be a twelve-hour day. By the end of it, he had completed his accident site field investigation, interviewed the state police sergeant in charge plus the two PennDot maintenance men, arranged to receive a copy of the police report, taken fifty-two ASA 400 35 mm photographs of the entire scene, including both vehicles, and arranged for an accident reconstructionist to fly out from Columbus, Ohio.

In the afternoon he drove back to Pittsburgh to meet with the personnel director of Mon Valley Electric and pick up additional information on the survivor, George Kersten. While there he was given some unusual facts that influenced the claim file being created.

Ten days later, in a file review with his supervisor Greg Jeckel, Mark brought the facts of Kersten versus C/NC up to current status. The two men were in Jeckel's office, reading a three-dimensional computer reproduction of the paper claim file off Jeckel's CRT.

"I was at the hospital yesterday," Mark said, stretching his six-foot-eight frame. "Kersten survived his third surgery for internal hemorrhaging of the left lung. He had his first problem there some thirty-six hours after his initial trip to the OR. With the right one removed due to emphysema, the left's been pushed hard, but they have him stabilized. He's breathing on his own, so they've taken him off of the respirator. He's still on oxygen, though."

Greg watched the CRT screen, reviewing the medical records. "What's the prognosis on this coma? Kersten hasn't come around since they took him in."

"There doesn't seem to be any organic brain dysfunction. There was a concussion from the lateral impact to the left temporal area, but no fracture. CAT scans, three of them now, have shown nothing unexpected. Neurological referral comes up negative, except that this kind of reaction to blunt force trauma is not rare in accident victims."

"No permanency appears indicated," Greg mused, reading the neurologist's opinion.

"Not to the head, apparently. But the paralysis is a foregone conclusion," Mark continued. "It's pretty clear on that."

"Yeah, I can see that here," Jeckel said, not looking up. "Any change in the prognosis of the lower limbs?"

"Not much, as it sits now," Mark replied. "Claimant suffered a ninety-five percent transverse tear of the spinal cord at the fourth and fifth lumbar vertebrae. The neurosurgeon said the bone ripped through there like shrapnel."

"So what's the bottom line?"

"Presuming the lung remains stable and he comes out of the

coma reasonably soon, they think he can be rehabbed as a para, but no chance he'll ever walk again."

"Harmarville?" Greg asked, referring to the rehabilitation center for paraplegic and quadriplegic injuries located northeast of Pittsburgh.

"He'll be evaluated for that and will be transferred after he's had some low-level therapy at North Side. But his return to Mon Valley is out in the ozone right now.

"Problem is," Mark added, "we have a fifty-year-old high-wage earner, experienced and motivated under normal circumstances, but in all likelihood, he'll never return to any kind of gainful employment, let alone the almost six-figure-a-year income he enjoys now.

"Factor in the medical liens and the litigious nature of the claimant, and it doesn't look good."

Greg's last remark was a reference to the lawsuit George had brought against the drunk driver who had killed his wife and two sons five years before. George had won a plaintiff's verdict for three million dollars and had then given it all away to MADD. That unusual move had garnered him some statewide press.

"Costs are getting up here, too," Mark continued. "We're ten days post-accident, three surgeries, multiple special med teams, and ICU care. We passed the two-hundred-thousand-dollar figure two days ago, and it's still climbing."

"So we have probable, if not clear, liability on a catastrophic loss case, with permanent injuries and extensive wage loss. The claimant has a projected life expectancy of twenty-four years, and up to fifteen years of lost income, not counting future medical care." Greg looked at his young adjuster. "Given all that, what's your recommendation?"

"Well, both vehicles are clean. Our expert says the differential repair on the rig had nothing to do with the accident, and Kersten's Crown Vic was cool. Proximate cause of the accident was C/NC's driver exceeding safe conditions. We're liable on this one."

Mark leaned back and briefly rubbed both long hands over his face. It had been a long week. His hands dropped while he considered the company's exposure on this claim. Mark cocked a tired brown eye at Greg and shook his head. "If I were to settle this tomorrow, I'd need a hefty loss reserve. With the possibility or probability of litigation to follow, I'd say this is a limits case."

"I agree," Greg replied. He tipped his chair forward. "Add this to your formal report for the home office in Phoenix, and I'll endorse it up to the manager. We recommend reserves on this file be increased to two million dollars, policy limits."

FEBRUARY 14, CAREFREE, ARIZONA

Luther Sitasy's eyes opened a minute before the faint click of the radio alarm button, set to go off at 4:30 A.M. He lay motionless, feeling his senses kick into real time, awareness chasing the lethargy of sleep away with one large push. Reacting out of habit, he began to take stock of his immediate surroundings.

The soft breathing coming from below the foot of the bed, out of sight in the darkened room, signaled the presence of Khanh, his six-year-old black lab-shepherd mix.

Luther then sent out a full-senses probe of the house, not caring that the chances of actually hearing anything within the 20,000-square-foot home would be doubtful. He performed the exercise so automatically that it required only a trace of conscious effort. It was a long-established routine, this immediate need to secure the place he was in.

He felt rather than heard Myoshi moving around in the kitchen on the far side of the house. Nakato, her husband, would be close by. Satisfied that all was in order, he rolled out and sat on the edge of the bed, in the same movement reaching out to turn on the soft lights recessed in the curve of the ceiling above the round platform bed.

The movement brought a response from the dog, who sneezed, shook his head back and forth, rattling his collar, stretched, then rocked himself up off the floor.

"You make it sound better than it is, Khanh," Luther said in greeting.

17

Hearing Luther's voice, the large black animal walked down the side of the bed toward him, tail gently waving as he rubbed his length against the blankets. He stopped near Luther's hand resting on the edge and nuzzled it, looking up for the response he knew was coming.

Luther hooked his fingers behind Khanh's ears, digging them into the thick fur, communicating his affection for the dog through his fingertips.

Following routine, Khanh took another step forward and placed his head on Luther's thigh. He locked his dark eyes with the equally dark eyes of the man on the bed. He nudged him, paused, and did it again.

"Okay, okay, I hear you," Luther said, standing up. He stretched his arms while Khanh backed up and sat down, watching. Luther detected a bit of impatience in the dog's pose. Bending down slightly, hands on knees, he looked at Khanh. "You're a delicacy in Vietnam, you know," he said. "Was a time when we used to eat the likes of people like you." He leered at the dog, cocking an eyebrow.

Khanh's tail began to wag, then his muzzle slowly opened in a silent pant, allowing the soft light to illuminate his teeth.

Luther regarded the dog's face for a moment, then said, "Yeah, I bet you did, too."

He headed for the master bedroom, then paused, as he often did, to gaze at the framed photos on the shelf above the headboard. His eyes slid from one to the other, past his eighteen-year-old daughter, Mikki, her long red hair and lovely features favoring her mother, Jackie, Luther's ex-wife.

The second photo showed Jackie in a familiar pose, head tilted a bit to her left, loving blue eyes shining, before it all went to hell. A picture from another time, though not necessarily a better time.

He stopped at the last one, showing him and John Paraletto standing before the Huey UH-1D troop ship they had flown together. John had been Luther's copilot back then, and other crews had taken to calling them Mutt and Jeff, since John was six feet two to Luther's five-six.

Luther shook his head, smiling at the memories. "Exciting times, Khanh," he told the dog, and walked away, closing the bathroom door behind him.

18

Khanh, after sitting patiently through Luther's silent trip, got up and sniffed once at the bottom of the door. Then he trotted off to find someone more willing to meet his immediate needs.

Luther leaned against the edge of the marble counter and paused to study the image before him. Not that he was obsessive about age, he reminded himself, but he knew he didn't really look forty-two, even with the gray lightening his full beard and collar-length hair. He'd kept himself in shape, something he was especially proud of, given the tendency of things to generally head south in people his age.

He quickly finished his morning routine and left the upstairs suite for the kitchen. He had dressed conservatively, as was his nature, attired today in soft-topped dark gray bucks, medium gray slacks, a navy blue fitted shirt that displayed a soft blue pinstripe, and a maroon, gray, and navy regimental stripped tie. He carried a tweed blazer over his arm.

Perhaps because he could afford it, he wore little jewelry. On his left wrist was a gold Lorus watch, a moderate self-indulgence. There was nothing else except the memory of the heavy gold ring he had worn on his left hand. The ring he had given back to Jackie. The memories he held on to; they were his.

Luther made hardly a sound on the thick off-white carpet of the curved hallway, at the end of which was a stairway, a series of wide descending tiers spiraling down the outside wall of the seventy-foot-wide circular living room below.

Passing through the living room, he arrived at the kitchen, a large room of ceramic tile counters, carved cherry cabinets, and slate floors. A curved balustrade of heavy hand-carved teak served to separate the elevated cooking area from the dining space three steps below.

In the midst of that spacious area, working quickly, quietly, and most deliberately, stood a tiny female figure. Barely five feet tall, the mid-sixtyish Asian woman dissected a variety of fresh fruits with short, precise cuts.

Myoshi Arutaka and her husband, Nakato, had worked for Luther for ten years. He had met and subsequently hired them while attending an international risk management seminar in Japan.

19

In what had become a morning ritual, Luther came up to her, stopped to draw his feet and hands together, and then bowed from the waist. "Good morning, Myoshi," he said.

Myoshi, familiar with this ritual, repeated Luther's gesture. "Good morning, Sitasy-san."

They straightened up together, Myoshi holding the smile she always had for Luther. Then she motioned him to the dining alcove set into the large bay window opposite the serving counter island.

Seated at his usual place, he looked out at the still-dark eastern horizon. At this time of year in Arizona the sun rose close to seven o'clock. At five-thirty he could see the first rose-tinted glow defining the tops of the McDowell Mountains east of Carefree.

The back patio lights revealed two figures on the far side of the inlaid brick area. Nakato Arutaka was kneeling before a miniature temple mounted on a short pole a few feet off the ground. He was hunched over, his clasped hands held close to his chest as he went through his morning ritual of prayers. Beside him sat Khanh, observing the old man.

Luther looked at the tableau. He respected Nakato for his religious devotion, and understood it. He had his own beliefs concerning God, although he subscribed to no particular faith.

"He thinks about the old times very much lately, Sitasy-san," Myoshi said, placing a plate of sliced fruit before him. There was a hint of concern in her voice.

"Is it nostalgia, or something else?" he asked.

"I'm not sure," she replied, looking out toward her husband. "Maybe it is only that, nothing more. He is always a little like this each year as the time to leave approaches. But the children are doing well, so there is no worry there. Sometimes I think he simply misses those days, even as hard as they were." She paused for a moment, then added, "For all of us."

Nakato, once a sergeant in the Imperial Marines, had survived the island campaigns ending in Okinawa at the close of World War II. Most of his regiment and many of his friends had not.

His resolve to rebuild his life after the war, to understand and accept the reality of those times, and to use that to go on with the

20

necessary challenge of living, had become an inspiration for Luther years later.

"When the two of you go back, maybe he'll find an answer for what bothers him," Luther said. "But if there's anything I can do . . ."

The small woman smiled quickly. It was the custom of the Aruta-kas that each year, from April to June, they would return to visit their home and their remaining family on the island of Honshu. The emerging spring and early summer provided them a time to renew their ties with their heritage.

Luther used the time to regroup on his own. In the last couple of years, he had come a long way in proving to himself that he had turned a corner in his life. He needed the months alone to remind himself that old wounds did heal, and that he could function on his own.

Myoshi pondered Luther's statement for a moment, then said, "I think he will find answers. I really think that time at home, in Japan, is all he needs." Then, again with the small smile that came so easily, "Old men need to be reminded that at one time they were young men. Do you understand, Sitasy-san?"

"Yes, I do," he replied, "and thank you for reminding me," he added ruefully.

"You are too young to worry of such things," she said coyly, nodding her head slightly before turning back to the island counter. "What time may we expect you this evening?"

"Should be the usual, but you never know," he replied. "The schedule yesterday didn't show anything but the normal routine, so if that holds, I might be able to get out of there by six."

Myoshi nodded her understanding. It was not out of the ordinary for him to return considerably later than normal business hours. She knew his work was both important and demanding, and that he took his responsibilities very seriously.

All of which was true. Luther was manager of the policy limits claims section of Trans Patriot Insurance, one of many departments that made up the company's claims division. Almost two thousand of the ten thousand employees who worked at the vast home office were involved in claims handling in one capacity or another.

Luther was responsible for overseeing the efforts of a staff of twelve who reviewed and audited policy limits claim files covering the myriad commercial, personal, and professional policies Trans Patriot provided in both domestic and foreign markets.

His group was required to monitor each policy limit case in litigation, including controlling the massive expenses incurred from defending these cases. They also had to determine the ultimate liability of their insureds in a particular claim and decide whether to continue to defend it or settle the loss.

Luther had worked for TPI for fifteen years and, out of his own habit, started his day at 6:00 A.M., normally continuing to 6:00 P.M. His management position within the claims department was unique to the company; it had been created a few years earlier in response to an increasing need for careful supervision of policy limits claims. The position had not been created specifically for him, but it might have been, since he took such pride in it.

Luther got up from the breakfast alcove just as Khanh and Nakato came in from outside. Nakato started to check his daily work schedule, which was necessary to keep the ten-acre estate operating.

Luther carried his plate over to Myoshi, who was scanning a shopping list on a computer monitor. He stopped for a moment and looked over her shoulder at the screen. "Italian?" he asked.

"Yes," she replied, taking inventory of the pantry items listed. "Something from the northern provinces," she continued, speaking as she wrote. Myoshi had a gift for creating absolutely authentic cuisine from any region or nationality in the known world.

"I leave it in your capable, and incredible, hands," he said, turning to Khanh, who sat patiently waiting for Luther's farewell. Luther stepped up to him and patted both hands on his chest once, another part of their morning ritual. The huge dog leaped up, balancing his front paws on Luther's shoulders. They stood almost eye to eye.

"Guard the fort, big guy," his master commanded, grasping the thick fur alongside Khanh's neck and affectionately shaking his great head. Khanh licked his bearded chin, then pushed himself back and sat down by the door. He would be there when Luther came home hours later. It wouldn't matter what time his return might occur. Khanh just knew.

Luther gave one more rub along the dog's head, then pushed open the door to the hallway leading to the garage.

The garage was a five-bay affair, crescent-shaped to repeat the general lines of the house. A substantial workbench ran the length of the house-side wall, with racks of tools in regimental order above, and shelves holding other equipment.

At the far end, sitting under a drab tarpaulin, was one of Luther's works in progress, a 1968 Shelby GT 500. He was slowly restoring it. He believed things should be used for the purposes for which they were designed, not sealed away. Next to it sat a two-year-old four-wheel-drive Chevy Blazer, its dark red surfaces gleaming under the fluorescent lights. The middle bay was reserved for his daughter's Camaro, on those weekends when she came to visit.

In the bay closest to Luther sat his pride and joy, a 1973 Mustang Mach I. He had purchased it new that year and rebuilt it twice in the years since. The latest overhaul had ended up a full-blown restoration upgrade, combining some high-tech changes the original had never had.

Luther had gotten the Mustang back only five days ago and had yet to see what the $30,000 restoration had done for it. As he backed it out of the garage, he thought that this morning presented an excellent opportunity to find out.

The Mach I prowled down the serpentine lane that wound through this semi-exclusive part of Carefree and emerged onto Pima Road, the major north-south thoroughfare that connected Carefree with Scottsdale. The Trans Patriot complex lay fifteen miles away to the south.

He slowed to a stop before pulling out onto the six-lane-wide expanse of concrete, idling the car and checking his rearview mirror for oncoming traffic. Ahead, in the shallow bowl of the valley below, the carpet of lights from Phoenix glittered.

Luther dropped his hand behind the T-handled gear selector and flicked the rocker switch, turning off the radar detector mounted behind the honeycomb grille.

"Take a chance," he said aloud and reached back to the shifter. He pulled it back to first gear and steadily floored the accelerator.

23

The entire car squatted as power was fed to all four wheels, and the ebony vehicle simply launched itself.

Luther felt the acceleration in his back and snapped his eyes from the road to the orange-on-black VDO instruments. G-force pushed him deeper into the seat, and he shifted quickly through second and into drive.

He watched the tach needle rotate past 4000 rpm, checked the speedometer, and saw 100 pass by. He let the tach go to 6000, still 1500 away from the engine's redline. A chorus of sweetly tuned low-frequency mechanical screams stabilized into a moan as the 427 cid engine spun over four hundred horsepower. Luther held the speed to 140 miles an hour.

The roadway edge flashed by in the probing glare of the car's halogens. To his left, the McDowells were black-edged against a cantaloupe-colored horizon fading upward into softer shades of rose, blue, purple, and black.

Luther began to slow down to the posted limit a mile before crossing through the intersection of Pinnacle Peak Road. At that point he reactivated the radar unit and shifted up into fourth gear overdrive. He hadn't seen a soul for the entire run.

"That answers that question," he said, patting the top of the steering wheel rim. "You'll do just fine."

The Mustang, the expansive custom-designed house, and a few other high-ticket big-boy toys were all part of a lifestyle Luther had only recently come to embrace.

His father, Nicholas "Big Nick" Sitasy, had always assumed that Luther, the youngest of three children, would follow tradition and pursue a career in the family shipping business, an operation based in Houston, which over the years had grown into a multibillion-dollar enterprise.

Nick's first two sons, Michael and Frank, had joined him. The youngest had not. Always the dreamer, as his mother once described him, Luther nevertheless had inherited the strong work ethic of those before him. He just wanted to direct that effort into something of his own choosing. His obstinacy drove a wedge between son and father and eventually pushed Luther out of Tulane University after his sophomore year and into a more than passing acquaintance with alcohol. Luther's immediate future was decided by the times when Southeast Asia and the United States Army reached out for him.

He obtained a stateside officer's commission first, then went on to survive two tours, the first on the ground, the second in the air. When he returned four years later and resumed college, he had settled down substantially. After Vietnam, college almost seemed to be a dream where the worst problem he had to face was finals week. He met and married another student, Jacqueline Arlene Mirany, his first semester back, and they quickly produced a daughter, Michelle. Luther eventually earned a degree in engineering, while Jackie graduated in journalism.

Readjustment from the war remained elusive, however. Luther's fondness for the bottle became an addiction as guilt and lingering nightmares day-tripped into his life at the worst times. His parents tried to intervene, for Jackie's sake and Mikki's, if no other, but Luther continued to refuse any help from them. While the marriage suffered, Jackie's career flourished in awkward counterpoint as she moved up in electronic media as a television news producer.

Luther finally landed a job as an insurance adjuster for Trans Patriot Insurance, the only work he could find in those recessionary times. In spite of himself and his slowly self-destructing personal life, he became an effective professional claimsman, taking the advances and promotions as they came, until Trans Patriot moved the family to Phoenix, Arizona, in 1980.

The spiral of dependency continued, pulling the marriage down, although Luther remained adept at hiding his drinking problem from those at work. Four difficult years later it was over for him and Jackie. The divorce was the prologue to what could have been Luther's final act, played out alone the night he hit bottom, burned out on booze and despair.

Stumbling toward the end of a twenty-hour-long weekend binge, Luther sat down in his tub, turned the shower on full blast, and pushed the muzzle of a .45 auto into his mouth. He never pulled the trigger, his finger stayed by a long-lost spark of self-respect and a battered instinct for survival that finally emerged from a forgotten

25

place deep inside. He laid the weapon down, crawled out of the tub, and went straight into detox and AA.

This new war was as difficult and frightening as the old one. He didn't stop crawling until he had defeated his alcohol addiction and buried the ghosts of Vietnam. His re-emergence into life brought a reconciliation with his father, who welcomed with some bittersweet hindsight the positive changes in his lost son. Nick resigned himself to the fact that Luther had finally chosen a course for himself, and let it go.

But blood was blood, and Luther was part of the family business, whether he wanted to be or not. Despite his son's protest, Big Nick set up his inheritance, as he called it, in the form of a ten million dollar annuity, renewed each year to maintain the balance. It was a sign of long overdue affection and would be available anytime Luther wanted it.

His return to self-respect allowed Luther to accept the annuity, even though he kept his work ethic, needing to be productive in something he was good at. But the money was for real, and he saw no reason why he couldn't enjoy the best of what his new life had to offer. He had paid his dues in full.

Some people, as expected, resented his wealth and his refusal to hide it, but by and large most saw it as part and parcel of the man. His performance and expertise in the claims business were excellent, and if anyone ever gave it a thought, his lifestyle only added a certain panache, even eccentricity, to his reputation. More important than what other people thought, however, Luther knew who he was.

The Mustang hummed perfectly as Luther continued south until he reached the turnoff for the Trans Patriot complex.

Making a left, he turned into the company compound, which the employees called "The Village." The Mustang's wide tires thrummed over the bricks of the tree-lined boulevard as he circled the perimeter of the two-hundred-acre campus, the headlights illuminating the lush desert and tropical landscaping.

The facility had been designed to replicate the look and feel of an eighteenth-century Spanish-style California mission. Ten buildings were visible, one- and two-story affairs of thick adobe walls, conical-tiled roofs varying in color from black to red to rust to brown.

The focal point of TPI's complex was a large white cathedral-like building, a twin-towered structure, its design borrowed heavily from the San Xavier del Bac mission near Tucson, known locally as the White Dove of the Desert.

TPI's cathedral—similar to the White Dove but larger, standing fully five stories tall—housed the corporation's executive offices.

The other mission buildings housed different division offices and support services for the company. The image of a Spanish mission, tranquil in the sun, was effectively complete.

But Trans Patriot's heart, the core that really made the company function, remained out of sight, literally. Fully 80 percent of the complex was, in fact, below ground, continuing below street level an additional seven stories. The parking garage was itself a four-level affair directly below the plaza, each level the size of three football fields.

Elevators, escalators, moving walkways, and maintenance tunnels connected the subterranean levels. In all, almost ten thousand employees worked there.

Putting the majority of the operating space below ground simplified the economics of maintaining the vast facility. Natural subterranean cooling was augmented by solar-generated air conditioning provided by surface-mounted solar panels. The same solar technology met all the other light and energy needs of the complex.

Luther directed the Mustang down one of the descending spiral garage entrances and rolled out onto the first level, reserved for executive officers. He then took the elevator down to the fifth level, one of two floors taken up by the claims department. Angling across the vast expanse of the floor, down complex hallways, he headed toward the north side where his office was located. Most of the lights were on; Trans Patriot conducted its around-the-world business on a twenty-four-hour basis. Even so, the late-shift troops were fewer in number, and the first of the new morning shift didn't start to show until seven-thirty. A few of the night owls raised their hands in greeting as Luther passed by.

He entered his ten-by-ten-foot office and turned on the lights. His

27

L-shaped desk took up the far corner opposite the door and contained a full-color PC and monitor. In front of the desk were two low-backed swivel chairs. He was reminded that his office, given a double bed, could stand in for every motel room he had ever seen. It retained a familiar feel of solidity, even of comfort, which was fortunate, since he spent almost as much time here as he did at home.

Luther took off his jacket and hung it over the back of his chair. He sat down, rolled up his cuffs a couple of turns from habit, and fired up his PC, beginning another day.

It was nine o'clock when he received the first mail drop and a printout of all new limits files being logged in that day. As manager he scanned every new file before assigning it to one of his people or keeping it for himself. The problem was maintaining control of all the open files without overburdening his people.

Luther scanned the new limits cases. The first was Kersten versus California/North Carolina Express, a bad car-truck accident. He noted the file number that put the claim with the Pittsburgh claims office.

He called up the opening file status, which gave the highlights, further noted the recommendation by the Pittsburgh claims manager, underscoring his adjuster and supervisor, that the file be reserved at policy limits. This prompted him to call up another screen containing C/NC's policy information. Quickly he confirmed the endorsements and limits of coverage. Satisfied with Pittsburgh's initial recommendation, he assigned it to Gordon Hatton, one of his staff, for follow-up.

At ten o'clock he stopped for his usual break. He stood up, stretched, and had started to walk around the desk when the phone rang.

"Sitasy, claims." The greeting was constant, automatic.

"Hi, Daddy," came the response.

"Hi to you too, gorgeous," he answered, glancing at his computer.

There was a pause. "Pop, you forgot, didn't you?" The tone was only slightly remonstrative, and like any father of a teenage girl, Luther backtracked quickly in his mind to find out what was it, exactly, that he had forgotten. And like any good father caught in the same position and unable to come up with an answer, he changed the subject.

"What are you doing calling at this time of the day? Don't you have a class or something?" Mikki was a freshman at Arizona State University, majoring in economics.

"Last semester I had classes in the morning," she explained patiently. "This semester I only have afternoon classes on Tuesdays and Thursdays. I was getting ready to leave for campus and thought I'd call you. To see if you remembered." Again that accusatory tone.

He surrendered. "I guess you're right, hon. What is it I've apparently forgotten in my advanced age?"

Exasperated now, the young voice came back, "Check your calendar, Daddy. It's Mom's birthday." She waited a beat and added, "And Valentine's Day, too, in case you needed even more incentive."

A quick glance at his desk calendar confirmed her admonition. "You're right, Mikki," Luther said apologetically. "Looks like I've done it again."

"I know I shouldn't ask," she added calmly, "but did you get her anything?"

"No, but that's easily remedied," he answered. "I'll take care of that immediately." Luther picked up a pen and wrote "flowers" on a yellow Post-it, peeled it off, and stuck it to the bottom of the phone. "Okay, I made a note. Listen, you all right otherwise?"

"I'm fine, Daddy," she said softly. "Will we be seeing you anytime soon?"

"Maybe," Luther replied. "Are you coming up this weekend?"

"I think so. This week's looking pretty light, study-wise. I could use a long run or two with you and Khanh."

"Speaking for both of us, that would be great," Luther replied, pleased with her answer. He waited a few seconds to see if there were any other reasons for her call. "Well, I guess I shouldn't keep you from your trek down to campus. Say hi to Mom for me, okay?"

"You know I will," she answered. Then she said, "I love you, Dad."

"I love you too. Bye, Mikki," Luther said, and broke the connection.

He stood for a short time, lost in thought, forgetting his original reason for getting up. Then he sat down and used the Yellow Pages to order a dozen pink roses for Mikki and a dozen long-stem dark red roses for Jackie. Delivery was promised by five o'clock.

29

Returning from a quick trip to the employee lounge, he paused a moment to ponder the company's response to the windowless environment it had created. Inlaid into the wall of his office at eye level was a tropical water fish tank, fully three feet high and five feet long. Luther sipped on a soda and watched the rippling colors of the fish pass lazily by. If nothing else, it helped relieve the cloistered feeling of the space, but mostly it just plain relaxed him.

At midday Luther rounded up Walt Golding, his department assistant manager, ten years his senior, and the two of them made their way topside to the plaza level, where the company cafeteria was located in one of the long single-story mission buildings.

The two men were partway through their meal when their conversation was interrupted by a familiar, slightly accented voice from behind them.

"Good afternoon, Luther. Might I share your table?"

Both men turned their attention to the young woman standing nearby, tray in hand, a slightly alluring smile on her lips.

"Dana, please," Luther mumbled, standing and quickly motioning her toward an empty chair. Walt remained seated, silently appraising the young woman. He did not know her well, but he recognized her immediately, and he did know her reputation. Even in a company this large—and sometimes impersonal—certain individuals could gain a certain renown. Luther was one, and so was this woman. Walt was surprised that she looked so young. From what he had heard about her, he assumed she must be older.

She was, in fact, twenty-eight, and she had earned a reputation as a man-killer. The stories of her conquests—and rejections—were legendary and, by now, greatly exaggerated. Still, she was beautiful, with a hint of the exotic thrown in, and just enough of a suggestion of danger to make her truly seductive.

Although barely five feet two, Dana Quinn carried herself with an air that seemed to lend her stature. Her golden bronze skin tones were enhanced by her long auburn hair, which cascaded thickly down over her shoulders. The reddish brown waves framed her high cheekbones and exotic features. Her full lips glistened with a dark cherry red that perfectly complemented her face.

Her thin nose had delicately arched nostrils that drew the viewer

30

to her eyes, which were her most arresting feature. They were darkly lidded, sweeping upward at the outside corners in an almost Asian way, the irises an odd, alluring mix of violet and crystal. The effect was one of bottomlessness.

As she sat, her floral-print skirt and long-sleeved white blouse hugged her body tightly. The V-neck cut of her blouse was modest but did little to hide her full cleavage.

Luther made the introductions: "Walt Golding, Dana Quinn."

Walt reached across the table to take her small hand. "Ms. Quinn," he replied.

"I know you," she said, repeating her earlier smile. "You work with Luther, don't you? And please, call me Dana."

"Yeah, I'm in Lute's department."

"Dana's one of the investors for TPI," Luther answered for her. "She gets to make money for the company," he continued, smiling at her, "as opposed to us claims types, who get to spend it instead."

"Well, actually," she corrected, "we *try* to make money. Sometimes it doesn't work out."

Walt was smitten by her looks and quiet demeanor. Forgetting his own meal for the moment, he leaned both elbows on the table and asked, "Forgive me, Dana, but I have to ask. Your accent, it's so . . ."

"What? Interesting?" she interrupted, amused by his question.

Now embarrassed, he leaned back in his chair. "I apologize," he said, flustered. "But you must get asked about that a lot."

"No, that's quite all right," she replied innocently, then leaned forward against the edge of the table. "That's tame compared to some of the things I get asked," she said, smiling as she looked at Luther.

Walt caught her expression and glanced quickly at Luther, who remained coolly silent, a smile tugging at his bearded face. Walt returned his attention to the girl.

"In fact, Walt, I'm Jamaican-British—Jamaican on my mother's side. But I've had American citizenship since I was ten years old. My father owns an import-export business in the islands, and he sent me and my brothers and sisters to school in the States. So between my parents' influence and college in the Carolinas, my accent has been a bit bastardized."

31

"Well, it's a pleasure to make your acquaintance," Walt said, then made a show of looking at his watch. "But I really have to get back to the department."

Luther looked surprised and started to speak, but Walt stood up and placed a hand on his boss's shoulder. "Got to get on to those reinsurance reports, Lute. See you back at the shop. Ms. Quinn . . . Dana."

She nodded, and she and Luther watched the older man leave.

"I hope I didn't run him off," Dana said, turning to her salad.

"Whatever gave you that idea?" Luther replied dryly. "But you do seem to have that effect on a lot of men, Dana."

"Perhaps," she said, and he caught a challenging light in her eyes, "but apparently I haven't affected you in *any* way."

Luther sighed and reached for his drink. "Look, Dana," he said, trying for the right emphasis. This was not the first time they'd had this conversation. "It's not that I'm not interested in you." He paused, allowing his glance to sweep carefully over her, something he knew she expected from him. "In fact, I'm extremely flattered that you seem interested in me, but . . ."

"You think I'm too young for you," she interrupted.

He shook his head. "You don't understand. It's not the age thing, it's just—"

"Oh, Luther," she said, suddenly brightening, and she reached over to pat his hand. "Please don't tell me you have other obligations. That's such a cliché, and it wouldn't do anything to enhance my reputation."

He looked at her questioningly, to which she replied, "I know what they say about me, and whether it's true or not, I don't mind. It keeps the amateurs away."

As Luther listened to her light explanation, he couldn't help watching her eyes, sensing that something else entirely was motivating her aggressive approach to him. He shrugged in reply. "Well anyway . . ." he said.

Dana returned his gaze. Finally she said, "Yes, anyway, indeed, Mr. Sitasy." Then she turned back to her meal.

• • •

After lunch, Walt Golding stuck his head in Luther's office. "Dana Quinn seems to be something of a handful."

"Brilliant, too," Luther added.

"I believe it," Walt said, hesitating. "Is there anything going on between you two?"

"No, not at all," Luther replied. "I kind of think she would like there to be, but I can't help but feel that it's just another game for her."

Walt chuckled. "She wants you for your money, not your body, eh?"

Luther leaned back in his chair, lacing his fingers behind his head. "To tell you the truth, Walt, I don't think she's after anything I have, not seriously. But still . . ." and he trailed off, not sure himself what it was about her that bothered him.

Walt pressed the issue. "You seem to know a lot about her."

"No big deal," Luther replied, his mild Texas accent coming through. "When someone looks like that and draws attention to herself the way she does, you're bound to hear things."

"So it's not all innuendo, then. What's her background, since you seem in the know?"

"She came here out of Wall Street a half dozen years ago, arriving at the same time as a fellow named Bloodstone . . . Norman Bloodstone who had worked in the same New York office."

"Bloodstone?" Walt said. "There's an interesting name for you."

"Yeah, one that's easy to remember," Luther agreed. "He was an interesting guy, too, quite the athlete. I used to play a little interdepartmental basketball. Norman wasn't that tall, maybe six feet, but he had these huge hands like Magic Johnson. Bloodstone could palm the ball like it was a grapefruit."

Luther realized he had strayed from the topic. "Anyway, Dana and Bloodstone were a couple of investment wizards, real Turks. They were hired into TPI's investment department, and did real well for the company, so I heard."

"I haven't heard of this Bloodstone character before," Walt said. "Is he still around?"

Luther shook his head. "He left a couple of years ago. I think he went independent, consulting on his own."

33

"So he and Dana were an item?" Walt said.

"They seemed to be when he was here," Luther answered. " 'Course, now I don't know."

"If he's still hangin' around, you'd better watch yourself, Lute," Walt replied sagely.

Luther waved it off. "Not to worry. I think Norman and I have different agendas."

"Whatever you say, boss," Walt said, and left.

As usual, Luther remained at his desk a couple of hours after his staff had gone home. Savoring the quiet that descended over the office, he finished up a few projects.

He called Myoshi to tell her he was running a bit later than expected, which came as no surprise to her. At seven-thirty he shut down the PC, left a pile of reviewed letters in the out-box for the morning pickup, and turned out the lights in his office.

And another day down, he intoned to himself, as he headed for the elevators for the garage. I wonder who won?

The Mach I waited, and in minutes Luther was prowling up the exit ramp, headed home. He keyed the remote for the CD player, and Dire Straits came on with "Water of Love." His fingertips tapped out the bass line on the steering wheel rim, and the Mustang tooled out onto the highway.

Khanh met him at the hallway door into the kitchen. He roughhoused with the dog for a moment while greeting Myoshi, then he sat down for his dinner.

While he was eating, Myoshi spoke to him. "Mrs. Sitasy-san called for you."

"Jackie? When?" he asked.

"Not fifteen minutes ago," she said politely. "She thought to reach you, but I told her you were a little later than usual." Myoshi looked at him with a hint of concern. Her protective instincts were always on the ready, especially when it came to Luther's ex.

34

"I know what you're thinking," he said. "It's okay. I sent her and Mikki some flowers today."

Myoshi raised an eyebrow slightly.

"For her birthday."

"Ah," she said, "yes."

"I'll call her back after I eat." He paused for a moment. "She did want me to call back, didn't she?"

"That was her wish, Sitasy-san."

Luther finished his dinner quickly and went to his study, Khanh trotting along beside him. The comfortable room, with its dark paneled walls and thick Persian rugs, looked as if it had been lifted out of a gentlemen's club in Britain.

He sat down at his rolltop desk, idly rotating the swivel chair in short arcs while he dialed Jackie's number. She picked up on the fourth ring.

"Happy birthday," he said. "Sorry I missed you earlier. Running late, as usual." The always awkward pause as he waited for her to answer. Or was there a pause? He hated himself for expecting it.

"Hi yourself." Jackie's voice still carried more than a little of her Louisiana accent. "As it happens, I was running late myself. The flowers were here when I got home. Mikki got back from class just as they were delivered. We both thank you, and I especially thank you. For remembering."

"You are most assuredly welcome," he replied, "but the credit goes to Mikki. I lost track of the date, typically. She called this morning to chew me out for it."

"Yes, I know. She told me." Jackie caught the slip immediately. "No, that's not what I mean." Now more annoyed than flustered, she said, "I meant that Mikki had called you, not that you'd . . ." and then she realized she was almost rambling. "Anyway, you know what I mean," she finished.

"Yeah, I do. Smart kid we have there, huh?" Luther dragged the conversation out a little longer. He liked hearing her voice. "Mikki suggested we all get together soon. What d'you think?"

"Sounds reasonable," Jackie answered, "as long as my schedule doesn't get in the way again." She paused. "Dinner, maybe?"

"Not a problem," he said. "We'll work something out. I'll give you a call, okay?"

"Sure." There was a long pause, both realizing there was nothing more to say, yet each holding on to the connection. "Well, I should let you go," she said finally. Then, "Lute? I really do love the roses, they're beautiful. Thank you again. It was very sweet."

"Yeah, well . . ." He hesitated, beginning to feel the tightness come into his voice. "But you're welcome."

"Good night," she said finally. "Call soon?" Not so much a question as a request.

"I will," he answered. "Take care of yourself, Jackie." He sat quietly for a few minutes after hanging up, wondering why this was always so difficult. "So stop it," he said to himself aloud.

Khanh, thinking the command was for him, raised his head from his paws.

Luther looked down at him. "Not you," he said, smiling, and idly scratched behind the dog's ears. "Come on, big guy."

He stood up and left the study, with Khanh following close beside him.

FEBRUARY 16, MOON VALLEY, PHOENIX, ARIZONA

The desk was set into what would have been the closet of the 12-by-14-foot room, filling the entire length of the open space.

A track-light strip mounted in the ceiling over the desk softly illuminated the work area. Built-in shelves along the back wall of the recessed space held boxes of floppy disks, files, paper, ink cartridges, and other paraphernalia, all regimentally organized.

Centered on the worktable was a Packard-Bell 386-SX 33. To the left of the PC was a Sony 25-inch television monitor linked to twin General Electric VCR decks. A 9600 telephone modem sat beside the big Hewlett-Packard laser jet printer. A white business-style phone console completed the hardware setup. Three-way stereo speakers were mounted above the closet, suspended just below the 12-foot-high ceiling.

Heavy wine-red drapes covered the only two windows in the room, effectively shutting out the bright midmorning sun.

The three remaining walls of the room were covered by floor-to-ceiling shelves made of the same polished maple as the desk. On them were hardcover and paperback books, journals, magazines in hard-spined ring binders, and videotapes, all arranged in precise order. Among them were legal texts and research journals, books on medical definitions, diagnostics, drugs, surgical techniques, research and position papers, and other reference works. Other shelves contained an array of commercial publications, novels, works of nonfiction in both hardcover and paperback, and magazines. A quick glance at the assortment of material gathered offered few clues to the profession of the occupant of the room.

A closer look, however, revealed one common thread running through all of this material, one topic: death. Specifically, death by unnatural causes. To a casual observer the complete absence of any other subject would at first have seemed eccentric, weird, then deeply unsettling. And "unsettling" was also the best single-word description of the lone occupant of the room.

He sat on a Scandinavian-designed caramel-colored leather office chair. He was at that moment using the PC to review a stock portfolio for one of his clients, his right hand resting on the mouse, skipping about the display at will.

The fingers of that hand were long, sensual, expressive, and almost balletlike in their movements. His hands might have belonged to a concert pianist.

He did, in fact, play classical music, as evidenced by the white baby grand piano that sat in another room of the rambling four-bedroom single-story villa. As an only child growing up in an affluent household in Boston, he had been given the best instruction. His teacher had predicted that, given his intense precision and concentration, he had the talent to be an exemplary musician.

But the playing of serious classical music required both technical excellence and an intense passion for the music itself. He had the technical mastery, but other passions had intervened. His emotions had become centered in other areas at an early age.

The real world being what it was, he had recognized that emotions could be as much a weapon as an essential element of the human soul. And in business—high-technology-oriented, winner-take-all cutthroat dealing—the ability to manipulate emotions could be a key tactical advantage. He knew people, and how to react to them, as the situation warranted. It was a behavioral quality that he had developed into an art form.

He was six feet tall with a swimmer's build, broad shoulders, long arms, a washboard-flat stomach, slim hips, and powerful legs. His hair was honey blond, chemically lightened to accentuate the tones. Of medium length, it was brushed back from a clear forehead, giving a sort of sophisticated surfer look to his face.

His eyes were the most distinctive feature in a face that was, by any standard, handsome. The irises were hazel with traces of gold in them. The pupil of the right eye, however, contained a genetic defect, an elongated spike that cut upward into a point that bisected the iris, giving a cat's-eye appearance. It was nonfunctional, with no adverse impact on the visual acuity of the eye, but he had learned at an early age that the perceived defect was unsettling to people. During conversations, he noticed that whomever he was talking with eventually directed more and more attention to his right eye, in the process sometimes losing track of the conversation.

He had taken advantage of this oddity by adopting the use of dark glasses. In a situation where he was ready to clinch a deal, make a point, or win a debate, he would remove his brown-tinted glasses and let the odd shape work subliminally on the other person, causing that minor distraction he needed to win. In most cases, the technique worked.

He favored casual, expensive name-brand clothes in pastels for a look that said simply "money." He could have been a model for an ad for a men's fashion magazine, and at one point had actually played with the idea of doing some modeling.

But that would have taken him away from investment banking, an occupation at which he excelled. It also would have taken him away from his other occupation, which was infinitely more interesting. And profitable. Its special appeal was a client list that was temporary. His clients would depart; only their money would stay behind.

His concentrated focus on the computer screen was interrupted by the burring of the telephone. He picked up the handset but continued to watch the screen as he answered.

"Yes," he said, almost absently. His voice was sensual, low-pitched.

"Good morning yourself," she replied. "We have another one."

His reaction was immediate. He cleared the screen, punched into another program, and quickly set up the modem. The screen remained blank, waiting with an electric blue glow.

"So soon?" he replied. "What brought this on?"

"It just came across," she said. "We were lucky to catch it at all, but it was too good to pass up. Wait, you'll see in a moment. Are you ready?"

"I'm ready. What do we have?"

"An auto accident victim, in a coma, and paraplegic. Liability is clear against the insured, a large trucking company. The event occurred February first; it just came in this week, Wednesday. The reserve is the policy limit, two million."

A burst of data appeared on his screen, arriving in one long stream, too fast for him to read, until the transmission was completed.

The laser printer hummed into life, delivering the information into hard copy. He lifted the first page of the printout, reading as more data was copied out.

"Kersten, George A.," he read, as the Trans Patriot claim file appeared on the pages unfolding from the printer. "Mmmm, nasty injuries," he said, allowing himself a smile. "Impressive," he mused, looking at the text.

"The medical picture is what's interesting," she replied. "I know it's fairly soon, but I really don't think moving now would throw off the stats."

"You're right," he said, continuing to read. "There's something in this medical we can expand upon, creatively speaking." He was silent for a few more seconds as he reviewed the surgical operating room summaries describing the massive injuries Kersten had suffered.

"But this is good," he said, almost to himself. "Oh, yes, this is very good." The enthusiasm in his voice was audible.

39

The printer shut off, finished with its duplication. In the sudden silence, he read, condensing the facts, "Widowed male, mid-fifties, no surviving family. Mon Valley Electric executive, high salary. Ah," he noted, "a significant prior medical history." He shook his head. "Goes to show you what smoking can do to your health.

"Let's see," he continued, "traumatically induced coma, indications of cranial damage, post-concussion onset. Right lung lost to emphysema, the left lacerated by the broken collarbone, collapsed, three surgeries so far, mostly to repair internal bleeding of that lung. Interesting." He spoke quietly, now completely absorbed in the file. "And of course, the spinal cord injury and paralysis. I see they've done whatever surgical repair can be done for that, too." His brows furrowed. "Latest medical? This is a bit old."

"Keep reading," she said. "The rehab nurse's report is farther on."

He scanned ahead and found the evaluation. Trans Patriot had had its in-house rehabilitation nurse act as liaison with the hospital and doctors to begin to arrange for the future care of the patient and to act as medical case manager. Her report was thorough and detailed.

"They've got him in a private room," he said with some amusement. "How very convenient. TPI does do a great job," he added admiringly. "I think that we can definitely use Mr. Kersten's investment. The reserve is perfect. Trucking companies do carry such high limits."

The long fingers of his right hand tapped a quick rhythm on the tabletop. "I agree it is a little soon; the Martine case is only four weeks since closure. Still, there are some very nice things here. I see our Mr. Kersten is an Orthodox Jew. That rings a bell, for some reason. I'll check that too." He marked that passage with an asterisk on the printout.

"The possibilities for a negative outcome, as presented here, wouldn't create an anomaly in the overall curve," she interjected.

"Statistically speaking, it should fit right into the national averages. This could be more of a challenge, actually," he added, drifting off in thought. "It calls for something a bit more creative. Yes . . ." He drew out the last word, hissing the sibilant.

"Don't get cocky now," she cautioned.

"Don't *you* worry," he said, vaguely annoyed. "I'll do some research, get the options clear. I should be able to take an afternoon flight out, possibly a red-eye. It'll be the usual routine. When it's done, I'll leave the message on the service." He paused. "If all goes well, I ought to be back Monday night."

She paused for a moment. "Be careful," she said. "You know how I get when you're not here." The sexual connotation was clear.

"Yes, well, we'll take care of that when I get back, won't we." It was a statement, not a question.

"I'll see you on Monday."

"Of course," he said, and broke the connection.

He immediately began his research, combing through several volumes of medical texts. Two hours later he was done. The plan was set. He found a travel agency listed in the Yellow Pages and dialed the number.

In a furnished but unoccupied one-bedroom apartment across town in Glendale, another telephone rang once. Exactly six-tenths of a second later the signal was rerouted through a sophisticated switching unit to the travel agency.

The lease agreement on the apartment, paid in advance for one year, identified the occupant as one Peter Bennett. The name was false, and the fictitious Mr. Bennett did not inhabit the apartment. At the moment he was completing his red-eye reservation to Pittsburgh, with a return the next Monday.

He thanked the ticket agent for her help and promised to call again, in reply to her cheery good-bye. He wouldn't, of course. He never used the same agency twice.

At five-thirty that afternoon the sectional door of the three-car garage rose, and a metallic bronze Porsche 911 Turbo backed out into the cul-de-sac, turned, and glided down the street.

Anyone watching the car would have had difficulty making out the driver through the tinted windows. If he had been visible, however, he wouldn't have looked like the same man who had made a reservation for a nighttime flight to Pittsburgh. Now he had longish brown hair, parted conservatively on the right, and he wore brown contact lenses that effectively hid the odd cat's eye.

He had packed a hard-sided leather suitcase in which some particular items had been secured inside of a small padded case. He also had a matching soft-sided suit carrier, which he would carry on. He was dressed in a simple off-the-rack gray business suit that was in keeping with his coach fare status.

He would pay for the plane ticket in cash, which was not uncommon. His motel reservation in Pittsburgh, already set before he left the house, would also be a cash transaction. He didn't want to use plastic on this one. It was too easy to track.

The flight arrived in Pittsburgh without any significant delay. He had packed his heavy coat and gloves and was thankful for them when he walked out of the terminal to his rental car, a white Ford Taurus. It was 4:16 A.M. when he arrived, and the twelve-degree temperature, wind-chilled to seven below zero, bit at him, blown along by a sharp breeze.

He checked into his reserved room at the motel in Greentree, not fifteen minutes from the airport. The drive into Pittsburgh, and Northside General Hospital, would take forty-five minutes to an hour. He planned to check out the hospital at midmorning. He unpacked and went right to bed, falling asleep within minutes. Saturday promised to be a very full day.

He parked the white Taurus on the upper deck of the multistoried parking garage on the east side of Northside General. The time was 9:15 A.M.

This morning he was dressed in a conservative blue business suit, a white shirt, a tie, and an overcoat. He carried a well-worn dark brown briefcase.

He took the elevator down to street level, exiting into the building annex that had been added on to the forty-year-old hospital some ten years before. A typical convolution of hallways took him into the main building, where he picked up a map of the hospital. After getting a cup of coffee in the cafeteria, he sat down to wait for the nurses' shift change, scheduled for 10:00 A.M. A circular clock over the entrance doors showed 9:25. He had plenty of time.

He unfolded the map and began to study it. He knew that George Kersten was in room 710, north wing, seventh floor. The map told

42

him that all of the patient wards were in the old section. The newer annex was taken up primarily by labs, offices, and operating rooms. Locating the claimant's room on the map, he noted the exits, both stair and elevator, as well as the position of the nurses' station.

While he read, the pace of the hospital's daily activities picked up. More people straggled into the cafeteria, waiting relatives, new patients early for check-in, and some staff members, the varied colors of their gowns and scrubs denoting their different occupations. No one paid him any attention. He had done this before and was adept at blending his actions in with the daily flow.

At 9:45 he took the stairs to the seventh floor, recording in the back of his mind how long it took.

He proceeded with total nonchalance to the nurses' station and took a seat in a nearby lounge area. Pretending to study a couple of meaningless file folders, he watched the shift change, noting which nurses went where, at what times, and for how long.

Without glancing at his watch, he noted how long it took each staff member to make end-of-shift checks on patients. He memorized the types and varieties of uniforms he saw, especially the green of the physicians scrubs as opposed to the medium blue worn by the OR nurses and other technicians and the pink-and-white outfits of the student nurses.

While the normal shift change congestion was going on, he stood up and, still referring to the file he carried, ambled down the north hallway, seemingly absorbed in thought.

During this trip, which took him to the far end of the hall, he noted the arrangement of the rooms. George Kersten's room was two-thirds of the way down from the nurses' station on the left side of the hall. The door of the private room was open when he walked by, but he refrained from looking in.

He was far down the hall when the shuffling of people generated by the shift change died down. He noticed a nurse enter George's room, he assumed on a routine status check.

She came back out and returned to the station without a backward glance. Neither she nor anyone else saw the man walk quietly into room 710.

George Kersten lay unmoving in his bed, eyes closed, the lines from four I.V.'s running into him, one in each forearm and one in the back of each hand.

To accommodate the equipment, his arms had been rotated elbows down and secured to short boards by black Velcro straps. All told, six plastic bags, filled or partly filled with various fluids, were shunted into the heparin locks.

Another plastic tube, thicker than the I.V. lines, snaked out from under the covers on the patient's left side, apparently from the side of his chest. It contained a bloody, bubbly fluid that oozed slowly down the length of the tube, which disappeared at its other end under the patient's bed.

Above the headboard railing was a squarish metallic panel containing several gas-line fittings, a couple of rocker switches, and gauge facings. Attached to one of the fittings was a long, clear, flexible hose that coiled down past the patient's multiple pillows and rose up over his upper chest to terminate in a small, clear mask securely strapped over his nose and mouth. It appeared to be supplying oxygen mixed with something else. The man recognized a urinary catheter that carried the patient's kidney output down to another plastic bag, resting in a stainless-steel pan under the bed.

The man approached and looked at George. His color wasn't too bad, he noticed, given what he'd been through. As he turned to leave, he looked down at the still figure once more. "So simple," he whispered, "when you know what you're doing."

He reached out and pressed the tips of his long fingers to the back of George's hand. The touch was almost a caress, and he felt it then —the faintest flicker, like a pulse of brightness that raced up his arm. He smiled.

"Tonight, I should think, Mr. Kersten. We have so much to share." He smiled again, pulled back his hand, then calmly left the room.

He walked back down the hall and took an elevator to the ground floor. He had made the visit without ever being noticed. It was a polished performance.

He was working on barely two hours' sleep since his arrival in Pittsburgh, although he had slept most of the way on the flight. Even so, now that the plan was under way, he didn't feel the least bit tired.

Prior to leaving the motel that morning, he had scanned the local

Yellow Pages for medical clothing stores. There were several near a section of the city called Penn Circle.

He found the area on the rental car map and went shopping. Purchases in hand, he took time for a leisurely lunch and then reviewed his agenda. Satisfied he was on time and on target, he returned to the motel to finish his preparations and then to nap. He wanted to stay sharp, even with the buzz of anticipation he was feeling. The game was going well, and he was looking forward to the final move.

FEBRUARY 18, PITTSBURGH, PENNSYLVANIA

At 1:30 A.M. the white Taurus stopped next to the curb two blocks north of Northside General Hospital. The driver was dressed in the same heavy overcoat, now worn over jeans and high-top Nikes. He also wore a soft-brimmed wool hat and round wire-rimmed glasses. A brown mustache further altered his features.

He folded a padded plastic shopping bag up as tightly as he could and jammed it into the large left-side pocket of his overcoat. His right hand went into the other pocket, and he raised his shoulders to ward off the freezing night air.

The late hour and the cold night worked to his advantage. He saw no one as he began his solitary trek to the hospital.

He entered through the main doors and walked quickly down the quiet hallways to the same stairway he had used earlier. As he climbed three floors, he listened for the sound of others in the stairwell. Hearing no one, he paused at a metal trash container. He stripped off the heavy outer coat and hat, having no difficulty despite the skintight surgical gloves he wore. He then kicked off the Nikes and peeled off the jeans. Underneath, he wore the surgical green scrubs he had bought earlier.

From the plastic bag he took out a cap and smock. Then he put the Nikes back on and slipped on the disposable shoe protectors commonly used in the operating room. He straightened up and patted

45

the side pocket of the long smock, satisfying himself that the small bundle was still there.

He folded the discarded clothes and jammed them into the large bag, which he pushed into the trash can. There would be no trash pickup before 7:00 A.M. He'd already checked.

He hadn't shaved since his arrival in Pittsburgh. That, coupled with some dark eye shadow rubbed lightly under his eyes, gave him the haggard appearance of a surgeon who has spent the last several hours in a grueling session in the operating room.

After climbing the remaining floors to the seventh, he checked his watch. The nurses' shift change was scheduled for 2:00 A.M.

At precisely 2:03 he pushed open the exit door and stepped out into the hall. Nurses were talking two and three to a group, comparing charts, checking orders, and performing their normal tasks. He counted fewer than twenty people covering the three wings.

He walked past the nurses' station, his steps tired but purposeful. He was a doctor going to check the progress of a patient. The game was precisely on schedule, and he was coolly in control. He casually angled across the hall and walked without pause into George Kersten's room.

His luck held, as he had known it would. There was no one in the room but the patient.

He walked straight to the side of the bed, positioning himself so that he could see the door. Then he pulled the small bundle out of the pocket of the smock.

He flipped open a plastic case and extracted a hypodermic syringe. It was loaded with 25 milliliters of Marcaine, a powerful anesthetic meant to be injected in much smaller doses as a pre-op medication.

Placing the tip of the needle against one of the unused rubber shunts on the heparin lock where the I.V. ran into George's arm, he slid in the needle. Immediately he fitted the plunger into the barrel of the syringe and pushed it home.

When the cartridge was empty, he removed the plunger and the empty container, loaded another with the same dosage, and pushed it into the line.

Smoothly, silently, he removed the needle from the fitting and replaced the blue plastic cover over the point. The empty syringe and cartridges went back into the case, which he pocketed.

It was then that he took his first look at George. Leaning over, his face inches away from that of the unconscious man, he let his eyes dance over George's features, still, calm, and quiet.

Calculating that the Marcaine would take less than thirty seconds to begin to show its effect, the man crossed the room to check the hallway. He didn't expect anyone to come in. His earlier surveillance had told him he had at least fifteen minutes before anyone would come back.

He looked at his watch and felt the first rush of his own adrenaline and rising pulse rate. But it wasn't from what he had just done. Rather, it was in anticipation of what was to come.

This was the part that always excited him. He flashed back to the first one he had done, and the look of surprised pain on the face of the girl, who was only—what? twenty-six years old? He remembered the visceral thrill that had shot through him, the rush that had come from having absolute control.

Now he was blooded, and with each new killing, the feeling of power was more pronounced. It had reached the point where he needed to actually touch them now, to close that connection with them as they gave up their lives to him.

He chanced a glance back at George and saw the first tremor. He had calculated the amount of the Marcaine required as a 75 percent solution, given the patient's body weight and postoperative status. Incorporated into 50 milliliters, that ensured a lethal overdose.

The first effect of the anesthetic would be paralysis of the central nervous system, followed by cardiac arrest and convulsions. Death was certain within sixty seconds.

The tremor he saw was the signal, but he maintained his vigil at the doorway. He had to be sure. Anxiety mounted now as the seconds slowly passed. Still, he was safe. There was no sign of movement from the nurses' station.

He dared another look at his victim and saw a major tremor convulse the unconscious form. The paralysis from the accident confined the twitching and thrumming to the upper half of the body.

Unable to stay away, he quickly went back to the bedside and placed his large hand on George's. He locked his gaze on the closed eyes of the man in the bed and began to feel the beginning of the end, the life force eddying within the convulsing body.

George's upper body spasmed again, then seemed to vibrate; his breath became labored, and condensation collected behind the clear mask over his lower face. Suddenly there was a rapid series of strong rhythmic shudders. His shoulders and head snapped up off the pillow, and his sightless eyes flashed open.

Given the prior internal damage, his body couldn't cope with this new onslaught, and things let go inside. Bright red blood exploded out of George's nose and mouth, spraying against the mask. Seconds later everything stopped.

The body dropped back onto the bed, quiet and still. The eyes closed partway, neurological shutdown leaving one open a fraction wider than the other. Neither eye saw the figure beside the bed let out his breath carefully as his fingers stroked the lifeless hand beneath them.

The fingers next pressed against the jugular at the side of George's neck, feeling for a last pulse. There was none, but then, he hadn't expected to find one. He had felt the force leave the body.

It was over, once more. The passion he felt for the moment brought a swelling of emotion for the gift he'd received. With moistened eyes he bent over Kersten and kissed his forehead.

"Thank you," he whispered, feeling the quiet of the body through his lips.

Awareness filtered back in. With one last look back, he left the room. Two nurses noted the passage of the gowned doctor, so obviously fatigued.

"Looks like he's had a long one," one said with a sympathetic nod of her head.

"Bet he's got great buns," the younger of the two replied appreciatively, though the doctor failed to hear her comment. Neither nurse noticed that he left the hallway through the fire exit. But then, it wouldn't have raised any suspicion; everyone did it.

He descended to the third floor and retrieved his belongings from the trash can. He quickly stripped off all the doctor clothing and put

48

everything back into the shopping bag, then dressed just as quickly in his jeans, Nikes, and overcoat, feeling the absence of a shirt immediately. He kept the rubber gloves on. The neutral color made them virtually unnoticeable, and he would need them until he was clear of the hospital. Then he walked calmly back down to the ground floor, and left through the main entrance.

Before returning to the motel, he made one more side trip, this one to a public municipal furnace disposal yard, where he disposed of the shopping bag and its contents.

That task completed, he drove to the motel, already planning a little sight-seeing expedition before catching his flight back to Phoenix on Monday. There was so much to see in Steel Town, U.S.A.

FEBRUARY 19, MOON VALLEY, PHOENIX, ARIZONA

Dana Quinn was almost done with the strenuous aerobic routine she followed every evening between six and seven o'clock. The heavy bass line to Robert Palmer's "Addicted to Love" thudded out from the four stereo speakers. Her breathing came in controlled bursts as she coordinated her movements with the music. For the fourth time in less than fifteen minutes she shot a glance at the blue digital numbers of the clock on the front of the Panasonic receiver amp.

"Six forty-seven," she huffed through gritted teeth. "His message said six-fifteen. Where the bloody hell is he?"

Luther's description of her had been more accurate than he knew. Dana didn't play the field so much as she enjoyed the nuances of the game. Subtle flirtations allowed her to control those reactions she had come to expect from the opposite sex, and on rare occasions she was not averse to going a little further.

But she kept those infrequent liaisons strictly on the physical plane. From her perspective they were purely recreational, just a part of the process, a reinforcement not of her femininity—something in which she was wholly secure—but of what her femininity could accomplish, the power of it. She knew she was stunning, and she had learned that appearances, on occasion, were a crucial element of the game.

The attention she had given to Luther was nothing more than a continuation of that game, although she did find him interesting and she was impressed both by his obvious wealth and by the fact that in spite of it, he still put in a heavy work day. On top of which, she thought with a smile, he wasn't bad looking. Had he given any hint that he wanted her, she would have welcomed him into her bed, just to see.

She played the game well, but despite her proficiency, she was loyal to the one man who had gone beyond the mere physical with her, the man she now awaited. She hated this part the most, the days and hours he was gone. A thousand times she had fought the voice inside her that danced around, hinting at the worst. She had listened to all the what-if's, wondering whether this case was the one that would catch up to them, the one that would turn on some minute, crucial detail they had somehow failed to consider, and he would be gone from her, possibly forever.

And each time she would shout the voice down, because she was confident they hadn't been careless, they hadn't overlooked anything —their game plan had been too carefully constructed. Besides, she assured herself, taking comfort in this one absolute truth, he was the best, the absolute best.

Absently she continued to watch the progress of her routine in the mirrored wall before her, admiring her body, the way it responded to the pulsing rhythm of the music, the color contrast between her skin tones and her spandex suit, the way her thick hair whipped around with each sideways snap of her exquisite head.

She became so engrossed in observing her own performance that she almost missed the faint rumble caused by the garage door opening. Dana turned the volume down in time to hear the distant thump of the front hall closet door closing.

She turned expectantly toward the door as his voice called out, "Hello! Anyone home?"

Relief at the sound of his voice caused an anticipatory shiver to course through her. Her nipples stiffened, pushing strongly against the tight elastic of the mesh sports bra under her suit. "Back here, love, in the exercise room." Looking about quickly, she took advantage of the track lights above the mirrors, and arranged herself in a hipshot pose, hand casually curled around the ballet barre running the length of the mirrored wall. She leaned forward a little, enhancing the curves of her wide, firm breasts accentuated by the scoop neckline of the leotard.

His footsteps carried down the hall, sounding eager on the Mexican tile floor. They stopped in the doorway. "Well," he said, "I'm back."

He stood grinning at her, the successful businessman, dressed in a gray suit, striped tie impeccably knotted, russet loafers gleaming softly, blond hair brushed back in his usual fashion.

He reached up slowly and removed his sunglasses, then he smiled at her. The pupil of his right eye stared at her with its odd combination of cat's-eye mystery and lust.

"Norman," she breathed, "welcome home."

Norman Kearney Bloodstone dramatically flipped the glasses over his shoulder, took two steps toward her, and then picked her up in his long arms, squeezing her tightly.

"God, Dana, you should have been there!" he exclaimed, his words muffled as he buried his face in her hair. "This may have been the best one yet."

"Yes!" she answered, disengaging herself from him slowly, letting her hands trail down the length of his arms. Then she looked up at him, her face glowing, radiating her happiness to be with him again. She released his hands and took a deep breath, pushing her chest out toward him. "Start at the beginning, darling," she prodded. "I want to hear everything."

Norman's face became animated. "The operating room records were the real key, since they explained all the procedures used on George. That's where the Marcaine was mentioned."

Dana, capturing his eyes with her own, began to remove her striped leotard. She shrugged one shoulder, then the other, freeing them from the shimmering fabric. Then she pushed the garment deliberately toward the floor, stimulated by the details he related and the sensual show she was giving him.

"Once I'd decided on the drug, the rest seemed to fall into place,"

51

he continued, beginning to respond to the show she was offering him.

Dana, now wearing nothing but the sports bra, curled the tips of her fingers under the bottom edge of the front band and lifted the tight garment up and over her full breasts. The band pulled across her stiffened nipples, catching on them for a moment, then snapped over them, causing her breasts to jiggle slightly. The movement forced a small hitch in her breathing, but still she stood back.

"Buying the stuff was no problem," Norman said, now eyeing her naked form with undisguised interest, the lust evident in his face. "I simply called that distributor in Mesa I've used before. Told him I had a customer I thought might like a few samples. Said there could be a big order in it in the near future. He had it ready by noon," he added, proud of the subterfuge. "Setting up the cover of a medical supply salesman was a very smart move."

"I always knew it was," Dana replied, finally touching him and raising his elegant hands to her mouth.

She placed a finger between her soft lips, swirled her tongue around it, then moved on to the next. Her eyes were closed in sensual bliss as she made love to his hands.

Norman groaned, now ready to match her passion with his own. He had spent hours thinking about this particular homecoming, one more triumphant return. Now that same passion had a peculiar augmentation, driven by the exceptional circumstances that bound them closer than any personal feelings ever could. He allowed her to continue to stimulate him as he merely told her about his preparations.

Dana then placed his hands on the sides of her face and alternately kissed both palms. Next she drew them down her neck and over the twin arches of her collarbones, settling them on her breasts. Even with his extraordinary reach, his hands could not fully span the round globes. She encouraged him to caress her in circles. Once his hands had taken up the movement, she reached up, unknotted his tie, and pulled it loose, dropping it on the floor.

She pushed his suit coat off his shoulders. Norman assisted with a small shrug, letting the coat join the tie on the floor. Dana continued to undress him, as he told his story, giving her all the details, arousing her with his graphic descriptions.

52

She ran her hands around his shoulders, leaning forward to kiss the center of his chest, her excitement heightened by his words. Moving her hands slowly, she drew them down his chest, across his hard stomach, tracing the ripple of muscles there. Then she continued downward, bringing her fingers together until she found him, touched him, felt him harden in her small hands.

"I watched him when I pushed the plunger in." He sighed hoarsely, underlining his words by moving one hand down her body, leaving the other to its sensual erotic work.

His hand stroked the tops of her thighs just under her softly curved abdomen. Back and forth his fingertips glided. The tips made tiny patterns on her skin, swirling, tapping, his hand moving spiderlike, his fingers spreading wide, then closing, pulsing over her heated skin, making her jump with minute shivers. And all the time he moved toward her center.

Closing his eyes for a second, Norman spoke slowly, reverently. "The Marcaine went in smoothly. You could just feel the magic flow into him, deep, deep inside."

Dana moaned, her legs suddenly weak. She clung to his upper arms and buried her face against his chest, reveling in the waves of pleasure that rolled through her.

"Deeper," he said, his fingers punctuating his words.

"Yes," she whispered, "please . . ."

She pulled him to the floor and lay down beside him even as his fingers stayed within her. She felt the first rush, then the fine explosion that made her suck in her breath, her body rigid from the attack.

"Oh, God, yes . . ." Dana moaned softly. She pushed him down flat on the floor and hastily disengaged his hand, needing him, wanting him. She knelt astride his waist, reached back and fitted him to her with vibrating hands, encouraging him inside with urgent strokes of her long nails.

She sat upright, controlling his actions now, choreographing the scene. She began to move her hips against him. She leaned forward, palms on either side of his head, offering her pendulous breasts to him.

"George began to quiver," he said through clenched teeth, wanting to feel once again that special lust he had for his victims, so similar to the feelings she aroused in him.

"Hush," she said, responding. She didn't need the words now. She had him. Her body melted into him, rocking with his thrusts.

"I touched him, just like all the other times," he panted, ignoring her request for silence, needing to continue. He had to share all of it with her, let her feel what he had done for her. "It was there . . . like a current. . . . I could . . . feel him go."

"Yes, love, yes, love, yes," she chanted, not fully understanding, and not for the first time, her exclamations matching the motions of his body beneath her. She wanted him to squeeze her breasts in time with his thrusts.

Norman felt it, felt the underlying edge, and wanted more, wanted to take it further. In one swift move he grasped her tight to him and rolled, pinning her beneath him.

She looked at him, saw the exertion on his face, misinterpreting it as a reflection of what she felt for him. But this time his passion was not solely for her. His eyes were closed, his eyebrows lifted, his face suddenly benign yet tense. He clutched her as his breath froze. Then he groaned beside her ear with the beauty of it.

"Oh . . . darling," she whispered, letting her own eyes close with the heat thrill that washed over her. He didn't hear her.

"Norman," she whispered. Then "Norman," louder yet, and again, "Norman!" Her voice cut through to him. His eyes opened slowly, reality drifting in. He slowed within her, became aware of her voice, stopped moving, focusing on her.

Dana saw a light in his eyes she hadn't seen before—bright, distant, dangerous. Then it dissolved, and he smiled at her and relaxed. His arms beneath her relaxed, holding her to him.

"That was incredible," he murmured.

She looked up at the ceiling. A worried expression flitted across her face.

"Yes," she agreed slowly. "Yes, it was."

Much later, over supper, their conversation swirled around this latest investment in their unusual, and deadly, business.

"So what was the significance of Kersten being Jewish?" Dana inquired.

54

"Orthodox," Norman reminded her with a smile. "I knew there was something to that." The smugness crept back into his expression.

"Orthodox Jews have to be buried within twenty-four hours after death." He grinned to himself. "Not enough time for an autopsy, as I guessed. Ol' George is already planted by now."

Norman tapped his fingers in a tight pattern on the surface of the dining table. "That's what fit so well. Even if they did manage to find any evidence of outside intervention, it would appear to be a medical problem, a tragic overdose, mistakenly administered, nothing else." His smile widened. "It would look like the hospital killed him."

His face sobered abruptly as he addressed the next topic. The fast physical change in his features struck a warning chord in Dana's mind; the difference between the two expressions was distinct and was made without any transition.

"Do you think Kersten's power of attorney will be a problem?"

She took a sip of wine, then answered. "The employer in this case has power of attorney, and there aren't any relatives to provide the emotional decision necessary to prosecute a wrongful death action.

"For Mon Valley Electric, it boils down to sheer economics," she went on. "Their only financial loss to date has been payment of the hospital expenses, which is sure to generate a lien on the file. But with the claimant dead, the amount of the lien is now a fixed cost, easily covered. Once it's paid off, the file will be closed, probably within thirty days, forty-five at the most."

She sat back from the table, finished with her meal. "After that, it will be business as usual," she said matter-of-factly.

"The loss reserve money will be released when the file's closed," Norman said, "and it will be transferred to your department, to be dispersed among the staff."

They referred to the procedure most large insurance companies followed for handling this type of circumstance. The money estimated to be paid out on claims over the course of a year was reserved, accounted for at the beginning of the year by the company actuaries. If the claim was then closed during the year with no payment made on the loss side, such as when a lawsuit was dismissed by the court or settled for a sum substantially below the reserved figure, the extra unused balance became basically found money.

Already accounted for, it was invested into various markets to bring in the maximum gains allowed under the complicated laws of high finance. For a large corporation like Trans Patriot, diversified into a number of markets, it was just another source of profit, looked over, in this case, by the investment department.

"In due course," Dana continued, "my allocation will end up in some very solid areas."

"And Kallang, Limited, will show an additional profit this year," Norman finished. "We're getting close to our goal."

Kallang, Ltd., was a small, solidly successful foreign investment broker, headquartered in Singapore. It had the appearance of a legitimate brokerage, which in fact it was. But it had been created by Dana and Norman, the real owners, who used it for a specific purpose: as a middleman broker, Kallang located single investors unable to fund an investment project on their own but wanting to ensure additional protection for their investment by sharing the risk with other partners.

Dana Quinn, working on the inside at Trans Patriot, used her position to advantage by seeing to it that Kallang, Ltd., occasionally received some of Trans Patriot's business. Dana and Norman controlled the deal from a distance, safely hidden behind mountains of paper and red tape, shielded even from the manager who ran Kallang's office in Singapore. They put together deals with TPI and other investors and pocketed the commissions paid back to the broker by the various partners. That was the first part of the scam.

The second came from the deal itself. Dana saw to it that the joint venture consortium bought into a solid deal, as risk-free as possible, promising a healthy return on the investment put in. Then she had Kallang, Ltd., buy into the deal, too, as another partner. Once the transaction was turning over a fair profit, Kallang would sell off its proceeds. Dana kept an eye on the particular market she was working in, to be sure that there were no restrictions that would keep Kallang from participating beyond simply brokering the idea.

So far, over the course of four years, Kallang, Ltd., under the watchful eyes of Dana and Norman, had turned a handsome profit of just over seventeen million dollars, the proceeds residing in a numbered bank account in Bern, Switzerland.

As the creators of Kallang, they had been careful to incorporate their company overseas, effectively losing it in the convoluted and complex paperwork that was part and parcel of foreign trade. Anyone trying to track down Kallang's business pedigree would be a long time in the process. And by the time he got there, he would find the principals long gone.

Norman and Dana called it, simply, "the game." They played for high-stakes money, and their strategy had turned bloody, thanks to a quirk in the evolution of their greed.

"I'll be taking a trip for TPI to New York, soon," she said. "They just told me today."

"That's interesting," he said. "How would you like it if I came along on this one? It's been a while since we did the Big Apple together."

Dana blinked suddenly, caught unawares by the question. She recovered smoothly. "Why don't we wait just a bit? It's so bloody cold there this time of the year. Besides, I'll have other business to take care of for Trans Patriot, what with the brokers I'm to see."

She reached across the table to press her hands against his. "But I love the idea," she murmured. "We could have some fun."

"Yes, I suppose you're right," he replied, wondering at the quickness of her objection. "I'll find something here to amuse me while you're gone," he said, already making up his mind. "How soon is soon?"

"The company's got the trip set up for the second week of March."

"All right," Norman said, his plan taking form behind his golden eyes. "Maybe New York won't be as cold as you suspect."

The next morning after Dana had left for work, Norman sat down at his PC and pulled up the Kersten file. Smiling as he went, he began to enter a narrative description of the murder. It was detailed, precise, and exhaustive, and Bloodstone was pleased with the effort when he was finished.

He saved the information as part of the permanent file, then slid a formatted diskette into the machine. In seconds he had transferred the file contents onto the floppy disk and deleted the file from the disk drive's memory. Norman stood up, reached to the top shelf above the computer, and unlocked the small fireproof safe located there. Taking out a plastic file-card box, he placed the diskette in the alphabetized slot for Kersten, George. The box held twenty-two identical disks.

Had Dana known about them, she would have fainted dead away, considering the detailed and incriminating evidence they contained. They held the entire record of each murder, preserved by Norman not as evidence but as trophies, lasting reminders. He needed this connection, this last contact with each claimant. It served to verify his skill and expertise in the ultimate challenge, the game within the game.

MARCH 2, TPI, THE VILLAGE

Luther Sitasy received the report of George Kersten's death in the normal course of business. It arrived with the morning mail.

The report, written by the Pittsburgh file handler, Mark Alexander, indicated that his office had been notified by Mon Valley Electric following their notice by the hospital. Death apparently resulted from surgical complications. There had been no autopsy. The adjuster's closing report would follow as soon as the medical liens had been resolved. There apparently would be no wrongful death litigation. It was all fairly routine.

Luther initialed the report and entered it into the home office file on Kersten, another page in the daily paper shuffle. The insurance industry had reduced the flesh and blood of a man to numbers on a computer disk.

The premature closing of Kersten's file did have one ancillary effect that neither Norman nor Dana nor even Luther had anticipated. The ramifications, though, would prove to be critical, and ultimately terminal.

A typical policy limit file lasted a minimum of two years. Most averaged three to four. Everyone wanted to avoid having a large amount of time elapse before a file was closed, with a correspondingly large amount of money committed to paying lawyers on both sides. That money could be put to a better and more profitable use.

Luther's curiosity had been tweaked by George Kersten's death. He wondered if there was a way for TPI to predict at the outset the exact case life of a limits file involving a potential fatality. The ability to predict file reserves and litigation costs more accurately would be an important cost-saving tool.

It seemed to the claimsman, with his analytical mind, that some common parameters might be worked out, that it might be possible to develop a standard profile to support his hypothesis.

He mulled the question over during the morning. Of all the people on his staff, Gordon Hatton, at thirty-seven, an eighteen-year veteran in claims, had the heaviest background in systems analysis and accounting.

Luther invited Gordon to join him for lunch and pitched his idea, unsure if it had any merit and, if it did, whether there was any practical way to develop a statistical profile.

"The idea is sound," Gordon replied to Luther's proposal. "The question must be asked, given the way claims are handled in general, why this hasn't been done before." Then he paused before adding, "Ideally speaking, we set the initial reserves, try to get a claim investigation over quickly, ascertain the pertinent facts to establish negligence, or the lack of, for our insured. Then we adjust that reserve as needed over the duration of the legal discovery, and decide to defend or settle."

"Right, that's the ideal," Luther agreed, "but as a rule of thumb it doesn't apply to our types of claims—at least not all the time. A non-litigated claim may be extraordinarily complex, or there could be discovery forced by a lawsuit, both of which can add years to the case life."

"I understand that," Gordon replied. "We've got to factor in the complications of situations with multiple defendants-plaintiffs, cata-strophic injuries, massive medical treatment and attendant costs for that treatment, excess carriers, reinsurance levels, et cetera." He took another bite of his sandwich and added, "But it is a hell of an idea."

Luther slowly swirled the ice inside his cup. "So you think such a profile could be worked out?"

Gordon reached for his own soda. "I don't know, right off, Lute. There are so many variables. If we use the very things that make these cases so dissimilar as the common factors, we should be able to graph them as a generic model." He paused for a moment, considering the equation. "What I think is, even though these are policy limits files, they all share certain traits, enough to see if your theory holds water. What the hey," he continued lightly, "if we can predict the actual statistical life span for a given group of cases like these, the pencil pushers in accounting will love us. Look at the savings."

"Exactly my point," Luther said. "The analysis of these claims could be significant all by itself. I don't think Trans Patriot's ever had it done before, at least, not to look for what we're going to look for."

"As I said, it ought to be interesting." Gordon finished his sandwich, washed it down with his soda, and said, "Let me get with the systems people and see if we can hammer out a program. How soon would you like to see this?"

"No rush," Luther said. "It's just something that came up almost by chance. If it turns out to be something we can use, great. If not, no big deal. We've lots of other things to keep us busy without adding anything more to the mix." He considered this last thought in light of Gordon's caseload. "I wouldn't want this to interfere with whatever else you have on tap," he cautioned.

"Not to worry, Lute," he said. "We'll work something out."

That was the answer Luther had expected.

The following Tuesday Gordon stuck his head into his boss's office. "Got a minute, Lute? Looks like we have that program worked out for your profile."

Luther motioned him in. Gordon entered, accompanied by an attractive young woman who carried several folded computer printouts.

Gordon made the introduction. "Luther Sitasy, this is Sheri Moradilo. Sheri, my boss, Luther."

Sitasy got up to shake hands with the young woman as she set the papers on the side of his desk. "A pleasure," he said, taking her offered hand.

"Nice to meet you, too." She smiled brightly.

"Thank you for taking the time to help us with this project," Luther began, rightly surmising that Ms. Moradilo was from the company's systems department.

"No trouble at all." She beamed at him. Her smile was infectious. "When Gordo called with the outline, I was intrigued." She turned her smile on Gordon, who returned it with the same intensity.

Doing a slight double take, Luther asked, "So what did you two whiz kids come up with?"

Sheri spoke first. "Actually, the problem was not all that difficult, once we worked out the common factors of the program."

Gordon joined in. "Establishing the baseline took some time. We had to use all the data we could find on every policy and every policy limits claim file applicable. That produced a pretty complicated program, sort of like fuzzy logic."

"It's a new computer science, but perfect for this application," Sheri said. She reached for the computer sheets and began to arrange them on Luther's desk.

"Our baseline takes into account the standard national average stats for accidental death and death by natural causes or by other means."

"Also," Gordon said, "we factored in claims that were closed early, like voluntary dismissals of the lawsuit, failure to prosecute within the statutory time allowed, things like that."

"For our purposes, data not directly linked to a fatality was considered less important as regards this particular profile," Sheri added, throwing another warm glance at Gordon.

"Of course," Gordon agreed, returning the look.

"Of course." Luther was starting to feel like a third wheel in this conversation.

Gordon continued. "We correlated the national average stats from the U.S. Census Bureau with those from national insurance industry life tables. That gave us a starting point."

"Then we redefined that data with those stats taken from Trans

Patriot's records," Sheri broke in, "and came up with what we think is the definitive baseline for the survey." She pointed to a series of figures on one of the sheets.

Luther had followed the dual performance with interest and some amusement. Now he nodded his understanding. "When will you run the first survey?"

Gordon answered, "Let's see, you wanted to go back—what? two years initially?"

Luther nodded. "That ought to be enough to see if we're on the right track."

Sheri collected her papers and turned toward Gordon. "Running this program for two years' worth of claims shouldn't take too long." She paused in mid-thought and added, "But I think you're going to need more data."

She glanced again at Gordon, then directed her attention back to Luther. "I should think Thursday would do it, maybe sooner if Gordon would like some help."

Gordon didn't hesitate. "Yep, I could use the help, and Thursday sounds fine with me, too. That'll give us a chance to work out any bugs in the program. I'll put the results into graph form so you can compare the ratio of premature closings with the baseline norm."

Luther considered the direction in which their discussion was going. "Don't forget that the main reason for these closings so far has been the demise of the claimant-plaintiff, for whatever reason," he cautioned. "Don't get sidetracked by other details."

Sheri nodded in understanding. "We've taken that into consideration, Mr. Sitasy."

"It's Luther," he replied, "and you're right: I should have known. In any case, thank you both again for the quick work on getting this started. I really do appreciate the effort."

"Oh, Mr. Sitasy," Sheri responded enthusiastically, "it wasn't any effort at all. In fact, the pleasure's been all mine so far." She cast a sideward glance at Gordon.

"Yes, well," her partner said quickly, "any time, boss," and ushered Sheri out of the office.

Luther stood up as they began to leave. When Gordon approached the doorway, his boss said, "Gordo? Is there anything I should know?" He smiled as he pointed in the direction of the now departed young woman, then back at Gordon.

Gordon shrugged. "Nothing to report, boss. We just sort of hit it off. You know how it is." He glanced down the hall quickly, then added, "She's a neat lady, Lute. I like her."

"Beware the office romance," Luther intoned deeply, raising an eyebrow.

"Hey, no problem," Gordon said with a grin.

Early in the morning only two days later Gordon called his boss. "Got the survey done, Lute. Got time to see it?"

Luther glanced at the work already waiting on his desk. "Give me about forty minutes, okay?"

At the appointed time, Gordon walked into his boss's office, still studying the printouts he carried.

"Where's Sheri?" Luther asked, noticing the absence of the energetic systems analyst.

"Out and about," Gordon said, preoccupied with his reading. "She's wrapped up in another project. Anyway, here's the first analysis," he continued, laying the chart on the desk. He pointed to the graph. "As you can see, we ran the number of fatalities, which included other closing sources, up this way." He indicated the direction. "There were one hundred sixty-three deaths during those two years."

"And the baseline represents the average claim file life?"

"Right, but only for these two years."

Looking at the graph, Luther noted the slightly fluctuating but rising line above the baseline. "Appears we have an increase in the number of deaths recently."

"It kind of looks that way," Gordon agreed. "But note also that the rise is fairly narrow compared to the overall average." He tapped the paper with his pen. "I checked the figures. Statistically it's almost a random increase. No apparent reason for it."

"So you're saying that the rise is there but it could have been caused by any number of variables at this stage?"

"Exactly," Gordon replied. "But I think we need a longer time span than the two years we've covered, a bigger sample, something to give us a better bite at the figures." He stood up. "So far, what we've got is a statistical analysis that shows a marginal rise in death claims over a given period of time. Unfortunately it doesn't explain why. I'm afraid as a predictor for the average life span of a policy limits claim file, it's a bust."

Luther remained seated, studying the graphs, while he weighed the parameters and possibilities in his mind. Gordon's information wasn't what he had expected.

"Okay," he said, "let's take this back five years. That ought to give us more data to prove this out."

MARCH 12, TPI, THE VILLAGE

Luther arrived at the office at the usual pre-dawn hour and parked the black Mach I in his space in the underground garage. He proceeded through the deserted complex to his office and got no more than fifteen minutes into the weekend mail piled on his desk before Gordon walked into his office, knocking twice on the open door as he passed through it.

"Mornin', Lute," he said, taking a seat in front of Luther's desk without being asked.

Luther sat back in surprise. "Uh, good morning, Mr. Hatton. A tad early for you, isn't it?" He smiled at the preoccupied expression on Gordon's face.

"Under normal circumstances I should just about be getting up now," he replied absently. Then he launched right into the reason for his early arrival. "I finished your survey over the weekend. Yeah, I know," he said, cutting off his boss's protest. "You don't like us working weekends. But I really wanted to get this project done. Anyway," he continued, "there's something really weird about these latest results."

Luther noticed that Gordon hadn't brought any computer printouts. "Whatever it was, it was enough to get you to come in this early."

Luther studied the other man's face. "So let's take a look at what we have."

"May I?" Gordon asked, gesturing at Luther's PC. He nodded. Gordon got up, swiveled the unit toward him, and pulled the keypad around. He turned the system on and accessed his own coded files. A graph appeared on the screen, a duplicate of the printout Luther had seen the week before.

"I ran the survey back five years, like we discussed, looking for more similarities for the profile." Gordon rolled the computer mouse, touched the button, and the graph filled in the data lines. "This represents the number of fatalities on TPI's policy limits cases from 1985 to 1987," he said. "You can see that our cases number a little bit higher than the national average of recorded claim fatalities."

Luther looked at the wavering but slightly higher line. "Significance?"

"That took a little fiddling around," Gordon said, "but I figured it was the types of coverages that we write. We've got some pretty hairy risks out there, as you know. And when something goes bad with one of them, it's generally very bad."

He continued. "So if you use that as a constant for strictly TPI's cases, it explains why our case costs tend to run a little higher than the average, what with the special risk factors included."

He paused and tapped in another command. "Okay, this is where it starts to get strange." The data changed on the display. Now the baseline, a medium blue against the black background, was measurably higher than before. A new line, wavering above it, was a brighter electric blue. "What you're seeing here is a new baseline, using only Trans Patriot's cases. It represents all the coverages we write."

He tapped the screen with his finger. "From 1985 to now, there were over three hundred fifty-six thousand claim files worldwide, seventy-eight hundred of which were policy limits claims. Three hundred twelve claimants died during that time. The line's getting higher, shows more fatalities."

He entered a new command, and a third data line appeared, layered over the first two. The new one was in red.

"The red line represents death by accident, the bright blue line deaths by natural causes. Both are compared to the national averages and to TPI's averages."

Now the baseline extended sideways. Luther noted the graph now encompassed the years 1988, 1989, and 1990, up to February 28. The electric blue and red lines extended also, as they bled into 1988, then took a dramatic turn upward.

Captivated by the display, Luther leaned forward in his chair, studying the figures that glowed back at him from the silent monitor. "What the hell is that?" he asked, lightly stroking his beard.

"This is the weird part I told you about," Gordon said, standing beside him. "What you're looking at, Lute, is the number of fatal claims for TPI, specifically our policy limit claims, beginning in 1985."

There was silence while Luther focused his attention on the screen, processing the data. His eyes returned to that point in 1988 where the data curve bent upward. "Obviously, something happened in 1988," he said finally, breaking the silence. "Whatever it was, there is a measurable increase in the number of accidental deaths. So what is it?"

"Damned if I know." Gordon's voice betrayed his frustration. "Don't forget that there is an increase in deaths by natural causes, too, but nowhere near as great." He remained standing beside Luther, leaning on his knuckles over the top of the desk. "I checked and rechecked these stats ten times. It comes out the same way every blessed time."

"Why didn't we see this on the earlier survey?"

"I thought about that, and it looks like there's two reasons. First, that initial sample was for '88 and '89 only. Since the increased numbers had no prior stats to work off of, we went into that survey with an artificially high curve to start with. We just didn't know that this data"—he indicated the screen—"even existed."

"And the second?"

"The second is that the first survey's baseline represented the insurance industry as a whole. This one is strictly Trans Patriot's figures."

"I don't see any kind of predictability, any logic, to the death dates," Luther said.

"There doesn't appear to be any recognized frequency," Gordon agreed. "Despite accidental versus natural causes, each death listed occurred completely at random."

"How many cases account for this increase?"

"Between twenty and twenty-five more fatalities over these two years than there should be. It's too random to pin down exactly."

More fatalities than there should be, Luther thought, and exhaled sharply. "Jesus, this is bizarre. And there's no readily apparent reason for the increase?" He realized he was repeating himself.

"None. And something else, too. The survey covers all markets, domestic and foreign. But the additional fatalities are all in the U.S., specifically the lower forty-eight states; none have occurred in Hawaii or Alaska."

"Any particular concentration among a group of states?" Luther asked.

Gordon rubbed his palms slowly over his eyes. "None that I could identify. They seem to appear all over the country. What we have here, boss, is an awful lot of dead people. I don't know why, but for damn sure there's a reason out there. I just haven't found it yet."

Later that morning, Luther called Gordon into his office. He had made up his mind.

"Have you talked to anyone about this survey?" he asked.

Hatton shook his head. "Didn't seem to be any reason to, why?"

"What about Sheri?"

"She was in on the original program, but she doesn't know what I've done with it."

"Good," Luther replied. "There's nothing solid I can put a finger on here, but it's got me thinking."

"I know what you mean," Gordon said without humor. "It's been bugging the heck out of me since the weekend, too."

Luther leaned back in his chair. "Well, the only way I can see to try and resolve this is to go back to the basics. Do you have anything really pressing on your caseload for the next couple of days? Trials coming up? Settlement conferences?"

Gordon thought for a moment, then replied, "I'll check my calendar real quick, but I can always shuffle things around."

"Good, 'cause you and I are going to be busy,"

"I had a feeling something like this was going to happen."

"Just trying to give you job security," Luther said, smiling. Gordon smiled at the joke, too, job security being one of the least reliable things about working in insurance claims.

"There were three hundred twelve fatalities in four years, one-hundred sixty-three from 1988 to now," Luther went on. "We need to review every file and go over them line by line. There has to be something there, some common denominator."

"I had the same idea myself."

"Cover every aspect of each claim in detail, including the accident itself, the medical records, litigation, activity checks, family biographical info, work situation, prior injuries—the whole nine yards," Luther said, "especially the death certificates, and autopsies, as they apply. One way or another, we're going to find out what happened with—or to—all those people."

Gordon stood up to leave, then stopped. "Any particular way you want to split them up?" he asked from the doorway.

"Easiest way I know. Make a list and tear it in half."

"Works for me," Gordon said, and left the office.

The two claimsmen spent the rest of the week reading every fatal claim file used in the survey. Other tasks pulled them away temporarily, but at Luther's insistence, they continued their research.

It was painstaking, mind-numbing work, going over every file note, status report, legal plea, and motion filed. They took apart each accident investigation, reviewing witness statements and field reports. They read scores of medical reports, doctors' office notes, and OR summaries, along with coroners' death certificates and autopsies. Their constant goal was to find out why over twenty claimants, who shouldn't have, had died.

At the close of business on Wednesday, Luther called a strategy meeting with Gordon in the cafeteria after most of the daytime staff had gone home.

"How you doin'?" he asked his obviously weary associate.

"Hangin' in there, Lute, how about you?"

"About the same," Luther replied. "You know, with some four thousand open files in the unit, you wouldn't think that a few hundred fatals, spread over two years, would be all that many."

Gordon concurred. "Makes a big difference when you have to field-strip each one, more so when it's a file you haven't seen before."

"Speaking of going over someone else's files, has anyone asked what you're doing?" Luther inquired.

"Diane Folmer came by this afternoon and asked, sort of off the cuff. Said she had seen the extra effort and was mildly curious. None of the others seem to have even noticed."

"What did you tell her?"

"Only that it was a research project, and that I was unlucky enough to have been the one picked for it." He held up a hand. "Just kidding."

"I appreciate it," Luther said with a smile. "It wasn't my attention to shut anybody out. I'm still not sure what we've stumbled into here, but until the picture gets clearer, there's no sense tying up any more extra time, or people, in this."

"I don't mind the work," Gordon said, "since it's my program that got us into this in the first place. I just wish something would shake loose."

"Your program, my theory. How many files have you gotten through?"

"Forty-one," Gordon replied. "How many for you?"

"Thirty-eight," he said. "For a minute there I thought I had something, too. Came across a couple of files where the claimants died of accidental causes. One was a fall down some cellar steps. The other was a single car crash, with fire. Total loss to the vehicle as well."

"What was special about those two?"

"Nothing, really," Luther said, "but some of the notes made by the handling adjuster looked different, or sounded different . . . something."

Gordon leaned forward, resting his elbows on the table edge. "All right," he prompted, "what, exactly, didn't ring true?"

Luther gestured dismissively. Gordon ignored him. "Let me play devil's advocate, Lute. What the hell was it?" he persisted.

Dismissing the nagging feeling that he was being paranoid, he answered, "Well, in the one with the auto fatality, it was the fact that it was a single car crash, no witnesses, little-used road, two-lane rural blacktop, et cetera, et cetera."

"What's the et cetera stuff?"

"Oh, hell, I don't know." Luther sighed. "It just seemed to be so" —he made a twirling motion with one hand—"so . . . convenient." He paused. "But maybe that's not the right word."

"Gotcha barking at shadows, eh?" Gordon observed. "Don't feel bad, Lute. I've had a couple of squirrelly thoughts myself. Too much eyestrain. Your mind starts making up scenarios, playing with the input."

"I know, I know," Luther agreed. "Real life liberally sprinkled with a dose of Agatha Christie."

Getting back to what his boss had said a moment ago, Gordon asked, "You mentioned another case, something about a fall down some stairs?"

"Oh, right. That one was closed over a year ago. There was a note in the file from the handling adjuster wrapping up the final details." Luther became more animated as he remembered the note. "It was a summarized interview with a neighbor who was close to the claimant. There apparently was a formal investigation after the fact, as the claimant's body wasn't discovered for a couple of days. He lived alone."

He shook his head slowly at the memory of what he'd read. "The claimant was old—seventy, seventy-one. He'd been hit in the head by a forklift some fifteen years earlier. It left him with an immobilized left side and the IQ of an adolescent. His lawyer, prosecuting the civil lawsuit against our insured, called the authorities and asked them to check up on the old guy when he didn't hear from him."

"Man, that's tough," Gordon said. "What happened with the suit?"

"The lawyer shut it down. Dismissal with prejudice. Had second thoughts about pursuing a questionable-product liability suit now that his meal ticket was gone. At least, that's how the field adjuster read it. Legal vampires." Luther smiled grimly. "Anyway, the second accident seemed as odd as the other one. No witnesses, a single claimant, and a neighbor's statement. The adjuster indicated the deceased had a fear of the stairs, according to a neighbor who helped out occasionally. She was suspicious after the accident and said so to the cops who answered the call."

"What did the official report say?"

"Accidental fall, per the coroner's investigation. They discounted the neighbor as a friendly but snoopy old woman."

"Case closed."

"So it would seem," Luther agreed, although with perceptible reluctance.

"Time for us to close it, too. Let's take it on home. It's more of the same tomorrow."

"Sounds good to me, pal," Gordon replied. "If you're going my way, sir, I'll let you accompany me to where my trusty chariot awaits."

Luther stood. "Lead on, troop."

"So, Gordo," Luther said, as they walked to the garage, "how goes it with the good Miss Moradilo?"

"Just swimmingly, thank you," Gordon offered. "It's a real kick to be around someone so caught up in enjoying life." He looked over at Luther as they walked into the elevator. "Know what I mean?"

"Yeah, I do," Luther replied. The little voice inside him was nudging him again. This time he decided to listen.

MARCH 12, SKY HARBOR AIRPORT, PHOENIX, ARIZONA

Dana Quinn, dressed in a peach-colored business suit, checked into the early morning TWA flight to Kennedy Airport in New York with twenty minutes to spare.

On board, the first-class stewardess hung up Dana's heavy cashmere winter coat while Dana took her assigned window seat and immediately settled in with a romance novel, one of two she habitually carried on trips.

Dana always flew first class, making up the difference out of her own pocket, since the company only paid for coach. She felt she deserved the luxury and the service, and the extra money was not a problem.

While she was settling in, the stewardess approached her. "All the way to New York, or will you be getting off at our St. Louis stopover?" she asked cheerfully.

Dana looked up, returning the smile. "New York, actually."

She nodded. "I should tell you that the seat beside you will be empty for the entire flight, so feel free to spread out your things." She shuffled a stack of magazines, holding the titles toward Dana, who declined them all.

"Something to drink, then, before takeoff?"

"Chablis," Dana said, and settled back.

"Certainly." The stewardess pulled down the serving tray, then said, "Pardon me, but you're from the islands, aren't you? Jamaica, right?"

Dana smiled at the directness of the question. "That's right. I'm afraid it's pretty obvious sometimes."

"Oh, I think your accent is fabulous," the stewardess said. "The reason I ask is that my husband and I spent our honeymoon down there. It was just wonderful; we'd go back in a heartbeat. It's so lovely."

"Yes, it is, although I don't get to go back as often as I'd like."

They spent a few more minutes in amiable conversation while Dana patiently listened to the stewardess's stories of what had been good, bad, and indifferent about her honeymoon. Dana offered to provide her with a list of out-of-the-way, non-touristy places to see, should she and her husband ever go back. Her offer assured her of special service for the remainder of the flight.

Airborne after a thirty-minute delay, she checked over various investment portfolios, stock plans, and other transactions to which she had committed TPI's money. She confirmed her schedule with the brokerage houses she would visit over the next four days.

One appointment wasn't listed: a meeting with a law firm in Manhattan, on 39th Street. Dana smiled to herself when she thought about this meeting, for in a direct way, it was related to TPI business. It just wasn't known to anyone else in the investment department— or to Norman, either. The individual she was to see Wednesday of that week was Allen Parkman, one of the senior partners of Kast, Litz, Wallesen, and Parkman, a firm that specialized in corporate law, licensing, contracts, foreign trade, and overseas investments. Eighty-nine partners, half as many associates, and a battalion of paralegals, law students, and secretaries handled several thousand business clients in the United States and abroad.

Allen Robyn Parkman, fifty-two and divorced, had handled the business account of Strangeways, Ltd., a personal client, for over twenty-five years. Strangeways belonged to James Evan Quinn, Dana's father, who had built up a successful import-export business in Jamaica after World War II.

Allen was tall, just under six feet tall, beginning to gray, and fighting the good fight with his waistline. He was respected professionally, conservative in his politics, exacting in his culinary knowledge, occasionally existential in his recreational reading, and fanatical about his collection of Jaguars, half of which he had lost in the divorce, something that hurt him more than the alimony. Fortunately he had managed to hold on to the beachfront Tudor mansion in the Hamptons. The country house, however, had been a casualty of the divorce.

Divorced for ten years now, Allen fancied himself a late-blooming ladies' man, not realizing his personal income had more to do with his success in getting nubile creatures into his bed than his personality.

He had known Dana Quinn since she was a child, and thought her the most exquisite creature he had ever seen. He had offered Dana's parents advice on colleges for all of their children and had been instrumental in helping Dana gain acceptance at Duke University.

She had blossomed during her four years there, and Allen had been of further help upon her graduation in landing her her first job on Wall Street, calling in a favor from another client of the firm.

Dana's physical attractiveness had always been apparent to Allen, but it wasn't until some time after his divorce that he began to look upon her with a different eye. He had reminded himself, during a round of brandy-assisted self-revelation, that the desire he was beginning to feel for her, given his connections and relationship to the Quinn family, bordered on the incestuous. But the feelings continued, although he was careful to hide them from everyone, including Dana.

Then, four years ago, the unthinkable became the unbelievable for Allen. That his fondest fantasies became reality was all the more surprising because Dana had been the one to initiate their liaison—in return for a particular, and illegal, favor from him.

Consequently, each visit Dana made to New York was, for him, preceded by several days of lustful anticipation.

Dana arrived in New York in the late afternoon and took a cab from JFK to the Plaza Hotel on Central Park South, another luxury she paid for herself.

She unpacked at her leisure, thinking about how far she had come in her career and what she'd had to do to get where she was. In retrospect, she regretted none of it.

Dana Lenore Quinn had developed an awareness of her exotic beauty at an early age. She had discovered that her sensual charms, a gift from her mother's side, attracted a great deal of attention, whether it was desired or not. She had soon found that she could get whatever she wanted by a selective and discreet use of her physical charms.

She was not promiscuous, nor was she encumbered by a gold digger's mentality. She simply knew what she wanted and developed a plan for herself that worked each time.

After finishing undergraduate school at Duke at age twenty, she went to Harvard where she obtained a master's in finance. After that, the few things her intelligence could not do for her, her body could. She had an almost unlimited appetite for sex. There was little she had not tried by the time she interviewed for and won her first job with a mid-level brokerage house on Wall Street.

Her first year, however, she did not have to rely on her sensuality. There literally was no time for that activity while she sweated in the trenches, learning her craft. Sixteen-hour days became her religion; money, or the pursuit of it, was her god. Dana had learned about the absolute power of wealth even before she became aware of her extraordinary beauty.

She had met Norman Bloodstone when he came to work for the same firm. Dana had never really considered a long-standing relationship. She hadn't had the need before, and was comfortable with her business-only lifestyle.

But Norman had invaded her comfort zone, shattered her self-possessed caution with his brilliantly orchestrated, excitingly dangerous approach to both business and pleasure—especially pleasure. His intelligence and ambition matched hers perfectly. His passion for money and what it could acquire actually exceeded her own. But his passion for her was even deeper, and she returned it in kind, until eventually they became inseparable, the natural progression of their mutual desires. She had found the perfect mate, and she gave herself over to him completely.

Norman's success record with the firm made him popular with his clients as well. He invariably turned them on to just the right investments at the right time, and he managed their accounts with a field marshal's gift for tactics.

Dana hooked on to him and, in the process of finding out who he was, let him get close to her. She found out that, like her, he had a sensual magnetism, and he possessed the ability to reach into her and to release erotic levels deep inside her that even she had not known about before. It was a perfect relationship.

The sexual side of their relationship amazed her. For the first time, she had met a man who could match her own appetite for excess, even surpass it. Dana realized that his dangerous, risk-taking approach to investments was reflected in his feelings for her, and she let her passion consume her.

Norman was intrigued by her response to him, and he recognized her intelligence, found it refreshing. When they met, he wasn't looking for anyone, and he revealed this much to her early on. But anticipation and reality were often separated only by circumstance, which Norman was quick to recognize.

He saw the sensual side of their relationship as a motivator, more for her than for him, however. For him, it became an extension of his ability to manipulate, an interesting tactical exercise that allowed him to see on occasion what turning her on could do.

The complex regulations governing their business provided the holes in the system that they needed. Recognizing these breaches, they came up with scheme after scheme to bend the rules, circumvent the rigid controls—"sneak under their radar," as Norman once put it. For him the exercise was a personal challenge. The more creative it got, the more he enjoyed it. He called it "playing the game."

Norman and Dana maintained their strict adherence to the rules of the game. Still, Dana had to caution Norman at times, gently though, as he saw their tweaking the nose of the system as a challenge.

They had been at their game-playing for over two years without a hint of anyone catching on to them. Others had not been as lucky. Major shakeups, brought about by a series of federal prosecutions, had dropped a cloak of paranoia over Wall Street.

So secure where they in the level of insider trading they had gotten away with that they had expanded into other areas of illegal endeavor, always keeping their adventures short and sweet, however. Even so, by choosing their targets carefully, they siphoned off an impressive six-figure alternate income.

But the risk had increased dangerously as federal investigators probed around. Finally Norman and Dana had decided to strike their tent and look for new camping grounds, preferably some distance away. They resigned from the brokerage firm a week apart, to avoid any suspicion of a connection. Since it wasn't unusual for people in their line of work to job-hop, their leaving raised no eyebrows.

It was Dana's research into the need for their skills in the private sector that led them to Trans Patriot Insurance. Interviews, arranged with a TPI headhunter in New York, led to their placement at Trans Patriot's home office in Phoenix.

It took only a few months before they began to think they had been let loose in the corporate candy store. At first they stayed straight, keeping a low profile, learning the ins and outs of the insurance business and foreign trade ventures. The opportunity Dana had predicted soon arrived. The playing of the game was renewed with the creation of Kallang, Limited, although the renewal at first presented a problem for Dana.

The critical part of the scam was coming up with the seed money to allow them to create the brokering company. Exhaustive auditing of their requirements determined that they would need a million dollars to get started.

Norman, ever astute, and more successful at the banking business than Dana, had managed to secure a sizable nest egg during his years on Wall Street. His half of the start-up funds was secure.

Dana had not been quite so careful in her long-range planning. Although her income had closely matched Norman's, a combination of an expensive lifestyle and fewer breaks in the marketplace had left her three hundred thousand dollars short.

Unknown to Norman, Dana had an alternate source of funds. Because of certain restraints, however, gaining access to these funds would be difficult. Difficult, but not impossible.

The biggest problem would be keeping her arrangements from Norman. She hated for him to think any less of her for not being as strategic in her planning as he was. She also couldn't afford to give him the impression, real or false, that she wasn't capable of handling a complicated domestic-foreign trade business venture like the scam they were setting up.

The source of her money was a trust fund set up for her by her father; it contained more than enough to make up her shortage. But the fund had been safeguarded from any youthful extravagances by a provision sealing the account until her thirtieth birthday.

Management of the account was the province of the family attorney, Allen Parkman, and therein lay the weak link. Under special conditions, the trust fund controls could be circumvented, but only by the lawyer. Dana thought she held the key to that lock. She had seen desire reflected in Allen's lascivious eyes. It wasn't hard for her to understand what lay behind it.

She had suggested to Norman that they put off finalizing their plans until she returned from one of her trips east on behalf of Trans Patriot. She didn't tell her lover of the other business she planned to take care of.

She visited Allen in his office a week later and presented her request for access to the trust fund. She had anticipated his objections and was not surprised when he turned her down.

"You know I can't let you into any of those funds," Allen reminded her. "The account's sealed until you're thirty; you know that, too."

"But you can authorize withdrawals, and I've got a real need for this money."

77

Allen was unmoved. "Can't be done, I'm afraid. Besides," he added, smiling, "I know you, Dana. I'd venture to say that your idea of need is in direct proportion to your spending habits. And even if I did open it, which I won't, the whole process is quite difficult. The auditors would have to be given proof of justification, and there are other considerations. Generally speaking, it's one major headache." He waved his hand in the air at the problems he envisioned surrounding her request.

Because time was of the essence, Dana drew her trump card and played it. "Allen," she said coyly, looking him in the eye, "do you find me attractive?"

Taken totally off guard by both the directness of the question and the abrupt change of topic, he was at a loss for words. It was exactly the effect she expected.

"Really now," she said, smiling disarmingly, "you've been divorced for what, six years? When was the last time anyone really rang your bell?" Dana directed her devastating charm at the center of his lascivious libido.

Allen mentally backpedaled, not believing what he was hearing, curious as to why she was so open about it, and finally, hoping deep down that this wasn't just a game with her.

Dana continued her attack. "I've noticed the way you've looked at me the last couple of years." She leaned forward in the chair beside his desk, giving him just a hint of her generous cleavage. "That's quite all right," she said, softer now. "I don't mind. In fact, I enjoy it. But why has it taken you so long to do anything about it?"

In an attempt to regain control of the proceedings, Parkman pushed his high-backed desk chair away slightly, easing his tightening discomfort. Finally finding his voice, he said, "Now come on, Dana. We've known each other a long time. Your family has done business with the firm since you were a child. I've watched you grow up. What makes you think that I would jeopardize that relationship?"

His finish was strong, but his eyes strayed to the top of her blouse. She sat up slowly, then deliberately reached up and unbuttoned the top two buttons of her blouse. "Because you want it, Allen," she breathed. "That's why."

His resolve took one last mental shout at his conscience, then vanished with a whimper. In the end, they both got what they wanted. Allen occasionally looked back on the episode, the first of many, with a twinge of guilt. Dana, satisfied with her performance, never looked back and certainly never with guilt. She had him, for as long as she needed him. She left New York at the end of the week with the three hundred thousand dollars.

Dana's relationship with Allen was more than physical. It certainly was for him, although he rarely took the time to consider whether Dana had the same kind of feelings for him. He was afraid to pursue that line of thought too far, however, finding it easier to bury it away.

Instead, their relationship included his invaluable assistance in filing with the State Department for the trade licenses for Kallang, Limited. In return for his expertise concerning foreign licensing agreements, she told him about the game she and Norman were playing. She knew the information was safe with him.

Allen surprised her by showing immediate interest in the project. His participation and professional silence were secured for a percentage of Dana's share of the profits. Business was business, after all, and the scam had great potential.

She juggled her relationships with the two men like a chess player. While Allen knew all about Norman's part in the scheme, Norman was kept totally in the dark about the silent partner in New York. He was led to believe that Dana's monetary contribution toward the capitalization of Kallang and the mass of forms and licensing applications came from her. The need to file these papers through a legitimate law firm was just part of the process. Norman never questioned her choice of Allen's firm. He had no reason to doubt her word.

In her Plaza Hotel suite, with a busy schedule ahead, Dana made an early evening of it. Her last waking thoughts were of the increasing strangeness in Norman's character. It wasn't his behavior that was changing so much—that had always been on the odd side. No, there was a whole personality change that had become noticeable with the extension of the game.

"Time is the problem," Norman had said in the beginning. They had set a goal of making twenty million dollars' profit from their game; then they would shut it down and disappear. "There is one variable that we have no apparent control over, and that is the availability of loss reserves at the right time. The lack of ready finances impacts on our opportunities to invest," he argued. "It's too inconsistent having to wait around for the claim file to close before we get the portion allotted to you."

Dana knew the genesis of his concern. They had had to pass on several very nice—and potentially very profitable—deals, because the reserve moneys apportioned to the investment department at TPI had not been in the pipeline when they needed them.

"My love, that is really out of our hands," Dana had replied pragmatically, though she shared his frustration with the system. "When they show up, they show up. It's not like we can go out and create the opportunities. We are, in a very real sense, at the mercy of pure chance, waiting for a claim to be tried, or settled, or for a plaintiff to pass on."

"But you can manipulate those odds."

"How?"

"By increasing the capital at the front end," he replied, as if the answer were obvious.

"How do you propose to do that?" she asked.

Norman sidestepped her question, however, answering instead with one of his own. "Did you know that TPI has some special risk policies that carry multiple millions as policy limits? Imagine what we could do with even a portion of that."

She knew instantly what he was driving at. Dana had often been frustrated to see literally millions of dollars passing through her department while she was able to use only a percentage of it. She thought for a moment about having access—easy, regular access—to the funds.

"Precisely," he said, seeing the desire in her face, his cat's eye glowing. "Increase the initial capital investment, thereby increasing the downstream profit, cut the time span—compress it, so to speak —without additional risk. It all falls within the realm of statistical probabilities."

"Get to the end of it, Norman. What's the bottom line?" Even she at times grew impatient with his love of financial mumbo jumbo.

"Elementary," he said theatrically. "Eliminate the claimant."

Dana looked at him in silent surprise. Then she smiled nervously and said, "But you're not really serious?"

He ignored her question. "I've already done quite a bit of work on this theory," he said without emotion. "Come into the study with me for a minute."

He preceded her into his book-lined workroom, where he sat down at his desk, booted up the computer, and slid in a floppy disk. While he did so, he spoke like a life insurance salesman.

"Do you know how many people die each year from accidental falls in the home? Or how many deaths are attributed to electric shocks, slips and falls, drownings, stair falls, gunshot wounds, auto accidents? How about deaths from 'routine' outpatient surgery, to say nothing of hospital maltreatment?" By then the monitor screen was filled with graphs and text. Norman tapped the screen. "These are U.S. government statistics on the number of people who die each year from accidental causes."

He rotated his chair to look at Dana, who stood beside him.

"Pick a scenario," he offered, "and I'll bet someone has been killed that way. And that's just the accident side of the equation. Look at death by natural causes: heart attack, stroke, cancer, embolisms, aneurysms, AIDS, kidney failure—you name it." He jerked his head at the screen. "It's astonishing what modern man is dying from."

"So what's the point?" she said. "It's not like we can predict that's going to happen."

Norman shook his head, again smiling in that way she found frightening. "You're not listening, Dana. I don't intend to sit around and wait; I'm going to prove the statistics. You know, make it happen. For real."

Dana turned away from the computer. Her violet eyes searched his for a long time. "You are bloody serious, aren't you?" she said quietly.

Norman remained silent, his eyes providing all the answer necessary.

She moved away from him and began to slowly pace the room. Norman followed her with his eyes.

"Call it an expansion of the game," he offered to her silence. "Pick a heavy reserved limits file completely at random. The facts don't really matter. An unfortunate accident happens, and the claimant is removed from the equation. The file gets closed, the national averages are proven to be accurate, and we get a few more dollars to use."

He waited as she continued her slow tour of the room. He could almost hear the wheels spinning in her gorgeous head. "Plan the event, make it happen, and leave no trace. The ultimate game." His voice was tantalizing.

She registered his euphemism for murder, wondering why she felt no revulsion at his proposal. His tone was so businesslike that it seemed absolutely natural.

"How would we do it?" were her first words in response to his suggestion.

Norman smiled; he knew he had her. "I've been thinking about that," he said, then went on to explain his plan. He would quit TPI, citing a better offer. That would free him up to operate without restraint. Dana would remain on the inside, targeting claim files, passing them on to Norman. Afterward she would make sure that Kallang received a certain percentage of Trans Patriot's business.

"How are you going to handle those cases in litigation?" she asked. "Most policy limits claims are open court files, you know."

"My research shows that the lawsuit could remain active after the death of the claimant," he explained. "But a great many of them get dismissed over time as a function of the courts, or the lawyer does it, since he doesn't have a client anymore, especially if there's no surviving family member to benefit from the suit."

"And what about those that don't get dismissed?" she challenged.

"The statistics apply to attorneys, too. Accidents can happen to

82

anyone," Norman continued. "Geographic distances will work to our advantage. Logistics are easily handled, but random statistical choice is the biggest consideration."

The look on Dana's face answered his unspoken question. Her response confirmed it. "When do we start?"

Dana kept any remaining reservations to herself, although they remained—until the loss reserve of a million dollars on their first successful case had been released to the investment department following the dismissal of the lawsuit, just as Norman had predicted.

The scheme had involved a land development deal in Malaysia, brokered by Kallang, Ltd. Afterward she had directed Kallang to sell off its interests in the venture, and collected a quarter of a million dollars for the effort.

But the real thrill for the two of them had come when Norman returned from that first execution and told Dana, in detail, how it went. The sexual celebration that resulted had surprised her more than him.

And the celebration had been repeated each time after that. Norman got off on telling Dana about their victims, and she got off on hearing all the lurid details. It was safe then, no more to her than exciting hearsay, her direct participation in the game a matter of facts and figures. The reality of what she and Norman were doing never bothered her, or so she believed. She was convinced she had removed that thought from her mind.

The consequences of what would happen to them if they were caught were not considered. Dana very much appreciated the danger facing them, but she balanced the profits they were making against the odds of discovery. The ledger still favored their side in the game.

What bothered her was Norman's apparent pursuit of something else. He seemed most alive in the planning of each new execution, in custom-tailoring the demise of the claimant. His depth of research had risen almost to the level of fanaticism. He had volumes of books, tapes, and journals on the subject of murder, and had taken to honing his field skills with weapons at local shooting ranges and clubs. More than once he had referred to the process as a safari, and Dana had a feeling that if he could have, Norman might actually have mounted the heads of their victims on the walls.

In her Plaza Hotel suite, waiting for sleep to come, Dana considered what to do about Norman, and his unsettling changes of late. "Oh, Norman, my love," she said to the pillow, "whatever will I do with you?"

MARCH 14, NEW YORK CITY

Dana gazed out of the window of the cab that was carrying her to a ten-thirty appointment with Allen Parkman. She had awakened with an answer to her Norman dilemma. To resolve it she would need overseas connections and Allen's assistance. She would need to provide a little something extra as an incentive to ensure his compliance. She smiled seductively as she considered the possibilities. She had an answer for Allen, too.

Allen Parkman, nattily attired in a gray pin-striped three-piece suit, was already up and moving around his desk when Dana entered his office. The view behind him was magnificent. Ceiling-to-floor windows created a thirty-foot-tall wall of glass encompassing both corners. Beyond and below lay the concrete grandeur of Manhattan.

"Dana, my dear, how good to see you again." His voice was professional, richly modulated, in keeping with his position with a favored client. His pulse rate took a couple of quick spikes upward when his right hand briefly caressed hers.

"Allen, always a pleasure," she responded as she sat in the chair he indicated. He circled around behind her chair and bent down, placing a quick kiss on the nape of her neck. He whispered, "I could eat you where you sit."

She smiled up at him and silently mouthed the word "later." Then for the sake of propriety, and for the benefit of anyone who might overhear their remarks, she continued in a businesslike voice. "Yes, well, as usual, it's that time again. I hope you don't mind this interruption in your busy schedule."

"No trouble at all, Dana, I assure you. I suppose you'd like to start with the quarterly reports," he said, playing out their long-established charade. He retrieved a dummy file from a credenza near the desk.

She reached for the thin stack of folders and made a show of going through them. "Would you mind if I take these with me for review? I'm afraid I am a bit rushed today," which was true. Her legitimate business for Trans Patriot was waiting.

"Certainly not," he answered, hiding his disappointment at her brief stay. "Please take as much time as you need. You'll find the usual summaries on top." Allen relaxed a little. He knew that the real discussion would come when he walked her out to the elevators. Then she would actively seek his advice, ever the trusted counselor. The role came easily to him. Acting was a prerequisite for any successful lawyer.

"I hope your trip hasn't tired you too much to accept an invitation to dinner tonight."

Dana's response was equally smooth. "No, not at all. I'd be delighted."

"Fine," he said. "I have some work to do that will keep me here a bit late, so I went ahead and made reservations at Fellini's for nine, if that's acceptable."

She nodded her silent assent. It was his cue. "Well then, perhaps you could meet me here at, say, seven-thirty and we can have a drink somewhere before dinner?"

Dana caught the inflection in his voice and gave him a quick suggestive wink. "That will fit in just fine with my schedule. Seven-thirty it is."

She picked up her briefcase, slid the fake folders inside, and stood, preening a little for Allen.

"It really is wonderful to see you again, Dana," he remarked, already beside her, leading her toward the door. "I'll just walk her down to reception," Allen said to his secretary as they emerged from his office. He helped Dana on with her coat.

"We have to talk about Norman," Dana whispered to Parkman through a set smile as they neared the front reception area of the firm's foyer.

"What about him?" Allen demanded in a hoarse whisper.

85

"Not here, no time. Later, tonight. We'll need to go over the latest audit of the Geneva account as well."

"All prepared," he told her, getting on to part of her real business with him.

Near the elevators, he spoke up in a conversational tone, "And if there's anything else I can do for you while you're in the city, don't hesitate to call."

Dana turned her radiant smile up a few watts. "You're too kind," she replied softly, and entered the elevator. She smiled when she thought about how their evening might go. Business and pleasure, she thought.

At precisely 7:20 P.M. Dana returned to the lobby of Allen's building. She proceeded directly to the express elevator for the top floors, where the lawyer awaited her. The elderly uniformed security guard confirmed her name on his authorized list and ushered her inside, touching his fingertips to the bill of his cap as he did so.

Seconds later the elevator doors slid open, and she stepped out into the empty, partially illuminated reception area. Most of the staff had gone home by now.

Dana unbuttoned her winter coat and walked down the quiet hall to Allen's office. One of the tall paneled doors to Allen's office stood ajar and Dana could hear his muffled voice as she got nearer. She knocked once, pushed the door open, and entered.

Dictating the last of a letter into a handheld microcassette recorder, he nodded to her as she approached his desk across the wide expanse of the office.

Dana stopped behind the leather chair she had sat in that morning. Nonchalantly she shrugged off her heavy coat, slid her woolen scarf off with it, and draped them over the back of the chair. She remained standing so that Allen would get the full effect of the dress she wore. Made of jade-green silk, it had a low neckline and a clinging skirt that ended at midcalf and was slit on the left side to well above her knee, exposing the lower part of a rounded thigh. Her feet were encased in slim russet calfskin ankle-high boots. The dark richness of the dress was offset by a triple strand of pearls with matching earrings that swung slightly from her tiny earlobes. Her auburn tresses had been pulled up in an elegant style. Dana rested her hip against the chair arm, her body a sumptuous jade curve.

Allen did a fast double take, and felt a tingle scamper down his spine. He rushed through the end of the letter and flicked off the recorder, not sure he had actually signed off. He was unable to take his eyes off the enticing figure before him.

"Finished?" she asked, maintaining the pose.

"Uh, yes, well, actually," he stammered, "I suppose I am." He glanced at the gold and silver ship's clock on the desk. "Right on time, as usual," he said, lacking anything witty to say. She always had this effect on him, and he always hated himself for melting so quickly each time.

Still, there was that look. He tried a feint: "So what's the problem with Norman?"

"I thought we'd talk about that at dinner," Dana replied, leaning smoothly away from the side of the chair.

Sustained, he thought, and rose to meet her. She walked right up against him, molded the front of her body to him, and murmured, "As it's been a while, I thought you might like to forgo drinks before dinner, for . . ." The rest of her sentence went unspoken as she offered her full lips to him.

Allen might have been a gentleman, but the lecher in him won out. He wound his arms around her and kissed her passionately several times, all rapid-fire. His libido was running merrily away with his self-control.

She broke the kiss, touched a finger to his lips, and said, "There appear to be too many lights on in here. Could you . . . ?"

Allen looked confused for two seconds, realized what was going to happen, and almost dislocated his knee in his rush to hit the wall switch near the office door. He just as quickly crossed back to the desk, and the woman, and clicked off the yellow glow cast by the banker's lamp.

The room was suddenly transformed, the sparkling lights of the city creating a glowing curtain behind the desk, casting their beauty and mystery into the darkened office.

Allen heard the soft rustle of silk as Dana walked closer to the

87

windows. She looked out at the magnificent view. The ambient light reflected on her outline as she pressed herself against the glass. Then she turned to him. "Come here," she commanded softly, holding out her hand. On suddenly shaking knees, he approached her.

She stopped him at arm's length, turning back toward the glass wall. "It's beautiful, isn't it?"

"Yes," he replied, looking at her and answering a different question. "Dana—" he began, but she silenced him with a motion of her hand.

"Right here," she breathed, her back still turned to him. "Right now."

His pulse leaped as he watched her reach up and over her shoulder to disengage the zipper of her dress, then readjust her arm to pull it down. The tiny brass pull made a faint hiss at it descended all the way. The sound was an instant aphrodisiac.

For a man of his age, Allen had kept in reasonable shape. He knew he looked younger than he was, and sometimes he felt younger. His reaction to her eroticism was like that of an eighteen-year-old.

He began shedding his own clothing, throwing each item aside absently, the whole time keeping his eyes welded on Dana and the show she was putting on for him.

She half turned toward him, slid her hands up over her shoulders, and slipped her dress down. Dipping her shoulders forward slightly, a movement that pushed her ample breasts together, she let the dress glide straight off her body.

Allen felt another surge rush through him as he stared at her shadowed nakedness. Dana glanced down at him, smiling appreciatively at his pulsing readiness. She reached out for him, gently touching him, closing her fingers around him, causing him first to jump, then to moan quietly.

Pulling him to her, she turned back to the expanse of glass, reveling in the sight before her, and in the image of the sight she made, standing in all her sensual glory, bared to the glittering city below.

She leaned up closer to the window, as Allen moved behind her. Dana felt his hands on her hips, and his body pressed against her while his lips sought the base of her neck. Her hands rested against the coolness of the tempered glass at shoulder level, and she let his weight press her forward. The ends of her swelling breasts, pendulous now, pushed up onto the thick glass. Immediately her nipples contracted and hardened from contact with the cold, smooth surface.

Feeling Allen's hot breath on her neck she pushed away from the window. She urged him back a step with her hips, maintaining close contact with his straining body. It was time, she thought, succumbing to the electric thrills lacing through her body as he continued to caress her.

Allen couldn't believe they were actually going to do it, standing up like this, in front of the whole city, but he wasn't about to stop.

He felt her move her legs apart, felt her hand slide behind her, finding him, pulling him into her, urging him on to find the most sensitive part of her.

His legs were quivering again as he found her entrance, centered himself, pushed forward. Dana groaned as he began to move, his fantasy thoughts ripped away by the surging reality of the moment.

And like an eighteen-year-old on his first time out, he found that reality was irresistible. Much to his surprise, his charging body propelled him to a finish quicker than either of them expected.

Embarrassed, apologetic, and angry with himself for his schoolboy performance, Allen remained behind her, holding on to her as she quieted his words of apology, telling him over and over not to worry, there was always later.

Shortly thereafter, dressed again and greatly subdued, Allen escorted Dana down the darkened hallway into the elevator and out into the almost silent lobby, finally smiling at her efforts to make him feel better.

Outside she walked close to him, her arm linked in his. They hailed a cab, and Allen opened the back door with a flourish. Dana kissed him softly on his cheek as she entered, then slid over to give him room.

"Fellini's," he said to the driver as the cab pulled away from the curb and glided off into the night.

• • •

"Dana, you beautiful, conniving bitch, I love you."

Norman had decided weeks ago that he would follow Dana to New York and surprise her. Despite her admonitions that this was after all, a business trip, he knew that his surprise visit was something she would really enjoy.

That at least had been his intent when his taxi pulled up to the Plaza Hotel on Wednesday morning. He had paid the driver and was opening the door when he saw his partner come out of the hotel, signal to a standing cab, and quickly get in.

Norman was caught off guard, but decided to follow her to that morning's appointment, and catch here there.

He amused himself by imagining her surprised look when he appeared next to her. He expected she was heading for one of the downtown brokerage houses that TPI used. Norman was familiar with most of them. It hadn't been that long since he'd made similar trips for the company.

When Dana's cab stopped at a building on 39th Street, his curiosity was aroused. He wondered if TPI had acquired a new broker. The Midtown location was a bit odd, but brokering was, after all, an ever-changing business.

He followed Dana into the building, staying close enough to see her walk into the private express elevator on the far side of the lobby, away from the bank of public elevators, but too late to join her. He sought out the building directory mounted in the lobby, trying to identify Dana's destination. He found that the law firm of Kast, Litz, Wallesen, and Parkman was the only occupant of the top three floors. That seemed to him the only logical place she could be going.

He was openly curious now, and allowed the first inkling of suspicion to intrude into his thoughts. He could think of no reason for Dana to go there. His past experience with Trans Patriot told him that much. On the other hand, maybe there was some new business connection between TPI and the law firm.

Finding a public phone and a business phone directory, Norman leafed through it until he found the law firm's advertisement. According to the ad, they dealt with business accounts, tax law, corporate finance, and foreign trade services.

There might be a connection to TPI's business interests, he reasoned, but his doubts were increasing. Norman knew that Trans Patriot rarely used outside firms in their investment dealings, as the company's own in-house legal department was fully capable of handling virtually any legal situation or technicality.

Norman found a coffee shop that faced the lobby floor and sat reading a newspaper until he saw Dana cross the lobby and head outside. He let her go and finished the bagel he had ordered as he finalized the next step in his new plan.

Norman, dressed in a charcoal-gray business suit and a heavy topcoat, like just another nameless businessman, left the coffee shop and walked down the street. The suit was fine, but additional trappings were needed. Within three blocks of the building he found what he was looking for in a small luggage store.

He came out carrying a thin, costly leather briefcase. He had left his real one at his hotel along with his laptop computer, having no thought of needing either at the time. The new briefcase, however, completed the look he required.

He returned to Allen's office building, ambled over to the express elevator, and told the security guard posted there that he had business with the law firm—a tax matter. He got on with several other people and was whisked to the top floor. He got off, and approached the reception desk.

"Hello, I'm George Marshall," he lied easily. "I was supposed to meet a business associate of mine here, but my secretary failed to get the name of the attorney she would be visiting." Norman made a show of looking at his watch twice. "I'm also running a little late, and I'm afraid I may have missed her."

The young receptionist had already classified the tall, good-looking visitor before her. She was unable to see his eyes through the shaded glasses he wore, but the cut and fit of his suit strongly suggested that he was legitimate.

"Perhaps I could check the appointment calendar for you?" she suggested helpfully.

"That would be most kind. My associate's name is Quinn. Ms. Dana Quinn."

The receptionist entered Dana's name into a PC near her station. In seconds the screen gave her the information she needed.

91

"Your associate was in to see Allen Parkman an hour ago."

"And his office is where?" Norman asked, eyebrows raised innocently.

"Down the hallway to the end"—she pointed—"and left. He has the first corner office. Just a moment and I'll ring for you." She picked up her small handset, tapped in the office extension, waited a second, and he heard her say, "Helen? Ruth . . . Yes. There's a gentleman here who was to meet Allen's ten-thirty. Is she still there? . . . I see. When was that? . . . Very good. Wait a moment, please."

She spoke to Norman. "I'm sorry, Mr. Marshall, but Ms. Quinn left the building about forty minutes ago. Is there something specific that Mr. Parkman could help you with?"

Norman continued his role-playing. He smiled at her and shrugged. "No, but thank you anyway. You've been most helpful. I suppose Ms. Quinn has taken care of the matter. I'll just catch up with her later."

On the way out of the building, he mulled over what he had found out and what he had to do. He knew who Dana's contact was; chances were that Parkman's office would be clear at lunchtime. He therefore planned to return shortly after twelve. He smiled as he left the office building and walked down the busy street. Dana was up to something, and he intended to find out what it was.

At twelve-fifteen Norman stepped out of the elevator one floor below his destination. By taking the inside fire exit stairs up to the next floor he was able to bypass the reception area. He had gambled that here, as in many high-rise office buildings, someone would have kept the exit door illegally unlocked. He was right.

He followed the directions the receptionist had given him earlier and easily located Allen's corner office. His timing was perfect; the place was virtually empty. For at least an hour there should be no one to interrupt him. He went immediately to Parkman's secretary's desk. He was working on the presumption that she would have a list of her boss's computer codes. Human nature being what it was, he knew few people bothered to memorize the ever-changing code numbers.

His search turned up nothing, however, so he began looking around for other possible hiding places. His irritation began to peak into anger. Parkman's secretary, if the truth be known, was considerably more efficient than Norman had expected. She had no need to write down the codes required of her. She had simply filed them away in her neatly arranged photographic memory.

Norman was quickly running out of options and time. The double doors to Allen's office were open enough to reveal the edge of his desk on the far side of the room and the electric blue glow of the PC sitting on the credenza behind it.

After looking back down the hall and seeing no one, Norman entered the office and crossed swiftly to the other side. He looked down at the PC and smiled. Underneath the clear Plexiglas sheet protecting the top of the cabinet was an index card, and on it, in neatly typed rows, were the lawyer's codes, his secretary's, and four names—associates, Norman figured, who worked for Allen.

He quickly wrote all of them down in a small spiral notebook and was slipping the book into his inside suit pocket when a voice startled him.

"Is there something I can help you with?" Standing in the doorway was a young man, a thin file and legal pad held in one hand.

A smile jumped onto Norman's face, and he straightened quickly, crossing the room to the other man, extending his hand in greeting as he approached.

"John Thomas," he lied smoothly, instinctively coming up with a name different from the one he'd used before, "of Farber and Haskins in Kansas City. We were just having a bite with Allen, and he'd forgotten to bring along . . . Oh, I'm sorry, I didn't get your name?"

Thrown slightly off guard, but remaining in place, blocking the door before this eager stranger, the young man replied, "Charles Schotte. Mr. Thomas, was it? I don't recall Allen mentioning anything about a luncheon with any firm from—"

"Quite all right, happens all the time," Norman interrupted, moving out the doorway, while Schotte yielded, taking a step back. "No reason he should have mentioned it, I suppose. We only found out we would have time to get over here, what with the depositions in the Brice case being canceled and all." He kept moving now, walking down the hall, away from the danger, eager to get clear. He had not counted on this glitch in his plans.

"Listen, Mr. Thomas, perhaps you'd like to tell me what it was Mr. Parkman was supposed to have left, and I'll—"

"No, no, that's quite all right, really. It isn't there, it seems. I'm sure Allen will find it when he returns. I must get back, though, so if you'll excuse me, Mr. Schotte?"

And with that, Norman headed determinedly for the elevators and escape. In his wake stood Charles Schotte, a bit befuddled and not completely convinced.

Norman, still rattled at having been caught, left the building and took a cab back to his hotel. In his room he unpacked the laptop computer, set up the modem, and booted up the system. He took out the codes for the law firm and laid them down next to his keyboard, then dialed into the law firm's computer.

When he got in on line, he entered the access code, and once inside, he used the lawyer's personal code. He scanned the selection of available files and chose Allen's client list.

He was mildly surprised when he found no records for Trans Patriot Insurance.

He tried the firm's general client list and ran his request a second time, but again the search came back negative.

Trying a different tack, Norman entered the name Quinn. Immediately he got back a series of topic lists, including headings for Strangeways, which he recognized as Dana's father's business. There were also records on each member of the Quinn family.

Beginning to enjoy himself now, he took an electronic tour through the family's personal and business records until he uncovered the trust funds set up for Dana and her sisters.

Dana had never told him about the trust fund, and, considering the amounts involved, that fact bothered him. He searched the account until he found what he was looking for.

Three hundred thousand dollars had been withdrawn with the explicit authority of the administrator, Allen Parkman. The date of the withdrawal, four years ago, was familiar. Dana had taken a trip to New York then, when they were finalizing their plans for the game.

Norman backed out of the file and quickly accessed Allen's appointment calendar. The computer record showed Dana's name, exactly as he knew it would.

Not wanting to believe what the silent screen was telling him, Norman took the appointment dates further back, when he and Dana had started with Trans Patriot. He found only one entry, which could have meant anything; the date held no significance for him.

Norman kicked the search into the lawyer's calendar, covering several years, up to the current date. He was stunned to see that Dana had had appointments with Allen nine times over the years.

Without having to check further, he knew by the spacing that each one coincided with a trip she'd made for Trans Patriot. The evidence was clear for anyone to interpret. And with Allen's name, the final recognition thumped home, heavy and cold inside him: his name had appeared on the licensing applications for Kallang. Norman had thought all this time that Dana had handled that part of the initial setup on her own, courtesy of the experience gained from her father's business. Clearly that wasn't so. A lot of things weren't so.

He had a silent partner, and Dana was concealing that fact. Her lack of trust was a small jab, understandable in a way. After all, she was dealing from a more emotional level than he was. What really bothered him was her obvious disregard for his ability to understand her problem. Dana had never tried to explain it to him so he could help her choose the right course. Obviously she didn't trust him.

We really aren't equals in this, he thought, confirming something he had always known. She hadn't had the capital to begin with, and she had gone to Parkman to get it. What did she offer him? he wondered.

The answer he arrived at was one he didn't care for. The only explanation was that Dana had cut Allen in on the profits from the game, which meant that he must know most of the facts. Hell, he said to himself, Allen must know everything!

A flash of anger jolted through Norman, but worse than the anger

95

was the betrayal he felt. How could she do this? he raged. There was a sudden numbness in the center of his chest, a physical coldness that he thought was a hallucination at first. Then, almost as abruptly as it had appeared, Norman's fury cooled, and the calculating side of his brain took over, assimilating the data, fitting it to a new scenario in which there were now three players.

"The real sixty-four-thousand-dollar question is," he said aloud to the empty hotel room, "does Allen know about the murders? And how much of a threat is he? He hasn't gone to the authorities because he's too deeply involved, but he's a threat to the game and, by extension, to me."

Norman's mind whipped through several permutations of this new equation, fitting in what was logical, discarding what was not. Immediately there appeared thoughts of retribution. They came from the darkest part of him, and he let the cold sweetness of the emotion they generated flow through his mind. An entirely fitting retaliation was needed.

After a while Norman became aware that he had been sitting in front of the laptop computer for several hours. Outside his hotel windows, early evening darkness was descending over the city. He didn't mind, however; the time had been well spent. He had devised a response to this disturbing situation. He smiled openly at the poetry of it, playing it back, imagining the physical execution of the complicated stratagem he had concocted.

Norman's conscious mind was almost willing to accept Dana's treachery, but his darkly shadowed subconscious reacted differently. Strangely, he didn't fully understand the feeling. No one had ever betrayed him this way before. Bend with it, he thought. Deal with the unexpected and apply it to the expected. Work with it, and the end result will work out. It all had a purpose.

Norman got up, walked over to a window, and looked down on the winter evening. The darkness reminded him of the time. According to the entry in the computer's calendar, Dana was to meet Allen Parkman for dinner in a little while. Norman packed away the laptop and left his room.

Outside, he hailed a cab and directed the driver to the Plaza. When they arrived, he instructed the driver to wait on the side street.

Dana came out shortly. "Follow that car," he told his driver, and laughed at the old movie cliché. But the sound carried no humor with it, and the cabby glanced at him in the rearview mirror.

Thirty minutes later Norman was waiting outside the lawyer's office building when Dana and Parkman came out, arms locked together. Seeing them linked like that only confirmed what he had already surmised.

He watched them leave, then ordered his driver to return him to his hotel. There were reservations to be made and other things to do. He wouldn't be returning to Phoenix ahead of Dana. He had another stop to make first. A bit of new business seemed in order, given the circumstances.

Two days ought to do it, he figured, then smiled. Two days to work it out, and perhaps enjoy other diversions as well. Why not? The climate was always more agreeable there, especially this time of year. He thought of Dana, and Allen Parkman, and his smile tightened. He closed his mind against the hollow pain inside, the worst pain of all. He knew the source. He also knew the cure.

MARCH 16, PHOENIX, ARIZONA

Luther struggled all day with the information he and Gordon had acquired. He was rolling the latest bit of news over in his mind as he tried to keep up with the day's routine, and at the same time finish the file reviews the two of them had been working on all week.

Gordon had come in to see him the day before. "Got another strange item," he had said.

"What now?" Luther replied, irritation showing in his voice. This project was getting to him.

"I was going over one of the last claims on the list, and I found a newspaper clipping that was sent in by the handling adjuster—an article about the death of the attorney who had represented the claimant's suit against our insured. He was killed in an apparent mugging. Someone had tagged him near his home at the end of the day."

97

Luther sighed, shaking his head. "The operative word is 'apparent,' isn't it?"

Gordon caught his infliction. "You got one, too?"

"Not one, three."

"Perfect. Lawyers too? What the hell have we stumbled into here, Lute?"

"The answer to that is something I'd rather not have to deal with, I'm afraid. This whole thing is starting to really bother me. How many more files do you have to go through?"

"Just five. They'll be done tomorrow."

"Good, I've got the same number. Then I think we'll need a strategy session to go over this in detail. And for right now, we had better keep all of this between you and me."

Gordon nodded. Luther's warning wasn't just a reflection of paranoia. The black-and-white numbers of the profile made it clear that whatever was going on was far beyond the statistical realm of the purely accidental.

At noon the next day the two claimsmen met outside on one of the benches in the tree shaded plaza.

"I've finished my list," Luther said. "How's by you?"

"Finished a half hour ago," Gordon answered, "and I found another attorney down."

"Chalked up to what?"

"Heart attack. During the sixth inning of a Cubs game, last August in Chicago. Caused quite a stir when they carried him out of the ballpark, as I understand it."

In a flash of anger, Luther exclaimed tightly, "Want to make a bet on what really killed him?"

Gordon looked at his boss and replied softly, "Hey, Lute, lighten up a bit. We don't know anything for sure yet."

"You're right, I know, but it's all so damn coincidental. Look at it —we've got, what, between twenty and twenty-five claimants dead? Call it natural causes or accident, result's the same. And add to that at least five of their lawyers." He sat back, ran his fingers up over his temples and back through his thick hair. He held his breath for a long count and let it out slowly. "Coincidence only goes so far. I think we passed it a long time back."

"Would you like to hear what I think is going on here?" Gordon asked. "You're going to love it."

Luther indicated the open expanse around them with a wave of his hand. "You have the floor, sir."

"I've been working with statistical analysis for a long time," Gordon began. "It's a science I'm very comfortable with, primarily because it gives a rhythm to what we do. Risk management, loss histories, premium-to-loss ratios. Everything has a place in the grand scheme, if you will. But this scares the hell out of me. If I were a betting man, and I am, I'd say somebody right here at TPI has been very busy killing off policy limits claimants."

The silence between the two men was palpable. A slight breeze blew dryly through the orange tree shading them. Reality had forced its way into their conversation. Making their shared dread audible had made it real.

Luther noticed a pulsing sensation inside his ear. Adrenaline rush, he told himself automatically, then added, And why not?

"Has to be," he said aloud, his voice controlled calm, and commanding, in contradiction to the churning that had begun way down inside him.

"Amen, brother," Gordon acknowledged. "None of this is accidental. There's something very specific and, might I add, premeditated about all this."

Luther suddenly brought himself upright, and struck the top of the bench with his fist. "Damn! Why didn't this show up before now? How, with all the audits this department cranks out, could something like this go unnoticed?"

"Random chance, I think," Gordon answered slowly. "That and the fact that no one was looking for it, at least until now. You found it, Lute. If you hadn't ordered the profile, we'd probably never have come across this. It all fits the statistical averages, or at least it was meant to look that way. Whoever dreamed up this stuff has gone to some effort to make it appear to be random chance."

Gordon sat back, gazing up at a cloud formation for a moment. "It goes back to what I was saying in the beginning. Lost,amongst the industry stats, it's nothing. But if you compare it just to Trans Patriot's records, like we did with the profile, it stands out like a sore thumb."

Gordon allowed himself an ironic smile. "Hell, boss, you're probably the first guy to attempt to build a policy limit profile that could be used as a fail-safe predictor. I mean, the idea was terrific." The smile faded. "We just didn't count on finding this instead." He crossed his arms over his chest. "Jesus . . "

"You know what the problem is?" Luther said.

"Yeah," Gordon replied. "As we say in this business, what's the proximate cause? What's the point?"

"Exactly. Find the why and we'll find the who. Listen, you and I are still the only ones who know about this so far."

"So far," Hatton concurred. "All the graphs and stats are on my personal program."

"Good, keep it that way." Luther leaned back. "Does Sheri know?"

"No, not at all," Gordon replied.

Luther nodded. "Now comes the big one: what are we going to do about this?"

"I was hoping you'd come up with something."

Luther sighed. "Thanks for the vote of confidence, troop. I appreciate it." He drummed his fingertips on the bench back. "Actually, I do have an idea, but I'd like to think it over this weekend. In the meantime, it's business as usual around here, okay?"

"You got it, boss."

"No," Luther corrected, "*we* got it. And until we know for sure what 'it' is, security is the name of the game."

"Plus a little old-fashioned cover-your-ass. We could be involved in some serious shit, huh?"

Luther's features sobered, reflecting the reality. "Covering your ass is no joke, Gordo. Presuming this is for real, and we both pretty well think it is, what do you suppose would happen to us if the people doing this found out about the profile, and about us?" No answer was necessary, for his associate had already considered the possibility. Gordon's silence spoke volumes.

Luther nodded. "Yeah, that's what I thought." He looked off across the plaza. "We do have some options, but I need to think them over. I'll tell you on Monday what I have in mind."

They left the plaza and returned to their subterranean department to deal individually with their concerns and fears.

After most of the day shift crowd had filtered out, Luther slipped a formatted diskette into his PC and started to copy the statistical profile and all 163 claim files onto it. He had to use four disks in all, since there were hundreds of pages of documents. He made a second set as backup.

He shut down his computer, shrugged into his sport coat, and looked around his office, thinking about his options. Luther had been in the insurance business long enough to know how facts and figures could be manipulated. You could make them say almost anything to turn a case one way or the other. But this case could be read only one way, and the reality chilled him.

He grimaced. He and Gordon were right. Buried somewhere deep inside Trans Patriot Insurance was the answer, and they had to find it.

He put the disks inside his jacket and left the office. He was unable to shake the feeling that sinister unseen eyes were watching him. They followed him even on his drive home, until he forcefully suppressed them, angry with himself for his paranoid reaction.

He entered the house through the short hallway from the garage, stepping into the quiet, dimly lit kitchen. Khanh was waiting, eager to see him. The Arutakas had already retired to their separate quarters.

Too keyed up to sleep, he went upstairs and changed into faded jeans, a baggy white rolled-collar RAF-style sweater, and comfortable moccasins.

It was nearing eleven o'clock when he boxed playfully with Khanh as they descended the curving gallery stairs. The dog followed him into the expansive game room, where Luther paused before an antique red-and-white Coke machine, one of three similar coolers scattered around the room. He punched the selector, and the machine hummed, clicked, and sent a frosted sixteen-ounce bottle rattling down the chute. He caught it and jacked the top off with the opener on the side of the machine. Some things just didn't need to be improved on, he thought.

Despite his efforts to relax, his edginess stayed with him, and he

101

tried putting off what was moving around in the back of his mind. It didn't work. He thought he had a handle on what he was going to do about the profile and the files, but each time he tried to focus, to get serious, it seemed like so much science fiction. Then the reality of what he and Gordon had found would drive that impression out, and he would return to square one.

What he needed was a neutral opinion, someone off whom he could bounce ideas, someone who could react independently and without constraints to the information they had uncovered, preferably someone without ties to Trans Patriot. Until solid evidence was established tying the decision-makers to the deceased claimants, Luther and Gordon would be operating under glass.

Luther felt the pressure on him, and the desire for a drink, just a quick one, flitted through his mind, surprising him with the ease of its presence.

Not now, kiddo, he thought. That won't do any good. He briefly considered taking in an AA meeting. He knew where he would find one, even at that hour. Slowly he put that thought aside after taking comfort from it. No, what he wanted was trust, some honest conversation about the problem at hand. And counsel on what he should do. You trust her, his inner voice told him. Who better to talk to? He took a swallow of cola and looked at his watch. He told himself it wasn't that late. Or was it?

Stop it, and just do it, he chided himself. "Christ," he said aloud, and left the game room for his study. Khanh followed along, curious about his master's behavior.

Jackie picked up on the fourth ring.

"Hi, it's me," he said, staring across the room, studying his war memorial hangings on what he called his I-love-me wall.

"Lute, hi yourself," she responded. He could see her smile from the tone of her voice.

"It's not too late, is it? I wasn't sure you'd be up."

"No, that's all right. I just got in from the station. What's up? You sound a little down, preoccupied or something."

"Or something," he repeated, lightening his voice. "Listen, are you doing anything? I mean, getting ready for bed, or were you going to be up for a little while?"

102

"No to the first part, yes to the second. Why?" she replied, wondering what was going on with him. She could hear a change in his voice, a forced quickness to his speech, making his Texas accent more pronounced.

When he didn't answer right away, she pushed gently. "Hey, Lute, it's your dime, and you did call me. If something's wrong . . ."

"I thought I'd come over," Luther replied. "You know, just to talk." Before Jackie could say anything, he added, "Some things have been happening down at the shop; that's all. It's kind of important though."

Jackie could tell he was trying to gloss over his problem, whatever it was. It was a familiar trait, one he always exhibited when the issue was big. "So you're looking for a neutral opinion," she volunteered for him.

"Yeah, something like that," he agreed, and she heard the hint of relief. "I can be there in twenty minutes."

"Sure, why not?" Jackie answered. "Mikki's overnighting with a friend—big test in the morning—so it'll be us hardworking types. I could use the company."

"Great," he said, "I'm on the way. Thanks, Jackie."

Jackie stared at the telephone for a few moments. Communications had been reopened between them, one of those strange things that often grew out of a divorce. Seeing Luther now seemed somehow easier. Maybe that was because they had nothing more to lose between them, she thought. All the pain was in the past, something to be forgotten. Jackie realized she felt comfortable being around him, and she allowed herself an indulgent smile. Things between them had changed, maybe because they weren't together to stifle the process. She often thought they probably talked more now than they had during the last years before their marriage went bust.

But it was the experience of those darker times that had allowed this new relationship to grow. She had recognized the life-saving changes in him, applauding his fight to regain his self-repect and then pull his life back from the brink. She had even commented on them to him.

103

Luther, on the other hand, hadn't yet acknowledged seeing similar changes in her. Jackie knew the reason, for despite all the positive steps he had taken with his life lately, he had never come to terms with the guilt he still carried over his failure with her.

"Damn martyr complex," she said, sighing. Then she took a few moments to straighten up the living room before Luther arrived.

Headlights refracted across the wall when his Mustang pulled into her driveway. Jackie met him at the door and immediately saw the weariness in his face, the haggard look in his eyes.

"Jackie," he said, brushing his lips past her cheek as he greeted her, one arm going around her waist.

The kiss was almost brotherly, she thought, smiling inwardly, but the squeeze he gave her was something more.

Luther let go of her and took a half step back, as always enjoying being with her. Her red hair was shorter than it had been when they met all those years ago, but her full figure hadn't changed at all, something he was well aware of, even though tonight it was hidden under an extra-large sweatshirt. He felt a familiar tightening flutter in his chest, something he had never gotten rid of.

"You look tired," she said, taking his arm. "Not sleeping well?" She walked with him across the big living room, done up in southwestern pastels in keeping with her personal style.

They paused beside the long, overstuffed couch facing her console television. She had it tuned to her station, the NBC affiliate. Jackie stepped over and turned down the sound.

"Watching the crew?" Luther asked, referring to the production staff down at the station where Jackie was the news producer.

"Uh-huh," she answered. "We're following a double homicide over on the west side. I've got a mobile unit out there. It's a chance for the new anchor to strut his stuff. He'll do, so far." She turned and looked at him, tilting her head a fraction to the left, a characteristic pose for her. "So what's the deal, Lute? Tell me what's going on." She smiled as she said it, and fell back onto the couch.

He sat down with her, and immediately stretched back, lacing his fingers behind his head, eyes closed. Luther took a deep breath, held it a few seconds, and let it out in one long expulsion, feeling some of the tension go.

"This is so crazy," he began. He opened his eyes, but kept his hands braced against the back of his head. "You know what a policy limits claim file is, don't you?"

Jackie nodded, shifting around to face him more directly, and brought one jean-clad leg up underneath her. "Sure," she said, interest forming on her face. "What about it?"

"Well," he replied, lowering his arms, "it started with a simple exercise—an idea, really." He tried to smile, but the attempt failed, lost in his bearded face. He shook his head. "I was trying to save a few dollars," he said quietly.

Jackie saw that the lines around his dark eyes had deepened, matching the tension that seemed to cloak his body. "What happened?" she coaxed.

Luther then told her the whole story, holding nothing back, beginning with his initial theory and the statistical profile that Gordon and Sheri Moradilo had put together. He covered all of the evidence, as he had come to call it, that something was very wrong within the company.

"There are just too damn many of them, Jackie," he said, more animated now, using his hands to punctuate his story, driving his convictions into empty air. "More than twenty dead claimants over two years, maybe as many as twenty-five." He shook his head and settled back into the cushions.

"And they're only the ones we're reasonably sure about. It looks like even some of their attorneys may have been victims. The crazy part is, we can't tell which specific files pertain to the victims. All of these fatalities have the appearance of being accidents, or natural causes, or something explainable." He turned to her suddenly, his eyes bright with certainty. "But no matter how they happened, the simple fact is that these people are dead, Jackie. And they damn well shouldn't be."

She was fascinated. Part of her reaction was instinctive—she was, after all, a newshound by occupation—but mostly it was the source of the information that she found so exciting. She knew Luther and what he believed in. She knew that what he had described was true, and his involvement in it frightened her.

"All right, Lute. Let's take everything at full value, not just face value. You think that the orders have to be coming from within the hierarchy at Trans Patriot, right?"

He agreed, relaxing, knowing that she believed his story.

"So why does Gordon think it's at a lower level?" she continued, playing devil's advocate.

Luther smiled and this time it was genuine. He and Gordon had already had this conversation several times. "I don't know," he replied honestly. "If someone is actually ordering the systematic killing of claimants, for whatever reason, then that order has to originate pretty goddamn high up the corporate ladder."

He picked up the soda she had gotten for him during his explanation, then put it down without drinking. "But Gordon's got a pretty good idea, too, if you look at it from the money side. Start with another presumption, that reserves have something to do with it. I mean, they're all policy limits files, so that's a reasonable guess. A million or two, the usual amount reserved on these cases, looks big until you compare it with the daily figures TPI accounts for. There's tens of millions running through the system every twenty-four hours. We have thousands of interests all over the world, Jackie, and claims are only a part of it. That's a lot of money constantly rolling in and out. Over time, the amounts caught up in these fatality cases get lost."

She saw what he meant. "No percentage for the house, so to speak."

"Exactly. From that aspect, it doesn't make sense." He stared across the room, concentrating on Gordon's theory, chewing at the corner of his lip. "But if you apply a million dollars to an individual instead of to the company, it makes a lot of sense. Except how is a single person taking advantage of the reserves?"

"The perfect riddle," she said. "Whether from on high or down low, the decision is still coming from inside the company."

"Yeah, and people are still dying."

"So what's different for you? What makes more sense?"

He picked up the bottle again and finally took a swallow. He'd already thought about this angle. "I don't think it's the money at all," he said. Then he turned toward Jackie. "What I mean is, it is and it isn't. You don't necessarily have to have someone trying to rip off money. I keep coming back to that line from *The Godfather*—you know, the one where Michael says it's not personal, just business? If it's just business, it makes a lot more sense to me."

She was intrigued now. "How so? I don't follow you."

"It's like this. In insurance you have to keep several factors in mind, all of which impact on how well you do. Premium-to-loss ratios are one of those factors. If you spend more in claim losses than you take in in premium dollars, that's trouble. But there's something called incurred loss, which is the money reserved on a claim, not necessarily spent. A company like TPI reserves a hell of a lot of money, but we don't always pay all of it out.

"See, a claim is reserved based on potentials, what it *could* cost us. But the claim may resolve itself without anything being paid on the loss side. The claimant may drop it, or we might win at trial if we're sued, or the lawsuit might get dismissed, or we could settle for a lower amount." He looked at her questioningly.

"Okay so far," she replied.

"Good," Luther said, continuing. "What happens is the brokers and field agents out there are constantly watching the figures and corresponding with our underwriters. If a particular insured's incurred losses get too high, that policy could be canceled or the premium could get jacked up. That results in ticked-off insureds, who may cancel on their own and go elsewhere if their premiums get too high, or they could bad-mouth TPI out in the marketplace because they got a bad service rating and were canceled by the company."

"And the end result is lost business," Jackie said, seeing his point.

"Exactly," Luther replied. "If you can reduce the incurred-loss picture through risk management, that's one preventive system available. TPI does that. But once a claim is in and the reserves are set, a lot more variables on the final outcome of that claim come into play."

"So if you don't end up spending reserves, you're better off, insofar as it helps you in keeping business and renewing policies for the same entity, right?"

107

"That's the idea," he said. "So how do you keep from spending the reserve? Make the claim go away. And when you're dealing with million-dollar-plus claims, that's serious money."

"Killing the claimant seems like a pretty radical way of making that happen," Jackie said.

Luther raised his eyebrows and sighed. "Don't think we don't know that. Yet Gordon and I have the evidence staring us in the face. And if I'm right, then this whole scheme is purely business-based and, by extension, comes from executive row." He smiled grimly. "It makes sense to me. It always comes down to business, when you think about it. And there is one guy I have in mind, one of the senior VPs in claims, who might just be capable of orchestrating something of this magnitude. But I'll have to think about it for a while," he said.

Jackie was about to ask him for the man's name, but changed her mind. "What happens now?" she asked instead. "Or rather, what are you going to do?"

"That's the bitch," he said. "I've been wrestling with this for a while now."

"Explains the way you look," she said, wanting him to know she was worried.

"It's that bad?" he asked, thinking he had been handling it all fairly well.

Jackie reached over to pat his knee. "Noticeable, yes. Bad? Not really, but . . ."

He knew she was right. It was taking a toll on him. And on Gordon too. And this was only the beginning. "We're over our heads, Jackie. This needs to be turned over to the pros, maybe the feds."

She knew whom he meant, and she also knew he had made his decision. "You're talking about John Paraletto, aren't you?"

"Seems like the logical person," he said. "He's got the clout, and the assets. If he can't run it himself, I'm sure he can give it to someone in the Bureau who can."

"You've known John long enough to trust him," she said, seeing the relief way back in his eyes. She had given him the neutral opinion he had needed.

"Yeah, I think so. There are still some things I need to get straight, but John sure looks like the way to go."

"When will you talk to him about all this?"

"Soon, I think. I have something set up for myself tomorrow, a way to get all these little ducks in a row, so to speak. Then I think I'll have it pretty well laid out."

He looked at his watch and realized he had been talking for almost two hours. "Hey, it's pretty late, one-thirty. I'd best go home, let you get some sleep." He stood up.

Jackie felt a fleeting tug of regret that their late night was over, but she suppressed the thought. What was the point of opening that old line again, and besides, the timing was incredibly bad. Like the man said, it was over and done with. She chalked the feeling up to nostalgia brought on by the time and the conversation they had shared. That's all it was, she thought, shared problems.

"You're right," she said, "I'd better pack it in, too."

She stood up and stretched, the maneuver arching her back, swelling her chest for a few seconds.

Luther caught her fullness against the front of the bulky sweatshirt and looked quickly away. Pure instinct, he told himself, just a hormonal thing. Still, he felt the faint flush on his face.

"Well," he said, now intent on leaving, "thanks for letting me come by. It helped to talk about it."

"Look, Lute, I know this is serious business for you. If this is really happening, the idea that someone at Trans Patriot is responsible scares me. I mean, you're right there, and—"

"I know, I know," he said, stepping up to her. "But Gordon and I are being careful."

"There's another thing," she began, not sure how to bring the subject up. "This is one tremendous story." Luther started to speak, and she held up her hand. "No, I won't do anything with it right now. I wouldn't be that presumptuous. Nor would I want to put you in danger. What I'm asking is, when this is all over and you feel comfortable in telling it to the public, I'd like you to consider letting me do that for you."

His eyes narrowed, and he looked at her for a few moments. Finally he spoke, anger apparent in his voice. "Jackie, I don't have any idea where this is going to lead or how complicated it's going to get. And right now nothing could be further from my mind than its

109

potential as a news story. I'm just trying to make sure nobody gets hurt."

He sensed her hurt, felt her pulling away, and was immediately sorry he had been short with her. "Look, I'm sorry. You're right, this would make one hell of a story. When it's over, whatever happens, I'll tell you all about it, everything I can. You decide what you want to do with it. Fair enough?"

She stepped up to him, put her arms around his neck, and kissed him lightly on the mouth. "We'll talk about it when you're ready. Just be careful out there. If you want to see me before then for any reason —me, Jackie the person, not Jackie the news producer—let me know."

He saw the strength in her eyes and realized suddenly it had always been there. He wondered why he hadn't noticed it before. "I'll do that," he said, reaching up to take her arms down slowly. Her eyes never left his the entire time. "And now I really have to be going."

They walked together back to the door. "Mikki will be sorry she missed you," Jackie said, going for neutral ground.

"Tell her to come by this weekend," Luther replied. "I'll have Myoshi prepare something special for her." He stopped, his hand on the door. "The invitation includes her mother," he added.

"We'll be there," she said.

"Call me at the office," he suggested, opening the door. He popped a salute off his forehead to her, an old gesture. "Thanks again. I really needed the time to decompress."

"Me too," she said, arms crossed as she leaned against the doorjamb. As he walked to his car, she called out, "Lute, keep your head down."

He paused to look back at her, smiling at her use of one of his stock phrases. "Oh, yeah, don't worry."

He climbed into his car and backed out of the driveway. Seconds later he was gone. He hadn't heard her final admonition to him, spoken as he drove away.

"But I will worry, damn it," Jackie said. "I always do with you."

MARCH 17, FALCON FIELD, MESA, ARIZONA

The early dawn colors faded in, cycling from pale pink to lightening shades of blue, gradually defining the edges of things, still unfocused in the early hour of light.

The World War II fighter, a P-51D, sat silently outside its light green prefab metal-sided hangar. It faced north and greeted the morning sun obliquely as it rose over the rust-red hills east of the airfield.

The Mustang, one of two aircraft Luther owned, was the first he had purchased, three years ago. Luther had bought it from a north Georgia farmer who had tried to put together an aviation museum along fifteen acres of unused fields that ran parallel to the interstate above Atlanta.

An ex–army air corps crew chief named Dutch Oderssen and his company, Aero-Classics, had rebuilt the aircraft from the inside out. The Mustang had emerged a year later, finished in the subdued greens and grays of an RAF Mk.IV, as the D model was termed when it was in British service circa 1944. Luther's initials were displayed on either side of the fuselage, bracketing the tricolored roundels.

The other aircraft that shared hangar space was a restored V-tailed Hughes 500-D helicopter, configured to look like an OH-6 Loach, similar to the light observation helos in Luther's squadron in Vietnam.

Dutch was supervising the fueling of the P-51 when he saw Luther's car pull up next to the hangar. Luther was dressed in a faded orange flight suit and his old olive drab army-issue flight jacket. He unlocked the trunk and took out his helmet bag, then approached the fighter, calling out his greetings to Oderssen.

"Morning, Dutch. Good to see you again." He shook hands warmly with the older man.

Dutch was slightly taller than Luther, his short silver-gray hair

111

complemented by the gray work overalls he habitually wore. A black Jack Daniel's baseball hat sat squarely on his head, the bill curved like an arch, out of which shone his bright blue eyes. His face creased into a grin, the web of age lines testimony to too much sun and too many cigarettes, one characteristically balanced, unlit as yet, behind one ear. His thin frame was as hard as it looked.

"Just finished the fuelin', Mr. Sitasy," he replied. All of his clients were either mister or miss, no matter how long they had known him. His lack of a formal return greeting was also vintage Dutch. His primary concern was, now and always, his mechanical charges. The immaculate condition of the 51 was testimony to his care and to the expertise of his crew.

"We did a complete plug change since you last had her up," he said as they walked toward the plane. He indicated the maintenance log under his arm. "Also changed both mags. Everything else is in the green. Y'all set at Ops?"

"All set," Luther responded. "I filed the flight plan on the way over here. Just a VIR hop. I'll be out a couple of hours."

He stopped at the tip of the right wing, admiring the lines of the aircraft. "Care to accompany me on the pre-flight?" he asked. The invitation was a courtesy only. Dutch would have followed him any- way while Luther checked out the fighter.

"Be delighted," he replied.

Luther set the bag on the ground and began his careful visual check. Dutch quietly signaled to one of his crew, motioning with a finger toward the bag. The crewman just as quickly picked it up and climbed up on the wing root. He took out the helmet and oxygen mask and propped them up on the top edge of the windshield.

The two men finished the walk-around inspection. Luther signed the logbook presented by Dutch, then climbed up the wing root and into the cockpit. With the aid of another crewman, Luther was hooked up and strapped into it.

He checked the gauges, worked the controls, and looked out and down at the men around the plane. Dutch signaled all clear, and Luther lit off the big Merlin twelve-cylinder engine. The massive four-blade prop turned over slowly while the engine chugged, then roared into life, blowing clouds of blue-white smoke out of the exhaust stacks.

He waited for things to settle down into the green, then waved his gloved hand at Dutch, who waved back. With his white-helmeted head weaving from side to side to see over the long nose, Luther taxied the bird out, talking to the tower.

At the end of the strip, he gave a final check, the tower passed on his clearance, and he advanced the throttle, sending the fighter down the airstrip, gently toeing in a little right rudder to counter the torque of the prop.

He lifted off easily, letting the speed build up, and raised the landing gear and flaps. He pulled the control stick slowly back, the British-style spade grip comfortable in his hand.

Climbing quickly into the morning sky, he felt the pressures of the past few days already beginning to slide away as the ground retreated beneath the wings of the Mustang. He passed five thousand feet and leveled off the angle, still climbing. Beneath him the engine's powerful vibrations hummed through the airframe and the 51 oscillated gently in the thermals as it continued its mild climb to altitude.

Luther kept his right hand loose on the stick and turned his mind to the problem that had made him decide to take the plane out this morning.

His talk with Jackie had confirmed that his and Gordon's suspicions were correct. He also realized that his decision to take the investigation outside the company, and away from local law enforcement, was the only way to protect everyone.

If for some reason—one that neither he nor Gordon had uncovered or considered—these strange deaths could be accounted for, a federal investigation could quietly close the entire matter, with no one injured. That was the best way for Luther and Gordon to secure their positions at TPI.

But if John Paraletto and his agents found what Luther suspected they would find, the prosecution of those responsible would fall under federal jurisdiction. By Luther's calculation, the crimes had been committed in at least half of the states, so the feds would have the first shot at the case while the local courts lined up for their turns.

Another reason for taking the investigation outside the company was that he believed his theory was correct. Greed was a superb motivator, as he well knew after all of his years in the insurance business. But it came from all different directions, depending on circumstance and motive. He thought his hypothesis was dead on: ordering the deaths of some two dozen people had a certain cold-bloodedness to it that fit perfectly with a decision from a senior executive obsessed with the bottom line. Without a great deal of imagination he realized this could also be the result of some insane board decision. After all, wasn't that what the insurance business did with the real world? Reduced it to manageable figures, regimented markings on ledger pages?

His natural cynicism about big business plus the scale of what he and Gordon had uncovered convinced him that he was right. Still, Luther found it difficult to believe that a single person, bent on personal gain at murderous cost, could pull off a nationwide killing spree.

He leveled the Mustang out at twelve thousand feet and set a course generally northeast, toward the Four Corners area of the state. He had made up his mind. He had to give this to John; it was the only way. Wherever it goes, there isn't any other option, he thought, feeling the weight of his decision.

You could be bringing down the entire company, you know that? his internal voice cautioned, not for the first time. The possibility almost paralyzed him. If Gordon proved to be right, the company would weather the storm. But if Luther was right, the proof would destroy Trans Patriot as a viable entity, and a lot of people would be out of work.

Defining the duty owed was the problem. To whom did he owe his loyalty—his fellow workers or the nameless, faceless claimants who appeared as nothing more to him than words and numbers on a computer monitor?

He knew something about duty and loyalty, after all. When he was younger he had become intimately familiar with those values, despite decisions made by other executives far removed from him. And he had gone twice into that terrible cauldron, emerging from the experience both times having proven to himself that reality, that particularly brutal reality, was not a thing of numbers and words. There was nothing abstract about blood and pain. And he had dealt with both more times than he cared to remember.

He had made his decision then because of his recognized duty. And he made his choice again now. He was committed.

Holding the circular grip with his left hand, Luther looked down at the high desert mesa tops passing below the wings of his fighter. The aircraft bobbed gently, alive in its element. It seemed light-years away from the situation back at the company, but he felt the storm building, imaginary thunderclouds boiling into massive towers behind him, pregnant with destruction. Turning quickly to scan the brilliant sky behind him, he smiled grimly beneath his oxygen mask.

"As they used to say once upon a very long time ago, 'It don't mean nothin', troop, drive on.' " He remembered what those words used to mean, all those years ago. "Yeah, like hell," he added.

Luther rolled the 51 inverted, pulled back on the stick, and brought the nose up on the new southerly heading. Phoenix lay two hours away in the bright midday light.

MARCH 17, PHOENIX, ARIZONA

Dana unlocked the double front doors. The silence of the house didn't surprise her. Norman was out and about, possibly even out of town. Unable to reach him from New York, she had assumed that some legitimate leg of his business as an investment banker and counselor had called him away. He had left no message on their answering machine, but they left more intimate notes in another place.

Dropping her bags by the front entranceway, she walked back through the house, turning on lights as she went. In the study she turned on the computer, entered her code, and called up the message she was sure Norman had left her. They often used the computer's

115

electronic mailbox for just such a purpose. Her presumption proved correct when his message appeared on the screen:

Dana darling,

Off to L.A. Duty calls. Should be back by midweek. Missed you while you were gone. Hope your trip was profitable. We should celebrate when I get back. I really want to see you.

Yours, forever,
Norman

She tapped the screen with her fingernail, smiling at the words. "Ah, Norman, my love," she sighed. "If you only knew." She deleted his E-mail message and turned the unit off.

Dana stood for a moment, her finger still on the keyboard, replaying her time with Allen, and what she had told him about Norman. She had discussed her uneasiness over Norman's seeming preoccupation. That was a legitimate concern, but it also served to conceal her other concern—that she was losing control of him. Not that their relationship had been anything but equal in all things. But despite their intimacy and shared love, she still thought of her ability to manipulate as being applicable to Norman, just as it was to any other man.

Dana had suggested to Allen that Norman's increasingly strange behavior of late could jeopardize the security of the game. She was sure that her cat-eyed lover had allowed another intangible factor to enter into the overall strategy. What it could be had puzzled her for some time, but after his return from Pittsburgh, it had begun to frighten her as well. Despite the guilt she felt at her disloyalty, she had begun to make plans.

Without being specific, she had convinced Allen that Norman might develop into a threat to them. Allen was already familiar with the lengths Norman could go to in planning something, the detail and intricacies he calculated. If he was losing his concentration, allowing mistakes to creep into his schemes, he could place them all in danger. Allen, of course, was well aware of the ramifications of get-

116

ting caught. The promise of tens of millions of ill-gotten dollars had tempted the lawyer into joining the scam, but prosecution and jail were always on his mind.

Allen readily bought her concerns over Norman and her expressed desire to safeguard the Swiss account. He was the one who had pointed out the available options, dovetailing with Dana's intention to cut Norman out of the loop if necessary. Unknown to her, he felt a certain satisfaction when he heard her suggestion, for he could see the advantages coming his way. He had long resented Norman's hold on Dana, knowing as he did the depth of their relationship. Allen, as a part of his attempt to maintain a sense of chivalry, had never expressed to her his feelings about being the second man in her life. Granted, Allen shared Dana's financial riches with Norman, but the truth of it was, he wanted it all, and until now that hadn't seemed possible.

So he had stifled his feelings, hiding them under the mantle of legal protector, suffering valiantly in his silence, satisfied with his moments of passion with her as payment enough. But all the while he harbored the hope of a better, more permanent relationship.

Allen had gone on to explain what he had in mind. Swiss bankers were scrupulous to a fault, which was why a great deal of the world's serious money was still to be found safely secured in their hands. Allen knew that if the Swiss government notified a banker that the funds in a particular account were either tainted or the subject of a criminal investigation, the authorities would freeze the account. But business was business, even with the unflappable Swiss, and that was the key. Acting on instructions from their government, the Swiss bankers would need seventy-two hours to put the necessary orders in motion.

Allen suggested that they transfer the funds in their account by wire to the Cayman Islands. Blessed with less interference from outside sources, the Caymans offered a level of security even the Swiss couldn't match. The entire transfer would take no longer than the phone call to request it. So to be on the safe side, Allen went ahead and established a new account with a minimal balance in Georgetown on Grand Cayman Island.

Allen arranged the authorization to require dual codes to get access to the funds. He called it another form of insurance but didn't think she was fooled. Still, it solved the immediate problem of circumventing Norman. Allen figured he would have to take his own chances.

Presented with the plan, Dana had had no choice but to accept it. She also discussed ways and means by which she and Allen could leave the country on short notice, should it come to that.

She thought Allen's cloak-and-dagger reaction to the situation was a bit melodramatic, but she kept her opinion to herself. They agreed on how to arrange for alternate, legitimate identities, passports, and other forms of ID, all based on what she had learned from Norman.

Now, as she stood in front of the quiet computer, she considered everything that she and Norman had been through together, had planned together, had done together. She wondered at the apparent ease with which she had plotted to throw Norman over. She did love him, of that she was certain. But she realized, with no great trepidation, that if she had to, she could rid herself of him in a heartbeat. She wasn't sure what that said about her.

Then she shrugged and left the study to fix herself a late supper.

MARCH 19, TPI, THE VILLAGE

Luther and Gordon Hatton were having a dawn breakfast together in the company cafeteria. The sun rose earlier each day, a fast transition from the darkness of just a few weeks before. It was just clearing the tops of the McDowell Mountains a few miles east of the TPI complex. The long slanting light coming in through the wall of arched windows down the length of the building underlined the early hour.

Luther had called his associate from home the day before, asking Gordon to meet him at six-thirty to discuss his decision and to see what Gordon thought of it.

"I kind of figured we'd have to do it this way," Gordon had responded. "Given what we know, or presume, it's the logical choice.

Kind of intriguing in a way, you knowing someone in the FBI," he added with a conspiratorial wink.

"John's an old friend. I don't know if I've mentioned it before, but we go back a long way."

"Vietnam?"

"Yeah, my second tour. John was my copilot for most of it." Luther's attention was on the Formica tabletop, his fingertip tracing patterns in the condensation left by his glass of iced orange juice.

"John pulled me out of a bad situation," he said, smiling quietly. "Saved my life."

Gordon had never asked Luther about the time he spent in Vietnam, but now seemed like the time. "Care to talk about it, Lute?" he asked. "Or you can tell me to buzz off."

Luther smiled in response. "No, it's okay. It's been over and done with for years. The war, I mean. Actually," he continued, easing into the memory, "it was just something that happened. John was my third copilot. I'd lost two during the first few months of that second tour . . . been shot down twice before Johnny showed up.

"The squadron was inserting some American MACV advisers and a company of Vietnamese Regional Force troops, sort of like our National Guard. It was an early morning hop." Luther's eyes became distant. "Hell, seems like it was always early morning when things went bad.

"We hit a hot LZ, to put it simply. Lots of incoming mortars, Chi-Com 82s, heavy .51 caliber machine guns and lighter automatic weapons stuff. Red and green tracers were flying all over the place. Charlie knew we were coming, but then, he always seemed to have better intel than we had.

"They took out the lead ship and the number two in the string right off. We were the fourth bird in line and had just off-loaded our troops. Our slick—that's what we called troop-carrying helicopters —took some fire."

Luther's eyes were focused inside now, beyond seeing just memories. "The crew chief, Sergeant Blubaugh, and the door gunner, Spc.4 DiNardo, were hit." He didn't describe the terrible destructive force to their bodies when the .51 rounds struck. He could never forget it, but no one else would ever understand. "The transmission went. We lost power, caught on fire, and barely managed to crash the ship intact on the far side of the LZ.

"My leg was cut up pretty bad, and John carried me out while the ship burned. We called for an extraction, and while we were waiting, three VC tried to make a run at us. I got two of them with an M-14 rifle I got to packing along as part of my survival kit. John got the third VC right before he nailed the two of us. Shot 'im with a .44 Magnum he liked to carry instead of the issue .38. The Charlie'd tried to flank us while the other two kept us busy. It was John's first up-close-and-personal taste of the war."

Gordon was quiet for a few moments. Hearing Luther's story made him appreciate what his boss had done. Gordon had been too young at the time, and like many in that situation, he wondered if he had missed anything, despite the antiwar sentiment that had gripped the country. Seeing Luther's face just then, he decided he hadn't.

Luther took a quick sip of juice and sat up straighter, focusing once more on Gordon. "Anyway, John had his law degree from Georgetown before he got drafted. Went back for a doctorate in criminal law after the war and then got drafted a second time, you might say. The Bureau picked him up after a referral by one of his professors, and that was that. John never hung out his shingle."

"And he's at the FBI Academy now?"

"Yeah, working on some weapons research-and-development project."

"So how are we going to get this information to him?"

"Personal delivery. Seems like the safest way. I'm going to put in for a few days off. That shouldn't be a problem. Things are pretty much under control here, as far as the regular work goes."

Regular work, Gordon thought ironically, wondering if there would ever again be anything regular after this.

"I'll fly out to D.C. tomorrow, see John, and get this thing rolling," Luther said. "I copied the files last Friday onto some floppy disks. I'll take them with me."

"What do I do while you're gone?"

"Just maintain, best you can, Gordon. That's about all we can do right now. I'm not sure I can convince John that what you and I suspect is on track. If he accepts the information, then it'll be his ball game."

"And if you can't convince him?"

"Beats the hell out of me." Luther sighed. "In that event, troop, it looks like we're on our own."

Gordon thought about that. "Oh, swell," he murmured.

"Yeah, the whole thing's crazy. Who'd believe a story like this, anyway?"

Gordon looked back at him. "We do," he said.

"Amen, brother."

Luther called his boss, an older claimsman named Ernie Saylor. Saylor was the director of the special lines department and was the next level of management above Luther.

He told Saylor only that he wanted to take off a couple of personal days, and hung up thankful that Saylor had not asked him where he was going. He was also thankful that pulling a fast fade out of the office was no big deal, thanks to his level of management. "God bless our bureaucracy," he mumbled under his breath.

A half hour later he held a quick staff meeting with his people, explaining that he was going to be out for a while. At noon, with the last-minute business completed, Luther headed for the cafeteria with Gordon and Walt. He stopped at the elevator for the garage while they continued on. Gordon half turned and flashed him a quick thumb's-up. Luther returned the sign, his face displaying confidence, in contrast to the fluttering knots in his stomach.

The elevator arrived, and he stepped in and forcibly exhaled, letting out his pent-up breath. Then, breathing quietly, he willed himself to relax. As the elevator ascended, Luther gazed at his distorted reflection in the burnished copper control panel. "This is all really, completely crazy," he said, and the odd figure looking back at him nodded in agreement.

A few minutes later, the Mach I rumbled up and out of the underground garage and glided out of the complex. On the drive home, Luther contemplated his next phone call, this one to John Paraletto.

121

He had yielded to his paranoia and decided to make this call from his home phone. Trans Patriot's records could be checked, after all, and he didn't know who could be listening. There was no room for chances.

MARCH 19, FBI ACADEMY, QUANTICO, VIRGINIA

The report of the sound-suppressed 10 mm pistol reminded the sound technician, thirty feet to the left of the shooter, of the chunk-thunk made by the closing of an upright freezer door.

John Paraletto, forty-three, walrus mustached, thirty-five pounds heavier than he had been in Vietnam, light brown hair thicker and curlier, sat closer to the shooter, only six feet away. John's ears, covered by ovoid earmuffs, registered the shot as a flat, abbreviated crack, like a softball thudding into a catcher's mitt.

The big agent turned in his seat at his shooting table and looked back down range. He watched the bullet strikes follow the thin beam of the laser sight on the subdued target suspended at the end of the dimly lighted tunnel.

The shooter, Jim Zellis, sat hunched over the matte black semiautomatic, arms extended, elbows slightly bent, both hands gripping the weapon, resting against a sand-filled leather bag. The rested position steadied and supported the gun and allowed Zellis to concentrate on the placement of the laser.

He fired in a slow, rhythmic cadence, settling back on target quickly after each shot. John adjusted his mental count to the rhythm of the gun, ticking off each report until all seventeen shots had been fired. The metallic clack of the slide locking open at the end of the string was lost in the singular whap of the last shot.

From his position, looking through his range scope, John could see that a hole roughly one inch across had been blown out of the man-sized paper target. All of the shots were centered in the middle chest area of the generic "bad guy" figure.

The laser beam wavered up and out of the hole as Jim raised the gun. The beam was extinguished when Jim relaxed his grip slightly, thumbing the magazine release button. The empty magazine dropped smoothly out of the gun onto the table below. He tilted the weapon, visually checking the empty chamber, and laid the 10 mm down on a folded chamois beside the leather bag.

Jim turned to John, grinning as he took off his large-framed amber-tinted glasses. "By Jove, I think we've got it," he quipped.

"I think you're right," John replied, examining the target, which had run back on its electric track. The sound technician, monitoring the performance of the Knight's Armament sound suppressor, ambled over and gazed approvingly at the results.

John cast an inquiring look at the tech, who pointed back to his equipment.

"Air clap," the sound technician said simply, using the inside joke. At thirty feet and ninety degrees to the muzzle, the reduction in measurable sound was equivalent to one hand clapping against the wind.

John nodded and asked the shooter, "What'd you think, James?"

"There's a bit more noticeable kick with the suppressor over the compensator, but accuracy's identical. The last round of mods by ASP seems to have worked out the bugs. The single-double action cam selector works as designed. Carry it cocked and locked like a 1911-A1, or leave the hammer down on the firing pin block, and go double action each time. It allows a lot of flexibility either way."

"Okay, this one's a wrap," John said. "I'll get a new report off to Parsons. Now we can worry that the latest round of budget talks on the Hill don't deep-six the program. It'd be a shame to lose this now."

John left the range building, one of several in the vast training complex that made up the Bureau's Quantico academy. He reclaimed his car in the lot outside, sorry to be leaving the facility.

He had enjoyed his two years there, working in the SOARS, or Special Operations and Research Section, on a 10 mm pistol for the special action groups within the FBI. SOARS, responsible for all SWAT research and training programs for the Bureau, was developing a system with more exacting requirements, better reliability,

123

and target accuracy out of the box. All of this was a spinoff of the tragic Miami shooting in April 1986, when four agents were killed by two armed robbery suspects who sustained multiple hits from the 9 mm service round then issued.

John, who had been assigned to the Miami office at one time, had known all of the agents killed that day. His subsequent work with the SOARS unit had carried with it a personal obligation, and now it seemed that obligation would soon be met.

But with the end of the project came the end of his time in D.C. as well. John was slated to return to Miami as senior agent in charge of that office. In the long run, he welcomed the field assignment. Historically, a Bureau assignment to the Academy was considered a dead-end job, the end of the road for a career. John's involvement in the weapons project had been a plum, but continued time there would eventually lead nowhere.

He drove the short distance back to the academy side of the Bureau's complex, divided from the ranges by the main entrance roadway into Quantico. He'd hardly had time to settle in at his desk before the phone rang.

"Agent Paraletto," he snapped at the interruption.

"Damn, boy, if I knew you would be this cranky, I'd've sent a fax," came the vaguely southern-accented voice.

"Looter!" Paraletto responded enthusiastically. "Been a long time, buddy. How the hell are you, ya old Greek reprobate?"

"Probably better than you, you aging Maryland yuppie, but then, I always was."

John smiled broadly. Hearing his old friend's voice was a pleasant surprise. The closeness John felt to Sitasy came from those too-clear memories of the heart-stopping times they had shared.

"Man, Lute, it's good to hear your voice."

"Yours, too, Johnny. I've been meaning to call you for a while now."

"So everybody's fine at your end? Jackie and Mikki are okay?"

"Doing okay, mostly. Mikki's doing great at ASU. Jackie's still crankin' out the news. And your group?"

"Status quo, no problems. But it has been a while, bud. To what do I owe the pleasure, as they say?"

"I wanted you to know that I'm going to be in D.C. tomorrow. I hope we can get together. I've got something to show you."

The agent's professional interest perked up. "Where are you coming in? Dulles?"

"No, Washington National."

"So what's the deal?"

"Something important, Johnny, and"—he paused, not wanting to sound overly dramatic, maybe even ridiculous—"well, just say that it's unusual and serious. I think it's right up your line. At least at this point, it's probably more your line of work than mine." Luther realized his explanation had tumbled out in a rush, despite his caution. It was more than John needed.

"And you can't tell me over the phone, right? Are you in trouble, Lute? And is it personal or business?"

"'In trouble' is the operative phrase, I guess, and it's strictly business. I've got a bad situation, something the Bureau might be interested in." Luther listened to himself, and cringed at the melodramatic sound of his words.

"You'll stay with Cathy and me. No excuses, no objections. I'll meet you at National, main terminal. What time do you get in, and how long are you planning to stay?"

Luther gave him his flight information, then added, "Johnny, I hope I'm wrong about this, but I'm afraid the chance of that is pretty slim. I just need to show it to someone . . . someone, you know . . . safe."

"Hey, whatever you need. You know that."

"Thanks, man," Luther answered softly.

"You know how we do," John said. "I'll see you tomorrow."

MARCH 19, EAST HAMPTON, LONG ISLAND

Allen Parkman sat in a leather club chair, staring out at the waves rolling in from the Atlantic, visible two hundred yards away in the late evening darkness.

125

It was twenty minutes to twelve, and Allen had had a very busy few days. Unable to sleep tonight, he sat in the quiet of his expansive oceanfront home and replayed the events of the last week.

Dana had left him the previous Wednesday; since then he had thought a great deal about everything she had told him about Norman and his brilliance, which now appeared to be going in a dangerous direction. He had also thought a great deal about Dana Quinn, recognizing, not for the first time, how much of a black widow she could be.

Allen didn't doubt for a moment that her concerns over Norman were valid. She had said that he was getting so pumped up on his own ego, what with the success of their complicated investment fraud scam, that she didn't think it was a far reach to imagine him wanting to take a special risk—add to the excitement, so to speak.

Although Allen had never met the man, Dana had given him so much information over the years that he had a pretty clear picture of this other partner. He understood Norman's self-indulgent, almost maniacal personality and therefore fully appreciated the danger he could pose if he was, in fact, slipping his reality bonds.

Dana had assured him that Norman was still unaware of Allen's active participation in the scheme, but the lawyer had no doubt about what Norman would do if he ever found out. Both men shared more with Dana than mere illegalities. But Allen valued his personal well-being as the number one concern in his rather rich life, and after listening to her spin her tale of woe over Norman's strange behavior, he believed without reservation that Dana would have no problem throwing him over, right along with the brilliant Norman Bloodstone.

Still, he was surprised by his reaction when he thought about the possibility, not of being cast aside by Dana, but of losing her. Allen accepted the fact of his involvement with the Jamaican beauty as one of the perks of taking a little risk, a kind of payback. Arranging her access into the trust fund had been a fairly simple task. His financial growth as a silent participant in the game, simply for providing his considerable expertise in foreign trade laws, seemed at times too good to be true.

But his enjoyable dalliance had somehow turned into a real passion for her, the I-want-you-forever kind of passion that had hereto-fore eluded him.

His mouth twisted in a rueful smile at the memory of her compen-sation to him for arranging that initial financial indiscretion. At first he had regarded his need for these dalliances as nothing more than a character flaw, a temporary yielding to weakness. But they had continued, and now his involvement with Dana had taken him so far down that road that there was no turning back. He was hooked on her, perhaps even in love, in fantasy if not in fact.

"It's a bit more than a character flaw, my boy," he chastised him-self aloud, his words slowed by the effects of the smoky Scotch in the glass he held. Still gazing at the soundless sea beyond his heavy-framed windows, Allen raised his glass and murmured, "To the ex-quisite Ms. Quinn, whose passion is matched only by her greed. So very beautiful and so very, very, deadly. Your health, my darling."

He tipped the glass back, grimacing slightly as the fiery liquor burned down his throat.

"That's enough of that," he said aloud, as he stood up somewhat unsteadily and walked through the dark room to the windows, where he stood in silence. He could hear the quiet, feel the solitude. Out-side, far down the beach, the waves continued their perpetual sliding, rolling, skimming motion.

After a while, he sighed deeply and longingly. "Some things never do change, do they?" he said sadly. He took himself to bed, trying not to think about the source of the feeling of loss that accompanied him to bed that night.

MARCH 20, CAREFREE, ARIZONA

His own shouted exclamation tore him from sleep, snapping his body up and out of the bed, diving for cover onto the floor from the nightmare figure. Khanh, startled by Luther's shout, snarled once and huddled low, on guard, looking for an intruder.

Luther pushed over slowly onto his back, heart thumping, hands

127

shaking, his chest heaving with the adrenaline rush. He felt the cool rivulets of sweat tracking down his sides. The dog came over to sniff and lick at him, confused, wanting something to attack.

"Jesus, Khanh." He managed to force the words out, his throat constricted, hurting from the effort, and he knew it was from his rasping breath. He reached out to touch the animal, calm him down, calming himself in the process. Luther forced himself to take deep, lung-filling breaths, hold them, burning off his body's naturally produced speed.

"Oh, man . . . oh, man," he said, slowing down. "I haven't had one of those in a long time." He gave Khanh a final pat and sat up, wanting to remember the nightmare, trying to figure out why it had come back, but he could recall only a few familiar snatches, torn fragments of the dream.

"Some dream, man," Luther mumbled, feeling anger at it, and at himself, begin to surface. "You're supposed to be over this nightmare stuff, buddy. You took the cure, remember?" He sat on the floor and took another calming breath, holding his hand up in front of his face, able to make out enough of it in the dark to see if the shaking was subsiding.

Well, he thought, they say you never get over it; you only learn to deal with it. But the nightmare had come all the same, one of the worst, like the ones that used to ride with him almost nightly years ago. His consciousness recognized enough of it to know which one it was. And he knew why it had come.

Triggered by the pressure of what he had uncovered, Luther had experienced an escalation of temper, a thinning patience. He found himself apologizing for obvious slights he had made to people on his staff. He had tried to brush it off, claiming all he needed was some time off. Time off would surely help, but it wasn't the answer.

"So now we go back to this, too?" he asked aloud. "If it's getting deep enough to bring the nightmares back, what the hell am I going to do about it?" You're going to stop the self-serving self-pity and get on with it, his inner voice answered. Make the choice, man. You did it before. Hell, you do it each and every day. You get up, you square yourself away, and you go out there and take it each and every by-God day.

128

Luther sighed, got up from the floor, and lay down on the bed. He closed his eyes, waiting for the images to flood back in, the incredibly clear pictures of kaleidoscope death. But the images didn't appear when he tried to summon them. They were gone for the night. But then, maybe not. Maybe they'll come back, he thought, knowing it could happen. And if they do . . . ?

"To hell with 'em," he said, hoping they heard, hoping that deep in their graves they could actually hear his voice. "The war's over, isn't it?" But he wasn't sure it was.

MARCH 20, PHOENIX, ARIZONA

Luther was up and dressed by five-thirty in the morning, suffering no aftereffects of the fright to his system from the night before. He finished some written instructions to the Arutakas on items needing their attention and discussed them with Myoshi and Nakato. After a light breakfast, he said good-bye to them and to Khanh.

He had not yet confided in the Japanese couple what the nature of his trip was all about. Even so, he'd had to evade a few carefully phrased questions from them in the past few days. They knew something was bothering him, but trusted Luther enough to believe that he would tell them what it was, in his own time.

He drove the Mach I to Sky Harbor International and left it in the long-term parking garage. Half an hour later he was settled in his first-class window seat. While the aircraft leveled off for the slow climb to cruising altitude, Luther eased his feet out of his cowboy boots, stretched his legs under the seat in front of him, and turned his head enough to see out of the square window beside him.

He tried not to think about the diskettes in his bag, protected in their stiff holder. That the five-and-a-quarter-inch squares of magnetic vinyl carried the future of Trans Patriot Insurance was painfully clear to him. That knowledge gave him a sense of power he didn't enjoy in the least.

He thought about the nightmare, recognizing it as a symptom, a warning to be careful. Slipping back into that other mentality opened up all of the scary things that used to do more than go bump in the night. Horror had its own effect, when purely imagined. When based on terror once lived, experiences were remembered with such clarity that even imagination couldn't match the ugliness. Just carry on, that's all you have to do, he thought. It comes with the territory, so deal with it.

"Yeah, sure," he said under his breath, and pushed his seat back. With an effort he closed off his mind, relaxed, and summoned sleep. It came sooner than he expected, a physical need overriding the mental pressure. Luther let it take him into quiet unconsciousness for the entire four-and-one-half-hour nonstop flight.

MARCH 20, WASHINGTON, D.C.

Luther joined the crowd of passengers trudging through the skyway tunnel into the terminal, walking off the confinement of the long flight. He cleared the gate door, checking the little knots of welcoming families and friends. He shifted his bag from right to left, and felt the pressure of a large hand clamping down onto his shoulder. Luther turned to see the beaming face of John Paraletto above him.

"Johnny!"

"Hey, Looter," he said, and their hands came together, roundhousing into each other, gripping firmly, each man's eyes holding the other's, smiles creasing underneath the beard of one and the mustache of the other. Their grip changed, hands rotating to clasp the other's thumb, palms pressed tight, holding fast. Their grins widened, and they pulled together to clasp each other close and tight.

"Man, it's good to see you," Luther said, his greeting muffled by their embrace.

"You too, buddy. Been too damn long."

They held on to each other for a time, oblivious of the shuffling crowds around them.

They stepped back to see each other better.

"I'd've found you quicker if you'd had a little more height on you," John observed.

Luther returned the serve. "I see what they say about Washington fat cats is true, at least in your case."

"Hey, you don't like the look?" John swept his long arms wide, inviting more commentary on the extra girth he had picked up over the years.

"Who me? Naw, big guy. You look marvelous."

"Listen, I have this great idea," John said. "Let's get your bags and get the hell out of here."

"Already there," Luther replied, gesturing to his single carry-on.

"That's it?"

"That's it. Lead the way, Johnny."

Luther followed his friend's broad back through the crowds and out into the Washington sun.

Luther watched the highway signs, noticing that John was heading for I-95 south. "Where's this place you mentioned?"

"It's called the Globe and Laurel, down in Triangle. It's kind of a hangout for the spook crowd, plus the military and the Bureau. Place has a lot of history. You see a fair number of foreign types, too, on occasion."

John's eyes were busy, always checking around them, behind them, flashing up at the rearview mirror, looking far down the highway. It was a habit that had long since become second nature. Luther noticed it because he did the same thing.

"Place is run by a retired marine major named Spooner. He used to head up the Corps version of the army's CID. Hey, you still with us?" John asked.

Luther brought his attention back. "Sorry, fella, I was someplace else."

"I figured that. Anyway, we're here. Now's a good enough time to get into whatever it is that's brought you twenty-three hundred miles."

"May as well," Luther replied, perusing the outside of the building as they pulled to a stop near the front of it.

131

The two men entered the restaurant, and John watched the reaction on Luther's face when he got his first glimpse of the interior of the Globe and Laurel.

Plaques, awards, and decorations, all of military derivation, were displayed on every wall. There were more than a few CMHs, Congressional Medals of Honor. But the ceiling held the main attraction, for it was literally covered with the patches of thousands of military divisions, regiments, and brigades from all over the world.

"Really something, huh?" John said, indicating the room, just as a slim young man appeared, dressed in white shirt and black bow tie. He directed them to a table with a minimum of fuss, all the while exhibiting a starched, military bearing.

Their waiter, a mirror image of the one who had seated them, arrived and took their order. Luther wondered if any of them were moonlighting marines. The agent assured him they were not. Their bearing was simply due to the way Retired Major Spooner ran his establishment.

There was a pause, during which John appraised his friend and the tiredness around his eyes. "I suppose we've put it off long enough, talking about why you're here. You have the floor, Lute."

Finally given an opening, Luther chose to approach the subject indirectly. "How much do you know about what I do at Trans Patriot?"

"Only what you've mentioned before, that it's not just the usual auto claims or slip-and-fall stuff. You deal with municipalities, police, serious injury cases, things like that, too."

"By and large, that's it. Without a long dissertation of the particulars of TPI's internal workings, let me tell you what happened recently. A few weeks ago," he continued, leaning back to allow the waiter to set down their plates, "I got to thinking that we could get a better handle on the expenses involved if we could predict from the onset, right when it was first reported, how long the file might actually be around."

Luther proceeded to explain how Gordon and Sheri Moradilo had developed the profile. He ended with their expectations of what they thought they were going to find.

"And did it produce what you were looking for?"

132

"No, not actually," Luther replied, leaning closer to the table. "What we found is that, statistically speaking, there were too many fatalities among policy limits claimants and plaintiffs."

John started to ask a question, but Luther cut him off.

"We checked the data quite a few ways. I mean, we went in looking for one set of data, and ran into this. Using a controlled data base we found that in the past two years there'd been around twenty-three deaths that shouldn't have happened. All of them happened at random, and all apparently were caused by explainable circumstances."

Luther took a breath before continuing. "It gets better. We can't identify which ones don't belong, because all of 'em look to be legit. The only thing we are certain of is that someone has been, and may still be, killing off policy limits claimants."

John's face showed little reaction, but the change in the tone of his next question told Luther his statement had hit home.

"What's your proof, Lute?" he asked quietly, knowing that Luther would have covered every conceivable possibility.

"That's the crazy part, man, because it all appears to be circumstantial. Each of these deaths, from what we've been able to see, was directly attributable either to a confirmed accident or to natural causes. But balanced against that are the statistics. No matter how we ran the data—and believe me, we burned it up—the results are the same; there are just too many dead people out there." He shook his head grimly. Now that the story was out, he felt more comfortable talking about it. "Which is not to say that these deaths couldn't be legitimate—some sort of quirk in the averages, or whatever. But I have to add that the odds of what we found here being anything other than deliberate killings is almost off the charts."

"Coincidence?"

"As a factor?" Luther shook his head again. "Doesn't fit. The math's all wrong. And there's something else." He took a deep breath, quelling the nervousness that was creeping back underneath his control. He rested his arms on the tabletop, lacing his fingers together. "Gordon and I reviewed three hundred and twelve claim files, all fatalities. One hundred sixty-three of them happened in the last two years, including at least five plaintiff attorneys."

133

John's mind was working quickly on the data. "What happened to the lawsuits with these dead lawyers?"

"We found a small pattern there, interestingly enough. Each lawyer died *after* his client, not before, and all five suits were eventually dismissed. Causes of action can be maintained by the estate following the demise of the plantiff, depending on the estate situation and the jurisdiction. It's a judgment call whether it will be continued. Each of these was dismissed voluntarily. All five of these lawyers were sole practitioners or came from a firm of two or three partners."

"Sounds like someone was counting on the dismissals."

"Exactly. Now you're getting the idea."

"I suppose you've considered suspects?"

"That's where it gets sticky, and why I've come to see you," Luther said. "I think it's coming internally, from pretty high up, possibly even at the executive level. There's a certain senior vice president of claims who might fit the bill. He comes from an accounting background, which will make sense when I explain my theory."

He told John his idea, then contrasted it against Gordon's belief. "This VP's name is Branden Stennett, been with the company a dozen or so years, although he's got thirty years in this racket. He's a dinosaur, and his reputation is that he believes the bottom line is it. He's not particularly well liked; in fact, he's fairly nasty. But his technical knowledge of this business is absolutely first rate. It's why they keep him around, because he makes money the old-fashioned way, as they used to say. But how he does it is pretty ruthless."

Luther glanced around reflexively. "That's why I can't tell anyone above me what we've found. It's the classic problem of who do you trust? But Gordon thinks the source of the deaths goes lower down, motivated by individual greed, money. Frankly, I'm beginning to see his point. The possibility of ill-gotten gain makes a pretty persuasive argument. And if so, that puts this case into your lap."

"A logical conclusion," John observed, "but never overlook the obvious simply because it doesn't appear to fit at first. Prove it out. But never stop looking elsewhere, either." He smiled at his obfuscation. "Usually the motive becomes clear enough in the end. It's when the opposition gets cute that the fun begins."

"So you're going to look into this—'take the case,' I believe they call it in all the detective movies?"

John nodded briefly in reply. "What you've laid out has a certain ring to it, even though much of the evidence appears to be circumstantial. But it's worth checking out, if only to validate your statistical profile."

Luther visibly relaxed, finally having heard the words he had been anticipating.

"But prepare yourself for the other side of the equation, too," his friend cautioned. "It could just as easily end up totally explainable —no conspiracy, no ulterior motive. This guy Stennett may be nothing. For that matter, motive seems to be your biggest missing factor. If Stennett is a wash, then we'll have to look elsewhere."

"I've stayed awake many hours, thinking over exactly that," Luther said, toying with the remaining silverware on the table top near him. "I mean, this still sounds a little crazy and scary, and I'll admit to becoming paranoid over the possibilities. Man, I've literally got Gordon's and my careers on the line, besides the existence of Trans Patriot. If this goes wrong, it could destroy the company, and there are thousands of people that will be out on the street."

He cupped one closed fist inside the other hand, pressing tightly. "Think about it? Damn straight I've thought about it." He raised his eyes back to John, a combination of intensity and pleading shining from within. "I just don't know what the hell else I can do about it. All I can tell you is what I feel, what I believe. Something very, very wrong is going on here, and in order to find out what that is, and then to prove it, I may destroy a major company, along with the lives of a whole lot of people. But, Johnny, I've got no other choice!"

"You could walk away, Lute," John said quietly.

Luther stopped, chilled suddenly by his friend's statement.

"Sure," John continued. "Who would ever know? You could let it go. You've always said the company makes more money than God. In the grand scheme of things this body count's not that bad."

The moment stretched out between them. Then Luther smiled, leaned back, and stared evenly. "Would *you*?" he asked, his voice calmer.

John returned his stare, and both men knew. A half smile appeared

135

underneath the agent's thick mustache. "No. No, I wouldn't. I didn't think you would, either."

"So what do we do now?"

The agent picked up the napkin from his lap, laid it before him where his plate had been, and shoved his chair back.

"What we do now, buddy," he said, standing up, "is go out and get 'em."

Back on the interstate, heading south toward Fredericksburg, John noticed that Luther had lapsed back into his preoccupied state.

"Something else troubling you, Lute?"

Luther snapped out of his musing. "Not really . . . Well, maybe. It's just that I've put so much time into thinking about all this, worrying over it. You know, all the what-if's, and who's responsible."

"And?"

"And after all of that, I lay this on you, and, bam, you pick it up right away. I mean, you didn't ask that many questions, and here we go, off chasing the bad guys—if, in fact, there are any bad guys."

"And that bothers you?"

Luther nodded.

"Okay, I have an idea what you're saying. Let me try to clarify it. First off, you've been in insurance how many years now?" Not waiting for an answer, John provided his own. "A long time, long enough to have learned your trade pretty well. You consider yourself a professional, which you obviously are. You're good at what you do, or you wouldn't have stayed with it this long."

John shifted in his seat, watching his driving as he continued. "So what happened when you came up with something that didn't fit into the normal chain of events that make up your world? You started checking it out. From what you've told me so far, you did more than that. You field-stripped the data."

Luther acknowledged all of this.

"That's the professional in you," John went on. "Well, that works for me, too. The years I've put into catching bad guys have given me a certain perspective—call it an educated viewpoint—on the human condition.

"That advantage tells me that, as wild as it may all seem to you, to me it has a distinctive ring of plausibility, dark-centered as it may be. Not too much surprises me anymore, not when we're talking about what one man can do to another. It's a jaded outlook, to be sure, and you try not to let it get to you. But it's real, and I deal with it every single day.

"For what it's worth, you have something here, Lute, and I can guess what it's cost you to bring it to me. But this is just the beginning. Things could get a whole lot darker before it's over."

Luther listened to John's words. They carried with them a feeling, not quite of relief, but of promise. His problem was being observed from another perspective now, one that promised a solution. Good, bad, or otherwise, at least an end to it seemed reachable. The realization that he and Gordon might have been right all along lay like a sobering pall over his resolve.

"All right, I can accept that. So back to my original question: where do we go from here?"

"Tomorrow you and I are going to see some people in the Hoover Building. If you don't mind, I'd like to have you go over all of this again for them. We'll put some feelers out and see what comes back." John shot him a quick grin. "And while that's going on, I'll show you what we've been spending the taxpayers' money on for the last two years."

They arrived an hour later at the Paralettos' turn-of-the-century Victorian home, sitting on a gentle slope on a neighborhood street almost lost beneath the tunnel of branches from the oak trees lining it.

They entered through the side kitchen door, and were met by Cathy, John's second, and very young, wife. "Luther, so nice to see you," she said.

She stood half a head taller than Luther, and he was instantly aware of her lithe form. "I hope I'm not causing a problem, y'all putting me up like this," he said.

She assured him it was no trouble at all and embraced her husband. "Beat the bad guys again?"

John pinched her hip as she tried to dodge his hand. "As always, Cath. The late J. Edgar would have been proud."

137

Luther admired the couple and said so. "I didn't think it was possible, a bear like Johnny finding someone who fit him so well. You guys keep getting better every year."

"Thank you, kind sir," Cathy replied. "It has been an interesting four years."

"Four years, three months," John threw in, "but that's enough of that. I guess you just get lucky sometimes."

"Yeah, I can see that you do at that," Luther agreed.

"You've already eaten?" Cathy asked, and John nodded. "Well, I've got a few things to keep me busy while you boys talk shop. I'll see you in a bit."

"Yes, ma'am," her husband said, and motioned toward the hall door. "I believe we're dismissed, Lute. I'll put your bag in the front bedroom, and we can talk over our game plan."

"Sounds good," Luther replied, and followed him out.

A few minutes later they settled themselves in the family room and John outlined the next day's agenda. "We'll hit the Hoover Building first, Lute. After your call I played a hunch and alerted a team to meet with us. You can tell them the same story you told me.

"One of the things I want to check is the well-being, or lack of it, of all the plaintiff attorneys identified on all of those lawsuits. We'll use the results as a barometer of sorts to give us a better idea how widespread this thing might be. It might give us a clearer pattern, too."

"I'll be curious myself to see if the lawyers' deaths fall into the same parameters," Luther said. "Gordon and I only found a few, but at least one of them was a crime victim."

"We can check with local law enforcement on cases like that," John said. "The amounts of money tied up in these files still fascinates me. It's not just the reserve money, but add to it the costs of defending them. The buying public really has no idea the complexities that go into your business, or the wide variety of claims you handle."

Luther smiled wryly. "Yeah, if someone were to sit down and try to make up some of the claims we see every day, no one would believe them."

John shifted direction abruptly. "By the way, are you up on your shooting skills?"

138

Luther smiled knowingly. "I manage to keep my hand in," he said. "I had a small range built in the basement of my house. Nothing elaborate, just a hundred-foot tunnel, good for handguns up to .44 Magnum and rifles up to .308."

"Must be nice," John kidded.

"Got to have a hobby," Luther replied.

"Anyway, the reason I asked is that I'd like to run you down to Quantico tomorrow, over to the SOARS unit. I think you'll be impressed with what we're working on. We can do that after your briefing, while my guys are running down some of the lawyer information."

"Sounds good," Luther said.

Later on, Cathy joined them for conversation that was punctuated by shop talk from John, some amusing claims tales from Luther, and only one war story, toned down for Cathy's benefit. All through their conversation Luther felt a sense of real accomplishment. Now a bona fide law enforcement agency, arguably the best in the world, was involved. The FBI had the capability to get to the heart of the problem.

But as confident as he tried to feel, Luther knew that even more caution would be necessary. There were going to be more hands involved in the mix, more chances for mistakes. He hoped that wouldn't happen, but he resolved to be prepared for it if things went wrong. A lot was riding on what was happening now.

MARCH 21, WASHINGTON, D.C.

John drove them to the main headquarters of the FBI, arriving just before 8:00 A.M. The J. Edgar Hoover building imposed its modern, oddly angular gray presence on almost an entire block, near Tenth Street and Pennsylvania Avenue.

Its intimidating size stood as a physical reminder to the visitor that it housed probably the most formidable law enforcement agency in the world. Which made it all the more curious to Luther, as they approached the building, that just across the street of this bastion of

139

power, stood a series of porn shops and peep shows, garishly announcing their wares.

When he commented on this to John, the agent stoically replied, "Yeah, J. Edgar is probably rolling over in his grave."

John cleared them through a checkpoint with his security badge and drove down a ramp underneath the building, into the underground garage.

"Shades of TPI," Luther said, as they wound their way down.

"This is only part of it," John told him. "Most people don't realize how long this place was under construction before it actually broke ground level. One of the favorite stories going around is that all of D.C. is connected by underground passages. I wouldn't be the least bit surprised to find out it's true."

He pulled the Buick into a slot and stopped. "We're here."

John led them off the garage floor and down a long corridor to a security station, where he signed for a visitor's pass for Luther to wear while they were in the building. John then led the way into an elevator, which ascended several floors.

As the door slid open, Luther asked, "Are we still underground?"

"Not now," John replied, leading them through a maze of interconnecting corridors that rivaled the worst that the Trans Patriot complex had to offer. They stopped before a door of nondescript solid paneling. Small brass lettering proclaimed this the Field Investigation Division. John ushered Sitasy into the office.

Inside, Luther was disappointed to see a standard business office filled with desks and cubicles, although the sheer size of the floor space made an impression. "You could play football in here," Luther commented.

After finding an empty office to use, John left Luther alone for a few minutes while he rounded up three men. "Luther Sitasy, let me introduce David Armitage, Paul Gorley, and Dale Reichley." Luther shook hands with the men and felt their silent appraisal of him behind their uniformly smiling faces and warm handshakes.

"Gentlemen, Mr. Sitasy has brought an interesting scenario for your review and interpretation," John began, motioning for all of them to be seated. John explained who Luther was. Then he said, "Lute, if you'd give them the details of the profile?"

The claimsman's hour-long recitation was interrupted occasionally by questions. After answering them, he concluded his presentation. Dale Reichley and Paul Gorley finished taking notes while John stood up.

"You three men were chosen because of your familiarity with mail and investment fraud cases. That background should help."

John continued, "Split the country up into thirds. Check out each case that's in suit, ID the plaintiff's lawyer, and contact the closest field office. Find out whether the attorney is still among the living. If not, find out how he died and, if possible, why. Take note of anything else that seems significant. This is a preliminary survey. Advise the field office that additional information will be coming within forty-eight hours. We'll have a strategy conference at the close of business today, five P.M." He directed his next comment to Dale. "Do we have this room reserved then?"

"Taken care of, John," Dale assured him.

"Where will you be?" Dave, the older man, asked with his smoker's gravelly voice.

"Down at SOARS for a few hours. We should be back by midafternoon."

"Okay, boys," Paul announced, getting up from his chair, "let's go to work."

"Just like that?" Luther asked, impressed by their efficiency.

"Just like that," John answered, his small smile adding to the calculating light in his eyes. He took Luther in tow, leaving the others to sort through the files.

In the light of a glaringly bright day, they drove to Quantico, headquarters of the United States Marine Corps as well as site of the FBI training academy.

As they drove through the main gate, Luther noticed the preponderance of uniforms, both full dress and fatigues, and the formations of troops passing by, jogging together in double time or marching in stern-faced platoon-sized formations, black M-16s cutting diagonals across the ranks.

"Never changes, does it?" Luther remarked as they glided past.

141

"No, I don't suppose it does." John pointed out the academy buildings on the left. "Ranges are on the right," he indicated, "including the hostage rescue team area and the obstacle course. It's called the Yellow Brick Road, but Dorothy never walked down it."

They pulled up in front of a long single-story brick building and parked. "Our group should be in here," John said, getting out. "Wish we had more time. We have some really interesting live fire ranges farther down."

He led them through the double glass doors of the outside entrance and then through two steel doors into a long hallway that appeared to stretch the length of the building.

Luther heard the muffled whap of gunshots reverberating flatly in the hall. "Got some testing going on in some of the other bays," John explained, opening a single door and motioning Luther inside.

The room was roughly eighty feet wide and one hundred feet deep. A dozen shooting lanes gave the appearance of a bowling alley. Sturdy benches and tables anchored the near side of each lane, and several were occupied by shooters, all checking equipment. Other technicians were at work calibrating an assortment of instruments.

"Lets get some muffs and I'll introduce you around."

They walked down to the range master's cubicle, and John signed for two sets of hearing protectors, large bright orange cups that looked like hard plastic earmuffs.

Several groups of men busied themselves at tables across the back of the range. John took Luther to the nearest group and introduced him to a big man, who turned to greet them.

"Luther, this is Kevin Parsons. Kevin's been instrumental in developing some of the mechanics of our system. Kevin, meet Luther Sitasy. He's in from Phoenix on some business for the Bureau. I thought I'd bring him down here to show off our new toy."

"Well, in that case, you're just in time," Kevin responded. "We're getting ready to run some systems checks on the piece. If you'd like, you can sit in on the tests."

"Sure, love to," Luther replied. He watched as Kevin turned back to the shooting table. Next to a spotting scope sitting solidly on its small tripod lay three flat black oblong cases. He slid one of the cases toward him and worked the zipper around the edge, opening

142

up the soft case. He folded back the flap, revealing a gold plush lining, and turned the case around.

"This is it," he said, indicating the weapon lying inside.

"Looks like a Colt Commander or maybe a Springfield Armory variant of the same thing," Luther commented, appraising the black finish.

"Good eye," Kevin said, picking up the gun. "You know your weapons." He cleared the piece, making sure there was no magazine in the butt, and locked the slide back, confirming no round in the chamber before handing it over, butt first, barrel down.

Luther took the gun and checked for the same things. "Feels wider in the grip," he said, hefting it.

"What we started with here was a Commander-type 10 mm Omega from Springfield Armory," Kevin explained. "What the HRT people wanted was a high-capacity 10 mm pistol capable of firing either full-house loads or the reduced-velocity field load developed for the S&W 1006. Are you familiar with the Smith?"

"I've read about it," Luther replied, "but there haven't been any showing up on dealers' shelves in Phoenix yet."

"And there may not be," Kevin added. "We're starting to get reports back from the field, preliminary at this point. There are some problems. In any event," he went on, "this is strictly a special-use weapon. John's people called ASP to do an engineering and feasibility study on it."

"What's ASP?"

"Armament Systems and Procedures, Incorporated," Kevin answered. "We're a specialized civilian firm contracted to do projects for the government. Saves time and, more often than not, money, too."

He referred back to the gun. "We use a rotary bolt with a modification of Reed Knight's roller bearing blowback system. It allows us to use the full power of a 10 mm in a smaller package. The barrel acts as its own operating guide rod, in effect clearing that space under the barrel for a frame-mounted laser sight."

Luther whistled. "I'd say you seem to have hit your design parameters."

"Oh, we got more than that," Kevin said, picking up a loaded magazine. He signaled the range safety officer to clear the range for live fire. "Care to try it?"

"Be my pleasure."

They walked up to the firing line, a white strip a few feet in front of the table. Kevin laid the gun down on a small stand next to the firing line and pulled on his protective earmuffs. Luther did the same. He heard Kevin's voice, slightly muted through the muffs.

Kevin picked up the squarish magazine, tapped it against the edge of the stand to seat all the rounds, and loaded it into the 10 mm. "Slide and safety are ambidextrous, and there's no magazine disconnect. The laser is controlled through the grip; tighten just a bit to turn it on. On single action the trigger pull is very light."

"How light?" Luther almost shouted back unnecessarily, his voice sounding louder in his ears from the muffs.

"Like about two pounds," Kevin grinned. "I think you'll find it a bit of a surprise, but quite controllable. The compensator on it adds a little heft and works very well on recoil reduction." Kevin handed him the weapon, and stood a few paces to the side.

Luther touched the slide release, letting the slide chamber a round as it seated, and set the safety. He assumed a stance with both arms forward, the left hand wrapped around his firing hand, leaning into the gun. He thumbed the safety off and tightened his grip a hair, lighting up the laser. He steadied the red beam on the center of the target, a dark silhouette set against a darker background, and touched off the first shot. As Kevin had cautioned, it surprised him. His ear protectors diminished the bang to a flat whap.

"You're a little right," Kevin said, leaning toward Luther's ear.

The claimsman nodded, aimed, and fired again. The shot also printed right of his point of aim and a scant half inch above the first one.

"Looks like the laser bore sight could be off. Do you want to adjust it?" Kevin asked.

Luther shook his head and took aim again, holding a little left to compensate. In measured cadence, he started firing once more, getting into the gun as it recoiled, a sharp push into his hand. The remaining fourteen rounds blasted downrange, opening up a ragged two-inch hole in the center of the figure.

The slide locked open with the last shot, and Luther ejected the spent magazine, letting it drop to the floor. He lowered the weapon and checked it to be sure it was empty, then handed it to Kevin. "Nice," he said calmly, with a faint smile.

Kevin looked at the target with a practiced eye and agreed. "Sure is."

John stood with his arms crossed, chuckling. "I'd say you've kept your hand in real well, Looter," he said, taking off his hearing protectors.

Luther grinned back and looked at the target, which was being run up on its motorized overhead wire. "Yeah, maybe a little. Not bad for a middle-aged insurance type, eh?"

"I was going to ask what you did for a living," Kevin interjected. "Tell you what. If you ever get tired of doing what you're doing, give us a call. I think we can find you something to do at ASP."

"I appreciate the offer," Luther replied, flattered, "but I'm sort of involved in a few things right at the moment."

John was still smiling when they exited the building. "Glad you still have what it takes, buddy. Settles my mind a bit."

"It doesn't hurt to be prepared," Luther said.

During this time, the three agents back in the Hoover Building were compiling responses to their inquiries. Some of the answers were interesting, but not totally unexpected. Accustomed as they were to the vagaries of life, the emergence of a pattern only tended to underscore their preliminary suspicions.

David Armitage reviewed the information coming in and compared it to the file data on the claims already being entered into the Bureau's main computer records. Many of the agencies around the country were tapped into local UCR and NIBRS data networks. Some of the larger and more financially stable agencies used the CRIS system, making the FBI's retrieval of data easier. He smiled with grim satisfaction at the early results, lit another cigarette, and mumbled under his breath, "Son of a bitch."

Paul Gorley, leaning over his shoulder, having just taken a call from the St. Louis field office, commented at the data entered on the PC on Armitage's desk. "Big John's gonna love this. What's the count?"

"Six confirmed," Dave replied, blowing smoke at the screen. Behind them at another desk, Dale Reichley hung up, then called out a name and file number. "Make it seven. Rattagen versus Euclid Engineering, Incorporated. Dismissed six months ago. That was the Cleveland office. Rattagen's lawyer was mugged while jogging near Lake Erie ten weeks after the plaintiff checked out. Death certificate in the claim file said the claimant had a coronary. Cleveland PD still has an open book on the lawyer."

"Is it a coincidence that all seven came from sole-practitioner firms?" Dave observed, and answered, "I don't think so."

At the end of the afternoon Luther and John were back at the Bureau's headquarters, being filled in on the first solid bits of information gleaned from the fledgling investigation. "We ran all one hundred sixty-three files," Dave was saying, referring to written notes as well as the computer screen. "The last confirmation came in from Hartford, Connecticut, fifteen minutes ago."

"Disregarding the actual locale and the type of claim litigation," Dale interjected, "there are fourteen attorneys who have expired over the last two calendar years."

"Nothing before that?" John asked.

"Negative, John. All these deaths occurred after January 1988."

"Okay, how many apply to closed files, those with dismissals entered on the suits?"

"Eight," Dave replied dryly.

"How many died after the dismissal was entered in the court record?"

"Only one."

"Fine. It's an even bet that we will be able to discount that one, but keep it in for now." John smiled wickedly.

Luther felt a chill. "Now the big one: how many of those are confirmed homicides, where the locals have definitely ruled out both accidental and natural causes?"

"Five," Dale answered. "All of them are open and active homicide cases."

"Patterns?" John asked.

"Those five homicides occurred six to eight weeks after the demise of the respective clients, but before the suits were dismissed," Paul said. "Looks like whoever it was got a bit careless when dealing with the lawyers, like his standards dropped when it came to making these deaths look like accidents or natural causes."

"It's a presumption that bears looking into," John agreed. "Relationship of these lawyers to their clients?"

"According to the claim files, each of those claimants died either accidentally or by natural causes. Beginning to sound real familiar, isn't it?"

"Jimmy the Greek wouldn't give you odds on any of them right now," Dave observed. "We have some dirty business here, no doubt about that."

"I agree," Paul added. "Coincidence is coincidence, but it won't spell relief, boys. Also," he added for Luther's benefit, "thirteen of the fourteen lawyers were one-man firms with no partner to continue the suit."

"And the odd one is?"

"You guessed it. The one that died after the dismissal was already filed. Very neat, if you can believe it."

"There's the key," John reminded them. "This was supposed to fit into the national averages and get lost in the statistics. Someone who knows about statistics was being pretty clever. It's part of the operating plan. And it gives us a starting point. Keep in mind that all we have at this stage is confirmation of the numbers, or some of them. There's a long way to go yet."

The four agents exchanged glances, already knowing what was ahead. Luther remained standing, leaning against the edge of a desk, looking at the floor. His heart rate had picked up, prompted by the conversation. Inside he was chanting over and over, Yes, Yes, Yes. "Bingo," he whispered.

"You said it, brother," Paul replied. "The game is afoot, Watson," he said to John.

John exhaled and patted Paul on the shoulder. "Looks like you got your investigation, Lute," he said. "Let me run this by the old man for clearance, and it's show time. Dave, would you start putting the table of organization together for this project? I'll run it up the line for clearance."

Dale Reichley still gazed at the screen, clicking a pen against his front teeth. "You know, there's something else, too."

"Such as?" Dave Armitage asked.

"Why nothing international? Certainly Trans Patriot's got overseas claims, some as expensive and potentially as large as any of these."

Luther nodded. He and Gordon had asked themselves the same question, without coming up with a satisfactory answer.

"If the scheme, or whatever it is, works domestically," Dale continued, "why not export it? That would increase the return, if we're talking about money."

"Unless foreign profits weren't needed," Dave said simply.

"Or because it couldn't be done," Paul added. "Maybe the international markets were out of reach, logistically speaking. You'd also have to consider the red tape involved, plus the language problems, things like that."

"Meaning?" John pushed, guessing the answer.

"Meaning whoever is running this scheme either doesn't want to export it or doesn't have the oomph to get there. Keep in mind the size of the reserves we have here. Plus we surmise that the orders originate from within the company, given the specialized nature of the cases here."

"In a nutshell, that's pretty close," Luther agreed. "Which means that this may not be directed from the executive level at all, right?" he asked, catching the direction Dale was headed.

"Precisely." Dale smiled. "That's another possibility. It could explain the relatively small amounts of cash when seen from the perspective of each individual claim file's impact on the financial picture of the company as a whole."

"A lot of presumptions," John interjected, "but all based on finances. It generally comes down to the money, doesn't it? I'm going to ask for Drachman."

"Deacon? Good choice," Dale said.

"Deacon? Who's that?" Luther asked.

"Emil Drachman," Dave answered, lighting another cigarette.

"He helped bust Boesky and was in early on the California Savings and Loan scandal and the HUD fiasco. They call him 'Deacon' from his high school days," he added. "He went to divinity school before dropping out. Got turned on to high finance rather than God, I suppose. He's an independent, does projects for Securities and Exchange, investment banking, securities fraud, that kind of thing."

"And he's an absolute wizard on a computer," John added. "If he's free, we'll get him. This is looking like something right in his ballpark. We'll need a gunslinger like him."

He signaled an end to the meeting. For the next two hours they bustled about, all except Luther, who cooled his heels in an empty office while John met with Bob Killen, supervising director, who approved the initial funding for the group. John's request for Deacon Drachman turned into the first stumbling block.

"You can't have him" was Bob's immediate response. "Treasury's got him working on something at the moment."

"For how long?" John asked.

"You know those guys," Killen said. "They can barely talk to each other, let alone share knowledge with a brother agency." John rolled his eyes at that one. Infighting between governmental factions was legendary.

The big man mumbled a few choice words about rival agencies, then made the argument to free up Drachman anyway.

Bob listened for some time before holding up his hands in the middle of John's artful plea. "Come on, John, ease up. If I could break him loose, I would. You know that. You'll just have to go on without him for a while. Let me work on things; I'll let you know." Bob looked over his glasses at John, knowing he wasn't placated by the promise. "Listen, John, just give me some time on this, okay? I can pull a few strings, and we'll see what shakes loose."

John took that for what it was worth, which was something. Bob was an administrator, but his history was in the streets. John respected his ability to make things happen when they should, and let it go at that. "All right, Bob, and thanks."

• • •

149

John met with his team, including Luther, for the last strategy meeting of the day, precursor of many late hours to follow. He outlined what he wanted done next and in what order. The process went smoothly, like any other business meeting. They were, after all, craftsmen, master mechanics of their trade. Assembling the component parts was the hard part. And they were prepared for whatever they would find along the way, no matter how bad it might be.

Luther, watching them work together, hoped he was as ready. His little voice was murmuring to him daily now, in its cautionary way. Something's coming, it said. Remember who you are. The words cut into his memories.

John's voice faded back in. "Till we get Drachman, we'll be a bit hampered, but not by much. I want Trans Patriot checked out, with an eye on its financial solvency. Things can look good on the surface, but they might not be. Contact the Securities and Exchange Commission and see what they can tell us.

"Next, run down all of Trans Patriot's executives, notably this Branden Stennett, senior vice president. Luther's theory on losses versus premium versus maintaining a profitable account shows promise. Get me the full jackets on Stennett and any other possibles, both personal and business. Anyone who might have a relationship to policy limits files. Also—and Luther can help with this—we need to compile a list of everyone in the company who has access to these files, for whatever reason. Accessibility may be one of the keys. As for the files themselves, I'd like a match-up of every common factor, no matter how infrequently it may appear."

"Why not interface our system with Trans Patriot's and transfer the files en bloc?" Dale asked.

"I think I can answer that," Luther offered. "Even using the access codes I can provide, the end user of the transfer would leave a signature code, something that could be picked up. It's the one part of the security system I can't bypass."

Dale grinned. "Don't worry about that. They'll never know we're in there."

John continued running down his order list. "Our field offices will have to be brought in on this, so I've requested tight security. Open homicide cases will get turned over to us, which will cause friction as it always does. Let's see how diplomatic we can be about that, okay?"

He looked around at all of them. "We appear to have a serial murderer here, one who apparently knows quite a bit about the insurance business and who has the ability, whether through finances, or perhaps organizational size, to act in all fifty states. The body count is already excessive. You all know the drill. Let's find them. Or him," he added as an afterthought.

With the meeting finished, John and Luther left together. "Once you get back to Trans Patriot, I want you to keep as low a profile as you can," John instructed, "Gordon Hatton and Sheri Moradilo too. For now, with the volume of stuff to be checked out at first, we'll run command and control out of here. Later on, we many relocate to Phoenix, depending on what turns up."

"Yeah, a lot of this is too early to tell anything," Luther added.

"There's one factor that isn't new, though, and that's all those dead claimants. Man, if you hadn't run that profile, who knows how long this would have gone on? But I'll tell you one thing, my Greek friend: we're gonna get 'em, whoever they are."

"I sure hope so," Luther replied. "I honest to Christ hope we do."

The next morning found the Paralettos and Luther congregated in their kitchen. Luther was still impressed with how quickly John's team had put together a nationwide investigation. The information was rolling in, but the fieldwork required was going to take time. Many of the claim files had turned up active and inactive police files. Getting into them would require some finesse, since cooperation with federal authorities was rarely accomplished without some local protocol being changed.

Luther had accomplished what he had come to Washington to do. Events were basically out of his hands for the moment. It was time for him to get back to Phoenix.

"Well, we better get this show on the road," John said.

"Okay, big guy," Luther answered, standing up to put on his flight jacket. He adjusted the collar of his shirt underneath and turned to Cathy.

"Very stylish," she teased, appraising the leather jacket. "You look appropriately New Age preppy."

"Gee, thanks," Luther replied. "That's exactly the look I was going for."

Cathy smiled and stepped up to him. "Loved having you here, Luther. Next time you'll have to stay longer. Take care of yourself." She dipped her head slightly and kissed his cheek, allowing him to hug her.

"Certainly my pleasure, and thank you for putting up with me at the Hotel Paraletto. The accommodations are great, and who can argue with the rate?"

John gave Luther the "ready" sign, and they headed toward the car. At the front door, Cathy lifted up her face to him for an intimate kiss.

"You be careful out there," she advised.

"As always," he answered.

"Safe trip, Luther," she called.

Luther wasn't worried about the flight, only about what would follow after it. They were all committed to the investigation now. He hoped they could move fast enough to keep more people from dying. That one thought preyed upon him more heavily than any other. It's too late for second thoughts, he told himself as he got into John's car.

Once they were parked at Washington National Airport, John extracted a wide legal-sized brown briefcase from the trunk.

"Got your office with you, I see," Luther said.

"Something like that," his friend replied, his tone noncommittal.

They entered the main terminal and proceeded to security, where Luther passed through without a problem. He waited on the other side as John displayed his ID, confirmed he was armed, and opened up the case for the security guard. They walked in silence toward the passenger gate for the flight to Phoenix. John motioned them off to the side, away from the milling people.

"Uh, there is one more thing," John said.

152

Luther turned to him. "I was going to say good-bye, Johnny. I just didn't want to get all maudlin about it."

"So don't," the agent said. "Get maudlin, that is. I knew you wouldn't go without doing something embarrassingly emotional. It's the Greek in you."

"Ah, it's all in the mix," Luther replied.

"But that's not it," John said. "I brought you a going-away gift." He unlocked the strap locks on the case, reached in, and pulled out a flat russet-colored leather case. "Here, hold this."

"What's this?"

"Party favors," John replied glancing around to make sure the case wouldn't attract any attention. He tripped the locks and lifted up the lid. Inside lay one of the new 10 mm pistols, inlaid into a gray foam block. The case also held three magazines, a suppressor and compensator, a cleaning kit, extra nicad batteries for the laser sight, and a fifty-round box of ammunition.

While Luther looked at his present, John took a smaller cardboard box out of the briefcase. "There are two holsters in there. A nylon Bianchi cross draw type and a Galco International leather horizontal type. I didn't know your preference. The ammo is factory loaded, full house, two-hundred-grain hollow point."

Luther looked up at him, reading the meaning of the deadly gift from the intensity in John's eyes. "This is serious business, isn't it?"

"The only kind. Just call it a feeling, buddy. But we discussed it back at the shop, and Dave and the others thought it best that you have a little extra protection, government-sanctioned, as it were."

"What about Gordon?" he queried, closing the lid on the box.

"I don't know his qualifications with weapons like this," John replied. "You, on the other hand, can take care of yourself."

"I appreciate your concern, John. I hope I won't have to use this."

"You do what you have to do, Looter, until the job is done."

"I understand," Luther said, shifting the flat box under his arm. He unzipped his bag, and pushed the smaller box with the holsters into it. "When will I hear from you next?" he asked.

"Next week, probably the end of the week. I'll try to set up a regular weekly progress schedule. What you choose to tell Gordon is up to you. But remember that security on this is paramount. We're

153

going to be shaking things up out there, more than likely. The less Gordon knows, the better."

"Otherwise, business as usual."

"That's a roger."

"You know, I kind of figured it would be like this. But what the hell, that's why I dumped the case in your lap, Johnny."

"Gotcha covered, Looter. C'mere." John stuck out his big hand in farewell to his friend.

They shook hands and as with their first meeting days before, pulled close, embarrassingly tight.

"Take care of yourself, Lute."

"You too, Johnny, and thanks, man, again and again."

"Go on, get out of here," John said, nodding toward the gate.

"See ya next trip." Luther reached down for his bag. He cleared the gate, turned once to see his friend standing there, hands thrust into his overcoat pockets, a monolith in gray. Luther nodded and walked down the tunnel ramp.

On the return flight, much as Luther tried, there was no sleep for him. It was a curious reversal of his trip in. He was too keyed up, as if he were running at 78 rpm while the rest of the world was at 33⅓. He had turned second-guessing himself into an art form, and he allowed himself a quick trip down that road, wondering for the umpteenth time if he had put himself and Gordon, and now maybe John Paraletto, into grave danger.

The 10 mm pistol in his carry-on bag was a cold dash of reality underscoring John's concern about what might lie ahead. But was it a harbinger of what was to come? Luther flashed back to that time over twenty years ago when he lived with weapons every hour of every day. Doing so had been necessary for survival, and he had survived those times. Survived, and left the guns behind.

Now he was carrying one again. Luther didn't need to wonder if he could use it. Old capabilities were coming back on line, after two decades of lying dormant.

He was sure he could do it again, and the knowledge scared him,

154

but not because of the potentiality. For the first time in a very long time Luther felt the rush. His senses fed him information as if everything were in high-gain resolution. He was letting that part of him come back, like a beast awakened from a long sleep. He had lived that profession once before; he knew what it took to perform, and what his performance had cost. That was what frightened him.

There would be no way to put the beast back until this thing was done. And the final truth was, he didn't want to put it back.

MARCH 23, TPI, THE VILLAGE

Dana Quinn sat in her office before her sideboard-mounted CRT, immersed in the figures of a profit-and-loss report on a computer chip business south of L.A. Her violet eyes tracked down the columns of numbers, but her mind was busy replaying the events of the past week.

She had returned home on Tuesday night to discover the entrance to her villa jammed full of flowers. Roses, to be exact.

A fortune in large red, pink, yellow, and white petals layered the entire floor, from just inside the arc of the doorway to the beginning of the hallway into the house.

Bouquets of roses were arranged in vases of all types and shapes, some on the floor, some on tables or plant stands, reaching up as high as her surprised face.

The fragrance and colors were staggering, the sheer beauty of the display breathtaking. There was just enough room left for her to pass through a virtual tunnel of flowers into the hallway beyond. Centered there, beneath the arched opening was a final vase containing a dozen perfect vibrant yellow long-stem roses set upon a waist-high pedestal table. Propped against the scalloped edge of the bottom of the vase was a small embossed envelope. Dana withdrew the card it held.

It was a message printed in Norman's precise, machinelike penmanship:

155

Dana, darling

We seem to have drifted away from each other of late. I guess that is my fault. Considering how close we are to finishing the game, maybe the reason is the pressure we both seem to be under.

Why don't we take a few days off just to enjoy each other and our success so far? And in that spirit I hope you will accept this small display of my undying love for you.

Yours forever,
Norman

P.S. The yellow brick road leads to the Land of Oz.

Dana looked down and saw a trail of yellow long-stems leading toward the large master suite.

She picked up the first one, a delighted smile on her lips, and, like Dorothy, followed the road to Oz. Norman's show of affection displaced her misgivings, and she felt a shiver of guilt for her deviousness. But she suppressed it, preferring not to deal with that just yet.

She hesitated in the entrance to their bedroom to take in the sight awaiting her there.

Soft blue lights bathed the room in quiet shades, casting provocative shadows of plum and indigo across the queen-sized bed. The eight-foot-tall bedposts spiraled their carved bodies sensually toward the canopy, which was lost in the subdued light of the cathedral ceiling twenty feet above.

Her gaze followed the trail of roses into the room and across the floor to the edge of the bed, upon which, propped against several large pillows, lay Norman Bloodstone.

He held a final rose, which he ran languorously up and down his naked body. His leg was raised, bent at the knee, hiding the object of her growing desire.

"Hello, darling," he said softly, "I've been waiting." With that, he slid his leg down, and Dana saw how ready he truly was. The petals of the rose continued to play over his firmness, back and forth, back and forth.

156

"Norman, my love, you are so sweet," she replied. She took in his body, stepping closer, and her smile turned decidedly erotic. "My, but you have been a busy little boy, haven't you?"

"Only for you, love, always for you."

And it was at that precise moment that Dana, deafened by her affection for him, stopped listening to the murmured warning from her little voice.

He really has outdone himself, she thought, as the roses she carried dropped to the floor, followed by her clothing. "Oh, Norman, I don't know what to say."

"Don't say anything, not just now." His eyes devoured her. "Come here," he commanded in that same soft, sensual tone. "Do it," he urged. "Do it now, the way I like."

"Oh, yes, love," Dana murmured, her hands finding her full breasts, beginning the movements he liked to watch. "For you, darling Norman . . ."

She sat astride him, occasionally pumping her hips. With eyes closed, she leaned forward slightly and gently took his hands from her breasts.

Dana raised his left hand to her lips and licked his palm, then his wrist and forearm, pausing to nip little bites here and there, trailing the tip of her pointed tongue across his smooth skin, past the soft hollow of his inner elbow.

She welcomed him back, letting him use her in whatever way he desired. And he desired all of her, dazzling her with his expertise, arousing her in every imaginable way, while she gave him back in kind.

This is the best part, she thought languorously, to be this close to him, have him so . . . deep. She leaned down and touched his lips with her own, eyes closed in delirious pleasure.

"My darling Norman, I love you so much."

"And I you, Dana, always."

Her eyes remained closed. His were not, and she failed to see in them the dangerous light from within that reflected the lie in his pledge to her. His was a performance to be remembered for a long time.

• • •

That episode on Tuesday night had been the opening scene in a week filled with similar romantic dramas, all directed by Norman, who appeared unable to do enough for his love. There were candlelit dinners, quiet moments at out-of-the-way nightspots, on terraces overlooking the glittering lights of the city. They rented a room at an expensive resort hotel for one night only, giving absurd aliases, giggling at the charade behind the bellman who led the way to their room. They spent the hours with bodies entwined, coupled on the broad expanse of Mexican tiled balcony outside their room.

But Dana's most wondrous memories were of wild, incredible sex. It was quite unlike anything they had ever done before, including their initial courtship back in New York. Norman's appetite for her seemed insatiable, and he had her in some extraordinary ways, in every possible manner, time and again.

By the end of that fateful week, Dana had, on the surface at least, changed her mind about Norman and his strange obsessions. Though they might still be there, his latest obsession was clearly with her, and she reveled in it.

She didn't see even a hint of the aloofness she had noticed before, and she wondered at one point whether she had ever really seen anything strange there. On Thursday, as they lay in bed together, Dana had mentioned that it had been some time since they'd done a policy limit case. Considering how close they were to their target figure of twenty million, ought they not to look for another? He had agreed, as she expected, which led to her surreptitious review of claims files the following day.

By eleven in the morning she had screened three possibilities: a flammable fabrics case in Bloomington, a paraplegic gunshot victim in Santa Fe, and a brain-damaged surgery patient in Madison, Wisconsin.

Dana dialed up Norman's computer with her desktop modem and transmitted the data on all three claim files. They would review them at their leisure that evening. Although they looked promising on the surface, should none of them end up exactly suitable for their needs, she would try again. There were plenty of potential targets.

Dana returned home that evening to find Norman in his study, engrossed in reading the files she had sent. He acknowledged her arrival by trailing his long fingers down the side of her thigh as she stood near him, watching him read.

Knowing that his concentration should be absolute, Dana left him alone. She changed into a leotard and began her daily aerobic workout. Inwardly, she was pleased to see him working on the latest project. He seemed so much more like her old Norman.

The end result of his study was of no particular concern to her. The demise of yet another faceless, fleshless compilation of figures and numbers had no more effect on her than reading a ledger sheet. She had become jaded, if that word could be properly attributed to a serial murderer, by the successful execution of this part of the game.

After her hour-long workout, she watched Norman cook up a batch of chicken fajitas and rice, all the while discussing his review and his recommendation for their next target.

"It's an interesting selection," he said over one shoulder, slicing marinated strips of meat and laying them carefully on the broiler tray. "After weighing all the factors, I think the Santa Fe case is more interesting than the other two."

"In what way?" she responded, adjusting the towel she had wrapped about her damp hair. She had showered minutes before, and sat at the intimate kitchen table in the nook by the window in her paisley silk robe.

"First of all, it carries the highest policy limit reserve—two million, on a law enforcement policy. The others are only a million each. But the most intriguing fact about this particular case is that the plaintiff is being represented by her own husband, who happens to be a sole-practitioner lawyer."

Dana caught his meaning immediately. She had drawn the same conclusion during her perusal of the file earlier in the day. "The best of both worlds," she concurred. "On the one hand, there is the plaintiff, the paralytic survivor of a badly botched police drug raid, and on the other . . . ."

"You have her husband, the lawyer," Norman interjected, removing the heated flour tortilla shells from the oven. He unwrapped the towel covering them and arranged two each on matching plates.

159

"Eliminate both of them at the same time," Norman said matter-of-factly, "and all of the potential loose ends are tidied up. The claimant-plaintiff is gone, the suit gets dismissed, the file gets closed, and we"—he turned, holding the steaming plates—"get the money."

"Unless, of course, the case is settled in the interim," she cautioned. "Don't forget about the other defendants here. The file status notes indicate there has been some activity toward trying to settle this."

"I thought of that," Norman said a bit tightly, irritated by her interruption. Glossing over the slight to her by his tone, he recovered smoothly. "That's all to our advantage, actually. From what the file states, all of the defendants, including TPI's insured, are squabbling amongst themselves as to who should bear the majority of the liability here. And as long as they do that, whether they settle or defend remains a moot point. It looks like it will be some time before they get their collective act together, and by then it will be all over.

"Besides," he continued smugly, "given the negligence here and the degree of injuries, it's highly unlikely the plaintiff would be willing to settle piecemeal with any one defendant. I think she would rather hang them all together in court. But it may be enough of a hook to get close to them. It's a possibility."

Acquiescing to his analysis, Dana let the point go and brought up another concern. "When I read this one, I was bothered by the type of injury. Do we need another paraplegic? Considering the last one, might this not have an adverse affect on the accident statistics?"

"That's a legitimate concern, but one of little consequence here. Bear in mind the random statistical probabilities. Certainly, on the surface it appears suspiciously coincidental to have two similar injuries so close together. But this type of injury, again from a purely statistical point of reference, is entirely within the limits. It isn't enough of a concern to negate the benefits this file has to offer."

Dana considered his argument and nodded in agreement. He did seem to have considered all the permutations.

Norman thought so, too, but for an entirely different set of reasons. He wanted this case badly. Two life forces just waiting for him. He had never done a double murder before, and the possibilities were dazzling.

There had been times during the last two years when Norman had wished that Dana shared his passion for the blood sport. But hers was an interest kept alive from afar. So long as she was removed from direct contact with the "wet work"—a lovely phrase he had found in a spy novel—Dana's satisfaction came from living vicariously through Norman's lurid descriptions of the killings.

He smiled, thinking how simple it was to manipulate this conniving woman, once you knew which of her buttons to push. And in the last week he had pushed them all.

His calculating brain sensed that the Santa Fe case could be his finest piece of work. Properly done, it could be the crown jewel of his collection.

MARCH 26, TPI, THE VILLAGE

Luther returned from Washington and walked straight into a claims department audit by a group of reinsurers. It was a routine event, but as these matters went, it took up several days. As soon as he could steal a few minutes away, Luther met with Gordon Hatton and briefed him on his trip. He didn't mention the pistol John had given him as a parting gift. Both men already knew how serious their business was.

Gordon was generally relieved that the FBI agent had been receptive to their theories, but the reality of the step they had taken weighed upon him. It was also the first time he had heard Luther give a name to his suspect.

"You really think Stennett the Terrible is behind all of this?"

Luther played with a pen, twirling it between his fingers. "I don't know, Gordon. But his was the first name that came to mind. He might be capable of something like this. I know there are a lot of rumors about him, and I can tell you that a few of them are factually based. He's old line, remember, and this would fit right in with that ancient anything-for-a-buck credo of the old school. And if it's not him acting alone, maybe it's a conspiracy, some kind of final-solution

161

decision by the board, led by Stennett or someone who shares his business-is-all philosophy."

"I suppose you're right," Gordon said. "You've almost got me convinced. But there's still the ill-gotten-gains angle." He felt he was closer to the truth than his boss, but since both theories were being investigated, he was satisfied.

"And I can't fault that," Luther agreed. "Just between us, I hope you're right. It's going to be pretty bad no matter which way it comes out, but somehow your theory doesn't seem quite so bad."

"So there's nothing for us to do unless, or until, John calls?" Gordon asked.

"That's about the size of it," Luther replied.

"I kind of feel like we gave up something, like a control thing," Gordon said. "I understand what's been done, don't get me wrong," he added quickly, "but it's a little weird, putting your future in the hands of someone else when you're most vulnerable."

"I appreciate that, Gordo, really, but we didn't have any other way to go here."

Gordon nodded. He knew what his boss said was true, and he appreciated the danger involved. "Just for the record, I'm with you all the way in this. We'll play it by ear, as instructed, and hope the feds know what they're doing."

"You and me both," Luther answered. "And speaking of both, how are you and Sheri getting along?"

"Famously, I believe is the appropriate word," Gordon replied. "I think there's something happening there."

"Terrific," Luther said, genuinely pleased. "But keep in mind that we have to keep her completely out of this now."

"No problem, boss. It's closed business for her."

"Okay, but keep an eye out for any renewed interest, and see if you can steer her away with some generic answer."

"I hear you, Lute." He got up to leave. "Anything else?"

"Well, in the interests of keeping up a sense of normalcy, would you let Walt know that I'd like a short staff meeting at about nine, to catch me up on what went on here while I was out? I'd like to squeeze it in before this damn audit takes over again."

"Sure thing, Lute." Gordon took a couple of steps out of the office, then paused in the doorway, looking back. "Hang in there, boss," he said soberly, and patted the doorjamb twice.

Luther rocked back in his chair, lacing his fingers behind his head. "You too, Gordo," he said, holding his associate's eyes.

Gordon waited a moment longer. "Right," he answered, and left.

Luther stared at the empty doorway for a while, rotating in small arcs in his office chair. "Fuckin' A," he said, under his breath. He let the chair down and swiveled it back to his PC and the ever-present routine.

MARCH 28, HOOVER BUILDING, WASHINGTON, D.C.

"I don't care what kind of opposition the locals are throwing up," John Paraletto said into the phone. "Use some of those moves they taught you in Diplomacy 101, but convince them they better learn the definition of cooperation, or I'll start climbing over people." He hunched his big shoulders over the desk top. "And you can make it equally clear that if it comes to that, the body count will be an awesome sight to behold."

He listened to the reply from the other end. "Fine," he answered, and hung up.

"Who was that?" Paul Gorley asked, stopping beside John's desk.

"The SAC in Kansas, fellow named Reitel, on the Exeter versus Tri-Mini file. We apparently have some minor-level opposition to the feds getting involved with their unsolved homicide on Exeter's lawyer." He laughed suddenly, letting out the tension. "They all think they're Columbo or something."

"Did you straighten them out?"

"I think so. Anyway, we'll find out soon enough." He noticed the printout Paul held. "What have you got?"

"Forensic report on that Middletown, Ohio, file. We got the exhumation order. The body, according to our guy, showed evidence of bruising that was inconsistent with a fall, as originally reported. Turns out the original autopsy was done by the funeral home director,

163

in lieu of the county coroner, who was backed up at the time on a nasty multiple-death traffic accident."

"Didn't county review the report?"

"Yes, so our people say, but it appears to have been a once-over, at best. They released the body, approved the death certificate, and that was it."

"And now?"

"And now we got someone who appears to have been assisted down those stairs. There's a lower occipital injury that doesn't fit either the fall pattern or the stairway construction."

"Great, keep on it, Paul."

"No problem, John, but I have to tell you, we're getting over our heads with all this insurance high-finance stuff. It's dragging things down, the sheer volume of it and trying to define where to go with the figures, then link it to a suspect."

"I'll check on Deacon's availability, but that's the best I can do at the moment," John said apologetically.

"Yeah, well, until we get him on deck, this job is going to take time, boss," Paul warned, but it was only the usual rhetoric. He knew John was aware of how critical assets and time were on a project like this.

"Doesn't it always, though?" John replied.

"A little bit here, a little bit there," Paul chanted as he walked away.

APRIL 1, CAREFREE, ARIZONA

Luther and the Arutakas finished their light breakfast. The dawn light, arriving earlier each morning now, slanted strongly over the high rim of the McDowell Mountains east of Luther's broad estate.

The Arutakas' bags were already loaded into the back of the big Chevy Blazer. Khanh lay beside the hallway door to the garage, keeping his eyes on his master.

"Nakato is nervous this morning, I think," Myoshi observed with a smile, nodding toward her husband. "He really dislikes flying."

"And you?" Luther inquired, sipping his orange juice.

"Not so much," she replied, tilting her hand back and forth. "It is something that must be done."

Luther smiled at her over the rim of his glass. Her own nervousness at the beginning of the twenty-hour flight to Japan was apparent, as always. He found her evasive answer endearing.

"You will be well while we are gone, Sitasy-san?" Myoshi asked. She had repeated the question several times since his return from Washington, more often than concerns raised by the couple's annual trip usually warranted.

And for the tenth time Luther assured her that all would be well, even though he didn't fully believe that himself. Actually, with the way things were going at Trans Patriot, he was happy the Arutakas would be far from any danger that might arise.

"Things'll be just fine," he said. "I've got Khanh to watch out for me, and Mikki will be over from time to time. Jackie, too. We'll all have plenty to keep us occupied." He added a mental note to call his daughter and remind her not to drop by unless he was at home. He was trying to extend the safety zone without fully acknowledging his own rising unease.

Nakato caught his wife's eye and nodded. "As you say, Sitasy-san," clearly not convinced.

So they know something's up, but they don't know how bad it might be, he thought. Fine, the sooner they're away, and safe, the better. "Let's get loaded, then," he said aloud, thankful for any reason to change the subject.

Forty-five minutes later Luther pulled into the garage next to terminal three at Sky Harbor Airport. While he off-loaded the bags, the Arutakas said good-bye to Khanh. Myoshi spoke to him in Japanese and ruffled his fur, smiling when the dog responded with a low sigh. Nakato stepped up and looked Khanh in the eye as the dog sat before him. The old man held the dog's head in both hands, stroking his neck, and spoke quietly. Khanh, never flinching, returned Nakato's stare.

Nakato finished and laid his hand on the animal's head. When he raised his hand, Khanh huffed once, looked at Luther, and bounded back into the Blazer.

Wondering what message had passed between them, Luther rolled down the window a few inches on Khanh's side and admonished him to behave himself. Minutes later he and the Arutakas were at their gate, just as the first boarding announcement was made.

For a few moments the three of them stood awkwardly, unsure how to start the farewell act. This time it was different; they were all aware of an undercurrent of unease.

Myoshi finally broke the silence as the second call was made. She stepped up to Luther, and hugged him. "It is not traditional, but I don't think anyone will mind," she said, holding him firmly, speaking into his bearded cheek. She lifted her head and kissed him on the corner of his mouth. "Be safe, Luther," she said, surprising him with the use of his first name.

He squeezed back. "I'll miss you," he whispered, "but you know that."

"Hai, Sitasy-san," she said, and pushed back to arm's length. She continued to hold his upper arm, fine vertical lines appearing in the middle of her smooth brow. "You will be careful for these next few months." It came out as an order.

God love you, Myoshi, he thought. "I'll be fine, really," he responded. "Don't worry."

"Ah, but I will," she replied, still drilling him with her look. "Your assurances can't prevent that."

A small shiver scampered down his neck. Her perception was too sharp, as always. She knew him so well.

"Whatever is happening will turn out as it will," she continued. "You have come a long way. Just remember who you are, and you will resolve this trouble the best way for you."

They stepped apart, Nakato taking his wife's place. He bowed in the traditional way, and Luther returned the gesture. Then he held out his hand, and both men shook warmly.

"My wife sees many things," he said somberly. "But she is a

woman, and they are almost never right." He chuckled, deliberately breaking the solemn mood. Myoshi gave her husband a wry look.

"Well," Luther sighed, "you've got about twenty hours of flight time to get her over that last remark."

"Women are also very understanding and forgiving," Nakato added with a smile.

"Good thing for you," Myoshi admonished.

"Take good care," Nakato said, patting Luther on the upper arm. "We will pray for you."

"Thank you," he said, wondering if the Japanese gods held any special power his own God didn't. He didn't know how far prayer could go in this. "I'd like to call you sometime," Luther said suddenly.

Nakato paused, searching Luther's face. He had never made such a request before, confining his contact with them while they were away to a monthly letter. Luther didn't telephone because he respected their time with their family and didn't want to intrude.

The old man saw it then, far back in Luther's eyes, a look he himself had once had, a lifetime ago.

"We would be pleased if you did, Sitasy-san." Nakato gripped Luther's arm firmly, transmitting with the touch his understanding. Then he turned, took his wife's elbow, and directed her over to the line of people clearing their boarding passes at the gate. The flight attendant confirmed their first-class seating and motioned them to proceed. They paused in the doorway and waved a final farewell. Nakato's eyes narrowed, and he called, "Do what you must, but make that choice yourself."

Luther nodded and waved back. Nakato's words went to his heart, and he knew the older man was aware of what he was dealing with, without being told the specifics. He realized how far back he went with these two people and how thankful he was for their presence in his life.

They walked down the sloping ramp and were lost from sight. I hope my choice is the right one, he called after them, in a voice only his mind could hear.

He made his way back through the large terminal to his truck, feeling not quite alone but not whole, either. The feeling left him

167

unsettled as he pulled out into the morning brightness of a beautiful late spring day, Khanh taking up station with his black head pushed out the window.

Luther glanced over at his companion as he drove up Forty-fourth Street, the dog's fur rippling in the wind. "Looks like it's just you and me, big guy."

Khanh grinned open-mouthed at the passing sights, his day complete.

"Me too," Luther said, "me too," and rolled his window down, enjoying the wind that ruffled his hair and beard. He tried to ignore the sudden hollowness that rested, thick and empty, inside his chest.

APRIL 13, ROUTE I-25, OUTSIDE SANTA FE, NEW MEXICO

The bright beams and additional halogen driving lights of Norman's turbo Porsche stabbed through the darkness. He was just six miles from Santa Fe, running south toward Albuquerque, following the interstate signs for Arizona. He kept the car at the legal limit with difficulty, fighting the surging excitement inside him. His brain seemed to be on fire, lit from within by the scene he'd left behind, a place of blood-spattered carnage and profound revelation.

For a week, since April 7, Norman had stalked his latest targets. Margaret Larcalle, the plaintiff in the lawsuit, had named the White Rock County Sheriff's Department, insured by Trans Patriot, as one of the defendants. She had been paralyzed in a botched drug raid in which the county's deputies had joined four other police organizations. In a series of tragic events, the wrong house had been targeted, and Mrs. Larcalle was caught in the crossfire.

Her husband, Bentson R. Larcalle, a plaintiff's attorney of some reputation, was prosecuting her lawsuit against the defendant members of the drug task force responsible for his wife's substantial, and permanent, injuries. Among other allegations, the lawsuit stated that the drug task force was guilty of using excessive force and had been poorly trained and negligently supervised. The prayer for damages was several million dollars in both compensatory and punitive damages.

Norman Bloodstone had done his fieldwork, studying the details of the raid reported on the claim file Dana had transmitted and in the extensive coverage in newspapers, which he'd found in the Santa Fe and Albuquerque public libraries.

He had spent time observing the couples' expansive eighty-five-hundred-square-foot home, located in an exclusive cul-de-sac two blocks from the intended target of the raid, a known drug trafficker.

The simple transposition of two numbers in the address, a clerical error, had led to the faulty warrant and the poorly executed forced entry into the Larcalles' home. Mrs. Larcalle had been shot by over-zealous undercover officers. Forensic records had established that the four bullets that struck Mrs. Larcalle had come from at least three different weapons, one of which belonged to TPI's insured officer. Further, any one of the wounds could have caused the spinal cord injuries and subsequent paralysis.

Norman had further established that Margaret Larcalle had been the office manager for her husband's lucrative law practice and that the loss of expected income due to her inability to continue to work was a substantial part of the overall lawsuit.

Norman had followed Bentson Larcalle numerous times, establishing his work and travel patterns, watching for an opportunity to put his plan into play. The time had come that very day, April 13. Norman was going to commit what he presumed the local police would later determine was an armed break-in of the Larcalles' residence, or possibly a burglary that went wrong. They might even suspect a conspiracy by rogue cops involved in the tragic raid to eliminate the complainant.

He had remembered the phrase from the movie *The Mechanic*, when Charles Bronson's character referred to shooting an intended target as "cowboying." It had an intriguing sound to it, he thought. He was going to cowboy the Larcalles.

Bentson Larcalle—forty-eight years old, forty pounds overweight, his balding head covered by a thousand-dollar hairpiece—left his downtown Santa Fe office at precisely seven-fifteen that evening, as was his custom.

His later-than-normal business hours were a direct reflection of the success of his practice, the 110 percent effort he gave his clients, and the lucrative compensation he derived for the effort.

But the loss of his wife Margaret's business services, had made things difficult. Although he managed to continue, working with another office manager who'd been personally interviewed by his convalescing wife, it just wasn't the same.

No matter, he reminded himself for the hundredth time since the shooting, the bastards will pay before I'm through. His righteous anger accompanied him as he strolled purposely toward the small parking garage three blocks from his office building.

"Mr. Larcalle?" came the voice from behind him, causing him to start from his reverie and turn around.

He stopped when he saw the man approaching him. A head taller than he and impeccably dressed, the man had the look of corporate lawyer. His eyes were hidden behind brown-tinted sunglasses, dark at the top, clear at the bottom.

"Mr. Larcalle," the stranger began again, a smile lighting up his face, "thank you for stopping. I'm afraid my schedule almost made me miss you."

The tall man stopped before Bentson Larcalle, hand extended. "I'm sorry, sir. I'm Philip Cramer. My firm is representing the county for Trans Patriot Insurance." He pulled out a Gucci leather folder from an inside breast pocket and extracted an embossed card, which he held out to Bentson.

With those words, Bentson's momentary suspicions at being accosted on the street disappeared. He took the card, studied it, and recognized the name of the firm, his eyes narrowing. Bentson offered his hand after a moment. "Mr. Cramer," he said. "So you represent Trans Patriot's insured. And I suppose, judging from this 'accidental' encounter on the street after business hours, that this concerns matters best discussed off the record?"

Norman shook his head in amused respect. "I told them this would be a bit too transparent. I beg your indulgence, sir, and you are exactly correct."

170

"You get so you know what to look for," Bentson allowed good-naturedly. There was a message here, and it had settlement written all over it. This was a power negotiation, a possible split in the united front put up by the defendants, especially since Cramer's actions seemed directed toward keeping his activities secret from the co-defendants. Bentson decided to allow the other lawyer to present his offer.

"Actually, sir," Norman continued, "this does concern the litigation you filed against our insured. I was hoping you might have time to hear our proposal, one which I think might be in the best interests of you, your client, and our insured. Is there someplace we might go for a chat?"

Bentson's radar was up as he wondered what circumstances within the defendants' camp might have generated this unusual approach. It was obvious that the defendants' carrier was taking all precautions not to make this conversation a matter of record. If whatever this young lawyer had come to talk to him about failed, there would be no trail. But if it led in the direction Bentson thought it would, he stood to score some major funding, plus possibly break up the defendants' united front. The possibilities intrigued Bentson and led to his fatal reply, exactly as Norman had hoped.

"I was on my way home, as it happens, Mr. Cramer."

"Philip, if that's all right with you," the young man interrupted.

"As I was saying, Philip, I have a perfectly good office at home. I should think that this discussion would best be conducted there."

"Excellent, Mr. Larcalle. I was hoping you would say that."

Twenty minutes later Bentson's burgundy Cadillac Sedan DeVille nosed through the electronic gates of his house on the northern heights overlooking Santa Fe.

The two men had engaged in small talk about the business of insurance litigation, each feeling out the other as a prospective antagonist and negotiator, or so Bentson was led to believe. The older man had briefly considered inviting Philip Cramer to dinner, but discarded the thought. Better to keep their meeting purely business, which would maintain Bentson's stronger negotiating position.

Norman continued to feel confident as each phase of his carefully constructed plan was reached. He felt a quickening inside and found himself struggling to keep a hold on his excitement.

171

As the car glided into the well-lit multi-bay garage, Norman retrieved his briefcase from the backseat. Glancing around, he noticed the ramps built up from the edge of the concrete apron toward the house entrance, obviously to accommodate Bentson's wheelchair-bound wife.

Norman followed his host's lead and was ushered into the house, entering from the garage into a pantry as large as the bedrooms in smaller homes. He listened respectfully, keeping up his pretense, as Bentson preceded him into the living room, pointing out the south-western style and construction.

"Yes, well, I'm a New Mexico native," Bentson was saying, "and Maggie and I long ago decided to maintain our connections with our heritage."

"You've done it quite well," Norman said truthfully, impressed by the grandeur of the forty-foot-long room.

"It's home," Bentson said a bit pompously.

They passed through into a formal dining room, only marginally smaller than the living room. A long, heavy carved table took up center station, surrounded by a dozen matching high-backed upholstered chairs. The smell of cooking filled the air.

"I'm sorry," Norman apologized. "I should have realized you ate dinner late."

"Not a problem," Bentson said. "It will keep."

Margaret Larcalle chose that minute to roll out of the kitchen, pausing in the square beamed archway. "I thought I heard you come in," she said, her attention on Norman.

Bentson crossed over to kiss her cheek, then straightened for introductions. "Margaret, this young man is Philip Cramer. Mr. Cramer, my wife, Margaret." To his wife, he added, "Mr. Cramer represents the county. He's come to talk with us."

Norman stepped forward, taking her offered hand, which was firm and warm, in contrast to the cool look she gave him. "I hope I'm not intruding," he said, keeping his cordial-guest smile on.

"Not at all," she replied.

"I believe Philip wants to pitch us a settlement offer, my dear," Bentson said, ambling over to an ornately carved bar. He took out

172

three heavy highball glasses, then rummaged until he found a fifth of Scotch.

Margaret Larcalle studied her guest with renewed interest. Norman studied her back. She was a heavyset woman of medium height, in her mid-forties. The flesh of her face was doughy-looking. Her artificially colored blond hair had been carefully and stylishly permed, adding height to her round face. Her western ranch clothes—checked shirt, jeans, and boots—were strained by her body's weight. Her wardrobe carried designer label details, and she wore silver and turquoise jewelry, attesting to the Larcalles' good life.

Looking Norman up and down like a lab specimen, she spoke to Bentson. "I've just let Consuela go home, but I suppose if you gentlemen have business to transact, the dinner can wait."

Norman had previously confirmed for himself that their maid usually left by this time each evening. While Mrs. Larcalle talked, he walked slowly to the far end of the long dining table, away from the couple, and put his briefcase on the tabletop. He unfastened the leather straps and opened the bag while Bentson replied to his wife.

"We'll go into the study for a while. This shouldn't take too long."

"On the contrary, Mr. Larcalle," Norman said, his right hand rummaging inside the case, "it's going to take quite a while." His hand emerged, holding a flat cardboard packet, which he tossed onto the table. It struck the bare wood with a slap.

Bentson reacted with confusion for a moment, his attention on the packet, which appeared to hold a bunch of plastic laces. "Excuse me?" he began, not clear on the direction the conversation had just turned.

Norman motioned to the packet with his chin and reached into the bag again. "Those are the new plastic restraints used by police. They work just like the ones on trash bags. If you would be so good as to put one around your wife's ankles and another around her wrists?"

"Bentson!" Margaret said sharply.

"What is this!" the lawyer demanded, taking a step toward Norman. Then he froze. Norman had a gun pointed at him, a dull black automatic with a fat barrel, held comfortably at waist level. The way he held the gun told Bentson that he knew exactly what he was doing.

173

"This is a High Standard twenty-two caliber target pistol. It holds ten rounds. It also has, as you can see, a silencer, which is quite effective. No one, I assure you, will hear a thing, should I use this."

The room became remarkably quiet. Norman smiled his predatory catlike smile and removed his shaded glasses. His oddly spiked eye stared back at his prey.

"What . . . ?" Bentson began again, more subdued this time. His wife remained silent, numbed by the sudden thump in her chest as her control began to slip.

Norman gestured with the end of the silencer at the packet. "The restraints, if you please, and no heroics. I can and will put all ten shots in your head before you can finish a step. Just do as you are directed."

Bentson looked at the muzzle of the weapon, then back at Norman, letting the hate show through the fear. The broad, flat muzzle of the gun had taken on an absolute clarity, pulling his attention to it like a menacing magnet.

Norman saw the decision made in the older man's eyes, and nodded. He was also aware of the increase in his own pulse rate. Anticipation trembled through him.

"That's good, Mr. Larcalle. Very nice. Now . . ." He indicated the restraints one more time.

Reluctantly Bentson picked up the package and knelt by his wife's wheelchair. She looked at him in disbelief and beginning panic. "Bentson?" she beseeched him through tight lips.

He shook his head as he pulled one of the plastic bands out. "It'll be all right," he assured her, feeling the lie in his words.

"This may be unnecessary," Norman said evenly, "but secure her ankles tightly to the chair frame, please. Leave no margin for error."

Bentson did as he was instructed, moving on to secure his wife's wrists next.

When he was done, Norman, wearing an odd smile, reminded him of another point. "Would you be sure to set the brake? We wouldn't want Margaret rolling around now, getting in our way."

Bentson reacted slowly, his brain in overdrive, trying to fit this development into an equation that made sense.

Norman stepped away from the table and approached the couple. He pointed to one of the heavy dining chairs midway down the length of the table. "Pull that chair out, turn it toward Margaret, and sit down."

Still clutching the bundle of restraints, Bentson passed by Norman, acutely aware of the muzzle following his movements. The small black bore in the snout seemed as big as that of a cannon. He pulled the chair out, turned it, and sat down heavily in it. "You're not with Trans Patriot at all, are you?" he said to Norman.

"That's not quite correct, but we can discuss that later, perhaps."

The answer gave Bentson the hope that the worst might not actually happen, that they might just survive whatever this madman had in store for them.

Norman saw the thought race through his mind and felt another surge. He had known his answer would have that effect. "Now, if you would secure yourself in a like manner, please, beginning with your ankles."

Larcalle bent to the job, desperately trying to keep alive that glimmer of hope as Norman coached him. "Yes, very nice, just so. There. Tightly now about the other chair leg, and again, farther up, behind the knees."

When his legs were secured, Norman ordered him to strap his right wrist to the ornately padded armrest.

"I'm going to bind your free hand. I need not remind you about heroics, right?"

Bentson nodded and remained motionless as his other arm was tied down quickly and firmly. The young man added an extra band near each elbow for good measure.

"Better and better," Norman observed, stepping back to survey the scene. Then he returned to the briefcase, put the gun down, and took out a pair of surgical gloves, which he pulled on, smoothing the fingers down. He flexed his hands.

"You'll notice that I haven't touched a single surface in this house yet. These are just precautionary." Then he removed his suit jacket and laid it across the table next to the briefcase.

The two people stared at him, their fear quotient raised substan-

175

tially by the loss of movement. They sat helpless, facing each other. Bentson saw the panic and fear in Margaret's face, and tried to reassure her again with his eyes.

"Frightening, isn't it, to be trussed up like this, helpless, at the mercy of God knows what?" He grinned down at them as he reached back into the briefcase. "That's good, though—excellent, in fact. Let the fear grow . . . let the panic flow. You should fear for your lives, because that's exactly what this is all about . . . your lives."

Margaret moaned, hysteria building. Her heart thudded heavily inside her, adrenaline pushing its way into her racing bloodstream.

Norman encouraged her. "Listen to yourself. Forget these civilized surroundings. Your primal brain knows what's happening. Hear it. Listen. Believe it. Fear it."

Bentson shouted his protest, unable to take anymore. "What is it you want?"

Norman stopped, stared him directly in the eye, and said with controlled menace, "Why, you, Mr. Larcalle. I've come to collect you, shall we say." He smiled again, his teeth bared.

His answer shattered any hope, and Bentson gave in to his own panic. Confusion swirled over his features. Norman smiled condescendingly. "You don't understand. I realize that. I'll try to explain."

He took out a roll of silver duct tape from the briefcase and approached the lawyer. He pulled a strip off the roll, the sound ripping through the silence; then he carefully taped Larcalle's mouth shut.

He stepped over the short distance between them and repeated the process with Margaret. The taping pushed the couple further toward panic, paralyzing fear tearing through their minds. Adrenaline streamed into their systems as their blood pounded. Death was suddenly, scarily real.

Bentson moaned into the gag, no longer in doubt as to the intention of this frightful stranger. Recriminations for not recognizing the threat earlier tore into him, useless now. His mortality took on a sense of finality. His conscious mind tried to reject the thought, and failed. No one could hear the scream he uttered, but it echoed in his head, shone in his eyes, pounded throughout his body.

Margaret watched her husband, too terrified to look at Norman.

Her fear took its cue from Bentson's, and she understood with dread conviction what was about to happen. She rotated her hands in the tight, binding straps, futilely searching for escape.

The killer stepped back and retrieved the silenced pistol. "This journey is the most exciting one you will ever take," he explained, his words made tense by his excitement.

The couple looked on in mute resignation, recognizing the inevitable, horrible truth even as he rambled on.

Talking all the while, Norman approached Bentson's chair. "You have the great advantage of anticipation. I am only a catalyst for you, but we are to share so much. Hunter and hunted." He stopped just opposite the trussed-up lawyer's left side, facing him. Seven feet away, Margaret had a clear view of her husband.

With the pistol pointed toward the floor, Norman placed his other hand on his captive's head. Bentson's life force flowed out and up into his hand, tingling up through his fingers and arm, rushing into his brain, humming with a low intensity. Norman closed his eyes again, feeding on the sensations. "Yes . . . yes," he whispered. "Soon now . . ."

He felt the first quiver as Larcalle's muscles bunched together, ready to jump, to evade the trap. "What? Run now? Now?" Norman snapped, his tone cutting. "You don't understand at all! You can't run now! Don't you get it? Don't either of you get it? It's . . . too . . . late . . . for . . . running!"

Bentson threw himself against his restraints, a strong heave that moved the chair a few inches, and again he lunged, grunting with the effort, his breath muffled by the tape. His face shone with sweat, and he gathered his strength for one more attempt, one more final effort . . . and collapsed with a silent cry.

Norman took a step back, impressed with Bentson's performance. "You're asking why, aren't you?" he whispered. His answer came in that same calm, soft, maddening tone. "*Why*, since it seems so important to you, is the luck of the draw. *Why* isn't really that important. But of course I can understand that you might disagree."

He straightened up and continued. "The question of motive will be resolved by those who look into these things. They will assume that someone wanted you silenced for some reason. Logic will point to your lawsuit, and possibly your greed will contribute to that theory. This episode will appear to be a tragic continuation of the unfortunate events that have befallen your wife, and now you too."

Norman saw the question in the man's eyes, saw him desperately try to comprehend, to organize the horror into some acceptable format. "Oh, the mark of a truly logical man," he said. In the midst of chaos, the rational mind tries to circumvent reality, to bend the irrational into an acceptable configuration. Fascinating."

The tall killer smiled. "Let me tell you what else will happen. There will be a lot of finger-pointing from all sides, as each thinks the worst of the others. Accusations will fly. There will be hints of a police cover-up, possibly even criminal prosecutions. In the long run, though, no one will ever be found responsible for what is found here. No one will ever pay."

Norman's words had the desired effect. A series of moans, nasal whines, really, issued from Margaret. Her ability to comprehend was almost gone. She was in sheer panic, her life force bouncing and hammering inside her obese body, finding no way out, no escape. Her heart pounded, and her breath came in short, awkward, fitful gasps, sucked in through her nose. Almost unnoticed, the first pain tingled down her left arm.

"After a while," Norman continued quietly, "long after the smoke has cleared . . ." and Bentson's eyes flashed back at him, burning with hate. "Oops, sorry. Where was I? Right. As I was saying, after a while your file will be closed at Trans Patriot Insurance. There are no surviving beneficiaries, you see. All that reserve money will be free for our use. Business is business, in the end, and surplus money gets used. A certain associate of mine will put those funds into investments that will yield a substantial return."

Norman's eyes lost their focus as his thoughts turned inward. "Murder does have its rewards. That's so true." He sighed, blinked, and focused once again on the matter at hand.

"So that's it. Not much else to say, I'm afraid." He slid his left hand inside Bentson's suit coat, running his fingers down, feeling the ribs. Coming to the last one, he used the span of his hand to measure off a space below the curved bone and over the soft stomach.

Norman glanced at Bentson's wild eyes, timing the moment. He placed the fat muzzle of the silencer just under his hand, removing his flattened palm. "Wouldn't want to hit anything vital, now, would we?" and fired the first shot.

The thump from the weapon was matched by Bentson's convulsive jerk. His breath exploded out of his nose, and his hands flexed against the restraining bands. Shock rolled in after the gunshot, bringing a false calm. Heat spread inside him, and he looked first at Norman, then down at his side, his eyes oddly questioning.

Norman studied the reaction with interest, moved the pistol down a few inches, and sent a second silenced shot into the overweight abdomen of the bound man. Bentson moaned into the tape, screwing his eyes shut.

The killer lifted the muzzle away and inspected the damage, feeding on the fluctuations in Bentson's responses. Both shots had left burn marks on his expensive shirt. Pain washed over the lawyer, and he groggily looked down and saw the bright stains flowering around the wounds.

Norman's senses were turned full up, tuned in to the emanations radiating from the dying man. "Closer . . . that's it. You're getting closer." He panted as excitement coursed through him. He repositioned the gun lower still, settled it, fired again.

The convulsive jerk was not as pronounced this time. Bentson lowered his head slowly. His breathing was labored now, and a soft moaning began, repeating with each exhalation. Blood surged freely, soaking the bottom of his rumpled shirt, staining a horizontal band across his waist, turning it into a sodden dark red mess.

Norman's conscious ear heard Margaret's keening behind him, but he had no time for her just now. He paused, his own pulse throbbing.

He shifted the gun once more, this time to Bentson's right side, and fired. He moved too quickly, however, and in his haste he lost his cautious placement. The small projectile angled toward the spine, piercing the loops of lower bowel, and passed left of the fourth lumbar vertebra, cutting a ragged hole through the abdominal aorta.

Bentson's heart, already pumping all out, powered its life liquid in spurts out of the torn breach and into the abdominal cavity. He was dying quickly.

Norman, his hand against the man's chest, felt the sudden surge.

The bound man's breathing came erratically now, his chest heaving less and less often. The moaning had stopped, his chin rested on his hitching chest.

Norman knelt before him, knowing the end was near, and gently lifted Bentson's face, his fingers widespread under the jawline to keep his head up. His fingertips splayed downward, seeking the pulse alongside the neck. He found it and felt the sporadic thump under his fingers as the heart tried to keep up, but could not.

Bentson's eyes opened slowly, once, unseeing, and closed a last time. Norman felt the pulse fade altogether, saw the chest rise shallowly with the final breath, felt the body relax all over.

Inside himself, Norman was awash with energy, carried along by the spirit of this man. He felt a rush soaring through his body, too strong to ignore. And suddenly he knew what to do, what he had to do, to capture the fading spirit.

He ripped the tape from Bentson's mouth, then exhaled forcefully, purging his lungs of all air, and leaned into the dying man's face, as if he meant to kiss him, and waited. He felt the life force go, and inhaled deeply as the final breath of air rushed out of the dead man's lungs. Norman sucked it in, suffusing himself with the soul of his victim.

Norman held the breath, savoring it, elevated by it, the ultimate possession from the hunt. He held the soul of his victim inside himself, tasting the man's death, reluctant to let it out. He concentrated, forcing his diaphragm to be still, willing away the urge to breathe, his chest burning with the effort, letting the remnant of the dead man be absorbed by his own body.

When Norman felt Larcalle's spirit fading, he stood suddenly, throwing his arms out wide, trying to force the last glimmer out into the farthest cells and synapses of his being. The quick gesture propelled the .22 out of his hand, forgotten in the midst of the powerful transformation.

The weapon sailed across the dining table, slammed into an ornate mirror, and fell to the top of the heavy carved credenza, splinters of glass cascading around it. A ragged outline of the piece remained in the mirror, jagged lines jutting away from it, reflecting the room in disjointed, angular shapes.

180

Margaret Larcalle sat in stunned silence, uncomprehending. Her husband's body sat trussed and quiet before her, any hope that she would avoid the same fate stilled with the last shot. She waited for whatever was going to happen.

In medical circles it is generally conceded that one can literally be scared to death. At that moment Margaret was perilously close to proving the theory.

Norman, reminded of her presence, walked down to her end of the table and knelt before her. He reached out his long fingers to touch her cheek, gently caressing the smooth skin. He failed to notice her clammy pallor.

"I feel so much better," he told her, oblivious of her shortened breath, the wild look in her eyes, the increasingly gray color of her face. Pain shot down her left arm in spasms, spreading across her tightened chest. Norman's words came to her as if from a deep well. Vertigo tilted her world, and heavier, sharper pain thudded through her middle. She squeezed her eyes shut against it, the sudden rush of blood in her ears drowning out Norman's voice altogether. A light veil of sweat filmed her forehead.

"You are all so dear to me," he said soothingly, shifting his right hand to steady her face, gripping her chin firmly, thumb pressed into her cheek, fingers splayed across the other side. He moved his left hand to the back of her head. Her head was pinioned between his strong hands, the heavy flesh of her face bulging between his spiderlike fingers.

His gaze passed up over her, and he focused on something far off, well beyond the physical realm connecting the two of them.

A second massive bolt of pain shot out of Margaret's heart, radiating explosively, the final manifestation of the acute myocardial infarction that killed her instantly.

Lagging by only a millisecond, Norman twisted his powerful hands, snapping Margaret's head counterclockwise, breaking her neck cleanly beneath the base of her skull. The act was wasted. Death had already released her.

He allowed her head to roll gently forward, then let go of it. Norman rose quickly and, without a second look at either body, retrieved his gun from the sideboard and dropped it into his briefcase.

181

He slipped on his suit jacket and left the room. Passing through the pantry on the way to the garage, Norman picked up Bentson's car keys off a rack near the door. He left the quiet house in the lawyer's Cadillac.

Norman returned to Bentson's downtown garage and exchanged the dead man's car for his Porsche. Driving westward through the darkness, he concentrated on his feelings, the sense that he had been given a revelation. Something different had happened this time, something that he knew was profound, a new dimension to the hunt. He wanted to analyze it, go over every step of the killings in minute detail, and identify the thought that was skittering around in the front of his mind. He couldn't wait to get home.

APRIL 13, HOOVER BUILDING, WASHINGTON, D.C.

Two hours before Norman accosted Bentson Larcalle outside his Santa Fe office, John Paraletto met with his team to go over status reports on their progress.

Paul Gorley spoke first. "What we have a lot of is circumstantial evidence. Someone cleverly staged these deaths, including the so-called natural-causes cases, so that they would appear to be accidents. Very few inquiries were conducted at the official level to look beyond the obvious."

"We're getting some pathology reports," Dave Armitage added, "courtesy of some difficult exhumation orders." He tapped one pile of file folders. "Most of these were handled on their merits. Now too much time has gone by. We've lost too much hard evidence."

"Yeah, but we can still get a conviction on circumstantial if it comes to that," Dale Reichley cut in.

"Only if we have to," John replied. He pushed back in his chair, raised his arms, and laced his fingers behind his head. "Let's take it from both ends of the time spectrum. Take the newest fatals and work back toward the middle. Maybe the perp or perps started getting

182

complacent with their success. Could be there's something more obvious with the newer cases."

"Might be worth a shot," Paul agreed. "We could use a break. What was the last case again?"

Dave referred to his computer screen. "That was the Pittsburgh case, one George Kersten."

"Okay then. Let's light a fire under our people out there, talk to the medical types who treated the victim, the Trans Patriot adjuster, and anyone else mentioned in the claims file."

"Works for me, boss," Dale said.

"Not to change the subject," Paul said, "but what's the word on getting Drachman over here?"

"We're still working on that," John answered, "but SEC's got a pretty heavy situation, and claim they can't spare Deacon right yet. When I know, you'll know."

"Ho-kay, John, but the sooner the better."

Late that day, the resident agent in charge of the Pittsburgh office of the FBI called Washington to report that the Trans Patriot adjuster who worked on the Kersten file had some interesting information on the medical side of the case.

John called Thomas Tynes, one of the Bureau's forensic pathologists, and outlined the situation, and asked him to go to Pittsburgh with a member of the team. Dr. Tynes checked his schedule and confirmed he was free.

A quick drawing of lots found John to be the winner, or loser, depending on one's perception of Pittsburgh. Arrangements were quickly made, and the two men flew out on the same late evening plane.

APRIL 14, PITTSBURGH, PENNSYLVANIA

A meeting had been scheduled by Ralph Webster, the Bureau's agent in charge for Pittsburgh, after swearing Mark Alexander to secrecy. The Trans Patriot adjuster was confused, intrigued, and shaken to learn that the Bureau was interested in one of his closed claims files.

His easy cooperation had been ensured by a long-distance call from the manager of Trans Patriot's home office policy limits claims section. Luther Sitasy had made clear how important Mark's insights into the Kersten case would be to the FBI agents. After assuring Mark that he was not in any kind of trouble, Sitasy set up a meeting at the Sheraton Inn, near the Pittsburgh airport, for Saturday morning.

John Paraletto was immediately taken by the tall black adjuster. Mark Alexander's attitude conveyed cooperation, with a liberal dose of caution. John was careful to ask only questions related to Mark's field investigation, as a means of gauging the veracity of this particular witness.

Satisfied that Alexander didn't try to elaborate or otherwise embellish his facts, John turned over the discussion of the medical part of the file to Dr. Tynes, the pathologist. As soon as they were into it, John got the first inkling that the young adjuster might in fact have information that was worth pursuing.

"You know, losing Kersten like that came as a surprise to us," Mark said. "I mean, looking at his injuries going in, we didn't think the guy had a snowball's chance."

"Yes, I've read the medical records," Tom agreed. "The injuries were substantial, but seemed stabilized, save for the continued coma, which had no certain prognosis."

"That's the kicker," Mark said, feeling more at ease with the situation. He had expressive hands and used them freely. "After we got the word from Mon Valley that the claimant had died, I started my final wrap-up, getting the death certificate and whatnot to close our file. I talked with Kersten's doctor. We try to do that, if possible. Helps fill in the blanks sometimes."

"That would be Ann-Marie Distefano, I believe," Tom said, referring to the file. "She was the staff surgeon."

"Right," Mark said. "If you work in this business for a while, you get used to claimants passing on. It happens. As I said, it was sort of surprising to get the word on Kersten, and Dr. Distefano was really bothered by it. She was convinced she had him on the comeback trail."

The agents shifted their interest up a notch while Mark continued.

"The good doctor took an hour of her time to tell me in great detail just exactly what they had done for Kersten and what condition he had been in just before he died. She was pretty defensive about it, although she would not rule out the possibility that things might simply have gone bad for him at the end. Still, I got the impression that she saw no medical reason why he went that fast, with no warning, no downside indicators. Just . . ." He snapped his fingers.

"We know there was no autopsy," Tom said, "given the circumstances. So what is it exactly that bothers you about this?"

Mark shrugged. "It wasn't usually how these things go. I guess it was the meeting with the doc. She asked me to stop by, like she wanted to explain things. It was just odd, you see?"

"I think I'm beginning to," John said.

"One thing, though," Mark added. "Distefano had strong convictions about Kersten's prognosis. As I said, she was real defensive about it."

The three federal men wrapped up their business with the adjuster, again cautioning him to not talk about their meeting. John sensed that this meeting might have paid off. He hoped his optimism wasn't misplaced. It was time they got a break.

It took an hour and a half and three phone calls to convince the doctor's answering service, then Dr. Distefano herself, of the importance of meeting with the agents on a weekend. She reluctantly agreed to see them in her office at the hospital, and told them how to get there.

The team of federal agents arrived on time, shortly before noon.

Dr. Distefano was five feet four, in her mid-forties, with short, dark hair. She was dressed casually in jeans and a Nittany Lions sweatshirt. She looked quizzically at the three agents in their dark gray suits and listened politely as they presented their badges and introduced themselves. John noticed a hint of defiant hostility behind her energetic blue-green eyes.

The doctor's handshake, like her demeanor, was brusque, and she

185

got right down to business. "This is a little irregular, calling me out on a day off, to discuss one of my patients. It is doubly so to have the call made by federal agents. Perhaps you can explain this to me, or should I request counsel first?"

Ralph Webster picked up on her defensiveness and tried to defuse it. "First of all, we recognize how unusual this situation appears, and we thank you for allowing us to come by. I can assure you that you are not in any kind of trouble, but if you feel the need, you may certainly call for counsel. We'll wait for your lawyer to show before proceeding."

She understood the meaning beneath his words, thought about it for a few more seconds, and waved her hand. "Okay, then, let's get to it. I understand you have some questions on the George Kersten file." With a nod of her head she indicated a fairly thick file enclosed by a heavy, dark brown folder resting on her desk.

Tom Tynes had been watching her reactions and thought he saw something there. He decided to try it. "If you don't mind, John, Ralph," he said, shifting his chair closer to the doctor's desk.

"Dr. Distefano," he began, holding her eyes with a steady gaze, "we don't have a whole lot of time to dance around this nicely, and you don't have a lot of time to be defensive about it. We have chosen this setting to keep this inquiry as inconspicuous as possible, but we have a serious situation, and we believe you can assist us. Let me explain.

"Your patient, George Kersten, may have been murdered as part of a widespread scheme involving the insurance industry." He sat back a little. "At least it appears that way."

The doctor looked from one man to the other, studying them as they sat across from her, separated by her neatly arranged desktop. She opened her mouth to speak, momentarily changed her mind, then said, "I was about to ask how serious you gentlemen were, but that question is clearly unnecessary."

"We would like you to tell us, as chief surgeon on Kersten's case," Tom continued gently, "in your expert medical opinion, how he died, number one, and secondly, why you think he died."

She considered her answer for a while. Then she glanced at the heavy file again and asked, "How much of this goes on the record?" and John's internal bell rang again.

"Depends on what we find out," John replied honestly. "If the cause of death was natural, to your complete satisfaction, we'll be gone, and nothing will turn up on the record. But if there is anything, anything at all, that we can link to a third party, you could be required to swear to it, and possibly testify."

The silence in the room stretched on longer than it should have.

"Are you reconsidering counsel?" John prompted

Her answer surprised him. "No, I don't think that will be necessary." She picked up the file, weighing it gingerly, as if it might explode, then set it down and slid it over toward Tom.

"That is the record on the treatment rendered to Kersten, minus the radiology films, which I can get for you, if you need them." She laced her fingers together on the desktop and sighed softly. "But it's not quite complete. Certain lab results were withheld. I'll try to explain that.

"Simply put, George Kersten died by drowning in his own blood. From external evidence and symptomatology, while he was in coma something tripped inside him, causing violent convulsions. That reaction is consistent with the head injuries he sustained.

"When he was first brought in, cranial injuries included blunt force trauma to both the frontal lobe"—she indicated that area on her own head with her fingers—"and the left temporal area, which accounted initially for the comatose state."

She paused while the men nodded their understanding of this condensed briefing.

"Back to the convulsions, then. Because of their strength and duration, the internal stitches in the upper lobe of the left lung pulled loose, resulting in catastrophic bleeding. The lung collapsed, and that was that." She looked down at the file, which Tom had opened. "Before he was picked up on rounds, the damage had been done."

"He wasn't monitored, I understand," Tom said. "Any special reason why not, given his surgical history during the seventy-two hours prior to the event?"

"Because of his vitals," Distefano snapped. She caught herself and apologized. "I'm sorry. His vital signs were very strong, even after the third lung repair. There was no distress. He was breathing on his own, although we had him on an O_2 line. We had Dr. Karnes assisting as well," she went on. "Dr. Karnes handled the patient's history of emphysema and prior removal of the right lung. In his opinion, the remaining lung was pulling its own weight. There simply was nothing to suggest that the patient wasn't as stable as conditions warranted. EKGs were right up there; everything, save for the coma, looked good. Even with the coma, there was no neurological deficit. EEGs were clear. He was going to make it."

Tom nodded in sympathy with the surgeon. Still, he pushed for more answers. "Cause of death was established from an external examination of the body only?"

"That's essentially correct. With the limitations fostered by Mr. Kersten's religious status, we were limited in conducting the postmortem. As you know, the body was claimed fairly quickly by court order."

"Why didn't you argue for the postmortem, given the circumstances?" the pathologist asked. "Surely there wasn't that big of a rush to get the funeral over with."

She looked frustrated, and removed her glasses. "Believe me, Dr. Tynes, we tried. But Pittsburgh is a heavily ethnic town, proudly so. We don't tamper with traditions here. The employer's attorney was most specific that George had certain provisions in his will for the ceremony to be expedited. By the time we could have fought for a postmortem by an appeal of the order, it would have been too late. Apparently a swift burial was what the patient wanted."

"I understand," Tom said. "But what you've told us about isn't what killed George Kersten, is it, doctor?"

She froze, narrowed her expressive eyes, and immediately reappraised Tynes. She sighed tiredly. "Sooner or later . . ."

John's convictions rose.

"There are no accusations here," Tom added quietly. "We do need your complete opinion, Dr. Distefano."

A pained expression crossed her features as she wrestled with whatever internal conflict had arisen. Staring at her hands, she replied reluctantly, "From all of the lab reports completed on my

188

order," she said, emphasizing the last two words, "we found traces of Marcaine, primarily in the blood remaining in the chest drain tubes. The patient was sufficiently post-op that he should have been clear, especially since Marcaine was used only on the first surgical intervention. He'd been extubated pretty well, but still, there it was."

"How much Marcaine was present?" Tom asked, waving off Ralph's question.

"The sample we recovered was minute, a trace only, you understand. But considering how it got there and how quickly after cessation of all life functions we ran the tests, I would have to say that he received a sufficient amount of Marcaine to cause his death. To put it bluntly, we're talking overdose."

"What sort of time frame are you referring to?" John asked.

Tom answered for the doctor. "Depending on his physical condition and size, you can figure anywhere from sixty seconds to five minutes. Marcaine is quite capable of causing the symptoms Dr. Distefano described. It's a pre-op anesthetic, given intravenously. But if it was used only in the first surgery, it should have long been out of his system."

"So how did it get there? Unless . . ."

"We did it," Dr. Distefano answered in a small voice. "My staff killed him." All three agents stopped cold, her revelation coming out of the blue. She shifted in her seat. "I was mystified at how things had turned out. So I had further toxicology screens done on the effluents in the drain tubes and the collection bags, blood gases, urine screens, the works.

"There was no doubt about the results. The drug was introduced, probably as a result of a patient mix-up. Mr. Kersten was on a surgical floor, remember, and another patient scheduled for surgery failed to get the proper pre-op. I think that's when and where it happened." She finished. The effort her confession took was apparent.

"I took apart the staff," she went on, wanting to get it all out, "discreetly, of course. By the time I was through, I was absolutely convinced of two things. First, everyone on this hospital's surgical staff was completely correct in every procedure. The other patient had not received the necessary meds before surgery; that was true.

But that patient was not prescribed Marcaine. It was contraindicated for the surgery scheduled.

"Secondly, somehow, some way, Marcaine was administered to George Kersten in a dosage high enough to kill him. Obviously someone gave it to him. It was a tragic mistake, but a mistake. Possibly an order from another surgical floor got mixed up . . . I don't know," she finished quietly. She sat back, emotionally spent, dreading the results of what she had revealed, but knowing that the truth had to come out.

"Why say nothing until now?" Tom asked. "Surely holding on to such knowledge must have been devastating for you."

"Don't you think I realized that?" she shot back. "I agonized over what to do for weeks. I considered all the ethical arguments, all the moral responsibilities. But in the end, I had to weigh that against the competence of my people. I know what the physical facts were. But I also know what kind of a team I have here, how good and dedicated they are. They—we—care, very much, about the way we treat our patients. We like to think we do the best possible job every damn time. If this was a mistake, it was a tragic one, but just that . . . a mistake. Errors are made, things happen. But I have to believe nothing deliberate was done here. There was no reason to, don't you see?" Dr. Distefano swiveled her chair to look out of the windows.

"Ours is a litigious society, Dr. Tynes, as I'm sure you're fully aware. We didn't need the problems a malpractice lawsuit would have brought. George Kersten had no family left. It didn't appear that anything or anyone would follow up on this, so . . ." Her voice trailed off. She turned back to face them, her tone firmer. "It was my decision to keep it quiet. So be it. I suppose you gentlemen have the right to report this to the hospital's administration and to the Pennsylvania Medical Association."

Tom had no response. There was nothing professionally that he could say that would help the doctor now. The decision had been made and she was dealing with it, the best way she could. But her conclusions were not necessarily correct, and the agents knew that.

John answered for them all. "As we mentioned going in, Doctor, we have reason to suspect that your patient may have been murdered in a scheme that appears far removed from the business of this

190

hospital. Hypothetically speaking, given the test results you say you found, how much Marcaine would the killer have had to administer to cause Kersten's death?"

She thought about an answer, still struggling with her perceptions. "About twenty-five cc's would have been enough, Mr. Paraletto. The heart would have failed, and convulsions as described would have followed. Death would have occurred within, oh, probably sixty seconds. It wouldn't have taken very long at all."

She smiled ironically. "The trace we found probably was expelled by one of the last contractions. It was found inside the drain tube, not in the bag. If he had died any sooner, we might not have found anything."

"And if it was administered by someone who gained access to the hospital, someone who went unnoticed, that would explain it, too, wouldn't it, Doctor?"

"You mean someone just walked into the ward and did that, without being seen?" she asked incredulously.

"I daresay this hospital is top notch from a medical point of view, Dr. Distefano," John said, "but so far as security is concerned, perhaps that's not quite down your alley, so to speak."

"You think someone actually came in here, then?" she said, grasping at the possibility.

"We'd like to look into that possibility," John said. He had the information he needed now, and he was sure that the details would fall into place. Someone had indeed walked right in, and now John's team had the intruder's scent.

"I'd like to study this a bit longer, if that's all right with you," Tom said to the doctor, indicating the file.

She answered quickly, seeing a way out of her dilemma. "Surely, Dr. Tynes, if you think it will help. You may return it to my secretary when you're done with it."

The interview was over. The faceless entity they had been chasing had taken a partial step into the light. Now they had to illuminate the rest of him.

191

APRIL 16, HOOVER BUILDING, WASHINGTON, D.C.

Monday morning John briefed his team on the Pittsburgh findings, concentrating on the highlights of the discussion with Dr. Distefano. There were a few questions, and Paul Gorley was assigned to follow up on the continuing work with Webster's group.

"What do you have for me?" John asked at the end of his summary.

"Three things, John," Dave answered. "First, the good news. We got Deacon Drachman this morning. He finished up early with the SEC, and they sent him straight over here. He's just about through with the briefing now. The only thing is, we have to share what we get with SEC or they pull him out. I covered that with the attorney general's people. Unless you have an objection, that's the setup."

John paused, then replied. "Okay, I can live with that. What's next?"

"That was one and two. Number three is call Luther Sitasy in Phoenix. He's called here twice since last night, trying to track you down. Said he had something hot, but wouldn't give it to one of us, said he wasn't sure about it and would rather bounce it off of you." Dave's tone suggested the claimsman was just another civilian playing at cops and robbers.

John chose to ignore the insinuation. "Did he give you any details?"

"None. He just said he was anxious to speak to you."

"All right, I'll call him. Tom Tynes is going to go over the medical file on Kersten in detail to pick up what he can. Things are starting to roll. Anything else?"

"That's about it, boss."

"Let's get Deacon cranked up on the finances then. The key has to be in there somewhere."

"Will do."

John left the conference room for his office, dropped into his chair, and dialed Luther's office.

192

"Sitasy, Claims."

"Hi, Lute. Got your message, what's up?"

"John, thanks. Where are you?"

"D.C. We received some information on the Kersten file and took a quick run to Pittsburgh. It looks promising, the first substantial proof that one of these deaths was deliberate."

"That may not be the only one," Luther cautioned. "Looks like we have another one."

John crooked the phone into his shoulder and reached for a legal pad. "Where and when?"

"We got the report Saturday by fax from our Santa Fe office," Luther went on. "The file's styled Larcalle versus White Rock County, a bad police shooting case, drug raid gone wrong. Two victims, the plaintiff and her attorney husband. He was prosecuting her claim, a civil rights lawsuit charging excessive force, unlawful entry. You can look at the file later. The two of them were found Saturday morning by the hired help. As far as we know, the husband was shot to death, and the wife apparently died from a heart attack. We had a weekend skeleton crew that caught the report. Santa Fe PD called as a courtesy. At first they didn't think it was related to the lawsuit, but now we don't know." He paused for a moment.

"Look, John, this thing has really shaken up the locals. There are ugly rumors running around that someone wanted this couple silenced. No one is talking to the press, and the lid's been shut down tight. It doesn't exactly fit our profile, but it was a limits file. Seemed best if you knew about it, too."

"If it's as bad as your office reported, chances are we're already involved," John replied. "Something like this goes down, the feds usually get called in. Let me make a few calls, find out what's going down out there." He had another thought. "Has the claim file been brought up to date on the facts so far?"

"The report's here," Luther answered, "but I haven't sent it over to be entered yet. Why?"

"Presuming that there is a connection to the others, it'd be a good idea to keep this business as usual. Follow whatever routine you use to update the claim file."

"That's not a problem. The file happens to be one of mine, as it turns out. I can watch the request list to see who calls it up over the next thirty days or so."

"Exactly what I was thinking," John said. "In the meantime, hang tight, Lute. I'll get back to you."

"Roger that," Luther said, and broke the connection.

Things seemed much hotter in New Mexico. John had a strong feeling someone had just gotten real careless.

By close of business, John had been in touch with the Albuquerque agent in charge, Charlie Souza, who handled the Santa Fe area. Charlie had given him quite a few facts about the Larcalle killings. He confirmed that he and his group were maintaining control over the situation, moderating among the other law enforcement agencies. He also underlined what Luther had said—that Santa Fe was very hot at the moment and suspicions were rampant.

John had Dave Armitage fax out the outline they had prepped on the case to date, and suggested a team should fly out there. Charlie concurred readily, saying he would welcome any help from the home office, the sooner the better.

There was no coin toss on this one. John quickly made up a traveling team consisting of Dale Reichley, Tom Tynes for the forensics end, and himself. Travel arrangements were made for a midnight flight out of National, which gave the team members time to get home, pack what might be necessary, bid a quick good-bye to wives who were used to this routine, shag it back to the capital, and meet at the United Airlines terminal.

The Boeing 757 was only half full when they boarded. Tom took the window seat, John the aisle, with an empty seat between them. Dale took the aisle seat in the next row up.

The aircraft pulled away from the gate on time, and within minutes the lights of Washington fell behind, swallowed up in the solid cloud cover they climbed through. Dale tilted his seat back, and was asleep inside of two minutes.

John leaned back, but couldn't sleep. He looked over at the pathologist, who was reading pages from a file. John recognized the medical file on George Kersten. "Still not through with that, huh?"

"Not quite," Tom answered, pulling a number of eight-by-ten color pictures from a binder.

194

"Anything interesting?" John asked, welcoming conversation.

Tom shuffled the stack of photos taken of Kersten's body after his death. "Yeah, take a look at these," he said. "Dr. Distefano had them taken as part of her postmortem." He slid one of them out, pushed the armrest up and out of the way, and leaned across the empty seat.

"This one was taken an hour or so after death. See, you can see the discoloration in the skin tones, early rigor setting in."

John reached up and pushed the square button for the small reading lamp. The circle of diffused light fell on the photo, which showed the patient's right arm, minus all of the intravenous hardware. John didn't see the subtle shadings Tynes had mentioned, but nodded in agreement anyway.

"The general bruising around the needle marks is typical," Tom went on. "Now look at this one." He placed another picture over the first. It was a close-up of Kersten's right hand and wrist. In the shot, the hand and wrist were rotated slightly, revealing the inner edge of the wrist and forearm. The multiple needle marks in the back of the hand were plainly evident.

"Pretty bruised up," John commented.

"That's what I thought, which is expected, except for this area right here," Tom said, circling an area on the side of the wrist, using the tip of a ballpoint pen. "Here, at the base of the thumb."

"Not much there, just some shadows," the agent said, studying the picture, trying to see what the forensics man saw.

"More than that," the pathologist replied. He zeroed in on the photo with the pen tip. "See these shadows, as you called them? They're faint, but they're also bruises."

"Meaning?"

"Meaning that Kersten's pulse was taken by someone with a very strong grip. Look close, you'll see a line of bruises. They go right along the radial pulse, just there," he said. "Given how faint these are, and the time the picture was taken, which is marked on the back of each picture in the set, I can say with some degree of certainty that these marks were caused while Kersten was still alive."

John looked closer with a professional's curiosity.

"You got it, John. Someone was in the room, feeling Kersten's pulse when he died. If you take your own pulse, you don't need to

195

use much pressure. Whoever did Kersten was into it, enough to bruise his skin. Distefano saw this too, which is why she ordered the close-up. You wanted empirical evidence of foul play? I'd say Dr. Distefano has given you exactly that."

John looked down at the photo again. "Sometimes you just gotta be livin' right."

APRIL 16, ALBUQUERQUE, NEW MEXICO

The 757 touched down in the pre-dawn night. The three agents joined the slow-moving line of passengers trooping up the tunnel to the gate. They were met by Charlie Souza, sandy-haired, blue-eyed, and an inch or two taller than John, but forty pounds lighter. He looked worn out, underscoring the fact that in the last forty-eight hours he had managed only six hours of sleep.

John studied the red rims around the SAC's eyes as introductions were made. "How bad is it?" he inquired, as the three of them followed Charlie to the baggage claim area.

"Bad enough," Charlie answered, walking beside him. "The perp was interested only in doing the Larcalles. There was no break-in; nothing was disturbed. Apparently the lawyer let him in, or brought him in.

"Husband was shot up close and personal, small caliber, a twenty-two. Four hits. Not your normal gig at all. An execution, almost ritualistic. The woman died of a heart attack, but the killer still snapped her neck. Coroner says he did it after she died." He paused in his staccato delivery. "The victims were tied to chairs, facing each other. The killer wanted them to watch each other die."

"Jesus," Dale said, "what kind of psycho are we dealing with?"

"One who likes to kill," Charlie replied. "Watch this guy, John. He's fuckin' dangerous."

They waited for their bags to appear on the slowly circling stainless-steel carousel. Charlie turned to address them all, keeping his voice low-pitched.

"The rumors started almost immediately. You know about the fucked-up police raid and the victim's lawsuit against all of the participants? Well, given the mentalities prevalent out here, it didn't take much for people to jump to the conclusion that it was a cop who did it. Our brethren of the badge have circled their wagons. We've got your basic siege mentality going on, but there's a lot of scrambling, too. They want someone to pay, gentlemen."

They got the bags and left the terminal, loading up Charlie's Jeep Cherokee, which was parked immediately outside the main entrance. During the drive to Santa Fe, they discussed the facts known about the newest murders, and what the Washington, D.C., team had turned up in their investigation of the other Trans Patriot cases.

"When the story broke this weekend," Charlie told them in his tired baritone, "the media went into a feeding frenzy. Dan Melendez is the chief of the Santa Fe PD. He's caught the major flak over this, but he's hangin' in there. You'll meet him later this morning. There'll be a get-together at the coroner's office, as your man requested. I think you'll like Dan, but I wouldn't have his job right now for love or money. Someone's head is going to be on a plate by the time this thing's done."

"Well, if whoever pulled this off is the one we're after, it might get a few people off the political hook," Dale threw in.

Charlie nodded as he slowed the vehicle, and pulled into the large parking lot of a Howard Johnson's motel. "I read the summaries you sent out. The Larcalle case doesn't seem to fit what you've been looking at. This was no break-in gone bad. It wasn't anything other than what it was, a double murder."

"Maybe," John agreed. "The majority of the plaintiff lawyers taken out on these cases didn't die by accident either. That's the double standard of the perp's MO. With the claimants, he used some imagination. But for the most part, the attorneys were just blown away. And this case does involve a policy limits claim."

The Cherokee rolled to a stop under the overhang of the motel entrance. Charlie turned to address the others over the back of the seat. "Let's get you registered. Meeting's set for ten o'clock. Any of you want to catch a few hours' sleep, no problem. If not, we can cruise down to the office, talk some more shop, get a bite to eat, whatever."

197

John checked his watch, quickly reset it for the local time, and queried the rest with raised eyebrows.

"Unless you need me for something specific," Tom said, "a couple hours of sleep sounds fine to me."

"I'm okay," Dale said.

John nodded once. "Okay. We'll check in, drop Tom off for a while, and pick him up in time for the meeting at the coroner's."

"Works for me," Charlie said. "Let's go."

Ten o'clock found the four agents at the office of the Santa Fe County coroner, a two-story adobe affair. They were joined by Chief Daniel Melendez, two of his officers, the county sheriff, Cecil Nosse, with two of his deputies, and at least six other officers, half in uniform, the rest in plain clothes. The plainclothesmen were the ones who had participated in the drug raid, and their hostility was evident, hanging in a charged cloud as they crowded into the outer office.

Daniel Melendez—average height, black-haired, mustached, smooth-looking in a dark blue suit rather than a uniform—made quick introductions to the tight-lipped men in the room. John felt the heat go up a notch as the locals realized more federal agents were treading on their turf. Dale half expected someone to challenge his presence there. Territorial feelings pulsed strongly.

The tension was immediately cut by the appearance of Ben Welch, the coroner. He was in his mid-fifties and overweight. Square-frameless bifocals were perched on the top of his bald head. Looking at all the uniforms, hardware, and badges, he said with a wry smile, "Back again, eh, Sheriff? We could have had a cake delivered."

Sheriff Nosse cleared his throat to speak, but Dan beat him to it. "Ben, these are the federal agents, here to view the bodies. They have a theory this mess is connected to a case they're workin'. I appreciate your takin' the time to let us come down."

Welch waved a pink-palmed hand. "Always a pleasure, Dan. But you boys"—his voice took on an edge as he pointed to the uniformed and plain clothes police and deputies—"can cool your heels outside. There's enough brass in here without you adding to it. The way

198

things have been, I wouldn't want one of those cannons going off 'by accident.' "

Some faces tightened further at the implication. Other officers narrowed their eyes, and some of the men flushed, but all remained silent. They looked at their superiors, who silently indicated the door. Ben waited while the rest obediently trooped out.

"Maggie?" he said, speaking to his secretary, who had entered the room and sat off to the side. "We're going to be busy for a while down the hall." He swept his hand around the room. Then he pointed at the door through which the cops had just vacated. "If any of those boys outside stick their heads in, give me a holler."

"Yes, Doctor," she replied. There was no question who was in charge here.

"Gentlemen?" Dr. Welch turned and led the way out into the central hallway of the building.

Tom decided on the spot that he liked the man. "Things seem a little tense around here," he said, moving up to walk beside the coroner.

"I must apologize for my indelicate choice of words," Ben Welch replied. "Since this whole thing got started, those men have all been sniping at each other. Suspicious cops stop thinking like they should and start reacting like they shouldn't. It ain't good."

They pushed through a double set of metal doors. Judging from the equipment in sight, this was the forensics lab. Ben pointed at another set of identical doors across the room. "Morgue's in there," he said. "I've got the bodies set up for you. I think you'll find this interesting."

Charlie Souza turned and said, "Dan, you might want to wait out here, since you've seen all of this—unless you want to come in, of course."

"I'll wait," Dan replied, while Ben led the agents into the morgue.

Both bodies lay in unzipped dark green rubber bags on coffin-shaped stainless-steel autopsy tables, dished out slightly. No body fluids were visible along the center channel of either table. The surfaces were dry. The serious work had already been completed.

Ben, pleased to have a visitor who spoke his language, motioned

Tom forward to the table holding Bentson Larcalle's body. It showed the rough signs of a standard autopsy, including the long horizontal incision around the head to remove and expose the brain, and the large Y-shaped incision from the shoulders to sternum to pubic bone, closed now by heavy running stitches. The four ragged gunshot entrance wounds were evident on the pale gray skin of the lower abdomen.

"Fairly straightforward, Dr. Tynes," Ben began.

"Tom," he corrected, making a visual check of the body. He had read the coroner's report given him by Charlie that morning.

"The weapon used was a twenty-two," Ben went on. "The shell casings recovered at the murder scene plus the slugs recovered from the body confirmed long rifle hollow-points, manufactured by CCI. Disruption of the tissues, burn marks, presence of cordite gases, fabric, and high-velocity subdural striations suggest that the muzzle, probably fitted with a silencer, was pushed up tight against the body when the shots were fired."

"Methodical, then," Tom observed.

"No doubt. Whoever did this knew what he was doing, up to a point. He wanted the victim to last awhile."

"Takes all kinds."

"Yes, well, everything was going as planned until the last shot here," Ben said, indicating the wound in the lower right side, above the hip. "From the angle of this one, compared to the first three, I'd say the shooter hurried it. He appears to have something more than a rudimentary knowledge of anatomy and tried his best to miss anything immediately vital, until he got here." He straightened up and pointed at the wall a few steps away, where a row of illuminated viewing boxes held several X-rays. Tom walked over with him; the other agents followed.

"You can see the fatal wound here," Ben said, stopping in front of the first screen.

Tom looked at the hazy white lines, backlit by the fluorescent tubes. "The last shot clipped the abdominal aorta," he concurred.

"And that capped it. Exsanguination. Abdominal cavity filled up, pressure dropped, and that was that."

Ben turned back to the table and picked up a portable high-

200

intensity lamp from a lab table. "Your killer was right-handed, and something else, too: he liked what he was doing." The crowd gathered behind him. The coroner held the light while turning the body's head slightly. Dale thought the light was overkill, given the glare of the bank of lights suspended over the table.

John, intrigued by Ben's last statement, stood near the two doctors.

"Look just above the chin there, and again here, along the carotid," Ben said.

Tom bent closer to see, taking in every minute detail. He saw what Ben indicated, and motioned to John with his left hand. "Look at this," he said. "What d'you think?"

The agent leaned over to study the area of the corpse that Tom pointed to with his little finger.

"Remember the pictures in Kersten's file, the ones I showed you last night on the plane? This looks similar."

John peered closer. "Yeah, I see what you mean. It's close."

"You boys found something like this?" Ben asked.

Tom removed the medical file from his briefcase and took out the photos of Kersten's body. He flicked through them, pulled the two he wanted, and handed them to the coroner. "What do you make of these?"

Ben studied them for several minutes, tilting them a few times, going from one to the other, then looked at the body again.

"Close, as you said, real close. My guy here, assuming it's a guy, has extraordinary hands. The width of his finger span is eleven and a half inches, measured by the spacing of the bruises. But that's just an observation . . . you can see it clearer on the woman. It's the alignment on the neck that's of interest."

"Same thing we have with the Pittsburgh case," Tom said, speaking to all of them. "The killer was feeling the victims' pulse when they died."

"That's a bit cold," Dale said.

"It's more significant than that," Ben explained. "Sure, you can tell by these bruises what he was doing. My guess is that Larcalle was close to checking out after the fourth shot, and the killer was actually doing this," and he demonstrated by placing his fingers over the marks on the dead man's face. As he held them there, he said,

201

"Remember that we found both victims tied to chairs, sitting up." The position of his hand became immediately clear.

John spoke first. "The killer was holding Larcalle's head up, watching him go."

"He was feeling Larcalle die," Tom said, "not just touching him."

"That's my guess," the coroner agreed, removing his hand gently from the body. "And he was into it. Enough to cause bruising, which is why I said he enjoyed it. I really think he did."

"How did you determine the size of his hands?" John asked, returning to that topic.

"That we really got from the woman," Ben said. "There were similar marks on her face and on the back of her head. You know he snapped her neck, but that was after the myocardial infarction. She was already dead, but I don't think he knew that. Anyway, I measured the span. This guy is either well over six feet six or has extremely large hands, like a concert pianist might have. He's not freakish looking, but it is an identifiable feature."

"Why did he bother to break her neck?" Dale asked.

"As I said," Ben answered, "I don't think he knew she was already gone. Hell, with her history, it was a matter of time. Her cardiologist said she had a questionable EKG on her last checkup, five weeks back. He'd warned her to watch her diet and stop drinking. Being locked into that wheelchair was an added problem.

"But I'm willing to bet that the husband went first, given the crime scene," he continued, "and that she watched every bit of it. Conjecture again? I think she was scared to death. Also, I think your boy may have been distracted. I think he meant for the woman to last longer. Snapping her neck like that doesn't fit with the way he did Bentson." Ben thought about it for a moment. "It's almost as if he didn't care about her. He just broke her neck to finish up."

Ben looked around the room at the other men. "Just a theory," he said, and smiled.

"We've really got a unique one here," Tom said. "This guy walks into a major hospital unobserved, kills a patient on a monitored surgical ward, and leaves with no trace. Then he pulls another vanishing act here." He shook his head.

"I take it you all are pretty convinced there is a connection between these two cases?" Ben asked.

"Pretty sure," John answered. "But it looks like he screwed up big time on this one. Dan says he left a ton of evidence behind."

"Yeah, we'll have an operating profile, both physical and psychological when we're done," Charlie replied.

"Up until now he's been careful," Dale said.

"But not careful enough," John said. "It's just a matter of time, sports fans."

"We keep saying 'he,' " Tom said, "but I wonder . . ."

"Me too," John said. "Anything's possible."

When the meeting broke up, Charlie took the Washington team out to the Larcalle residence to view the crime scene, with Chief Melendez running escort.

Yellow police barricade tape was strung across the property surrounding the Larcalles' rambling brick and stucco home. As they got out of their vehicles, more officers appeared from the perimeter of the house.

The chief motioned at them. "These are all my people. When this got reported, I shut the scene down ASAP, brought in the homicide boys, then called Charlie. We've done it by the book, man."

"Looks good," Dale observed.

"Wait till you see the inside of the house. Somethin' strange went on in there."

John hung back as they entered the house, letting the feelings wash over him, a habit learned years before. He wasn't psychic in any sense, but he knew that first impressions usually carried a vein of concrete fact, which could be followed, if one knew how to do it.

Inside the house, the absolute stillness testified that human vibrations no longer resided there. Dead house, he thought, not for the first time in his career, a coldly familiar perception.

They quietly entered the dining room, and Dan halted at the large, heavy table, near the place where the killer had stood. He took out the investigative file, separated the photographs from the written material, and laid them on the polished wood.

"Apparently Larcalle brought the killer or killers in with him.

203

We're not sure how or why yet. Margaret Larcalle had sent the hired help home earlier. Kitchen shows she was finishing the dinner herself when Bentson arrived."

Her wheelchair sat facing one of the carved wood chairs from the dining set. Most of the surfaces of both chairs displayed powder residue left behind for fingerprints. On the edge of the seat frame of Bentson's chair, and beneath it, streaks of blackened blood had pooled and dripped down, ending in a dark blackish purple stain soaked deep into the plush carpet, testimony to Larcalle's violent death.

Dan started passing around the pictures. "The killer managed to get them secured into the chairs here, using plastic cuffs. We're checking on where he got those from. Anyway, neither body showed signs of a struggle. The Larcalles appear to have complied voluntarily. Then the shooting started."

The agents fanned out, each absorbing the scene in his own way. John was drawn to the shattered mirror and the outline of the gun.

"What's the theory on that, if there was no struggle?"

"Can't say, Mr. Paraletto," Dan answered. "Makes no sense. Situation was obviously contained, and there's no evidence that anyone else was here, no fight or struggle. I have no idea why the gun was thrown like that."

John walked over to get a closer look at the shattered mirror. "The gun left a pretty clear impression. Get anything out of it?"

"Definitely a silenced semiautomatic, probably a target pistol. The grip angle is the same as that of a 1911 A-1, but the weapon is too small to be a forty-five frame with a twenty-two converter system, like the Ace target setup. Could be a Ruger or an old High Standard. Both of those duplicate the frame angle of the Government Model."

"Prints?" Tom asked.

"None. Smudges indicate that the killer wore surgical rubber gloves. We also found some traces of the type of talcum powder some manufacturers put in their gloves. That's being run down, too."

"Our guys did a laser scan of the carpet," Charlie added. "Impressions pretty well establish one other person besides Bentson, probably male, judging from the size."

"That checks with the three highball glasses that were set out on

204

the bar," the chief said. "Looks like Larcalle was fixing drinks and got interrupted. Hints that something social was going on, which means either he knew the killer or had a good enough reason to bring a stranger into the house. He had an office here. His staff said Larcalle sometimes invited clients home. We're looking into them, too."

"What about Larcalle's Cadillac?" John asked. "Wasn't it found downtown?"

"It was in his usual garage up the street from his office, but not in his usual parking slot. We looked at cab records, thinking maybe the killer hailed a cab from the garage. So far, nothing."

John had the situation almost straight in his mind. The killer had met with the lawyer under some pretense, talked Larcalle into driving him to his home, then pulled the gun, tied the couple up, and went about his business, apparently planning on taking his time. Then for some unexplained reason, he hurried the job, which included pitching the weapon into the mirror. Then he left in the victim's car.

"Information, maybe?" he thought aloud. "Was he here to get something out of the lawyer, and when he got it, did the wife and left? Was Bentson into anything crooked?"

"Nothing we know of," Dan said. "He was a pretty successful lawyer who made a real comfortable living—look at this place. But illegal? I don't think so."

"So we get back to our premise, that he was another victim in the Trans Patriot thing," Dale said.

"Looks that way," John agreed. "Sure looks that way. But why light them up like this? Why no attempt to make it look accidental, rather than what it obviously was, premeditated and brutal? There was no finesse with these two. These killings break the pattern."

"Unless he's losing it, John," Dale suggested. "Maybe whatever timetable he's working on, if there is one, got stepped up. Comes back to motive, which we still don't have."

"Could be," John agreed, liking the way things were falling in place. "We've got to find the connection, gang."

They stayed another half hour, finishing their review of the murder scene, then had Charlie take them back to the chief's office, where

205

they discussed what to do to pacify the locals. John suggested letting them in on what they suspected, and the connection with the Kersten case. Charlie thought the information would help elicit more cooperation from the various agencies, which would be a welcome change. Dan concurred, saying that giving his brother officers something else to think about would be a big help. The chief further assured them that he would see that the Bureau got every scrap of information available on the investigation of the Larcalle murders.

Satisfied that the New Mexico scene was well handled, John called the airlines to confirm their return flight to Washington. He passed a few more instructions and requests to Charlie. "I've got a feeling on this one," John said. "Our boy fucked up here, not a little, but a whole lot, doing those people like that. I can feel him. He's warped and dangerous and as cold as ice, but he's closer than he was. It's time we reached out and touched someone."

"Works for me," Charlie said. "Anything else I can do here, holler."

APRIL 18, TPI, THE VILLAGE

Luther had just finished a discussion with one of his troops on a claim that was far enough along in the discovery phase of the litigation for Trans Patriot to consider settling out their insured, a county hospital in Nebraska.

The discussion put Luther in a bad mood. The claim was typical of those handled daily in his department. A thirty-year-old mother of two had gone in for her scheduled pap smear, the results of which came back normal. Six months later she died of cervical and metastatic cancer, which her widower claimed should have been found by the hospital.

The lab reports were clear to the claims people at TPI and to the expert hired to review them. The hospital procedures were at fault; the medical staff had missed the correct findings. But still the hospital didn't want to give permission to settle out, on a case with tremendous financial exposure and a plaintiff's demand that was considered reasonable, under the circumstances.

"Hit them with the usual advisory," Luther had told the file handler, Tony Marline, one of his claims examiners. "We'll continue to defend, and try the case, but if the verdict comes in greater than the amount we can settle for right now, all we're obligated to pay by the terms of the policy is the amount we could have settled for today, plus defense costs up to their receipt of your notice."

Marline wrote the recommendation into the file notes. He would enter them through his PC for the permanent record later. "They can kiss their policy limit good-bye, if that happens," he said, knowing the procedure.

"Exactly right," Luther concurred. "Anything else?"

"Naw, that's it for me. Thanks, Luther."

"Sure," he said, and watched the younger man leave his office. He started to spin back to his own computer when the phone rang, easily the tenth call of the morning. He paused, glared at the offending instrument, muttered, "I could really use a personal secretary," and picked up the receiver. "Sitasy, Claims," he growled.

"Oh, excuse me," he heard Jackie say. "I was about to ask you if you wanted to have lunch. I've got a couple of free hours, but I see this is not the time."

Her voice calmed him down sufficiently for him to apologize. "Hi, Jackie, I'm sorry. It's been the usual hectic morning, y'know?"

"I sympathize, Lute," she replied, hearing the tension leave his voice. "No need to apologize. There's a lot of that going around today."

"So what's up?" he said, rotating in his chair to return to the file on his monitor. He kept an ear tuned into the conversation.

"Same old thing," she answered. "But like I said, I've got a little spare time. Care to do lunch? My treat," Jackie coaxed.

Luther smiled in spite of himself, grateful for her call. "On your dole? Hell yes, kid. Sounds like the best offer I've had all week. Name the place."

"Let's do Dutch John's," she said. "It's nearer to you, but the station's got a crew working a story in the east valley I have to check on. It'll work out great for me that way."

207

"You're on. Twelve okay?" he asked, checking his watch. It was just past eleven.

"Terrific," Jackie replied. "I'll meet you there. See you later, big boy," she kidded.

"I can only dream," Luther deadpanned back. He hung up and sat for a moment, feeling a little lighter than he had a few minutes before. "Why not?" he asked aloud, and his little voice echoed back, Why not, indeed?

He pulled into the parking lot and spotted Jackie waiting for him outside the double wooden doors to the restaurant. She looked professional in her business suit. She also just looked good, and he took a few moments to enjoy that as he walked over to her.

"Nice to see you could make it," she said. He was on time to the second.

"New watch," he replied dryly, holding the door open for her.

They took seats near one of the slatted front windows. The restaurant was a sports hangout, a favorite with the business crowd during the week. The bar took up an elevated position in the center of the building, with the tables scattered around the outside walls.

A waitress took their order and brought drinks while they waited. Jackie was pleased to see Luther order iced tea. She hadn't expected anything else, but she knew how tense he had been lately. She knew he took life a day at a time, as far as liquor was concerned.

Luther had been keeping her informed on the progress of John Paraletto's investigation into the policy limits files. Keeping his worries inside was not doing him any good, and she was pleased that he trusted her enough to let her in on what was going on. Still, she had seen the pressure building in him, and had been watching how he was, or was not, handling it. She had asked him to lunch to see how he was doing—and, she admitted to herself, just to see him again.

"Of course, what you're really doing is checking up on me," Luther said, reading her mind. He smiled and took a sip of tea.

"Am I that transparent?" she said, feigning surprise.

"Not at all," he said. "You've just been showing this motherly instinct lately, that's all."

"The last time I looked, I was a mother," she said. "Besides, maybe you do need some looking after." Jackie turned serious. "So how are you doing, Lute?"

He sat back and combed his fingers through his hair. "I'm doin', I guess," he said, then sighed. "I don't know, Jackie. I know John's people are well into this thing, but I don't know how far, where they're going, whatever. It's like Gordon and I are operating in the dark here, getting the information after the fact."

"Isn't John keeping you informed?" she asked, concerned.

"Yeah, he is. That's not what I meant." He paused when their waitress showed up with their orders. After she left, he went on. "No, John's been good about it. I have a pretty good idea what's going on and how much progress they're making, which is quite a bit, really. But the deal is, see, it's out of my hands. I don't have any direct control over what's happening out there."

Jackie started in on her crab meat salad. "Isn't that exactly why you took this to John in the first place, to get it outside the company?"

He nodded. "Exactly right, and that was the only thing I could do. But this is serious stuff, Jackie. People have been killed out there, and all of the murders are related to something that's going on in here."

"I understand now," she said, seeing his point. "You think the danger is closer than anyone suspects, and you have no way of protecting yourself from it, because you're not controlling the action. Is that pretty much it?"

Luther smiled briefly. There wasn't much amusement in it. "Now you're reading my mind."

"Perhaps a little," she said, and leaned closer, "but I know you, Lute. I know how you react to pressure, how you want to control the important things you get involved with. It's the way you are . . . always have been."

What she said, the way she said it, triggered memories for the two of them, and though their memories were different, they were both bad ones. Silence ticked away for a few moments.

"Okay," Luther said, shaking it off. "I'll admit wanting to get into things. This one, especially, has me wired pretty good. But I have to be alert, Jackie," he said, his dark eyes suddenly intense. "Christ, if

209

something happens, if there's a leak, or the people we're after get the slightest word of what's going on, it could get real hairy real fast. I just want to be sure we're safe . . . all of us."

It was clear to her who "all of us" meant. And she knew why. He was raising his protective umbrella, including his family under it. That, too, was the way he had always been. His caution answered one of the questions she had been thinking about lately and made her feel good.

"We will be, Luther," she said, believing it. "The good guys are going to win this one, too."

"I hope so, kid," he replied, unable to tell her about the feeling of foreboding he sometimes wakened with, or the nightmares that had come to visit again. "I just don't want anyone else to be hurt." He paused. "Change that," he said. "I want the people responsible for this. I want to turn the key on them myself. That, or throw the switch." He tried to lighten a moment that had grown somber too quickly.

"Twenty years ago we had a phrase for it—'light 'im up.' What the hell, it was our first rock-and-roll war. Killing someone was as casual as lighting up a cigarette." Luther grinned, a small twist of his lips that was quickly pulled away. "That's what I'd like, Jackie. Just one more shot at glory, you know? See if it's all still there."

He said it with a smile, but the part that bothered Jackie was not the bantering tone. It was the feeling riding under it, the one that said finding the ones responsible was exactly what Luther wanted to do.

The rest of the lunch discussion was lighter, almost by agreement. At the end of it, Jackie had found out what she wanted to know— that Luther was coping with the investigation, but it was taking its toll.

As for herself, she had tested the waters a little more and found that they didn't feel bad at all.

APRIL 20, WASHINGTON, D.C.

Emil "Deacon" Sargitoff Drachman—twenty-nine years old, five feet ten, thin and dark—had dark blue eyes that radiated his Russian ancestry. He was used to his nickname, the result of a fling with the priesthood in his high school years. Born and raised in Willoughby, Ohio, he had been smitten with "the calling," as the Ursuline nuns at his parochial school had called it.

His vocation had led him to Borromeo Seminary in East Cleveland his freshman year, where he learned that his affinity for numbers was greater than his affinity for the Lord. As a result, he had dropped out of the seminary after the twelfth grade, much to the chagrin of his parents, and enrolled at Miami University of Ohio with a double major in mathematics and finance. He had graduated in the top three percent of his class, with a new vocation and a love of numbers, bottle-slide guitar playing, and computers.

The government had heard about him courtesy of some work he had done jointly with a team of federal investigators and Cincinnati bankers. The Securities and Exchange Commission had brought him to Washington and put him to work as a special investigator for them, occasionally lending him out to other agencies on the Hill. His specialty was high finance fraud. He was the most sought-after expert for that type of work in the capital.

When he was notified that the FBI needed him on a new case, Deacon felt that he was returning to familiar ground, only with a twist: this would be his first active involvement in a homicide investigation.

The Bureau had given him all of the computer access codes they had for Trans Patriot, provided by Luther Sitasy. He could get into TPI's mainframe computer and that of the Bureau from the office that took up one of the two bedrooms in his Georgetown apartment. John had arranged additional office space for him in the Hoover Building.

The financial whiz was provided a three-man team of CPAs to assist in reviewing the mountain of tax records, portfolios, investments, and contracts related to TPI's substantial dealings in the markets.

In addition, he had requested and been given a sample of insurance policy jackets covering the nearly four hundred types of coverage that Trans Patriot wrote. A cursory examination of this material, and of the premium-loss ratio statements and underwriting information, quickly told Deacon that he would need an insurance consultant to help him wade through it all. The Bureau was in the process of finding one to add to the investigative team.

Deacon took charge of his part of the investigation out of his bedroom office. He dived into it, burning up one hundred ten hours the first week, most of that in establishing a database showing where Trans Patriot's money went and who sent it there. Such long hours were typical for him, as he functioned well on as little as three or four hours of sleep a night.

The insurance expert, a retiree from Miami named Gil Epstein, arrived at the end of that week and was briefed on the situation. Epstein had put in almost forty years as a multi-line insurance underwriter and had worked as a consultant for law enforcement before. He was used to long hours of slow-moving, mind-numbing work. As he put it upon meeting Deacon's team, "There is little sex appeal in an underwriter policy file," but he said that the answers to their questions would probably start there.

His response to his first sight of the material facing him was to send out for a pizza and some No Doz. Once both essential supplies had arrived, he announced he was properly equipped for the duration, and waded into the paperwork.

After six days Deacon had arrived at the same problem that the team of agents had discussed at the beginning of their work on the case. He brought it up at a briefing that Monday, in the Hoover Building.

"The problem is the amount of money represented," Deacon told them, sitting on the corner of a desk, a blank PC monitor glowing blue behind him. "Trans Patriot, like any well-established, well-financed corporation, has diversified itself into hundreds of spin-off companies and jumped into as many markets here and abroad. It's a massive financial institution, more bank than insurance," he finished.

"But that's the pattern with these hundred-year-old conglomerates, isn't it?" Paul Gorley asked. "You expect to see diversity if growth and stability are to be maintained."

"Exactly my point," Deacon replied. "If a group of people or a single individual had been siphoning off this surplus policy limit reserve money in order to channel it into some illegal scam, the perpetrator's motive would be explainable.

"Most of the fraud cases I've been in on over the years," he continued, "have pyramided down to one, possibly two, people with an enormous appetite for megadollars and few moral scruples about how they fed that appetite. Greed is a common denominator, and extremely persuasive. Money talks, and as a motive, money in these amounts—fifteen, twenty million or more—when applied to one man, makes a whole lot of sense." He looked around the office at these career agents. "Excuse the pun, gentlemen, but people will kill for that kind of money."

Dave Armitage snorted and lit up another cigarette. His smoke-tinged answer said it for them all: "And don't we know it, sonny."

"All right," John said. "This is not a new theory. But so far we haven't been able to tie any money motive in with the background checks on the people already in the mix who had access to the claims files."

"Which leads us back to Luther's idea," Deacon said. "Maybe this is more of a Racketeer Influenced and Corrupt Organization case after all."

"You mean we build a RICO case against Stennett, the claims VP, and forget about finding someone who's showing signs of sudden wealth?" Paul asked.

"Have you guys found anyone who fits that profile yet?" John said, beginning to be swayed by Luther's theory.

"Not yet," Dave answered. "But then, we didn't figure that whoever was running this operation would be dumb enough to start getting flashy with the cash. We still have a lot of offshore accounts and European depositories to check out. Getting warrants and State Department approval is going to be the usual headache."

"All right, then," John decided. "Let's redirect the effort for a little while toward tracking the corporate angle, assuming that the killings are purely business-motivated. If that doesn't pan out fairly soon, we'll switch back to looking for the individual."

"You got it, John," Deacon replied, speaking for the group. "And if we make no progress in that investigation, I can always go back to the tried and true method," Deacon said, and added, "starting at square one."

APRIL 20, CAREFREE, ARIZONA

Luther nosed the ebony Mustang into the garage around eight o'clock, and let the segmented door roll down behind him to close out another typical day.

He sat in the cockpit, decompressing, listening to the diminishing echoes of the engine noise, and sighed once. "Typical?" he said aloud. "What the hell is a typical day supposed to be anymore?"

The waiting had settled into a steady routine of nervous anticipation, a bottom edge of tension that underlined his waking hours and haunted his nights with old reminders of distant times.

His attendance at the weekly AA meetings had taken on added importance. The urge for a drink had become more than the normal quiet-voiced suggestion. Lately it had been flat-out arguing with him. So far he had kept it corralled, but he was sure to make the Tuesday night meetings downtown, too.

The nightmares hadn't returned with their old frequency as he had expected, not since that bell-ringer from a few weeks ago. Still, he had had a few more, each one different, each an ugly reminder that control of his emotions was a two-edged sword. Talking to himself helped, kept him on top of things. He was thankful he hadn't regressed any further into his past. But Luther also realized he was moving closer to that point, flirting with that dangerous slide back. He knew what he was capable of. He just didn't want it to happen again.

His hand dropped beside the console, touching the butt of the 10

214

mm pistol resting inside its nylon holster. He had taken to carrying it with him every day, as John had suggested. His new routine was to practice with it at least twice a week in his basement range.

Luther picked up the weapon and got out of the car. He hesitated with his hand on the car door. Something lay heavy deep inside the middle of him, part fear, a great part sadness, and just a little, he had to admit—just a little—the thrill of the hunt.

"Hell of a thing, ain't it?" he said to no one but himself, and entered his quiet home.

APRIL 26, THE VILLAGE, SCOTTSDALE, ARIZONA

Dana Quinn's attention was only partially on the luncheon conversation coming from the other three women at the table. Her thoughts primarily were on Norman and the obvious change in him since his return from Santa Fe, a change so pronounced that she'd had to admit she could no longer ignore it. It was even more unsettling than his behavior after the Pittsburgh murder, although he had seemed to pull out of that one after a while.

They had celebrated the latest executions in their usual fashion, attacking one another while Norman related the details of his encounter with the Larcalles, his graphic description turning her on. Yet throughout his sexual performance, she couldn't shake the feeling that he was being less than candid. There was an undertone to the way he acted, the way he spoke. She felt him slipping away, and despite her own self-serving plan to abandon him if she had to, the thought of losing him left a surprising ache in her chest, and she found herself harking back to their first months together, before they'd hatched any of their schemes, before the game had begun. In those days their mutual attraction had resulted from what they meant to each other, not what they could do for each other.

With a growing understanding, she realized their love had been more honest in the beginning, and that fact forced her to consider for the first time what it was that now kept them together. The answer she supplied, pulled from deep down inside her, was not very pretty. Was their relationship over, or could it be salvaged? she wondered. And the real truth, which saddened her more than anything, was that she wasn't sure she wanted to save it.

Her new misgivings nagged her, eating away at her shaky trust in him. He was preoccupied with something, of that she was certain. Did he know about her and Allen Parkman? Dana struggled with that idea, afraid of what it could mean if he did know.

"Afraid" didn't describe it, she decided. "Terrified" would be a more accurate word. She shuddered at the thought, since she knew all too well the violence he was capable of. But if Norman did know about her affair with Allen, why hadn't he said something? There was no way he could keep himself from reacting to such knowledge, she was sure of that. And he hadn't said anything, had he? So he couldn't have found out about Allen. She dismissed the thought, only slightly relieved.

If not that, then what had happened? What was she missing? As often as she had gone over everything in her mind, she couldn't pin it down. But in the long run it didn't matter. Norman was becoming a risk, a liability. She admitted that she would probably have to leave him. Her escape plan was well established. A simple phone call, and . . .

She smiled, then realized that the smile didn't blend with the current line of conversation at the lunch table. Luckily, it went unnoticed by her companions. She forced her attention back to the lunch-table conversation.

"So, Sheri, how did you and Gordon get together in the first place?" Betty McClean asked.

Sheri Moradilo started to answer as Dana swept an appraising glance over her. "Well," Sheri began, blushing slightly, "Gordon had asked me to help him on a stat project for the policy limits section."

"Sounds awfully romantic," Betty deadpanned, resting her chin on her palm.

Sheri ignored the remark and went on, capturing Dana's full attention with her next words.

"It was a little complicated to begin with," she said. "The project, I mean. Gordo's boss, Luther Sitasy, wanted us to come up with a

216

claimant profile that could be used to accurately predict the case life of a limits file. Seems the idea came about from an audit of closed files where the claimant had died."

The words, delivered in an innocent way, echoed around Dana like a thunderclap. She blanched and then felt an odd tightening sensation deep in her chest. Luther! she almost cried out, How! Carefully exercising control, Dana interjected, "This project you were working on, did it get completed? I mean," she hastened to add, feeling their eyes turn toward her, realizing her question might seem off base, "I look at numbers all day, and this sounds interesting, from a certain viewpoint."

She saw the questioning looks from the other women, except Sheri, who gladly gave up trying to explain how she'd met her new love, and took Dana's inquiry as an excuse to get off the hot seat.

"As a matter of fact, Gordon and I did complete the profile, as he and Mr. Sitasy called it, but I have no idea what they did with it." She went on. "There was a meeting with Gordon and Mr. Sitasy and me. We discussed some of the parameters, baseline data, whatever, and that was all."

"Will we be hearing wedding bells?" Linda asked, steering the conversation back to the more important topic.

Sufficiently embarrassed, Sheri said simply, "No comment."

"I knew it," Betty said, winking knowingly.

Dana, her mind spinning, searched quickly for a way to ask more questions about the profile. She had to find out how far Luther had gotten with . . . with . . . and then she saw the embarrassed look on Sheri's face and took the chance. "So you don't have any idea what became of that research project?"

Sheri looked relieved, to Betty's consternation. "I'm sorry, but no, Dana. It was just a temporary assignment. I helped out on some of the basic work, then the claims examiners took over. Gordon never brought it up again. I presume it didn't lead anywhere. The initial data we used was pretty raw. If you're really interested, you might give Mr. Sitasy a call."

"Yes," Dana answered, "maybe I will."

Abruptly she got up, patted Sheri on the back of the hand, and said, "Good luck with your romance, love. It sounds wonderful."

Then to the table at large, she said, "Sorry, ladies, but I must get back to the shop. A woman's work . . ."

"Yeah, we know," Betty said for them all. "Take care, Dana."

At five-thirty Dana was trying to downplay the sense of urgency and panic she felt. She had spent the rest of the day going over everything at warp speed, each tiny facet of the game, looking for the slightest indication that she and Norman had been discovered. Her head spun from the effort.

"Luther Sitasy," she whispered under her breath, "what have you gotten yourself into?" This would not do, not at all. She knew him, knew how intelligent he was—a match for her, possibly even for Norman, in many things. And now he had involved himself in their game. This was a serious and potentially dangerous situation. What had she and Norman missed that might have led Luther to this surprising gambit?

She imagined tiny flaws in their strategy, but they remained elusive, as much as she thought about them. Finally, after careful review, she had to admit that nothing had happened; there had been no mistakes. She realized that it was her guilt that spurred on her panic. No one has come knocking on our door, she told herself. There's been no policeman with a warrant. Maybe they haven't gone far enough in the files yet. We're all right. She tried to relax as she looked about her department and noted people pulling covers over their PCs and word processors. She started the same routine, closing down her desk for the day, nodding farewell to a few of her co-workers.

But still the doubts nagged at her. If discovery was imminent, like it or not, the only one who could do what had to be done was the master of the game.

Dana went straight to the study upon arriving home. Norman was at his computer, making notes off a new prospectus.

He greeted her with a brilliant smile, looking not at her but at the screen. She felt the snub, but ignored it. She knew he would come around when she told him about the statistical profile, so she launched right into her explanation.

His first response was a question. "When was this profile put together?" he asked, turning his chair away from the PC, suddenly all business.

Dana realized she had failed to ask Sheri about the date. She had no idea how long the project had been ongoing, and she felt annoyed with herself for letting something so basic slip by her.

"I don't know the date for certain," she finally said, "but it was several weeks ago, at least. This Sheri Moradilo has a thing with Gordon Hatton, who apparently set up the profile at Luther Sitasy's request."

"No matter," he replied. "If they put it together the way I think they did, they'd have found something by now. Mathematics is an exact science, and statistical probabilities are even more precise. Anything significant that they might have uncovered would have led them to us. That obviously hasn't happened."

He tilted back in the leather chair, his cool demeanor contrasting with her agitation. His attitude irritated her; obviously he hadn't fully registered the danger.

Norman read all of this in her eyes, and his lips assumed an amused curve as she propped her hip on the edge of the desk near him.

"You think I don't appreciate the gravity of the situation," he stated, watching her. He didn't wait for her to answer. "Ah, but you are wrong." He focused past her for a few seconds and then added, "This is a very interesting problem, and we'll have to deal with it appropriately."

Voicing her thoughts, he said, "First, we need to see just how much the three of them know, or think they know. If it looks like they've discovered too much, there could be a few more accidents happening, right here in Phoenix."

"What are you thinking?" she asked, sliding closer to him, rubbing her thigh alongside his chair.

"I'm thinking we need to know a whole lot more about these people, especially Hatton and Sitasy. Then we need to know why they are insinuating themselves into our game."

219

"And?"

"Well," he said, rotating back to the PC, "if they've managed to make a complete nuisance of themselves, we'll have to see that they can't do that anymore." He paused, seated in profile to her. "Statistically speaking, of course."

Dana had hoped he would suggest it. She had no qualms about protecting herself and Norman from discovery, but she was moved to caution. "Be careful, Norman. It's so close to home, and to us."

A flash of anger lit his eyes, and he swiveled upright in the chair. "Don't worry about that," he said. "I can handle it, same as always. There'll be no danger." There was a hint of condescension in his voice. He looked at her, and the anger remained in his eyes. "This is just a bit of business to be taken care of, that's all." He blinked once, and the predator in his eyes looked back at her for the space of a heartbeat.

As his gaze softened, Norman reached out and let his fingertips slide up the side of her leg, from knee to thigh and back. Despite her doubts, Dana felt the quiver of excitement his touch caused.

He directed his next question to his gliding fingers. "Can you get me the access codes to TPI's personnel files?"

"I think so, yes," she replied, letting him continue.

"And the codes for Sitasy, Hatton, and Moradilo?"

"That might not be possible. The codes are in the system, but only a select group of programmers would know them. Things haven't changed that much since you left the company, love."

Norman considered that, then said, "Okay. Just get me the personnel files. I should be able to hack into the records and get what I want."

His hand strayed higher on her leg, sliding underneath the hem of her short skirt. Dana's eyes sparkled with a hint of anticipation. This was the old Norman operating.

"We really do need to find out how this profile was developed and what they used it for," he said.

"Yes, I quite agree," she said, feeling herself giving in to his lazy caress.

"Why don't you let me worry about that?" he said, watching his

220

hand. "Besides, there are other things, right at the moment, that we could concern ourselves with."

"Oh, and what might they be?" she asked.

"Something like this," he said, and he showed her. Several times.

APRIL 27, MOON VALLEY, PHOENIX, ARIZONA

Norman, working at his computer in the soft lamplight, disconnected his modem from the wire link to Trans Patriot's computer. He had finished his research into the personnel records on Sitasy, Hatton, and Moradilo.

His search had given him literally everything on the three of them—information going back to their childhood. Using their Social Security numbers, taken off the company employment records, he had sent for credit checks, using a national credit network. While he waited, he pulled up Luther's DD 214, the standard military discharge form. He noted that St. Louis was the main records repository for the U.S. Army.

Norman rolled his chair to one side, reached up to a shelf behind the PC, and pulled down a three-ring binder. The notebook contained a series of codes he'd collected over the years, a hacker's directory of classified illegal information. The handwritten notes instructed him on how to gain access to the army's computers in St. Louis.

Once inside the net, he read Luther's army records with interest, fascinated by some of the after-action reports attached to the combat decorations. "Doesn't hurt to know your opponent," he mused aloud. "At one time in his life, Mr. Sitasy was a dangerous man. I wonder if he still is?"

Norman moved on to Gordon's background, finding a fairly clean, almost boring history and coming away disappointed with him. He made even quicker work of Sheri Moradilo, finding little out of the ordinary about the cheerful systems analyst.

Norman set the printouts aside and thought about his next step.

221

"Time for a field reconnaissance," he said, and took down a Thomas Guide to look up their addresses. While he wrote down the directions, he felt the familiar stirrings of excitement at the beginning of the hunt. The purpose this time was different, but the end result would be the same. The skills he required for this phase of the game had become finely honed. He considered himself a craftsman, an expert in the killing arts. He doubted, in fact, if anyone else could come close to his capabilities.

Sheri Moradilo lived in a convoluted complex of narrow one- and two-story patio homes northeast of Scottsdale, off Shea Boulevard. All of the white stucco and red-tile-roofed houses were identical, down to similar landscaping.

Norman didn't bother to get out and walk through the area, his boredom deciding the issue for him. There was no challenge there. He would need to plan something else for her, another location possibly. He moved on to Gordon Hatton's neighborhood.

Gordon lived in north central Phoenix in a four-year-old development of single-story ranch homes. Norman noted that the model homes were still open, pennants snapping above them in the light breeze. On a hunch, he stopped at the sales office and picked up a handful of floor plans, politely declining to answer the salesman's questions.

With his directions on the seat beside him, he soon found Gordon's home, and matched it to the appropriate floor plan. The house was a two-bedroom wood-frame structure, attractively landscaped with desert foliage in the front. A six-foot block wall hid the side yard and backyard from sight.

The placement of the house near the entrance to a cul-de-sac told him that he could gain access to the back of the property fairly easily, if he needed to. Thick stands of pampas grass, Mexican fan palms, and a sweet acacia tree partially masked the approach to the backyard gate.

On his drive through the neighborhood, Norman noted that the development was serviced by a natural gas utility. May be something there, he thought, making another mental note.

222

Norman checked his watch, saw that the afternoon was advancing, turned his car out of Gordon's neighborhood, and set out for the northeast side of the valley and Carefree, where Luther lived.

While he drove, Norman began to pencil in a plan for Gordon. As the premise took form in his mind, he smiled to himself. "A bit spectacular, but another tragic accident, all the same." He turned north on Pima Road in the direction of Carefree. "Sometimes, it's too easy," he said, laughing.

Setting Luther up was not quite so easy. Norman followed the streets off of Pima and soon found the white mansion. A curving drive led up to the entrance and to a parking apron around in back of the house. An eight-foot wall enclosed the property, hiding its features from the street.

Norman drove down the street a short distance to where he could observe Luther's mansion. He settled back, his eyes absorbing the locale while his mind flipped through various options. He examined, considered, and discarded several, but kept coming back to one he had thought of from the first. In a way, it was Luther's obviously lavish lifestyle that made the choice so natural. He slid the Porsche into gear and drove past Luther's home.

On the drive home, Norman considered the options he had in mind for his victims. There was no doubt that the three of them would have to be eliminated. The plans began to gel, and by the time Norman turned into his own driveway, he had it all mapped out, including some special items and tools he would need. He was going to have a busy weekend.

APRIL 27, THE HOOVER BUILDING, WASHINGTON, D.C.

John Paraletto was going over the new status reports from the Pittsburgh office on the Kersten murder investigation when he suddenly exclaimed "Yes!" and punched the air with a fist.

Dave Armitage glanced up at John's animated gesture, pulled his reading glasses farther down his nose, and regarded the big agent over the tops of his half-rims. "So, I take it you have good news? Maybe you'd like to share it with the rest of us?" he said.

"Webster's people turned up a witness," John said, reading to the end of the report.

Paul Gorley, walking by with a cup of coffee in one hand and a dozen printouts in the other, stopped near John's desk. "What's up?" he asked.

John swiveled his chair to address both of them, paraphrasing the report. "Webster had his guys go back and talk to all of the nurses who were on duty the night of Kersten's death. One of them, an older woman, remembered something. Seems when two of Webster's guys were leaving the ward, and this older nurse happened to take a look at the younger agent walking away, she remembered something."

"What, his ass?" Paul asked, grimacing over the taste of the coffee.

"You got it," John replied. "Boy-watching. Seems it jarred her memory, and that of her co-worker, a younger nurse. The two of them recalled seeing a physician—a surgeon, they were pretty sure—on the floor that night, about the time of the shift change."

He read the line from the report: "Witness Palmer said the physician would have gone unnoticed if it hadn't been for his 'great buns,' as the younger witness, Mulhern, described them."

"They're sure it was a *staff* doctor?" Dave asked.

"No, but they're sure he was a doctor. Palmer, the older nurse, remembered that he looked beat, ragged out, like he'd been in surgery for hours. Bloodshot eyes, beard stubble, the whole bit. But he was dressed correctly in greens, hat, whatever. The thing is, neither of them can recall ever seeing him before that night, and certainly not after."

"But he didn't raise their suspicions at the time?"

"Apparently not. Palmer said it's policy for the hospital to grant operating privileges to physicians who are not on their staff. Apparently it's a common practice, so he wouldn't necessarily look out of place."

"Time relation and significance?" Paul said.

"Matches what we've hypothesized," John said, "although they can't be sure they never saw him around the ward prior to Kersten's demise. The younger one, Mulhern, described him the best."

"You mean, as he was walking away," Paul said with a wink.

"Exactly." John grinned, and slapped the report down on the desk beside him. " 'Great buns' is the new operative phrase," he said.

"Does Pittsburgh have a composite yet?" Dave inquired.

"In the works," John said, then added, "What's the status with Deacon?"

"The kid's been working eighty, ninety hours a week, John," Dave replied. "Those extra people we brought in from accounting have been going over tax records, articles of incorporation, contracts, whatever, from all over the world. And Epstein has all but locked himself away. I think he's existing on pizza and Italian subs." Dave shook his head. "How does an old guy like him live on stuff like that?"

"They're tracking all the business transactions generated by TPI's investment department," Paul added, "looking for correlations among the players, any common thread linking the use of policy limits surplus dollars. Deacon's got a ton of paper stacked up all over the office down there, not counting what he has at home. I've been there, doing a bit of O.T., myself. Hell, his office looks worse than this place."

"Is he in the building now?"

"Yeah, I was on the way back down," Paul replied, taking a sip from his cup.

"Let's have him come up," John said, reaching for his phone.

Deacon at that precise moment was correlating the end of a statistical analysis brought up on his screen. He had found it among computer records documenting the thousands of investors Trans Patriot had been partnered with in the past five years. The phone rang as the last set of figures appeared on his monitor.

"Drachman," he answered, his attention on the screen. "Oh, John, well, right at the moment we're into something kind of interesting. . . . I suppose so, yes."

He turned his full attention to the data before him. "Very interesting," he said absently, then realized he was still holding the phone.

"No, I'm still here, John. Sorry about that. Listen, you guys ought

225

to see this. Can you bring your group down here? Yeah, that would be easier. I think you'll be surprised by this. Sure, give me five minutes. Right," and hung up.

The office space allocated to Deacon was two floors below John's, so John had his team of agents down there in under four minutes. They found him, along with a crew of five accountants and banking specialists, awash in reams of computer printouts, brochures, contracts, tax records, and bound financial statements.

Deacon, the sleeves of his dress shirt rolled up, was waiting for them. The excitement on his face was unmistakable, and before John or any of the others could offer a greeting, he launched into his impromptu briefing.

"I'm glad you all could come down to see this. It's really something." He stood up and ran his fingers through his longish hair as he organized his thoughts.

"Gentlemen," Deacon began, leaning back against the edge of his desk, "the beginning of your homicide investigation revolved around some twenty to twenty-five claim file fatalities which, as you know, were statistically out of the normal range." He paused, but the information needed no acknowledgment from the men crowded into the small office. He continued.

"Your theory was that somehow these deaths had to be connected to some form of ill-gotten financial gain originating from within Trans Patriot Insurance. Well, I think we've found your cases."

John shot a look at the others, who reacted in a similar manner. Deacon turned and sat down. He indicated the screen of his PC and a pile of printouts on one corner of his desk. "It turned out to be a fairly basic process of elimination," he said, and rested his hand on the mouse near the computer.

"I've remained bothered by the relatively small amounts involved with these policy limits files," he went on. "We've discussed this before. Translate those amounts into working capital and they're not large enough to signify any singular investment opportunity on the part of TPI."

He scrolled down through several spreadsheets. The agents gathered around him.

"But if you take the same amounts and include them in, say, a

226

joint partnership scheme, the possibilities increase mathematically. Which led to this," Deacon said, pointing at the screen. "I ran a search of every business venture TPI has been in on that had joint capital investitures as its basis. The time frame went back five years, one year beyond Luther's profile study."

"You're talking thousands of deals, I would guess," Dave said.

"That's correct," Deacon said "Then, just to prove the hypothesis, I took it back even earlier, from 1985 to 1980, and compared the findings with present-time investment records.

"What turned up was pretty ordinary, actually. You know, a corporation this size falls on a few losers. You can't hit on them all. Then there are those projects that turn a profit, sometimes a very good one. Those get tracked, so that when an opportunity comes along to work with the same group again, chances are they get used again. It's simply based on prior performance."

"Gotcha so far, Deacon," Dale said, "so where does it lead to our cases?"

"Right here," he answered, moving the mouse about. The screen displayed a complex flowchart filled with company and corporate names, all interlinked with the names of brokerage houses and law firms. He moved the cursor down beside an entry and tapped the mouse. "By concentrating on only profitable ventures, we turned up quite a few companies that Trans Patriot had never dealt with prior to Luther's artificial baseline of January 1985.

"What is significant here," Deacon went on, warming up to the topic, "is that out of all those companies—six hundred twenty-three, to be exact--only seven had never been seen before 1985. And those seven didn't surface until after 1986."

He moved the cursor again. "Here's the kicker, John," Deacon said, speaking over his shoulder. "Presuming a connection between claimant fatalities and investments, I ran that hypothesis into a new program that matched up the closing of the file and the release of the reserve money with all of the investments actually entered into by TPI from 1986 to 1990."

He swiveled his chair away from the PC and lifted the top sheet off of the printouts beside his elbow. He held it out to John and went on to explain the figures.

"The time frame, running from the actual point when the claim file was closed and when the reserved money passed through the investment department, varied from a low of thirty days to a high of one hundred twenty. Of those seven brokers with no prior history with TPI, only one shows up after the close of a policy limits fatality, and then only consistently after twenty-three, and only twenty-three, such files. This one company never gets involved in any other joint venture schemes. This is the pattern you all wanted."

John read down the column of data and stopped at one name. "Kallang, Limited," he read aloud.

"Yeah, Kallang Limited. Based in Singapore, listed on the Far East and European markets. Only been around for four years or so. I don't have all the genealogy on it yet, but we're starting on that. It'll take a while—there are a lot of trade laws, licensing agreements, and State Department records to go through. But I'll tell you this," Deacon said, coming to the end of his presentation, "Luther was right when his profile found twenty-three fatals that couldn't exist."

"More importantly," John cut in, passing the printout around the group, "the source we're looking for originates from TPI's investment department, and it's tied in somehow to Kallang."

Dave Armitage sat in silence, letting the financial wizard finish his briefing. Now he spoke up, trying to set it all straight in everyone's minds. "Since we're dealing with statistical probabilities here, could it be coincidental that this Kallang is the only oddball entity in your theory?"

"Anything is possible, Dave," Deacon answered. "I understand your point, but here's why I think this is not coincidence. If a working scam is turning a profit, why not use it, even at random, in other schemes?

"Problem is, the capital doesn't seem to be there until after the file's closed. At no other time does Kallang show up in any other investments. Only within the time frame I showed you, and only in direct relation to the distribution of the reserve-surplus funds."

He saw Armitage about to say something else and waved him to silence. "Also, you would expect to see one or more of the six other broker firms wrapped up with TPI. And you do here, but not with the same frequency. In fact, two of them show up on several other ven-

228

tures, but Kallang does not. The chance of that being a coincidence stretches the realm of probabilities."

"We get the idea," John said, holding both hands up. "Great job, Deacon. This will tighten up the fieldwork considerably, now that we can name the exact cases involved."

He spoke to the rest of the group. "As for TPI, let's concentrate on the investors. Someone is targeting these files. Try to define a window of availability on when those policy limits files were pulled for review, and when the claimant expired. Whoever requested those files was operating with a specific time frame in mind."

John thumped the desk top with a closed fist, signaling the end of the meeting. "It's max effort time, gang. Let's notify the appropriate field offices about those files Deacon's identified."

He turned to the analyst. "Deacon, when the data comes in on Kallang, let's discuss where to go with it. It could require a hands-on look. You better check your passport and immunization records. There might be a trip in your immediate future. Now, what has Epstein found recently?"

Deacon checked another stack of printouts before replying. "He came up with something just yesterday. He's been running figures on it. Ah, here it is." He paused to slide out several pages.

"Yeah, okay. What we have is a progressive period of nonrenewals for Trans Patriot over the last two years, primarily in workers' compensation, some commercial lines stuff, and some professional liability coverages."

"Meaning?" Paul asked.

"Well," Deacon said, "Epstein explained to me that it's hard to tell just by these market indicators if these gradations are merely the result of natural competition from other carriers, or something else. But the results are, in fact, measurable, and consistent with a possible attempt to stave them off by some radical means, if you factor in Luther's theory."

"You mean there's a change in the figures if you apply the idea that claims are being closed early by killing off the claimants?" John asked.

Deacon nodded. "But don't get your hopes up. These are really preliminary figures. We have to run all kinds of cross-checks and market-share studies before we can be sure we're on the right track. There are just so many variables, John."

"Yeah, but it sounds like a link for real," Dave said, pleased with Deacon's efforts.

"Could be . . . maybe. I just can't say for sure," Deacon said, letting his caution show. "But we'll stay on it."

They all stood up and began to file out. John, the last in line, paused to lay his big hand on the younger man's shoulder. "Thanks, Deacon. I just want you to know we all appreciate the hours and the effort."

Deacon waved it off. "Comes with the job, John, but thanks." His face grew serious. "Y'know, most of the time, the people I track are white-collar types. Most have no compunction about ruining someone else for financial gain. Greed can be one hell of a motivating factor. But this guy . . ." He took a breath, sighed, and turned back to his computer. "Find him, John. Find him and put 'im away."

The agent left Deacon sitting there, absorbed in his work. His parting words hung in the air, needing no reply. John had long since made his decision.

APRIL 28, GLENDALE, ARIZONA

Norman's Porsche glided into the football field–sized parking lot of the home improvement center on the west side of Phoenix, looking only a little out of place among the half-ton pickups and Japanese econowagons. This was Phoenix, after all, where Porsches, Mercedes, BMWs, and Audis were as common as Chevies and Fords.

Likewise, the tall blond driver who got out of the car, dressed in a blue denim shirt and faded jeans, failed to garner any special notice among the other shoppers wandering through the parking lot or browsing in the crowded warehouse-style store.

The cashier paid little attention as the man laid his purchases on the counter. The young girl, a part-time college student, saw no significance in the array of items as she zapped them with her handheld scanner. Norman watched his purchases pass along the counter. It was an odd collection: a battery-powered screwdriver, bags of wood and sheet-metal screws, a short, flat pry bar, a few sheets of medium-grade sandpaper, a box of blue-tipped kitchen matches, and some other paraphernalia.

She rang up the total, bagged the items, and looked up for the first time at her customer. She found him staring back at her with an oddly amused expression on his rather handsome face.

Unfortunately, his eyes were hidden behind tinted glasses, and she couldn't see into his eyes. Still, she had the vague notion that he was looking not at her but through her. The feeling was uncomfortable, and she pulled her eyes away.

Pleased with his purchases, Norman left the store. He unlocked the car, dropped the bag on the floor behind the passenger seat, fired up the engine, pulled out of the lot, passing other weekend handymen, and drove to a Class III firearms store that sold special weapons. He had been there once before and knew they would have what he needed.

While he drove, Norman lifted the lid on the center console and took out a driver's license. It was one of four that bore his photograph, but each carried a different name, address, and birth date. One of his movie tapes had illustrated the process of obtaining such documents: Visit a cemetery, and find a grave marker of someone of approximately your own age who had died fairly young. Get a copy of that person's birth certificate at the county courthouse, and use it to apply for a new driver's license, even a Social Security number. The process was surprisingly simple and provided legitimate identification.

Class III dealers sold full automatic and silenced firearms, legal in some states so long as each successive purchaser paid the annual federal transfer tax on the weapon. The driver's license Norman took out of the console had been used to purchase the silenced High Standard .22 pistol used on Bentson Larcalle.

He had other weapons, but his collection, unfortunately, was limited. He needed a newer piece, one that couldn't be traced back to the New Mexico killings. He also wanted a higher caliber weapon with a heavier punch to it.

Norman parked in the narrow lot of the small single-story brick

231

building. It was distinguishable from the other similar but nondescript shops in the L-shaped strip by the heavy bars over the windows and by the thick leaded-glass door with its security-alarm label and magnetic tape.

The interior of the store was lined with glass counters filled with full automatic firearms, submachine guns, and silenced pistols. Wall-mounted shelves behind the counters displayed other weapons, some cumbersome, others exotic, all deadly. Norman wandered to the back of the store and waited patiently for one of the three salesmen to be free.

One clerk finished with a customer and approached him. "And what can I help you with today, sir?" he asked, taking in Norman's clothing and relaxed stance, reading him for a possible threat. Robberies were a constant danger in a store such as this. It had happened twice the past year. He received no telltale signs from the tall man.

"Yes, my name is Michael Peregrine," Norman lied smoothly, using the alias on the license in his pocket. "I've been here several times. About two years ago I bought a High Standard twenty-two with a silencer for my collection."

The salesman stepped over to a computer terminal on the corner of the counter and said, "I'm sorry, Mr. Peregrine, I've only been here a year. Otherwise I would have recognized you."

He asked Norman to spell his name, then requested his address, which he confirmed off the driver's license. The salesman punched the information into the computer. "Yes, Mr. Peregrine, I have that now." He read back to Norman the date of purchase, make, model, and serial number of the High Standard.

"That's me, all right," Norman confirmed, and told the salesman what he was looking for.

The man behind the counter was professional and quick. "Pocket size or larger?"

"Larger, either nine millimeter or possibly forty-five."

"Suppressor? Perhaps compensated?"

"Definitely with a suppressor or silencer."

"Ah, in the nines you have a pretty wide choice," the salesman said, unlocking the counter's sliding door. "Here's a very popular piece." He removed a closed case, fifteen inches by ten, and placed

JIM SILVER

it on the glass countertop. He lifted the lid, revealing the dull black weapon lying on the royal blue felt lining.

"The Beretta 92F with an eight-inch Knight's sound suppressor," the salesman said, describing the handgun. "This is a very popular system. It's a natural for adaptation to the silenced condition, since the barrel extension allows the addition of a suppressor with full house loads, or a silencer, if subsonic ammo is used. Neither will interfere with the functioning of the weapon."

He lifted the gun out, cleared it, and handed it to Norman with the slide locked back. Norman let the slide go, slid in the empty magazine, sighted at a spot on the floor, and squeezed the trigger on the empty chamber. "Could I feel it with the suppressor attached?"

"Certainly," the salesman replied, accepting the gun back. He took the tube out of the case and pushed it onto the end of the barrel. "This is the new snap-on fastener," he explained, handing the gun back to Norman. "There's no need to thread the extension. The suppressor, of course, allows the use of full-velocity loads. While it won't completely silence the supersonic crack of the round, it will effectively mask the operative noise of the pistol itself. Much beyond thirty, thirty-five feet, you can't hear the report."

Norman hefted the weapon again and dry-fired it twice. "High-capacity magazine," he observed. "How many rounds?"

"Fifteen, and you can load another up the tube. The rounds are numbered on the back of the mag." He pointed to the figure on the other magazine in the case.

"Sixteen," Norman mused. "I like that. How much?"

"Cased with two extra mags, accessory kit, federal transfer tax, and sales tax—around twenty-three hundred."

"Done," Norman replied, never batting an eye. "I'll take it, and a half dozen boxes of ammunition, whatever works best with this setup." He took out a Visa card with the Peregrine alias on it. The card was legitimate. Norman promptly paid off all of his various charge cards. Unlike the purchase of airline tickets, where cash wouldn't be questioned, an outlay of several thousand dollars to buy a gun might raise some suspicions. He tried to be careful.

"Very good, sir, I'll do the paperwork and get you rung up. It'll be a few minutes."

233

"Thank you," Norman said, and looked around the shop. He noticed a shelf several feet farther down, and the rifle resting on it, canted at an angle on its bipod. Norman called out to the salesman as he walked over to get a better look, "What's this one?"

The salesman came back carrying the federal registration forms for the pistol. He noted the weapon in question. "You have an eye for the best, Mr. Peregrine," he replied. "That's a British-built version of the Belgian FAL. This particular rifle is the sniper model of the L1A1, as issued to the SAS. Heavy match-grade barrel, selective fire, auto-ranging 4x14 scope, and suppressor."

Norman gazed at its black beauty, barely hearing the salesman's pitch. He was mesmerized by the lean, deadly lines of the weapon. "What caliber is it?" he asked, unable to take his eyes off it.

The salesman saw the look and knew he had this sale in the bag.

"It's chambered in 7.62 NATO, same as .308 caliber. Feeds from a twenty-round box magazine. The bipod is civilian-manufactured by Harris, which works a little better than the military-issue one."

Norman made his decision, even though his plans had not included it. "Price?"

The salesman told Norman the cost, throwing in, along with all the accessories, a nylon camouflage vest with pouches for six extra mags, and a padded carrying case. The total was over seven thousand dollars. Norman agreed to the price without a murmur.

He left the shop with his packages and laid them on the backseat with his earlier purchases. Driving home he mentally scheduled some range time. He would need to familiarize himself with his new toys.

APRIL 30, MOON VALLEY, PHOENIX, ARIZONA

Dana sat cross-legged on the long couch in the living room. She wore a tailored jumpsuit, and her thick hair was pulled up and back. Fuming over Norman's lateness, she watched the refracted light flicker over the wineglass she rolled between her elegant manicured fingers. Another week had ended, another tough one, during which, as had become the pattern lately, she had seen little of her lover.

His unexplained absences worried her, as did his failure to do something about the policy limits profile and the people responsible for it, Hatton, Moradilo, and Sitasy. Dana presumed he had been working on some kind of plan, but he had yet to tell her about it. She accepted the fact that she had been foolhardy to ignore the many warning signs she'd seen in Norman.

But she was finding it hard to carry on without some kind of support from the man. She was losing him, she knew it. Her feeling was more truth than she cared to admit. She would initiate the breakup and leave first. If she left before he did, at least she wouldn't be his victim.

But she was reluctant to act upon her decision. She would give Norman a little more time, one final chance. But if he didn't respond immediately to this newest threat from Luther and the others, she really would leave him. One phone call to Allen Parkman and she would be on her way to Switzerland or the Caymans.

Her decision to distance herself from her lover had been aided by Norman's odd behavior of late. She had come to recognize in him a most unsettling change, which became apparent at the oddest times. Dana wasn't sure if Norman was aware of it himself. A predatory, animalistic, and arrogant attitude kept surfacing, and a glare would flash far back in the golden depths of his deformed eye. It was a moment of pure evil, completely frightening, and full of dark threats.

The idea that all of the killing necessary to win the game would not have an effect on either of them had never really been discussed; it had simply been assumed. She realized now that it had affected Norman, twisting him in subtle ways.

If that was true, perhaps he was gradually losing his fabled control. How much longer, then, would she be safe around him? The possibility of him letting loose the beast inside him made her shiver.

Hearing the garage door close, she looked at her watch. She cursed under her breath and took another deep drink of wine. The chemical warmth she felt merged with the heat from her anger.

Norman, in square-toed boots, jeans, and a khaki chamois shirt, entered the dimly lit room and saw her coiled in the far corner of the couch.

"Did we forget to pay the light bill?" he asked lightly, heading for

235

the black lacquered Oriental-style bar opposite the couch, "or are you setting some kind of mood?"

"Please," she said, holding up one hand, "we must talk, Norman."

Hearing her tone, he stopped short, did a brief double take, then continued over to the bar, where he prepared a Manhattan, taking his time. "This doesn't sound like martini conversation," he said over his shoulder. "Sounds serious. Is there a problem?"

Dana waited for him to turn around and, when he did, launched into him, her emotions guiding her words, which was not a particularly good way to start an argument. "You could say that, and the problem is you."

He blinked, then stared at her, saying nothing. Her look gave away her thoughts. So it's finally come, he thought, and felt a leaden thump in the pit of his stomach, which surprised him. After discovering her betrayal in New York, he had come to believe his feelings for her were gone. Not quite yet, my friend, he said to himself. With an effort he kept the hurt from his eyes as she continued.

"What are you doing about the profile program and about Luther Sitasy and his cohorts?"

"Like I told you, there's nothing to worry about. I tracked down everything they might have learned from that, and it came up at a dead end. The sign-out logs show that all they did was review the files." He smiled calmly, not bothering to tell her that without their personal codes, he had been unable to go further into their records. In reality, he had no idea what had been done with the profile. It didn't matter anyway. He had devised a solution to the problem.

"Whatever they did with the program, it had no impact on us or on the game," he continued, thinking this was what she wanted to hear. "Luther Sitasy appears to have been working on some in-house project."

"Yes, I know," she replied, letting the biting edge of her anger show through. "So you said. A special project, some kind of accounting exercise, you said."

"And that bothers you?" Tiring of the verbal fencing, Norman set his glass down on the coffee table. Let's get to it, he thought as he stood up.

"It bothers me that the profile was done at all," Dana said. "It bothers me that this is exactly what you have been espousing for years, statistical random chance. It bothers me that Luther's interference doesn't seem to bother *you* at all!" She half turned, and slammed her own glass down next to his. She looked up at him, her violet eyes smoldering with anger.

"I don't know what it is with you anymore," she said, avoiding using his name, which made it easier for her to say what she had to. But her feelings for him left an audible quaver in her voice. "The old you would have been more concerned by something like this, more tuned in to it, more . . . prepared, I guess. You would have done something about it by now, especially with all we have to lose now that we're so close to our goal."

Norman saw the direction she was going, but let her continue. She's really going to leave me, he thought, and again the reality of the situation jabbed him.

"But now you've become . . . different. Strange and different." She fixed him in her gaze, her anger conflicting with her concern as she looked for an answer from him. The seconds ticked by. "I don't think I know who you are anymore," she said finally, softly, the edge gone from her voice.

It's the money, he guessed, more right than wrong, jumping on that as a ready excuse, unable to face the fact that their affair was over before *he* was ready to end it. If it weren't for the money, we wouldn't be having this conversation, he thought. Norman shook his head, his mouth twisting at the corner.

She saw the thoughts running in his head, misread the signs, and said, "Please tell me something. Say something to prove I'm wrong. Tell me this business will be taken care of, that you can still do what must be done." Dana's face expressed her concern. "For us," she added.

For us indeed! he echoed. You're such a material girl, after all. But he saw a chance to do it his way, to hurt her. It was small pleasure at that moment, but it was all he had.

"This is all a misunderstanding," he said to her, sitting down on the opposite end of the couch. He was careful to avoid any hint of condescension. He had perfected the art of subterfuge over his lifetime. Using it on her was easy. He shifted, stretching his long arm across the back of the couch. "You're right, of course," he said. "I have changed. But if you think I'm not in tune with what's going on, with what needs to be done, you are mistaken."

He lowered his gaze, striving for the right effect. "This may be difficult for you to hear. It's hard for me to say it, and I want to explain it without giving you the wrong impression."

A slight shift in Dana's defensive posture told him he had her attention.

"All this planning, choosing which claimants to go for, stalking them, making sure every detail is exact," he said tiredly, feigning the fatigue he knew she needed to hear. "It hasn't been easy."

Norman glanced up quickly, then away. "Look, Dana, we both knew it was going to be hard work pulling this off. But maybe I never realized how truly difficult it was going to be." Nice touch, he thought, congratulating himself. He lowered his voice, striving for conviction.

"Maybe I . . . we just need a rest from it all for a while. I was even going to talk to you about that when this profile business came up."

She continued to watch him, listening quietly, letting him go on. He interpreted her silence as acceptance.

"The one thing we couldn't predict, not accurately, was the human factor—the possibility that someone would decide to do just what Luther and the others have done. So I've been taking the necessary steps to remove them from the equation, as we discussed." He looked at her slyly.

"But you said that days ago," she replied defensively. "This close to home, I urged you to do something quickly, Norman. So far, I haven't seen you do much of anything but disappear most days. It's like you've been hiding from me, or hiding what you've been doing from me. Either way, it's the same thing." She calmed herself with visible effort.

"Ah, but that's part of the problem," he said, fixing her with a look. "Because we are so close to home, as you so delicately put it, the matter has taken some finesse to figure out. Look, Dana, I don't want to be discovered any more than you do, but by the same token, nothing can be left to chance. Whatever 'accident' befalls Hatton,

238

Sitasy, and Moradilo has to be letter perfect if we're to avoid investigation by the authorities."

"So do you have it all figured out?" she asked, her doubt obvious in the ring of sarcasm in her question.

He reached for his drink and played with the glass for a moment. Finally he answered. "Yes, I do. This is probably the best plan yet." He paused, counting to four for effect, before continuing, "I've deliberately refrained from telling you about it, to protect you from any pall of suspicion that may result. I mean, you're in the lion's den, so to speak. Your conscience must be completely clear in case you're asked if you knew anything about what was going to happen to these three. My silence is for your own best interest," he finished, proud of the lie.

Dana sat back when he was done. He's lying, she thought immediately. He's still hiding his plans, keeping something from me. Something major.

Norman misinterpreted the look, thought he had her hooked, and cast out his last line. "And this will all work out, as long as I have your love and faith." The words were a challenge, and he knew it. He wanted to hear her reply, but in the darkest depths of his heart he already knew her answer. He reached for her hand and lightly stroked the back of it.

Yes, indeed, darling Norman, she thought. Love and faith. Even now you hide your thoughts from me, as you have for months. As for faith . . . Dana sighed inwardly at the resignation she felt, and outwardly at the pretense of it all.

Norman understood her sigh, and something inside him faded. Dana, Dana, he thought, wanting to feel more, but unable to dredge up the emotion. How did it ever come this far? He moved his fingers farther up her wrist.

This time, to her surprise and sadness, she felt no accompanying thrill. She watched him, trying to read the depths of his veracity, but unable to see beyond the cold golden sheen of his eyes as he stared back at her. The predator was gone now. She was aware of his fingers on her arm.

As if that will make me tolerate this cocked-up mess, she thought.

Still, if it makes him think he's succeeded, why not? Sex always was the best part of their alliance anyway.

"Look," he said, "we're almost at the end. Once the final investment is made, we should reach the goal figure, and we can shut down the game. Then the two of us can disappear, just the way we planned. What do you say?"

She smiled back at him, a mask for her feelings. "I wish you'd told me all of this sooner. I guess this has been a tremendous burden for you." She allowed his fingers to wander up her arm. Dana looked at him, her violet eyes softer, her sad decision made. Good-bye, my love, she thought, with only a quick tug of remorse. It has been interesting.

As Norman read the changes in her eyes, her duplicity became transparent to him. She never could lie well, he thought, careful not to let her see his thoughts. He knew what she was going to do. He moved his hand up her shoulder.

"Just stay with me," he said, sliding his hand along her throat. It would be so easy, he said to himself. A quick squeeze and . . . "We're so close now," Norman said instead, letting his fingers drop farther to toy with the tab of the long zipper on the front of her jumpsuit.

"Yes, there's no denying it," Dana replied demurely, encouraging his fingers. But her mind was on escape, and how she could time it to allow herself the best chance to get away safely. A few more days, she thought, letting him continue.

The zipper made barely a sound as Norman lowered it. His fingers crept inside her jumpsuit, gliding up and down her tight cleavage.

"You want me to stay?" she asked, breathing in, making her breasts swell, letting the sultry look he expected to see glaze her eyes. "Darling, whatever made you think I would want to leave?"

MAY 1, MOON VALLEY, PHOENIX, ARIZONA

Norman awoke at his usual early hour to find Dana already up, dressed, and gone to work. Probably gone for good, he told himself, thinking back to their argument the night before. And if she is?

240

He ambled into the study to check for any message she might have
left him on the computer. To his surprise, he found one.

Dearest Norman,

I'm sorry for the row last night. I hope you'll forgive me. We
shouldn't let things get so far out of hand. I just wanted this
business with Sitasy and Hatton over with. I trust you, my
love, and know you'll do what has to be done.

TPI has another trip scheduled for me—Atlanta this time. I
should have told you sooner, but things have been so, well,
hectic. You understand. Looks like I'll be gone Thursday
through Monday. I'll see you tonight. Perhaps we can make
up for the last few days.

Yours as always,
Dana

Norman read the message once and deleted it, feeling that the note
was barely window dressing, a sham to disguise what she was obviously planning to do. He picked up the phone and dialed her extension at Trans Patriot, double-checking. She answered after the first
ring, her response businesslike and normal.
"Investments, Dana Quinn."
He quickly hung up, intrigued that she apparently hadn't yet im-
plemented her escape plan. Her departure wouldn't be long in coming, he was sure. She's playing it cool, he thought, seeing his
advantage forming. Yes, this could work out very well for him. As for
Dana, well . . .
"So it's Mr. Parkman at last," he said aloud. "Atlanta, indeed.
And while I'm waiting here for your return, you two will be enjoying
all those millions in the sun."
Norman sighed as he turned and headed for the master bathroom.
All this time, and this is the best you can come up with, he thought,
disappointed in Dana's performance. He stepped into the glass-
enclosed shower stall and turned the water on hot and hard. As he
soaped his lean body, Norman reviewed the next steps he would

241

cover. He wondered what Dana would say when she returned that evening to find nothing but an E-mail message. His note would mention a trip of his own, to Seattle. But like her letter, Norman's message was misleading.

"Turnabout time, Dana," he said, head back, arms crossed, letting the spray drill across his wide shoulders. "It's time Allen and I finally met." His lips spread into a Cheshire cat's smile, water droplets hanging off his sharp white teeth.

MAY 2, EAST HAMPTON, LONG ISLAND

Allen Parkman backed the E-Type Jaguar out of his garage, heading for the nearby municipal airport and the commercial helicopter that he flew into New York. His mind was still jumping from the phone call he had received the day before from Dana Quinn. It had finally happened; she had told him about it with no hint of panic in her voice. She had sounded remarkably calm and in control. Her news, after all, was not entirely unexpected. She was leaving Norman, claiming that his erratic behavior was putting all of them in danger.

Dana had mentioned hearing about the statistical profile that Luther, Gordon, and Sheri had created. Still keeping the truth about the murders from him, she had told Parkman the profile was a form of audit into various joint venture deals, not a review of policy limit fatality files. Afraid the audit might uncover their scam, she had reported it to Norman. Although he had promised to come up with a way to stop it, he had as yet failed to do so. It was so obvious a danger, she said, but Norman didn't seem perturbed, paying only lip service to the alarm.

She was worried and tired of taking risks. While Norman procrastinated, time was running out. It was time for her to move. She had instituted her emergency plan and was already working on leaving Phoenix as quietly as possible under the guise of another business trip for TPI. Allen was to finalize his own preparations, wrapping up whatever needed to be done at his end.

242

The lawyer was in a turmoil, excited that what had been only fantasy talk before was actually happening. But anxiety tempered his excitement. They were finally doing it, he and Dana. Pulling the plug, he thought, his distracted mind seemingly running off in random directions. Could he really leave all this behind? A lifetime of work, the law firm he had built up? Surely there was a way to avoid such a permanent step?

Stop it, his logical voice chastised him. Think about what you're involved in. How do you walk away from investment fraud and embezzlement? No, you're in this far too deep to consider anything but running. And look what you will have gained from the effort—almost eighteen million dollars by now, which would buy one hell of a lot of secure anonymity.

He allowed himself a faint smile as he thought about the money. Yes indeed, that would pretty well take care of any remaining reservations he had about leaving. Everything he had ever wanted, anything that had ever been denied to him, was now within his reach. And he would enjoy his wealth in the company of the delightful Dana Quinn. That idea left a comfortable feeling amid his continued unease.

His preoccupation with how to handle his immediate chores filtered back into the forefront of his brain as he reversed gears and guided the Jaguar down the winding drive from the back of his Tudor mansion near the beach. He braked suddenly, finding his way blocked by a four-door sedan parked across the drive, a tall figure lounging against the fender.

The man was blond, his eyes hidden behind brown-shaded sunglasses, a half smile on his thin lips. He was dressed in a dark brown leather jacket, open to show the blood-red golf shirt beneath. His arms were crossed, his pose confident, even arrogant, and slightly threatening.

He pushed off from the side of the car, and Allen froze, the stranger's identity suddenly as clear as glass. Fear cascaded down his body in a fine icy spray. His hands tightened on the walnut steering wheel, and he felt his thighs twitch.

As Norman ambled over to the Jaguar, he removed his glasses carefully and made a show of putting them into the pocket of his jacket. He leaned over and rested his large hands on the sill of the open window. His smile broadened as he looked down at Allen's upturned face, which had suddenly been drained of color.

"Allen Parkman," he said lightly, enjoying the effect he was having. "We've been fucking the same woman." He glanced left and right, appraising the Jaguar's lines. "Or, to be more accurate, she's been fucking us."

"You're Norman," Allen managed, his eyes drawn to the asymmetrical eyes staring coldly back. His foot slipped off the clutch, and the twelve-cylinder engine shuddered and stopped.

"Very good," Norman said, noticing the slight tremor in the other man's hands. "Why don't you turn off the ignition, Allen? We have some things we really should discuss." He straightened up and took a step back from the car.

The lawyer twisted the key, willing his hands to calm down, and reluctantly reached for the door handle.

"Relax, Mr. Parkman," Norman said, letting him climb out of the car. He put an edge into his voice. "If I wanted to kill you, you'd be dead already." He slipped both hands into his jacket pockets.

Managing his fright, trying to quell the alarms clanging inside his head, Allen took a calming breath. "What—" he started to say, but his tongue was dry, and he swallowed. "What do you want?"

"Ah, that is the question now, isn't it? What do I want?" he repeated. "How about what can I give you, instead?" He withdrew one of his hands, and Allen saw that he held a thick stack of computer diskettes.

"Truth, Allen," Norman said, inclining his head toward the house. "Truth and knowledge. It's time you had both, for a change."

Gaining control over his shaken emotions, the lawyer preceded Norman up the drive. He had no choice in the matter, but his professional side was prompting him to play it cool. He might yet survive whatever this man had in store for him.

They adjourned to the study, a ground-floor corner room overlooking the beach. Norman sat the attorney down at the PC beside his desk and had him boot it up. He stood beside him absently shuffling the

244

stack of disks, his presence alone sufficient to keep Allen nailed to the chair.

"Tell me something, Counselor," Norman said, keeping Allen off balance, wanting him afraid, unsure of his visitor's intentions. "When the investment funds available to Dana began to show an increase two years ago, weren't you curious? With your years of experience in these matters, didn't that seem just a little odd?"

Allen started to answer, wondering why Norman had asked the question. "I'm not sure what you're—"

Norman cut him off. "I wonder sometimes how people like you survive," he said sarcastically. "Did you think she had suddenly found a money pipeline? Really, Allen, I expected more from you. I'm going to proceed on a supposition here. Stop me if I'm wrong, but I'm guessing Dana hasn't been exactly straightforward with you," and he reached past Parkman to slide in the first floppy disk. He opened the file and pointed at the monitor. "Watch the screen. Even you can learn something new."

Norman read the information as it came up. "Melinda Carlisle, age twenty-six, the first one. Second- and third-degree burns over seventy-three percent of her body, caused by a flammable garment fabric manufactured by Oxlin Industries, insured by Trans Patriot Insurance." He scrolled down the file quickly, but not so fast as to lose Allen, who kept glancing from the screen to Norman and back.

"Here we are," the killer said. "Melinda Carlisle died of a myocardial infarction. Or so the record says. The claim was reserved for a million dollars. Policy limits."

He waited while Allen read the narrative at the end of the file detailing the first murder. The lawyer was confused as the connection began to dawn. Unsure of what he was seeing, he had started to turn when Norman removed the first disk and inserted the second one.

"These are chronological," he said, and tapped the monitor. "Keep reading, Al. It'll make sense in a moment. Yes, this one was unique. Caused me a bit of trouble, working out the details, but there you are. Ralph Thorsen, fifty-six, brain-damaged."

Despite himself, Allen was drawn into the silent words on the screen. The warning bell suddenly clanged louder as his mind started to see the pattern. His eyes widened with realization, and he sat back from the screen in revulsion, denying what he was seeing.

"That's better," Norman said, smiling. Seeing once again this electronic record of his trophies was a thrill. "It's not so hard to figure out, once you get into it," he said, and slid in another disk.

Allen sat immobile, unwilling to accept what was unfolding in front of him, yet unable to tear himself away from the terrible narratives that appeared before him, one after another. Morbidly fascinated by the carnage that spilled into the quiet of the room, he cursed the primitive corner of his otherwise civilized brain that held his attention on Norman's exclamations and descriptions.

He was back on the roller coaster, his body tensing as each new disk clicked home and each new body was accounted for, the killer's voice taking on a singsong lilt.

"Oh, God," Allen moaned at one point, not sure he even said it, his senses reaching overload, yet still hammering at him as he read the horrible details kept from him time and time again by Dana. "Please," he said with an effort, his throat constricting as hot tears welled up, then flowed freely down his face. "Please . . . no more!"

Norman ejected the disk and held up another. "Last one, Allen. You'll love this one. Numbers twenty-four and twenty-five, a doubleheader; the lawyer and the claimant were husband and wife." The label on the disk read "Bentson and Margaret Larcalle." Norman pushed it in.

He patted the lawyer's shoulder. "What's the matter, Al? Aren't you having fun? Don't you get it? Don't you see what's been going on?"

The long narrative describing the double murder came to an end, and Norman removed the last disk. He placed it carefully on the top of the stack, rubbing a fingertip across one edge. He sighed, letting the emotional high subside, relishing the glow it left behind.

"You really should be enjoying this, Allen. Fun is when you laugh." His voice dropped suddenly, hollow and cold. "Not when your heart stops."

Devastated, feeling the darkness twisting away inside him, Allen's dispassionate professional mind calculated the final tally as Norman gave voice to it.

"Twenty-five, Counselor. Twenty-five counts of murder one. Of course, you'd be found an accessory after the fact, at a minimum." Norman turned around, leaning against the edge of the desk. "But while we're being honest, let's not forget the attorneys. There are eleven of them. They weren't going to dismiss the lawsuits soon enough, you see."

Allen rested his elbows on the desk, both hands cupping his face. "How could you . . . the two of you . . . how could she . . . ?" and he groaned through muffling fingers.

"She sure did, didn't she?" Norman said, feeling no sympathy for the man. "And all this time you thought *you* were fucking *her*. Isn't knowledge a great thing? Now we all know what happened!"

"Why?" Allen asked quietly, sitting back slowly, not really caring to hear Norman's answer, wanting this maniac to finish whatever he'd come to do.

Norman stood, surprised at the question. "Why!" he shot back. "You're kidding, right? Tell me you are, really." He turned his back on Allen and walked slowly across the study toward the casement windows.

"You almost joined the others, you know," he said. "It came that close." He snapped his fingers, the sound cracking dryly in the dead air around him. "But then I thought, No, why not show him what true treachery is? You asked the question, but I thought you knew the why of it."

He stopped before the leaded glass, sunlight through the diamond-shaped frames cutting him into pieces. Norman looked out on the gray-green waves sliding up the sand two hundred yards away. "I met guys like you on the Street," he said, almost to himself. "Always on the scam, looking for the same thing, ready to bankrupt a deal, sabotage an agreement, breach a contract, even destroy a man. For what? For the almighty dollar."

He turned to cast a withering look at the lawyer. "And you ask me why. We're the same, you and I, exactly the same, whether you choose to see the similarity or not. You work more slowly, that's all. You set things up, bide your time, and when the time is right, when the opposition is eliminated, you move in for the kill. I just found a quicker way to get there. In the end, we both arrive at the same spot."

247

Allen found a reserve of courage and challenged the killer's comparison. "We're not anything alike. I didn't set out to do . . ."

"To do what? Come on, Mr. Lawyer. Tell me again what you didn't set out to do." Norman approached him like a stalker, the predator glowing out of the golden depths of his deformed feline eye.

The look frightened Allen, and he cowered. He also felt the pain of the truth and his fear at what he had fallen into. "What happens now?" he asked, figuring the worst was yet to come.

"Nothing," Norman said, the light fading from his eyes. "My agenda is a little different from yours. Besides, your plate is pretty full at the moment." He caught just a hint of relief in the attorney's face. "As I said, I came bringing knowledge. I thought you'd be smart enough to use it."

He picked up the stack of diskettes and put them back into his jacket pocket. "Just remember who put you into this position, my friend. How you handle that knowledge is your affair." He chuckled. "Sorry, that was bad." Norman started to leave, then paused. "There is one more thing."

Allen tensed, fearing what was coming.

The killer smiled. "Don't you trust me yet? No, it's the money. You remember the money? The root of all this evil?" He reached across the desk and pulled the telephone closer to Allen. "I'd like you to call the account manager in Bern, Switzerland." Now he had Allen's full attention.

"Right. Have him transfer the money, all eighteen million dollars, give or take, to the new account in Georgetown in the Cayman Islands." He placed a slip of paper near the phone. On it was a series of numbers. "Not the account you and Dana set up. Yes, I know about that, too. Use this one. It's mine."

Allen's eyes flashed with anger, but it was far too late for that.

"You may have known Dana longer than I, but I know her better," Norman said. "Just do as I say, and don't bother thinking you can pull a fast one later, since you know my number." He leaned over and touched Allen's cheek gently. The touch was like an electrical shock, and he jerked back from it.

"Even you wouldn't be that stupid. Besides, there's no guarantee the money will stay in that account. It's amazing how funds can be

248

transferred clear around the globe in this high-tech age we live in. No, I wanted you to see just how badly you've lost in this game. You're just not in my league, Al. But then, few people are." He straightened up, obviously in command. "Now make the call."

Allen did as he was told, Norman watching the entire time. The call didn't take long, as predicted. He hung up the phone slowly, feeling as if his entire world had crashed straight into hell.

Norman stood, surveying the room, immensely satisfied. He had accomplished everything he had set out to do. He crossed to the door and paused. "As I said, Allen, give some thought to how you got into this mess. You're in a heap of trouble. What are you going to do about it? What can you do? There *are* some options left." Norman winked his cat's eye. "You'll think of something," and he was gone.

MAY 2, SKY HARBOR AIRPORT, PHOENIX, ARIZONA

At that precise moment Dana was parking her Mercedes in the long-term parking at Sky Harbor International Airport. She had checked her bags with the skycap at the curbside service, verifying her boarding pass for the flight to Denver. It was just after seven in the morning, and the cloudless sky already promised to be clear and calm, a typical spring day in the desert valley.

She got out and locked the car, thinking with a tug of sadness that this would be the last time she ever saw it. But she refused to let such thoughts get in the way. She would soon have a new Mercedes, an entire fleet of them, if she wanted. She had the money now, and her freedom from Norman.

Dana wondered what he would think when he returned from his trip to Seattle to find her truly gone. Even if he tried, he'd never find her. She had planned this too carefully to allow any error. She had learned from a master, after all. How fitting that Norman's skills in subterfuge had helped contribute to his loss.

But who's really losing? The thought came suddenly, and she almost whirled around to see where it had come from. "Stop that!"

she murmured under her breath, refusing to allow any more of *that*. "It's his loss, my gain," she said. Then she realized she hadn't said "our gain," to include Allen. Dana paused for a moment, then continued on. She was right the first time. It *was* her gain, all of it. So be it.

She shouldered her purse and headed for the elevators down to the concourse. She put her free hand up to check the black wig she wore, and adjusted the big-lensed sunglasses hiding her eyes, which were now brown, not violet. She wore oversized clothing—a loose blouse, a full skirt, and a light jacket—to hide her generous figure.

She would make several more changes in her appearance over the next few days. That part of the plan was a bit time-consuming, but she and Allen had talked about it, and it seemed like the safest way to go. They were working on the presumption that Sitasy and Hatton might have stumbled onto enough information to lead them to report their findings to the authorities. She had reminded Allen that it hadn't happened yet, but she agreed that they had to consider that possibility. The fact that Norman had not yet solved that particular problem added further credence to the theory.

If the authorities were in fact looking for them, they would check out airports and other exit ports out of the country while they pursued them. Allen had suggested that they take a few days, in that event, to skip around the country, independent of each other, to throw their pursuers off. They would meet up in Washington, D.C., on Saturday, and leave the country on the same flight, keeping their false identities and altered appearances.

The elevator doors opened, and Dana stepped out into the crowded terminal concourse, losing herself in the throng, leaving behind whatever residual feelings she may have had.

MAY 2, NEW YORK CITY

Norman relaxed in the first-class cabin of the midday Delta flight out of New York's JFK back to Phoenix. He felt exceptionally invigorated, more than pleased with the way things had turned out. It had been a very rewarding trip. The lawyer had turned out to be a pawn in the game, another type of victim, just as Norman had expected.

Hardly worth the effort of a proper hunt, he thought, remembering the abject fear in the lawyer's face when he recognized Norman. Whatever qualities and expertise Dana had taken advantage of in Parkman were useless now. The man's destroyed, he thought smugly. Still, it remains to be seen what he'll do with what he now knows.

Later, as he looked out the small window at the greening plains of middle America, Norman mulled over the lawyer's alternatives, only slightly curious about Parkman's future. No matter which way he goes, it won't affect me, the killer thought. I've got the money, and I'm rid of Dana, the conniving bitch, and her silent partner. All I have to do now is take care of Sitasy and Hatton and their damn profile, and it'll be over. I'll be off to retirement and new horizons.

He pulled the plastic shade down over the window, settled back, and put on his earphones. The movie was about to start, but he found his attention wandering to the millions of dollars waiting for him down in the Caymans. He had done just what he had warned Allen he would do. Shortly after leaving him, he had stopped in Bridgehampton on the way back to New York and made a call, transferring the funds into yet another account, safe from any eleventh-hour attempt by his former associates. He had set up both accounts on a fast trip to the islands months ago after he'd followed Dana and discovered her connection to the lawyer.

That was one bit of business off the list. His plans for Gordon Hatton were settled, and he looked forward to putting them into play. He had dismissed Sheri Moradilo as a minor inconvenience, an unworthy target.

Luther Sitasy, on the other hand, was a special case. Norman had finally realized what was so significant about the last killings: it was that final effort by Bentson Larcalle to fight back. As futile as Larcalle's effort was, it had surprised Norman. Not for when it had happened, but for what it was.

None of his other victims had ever fought back. Granted, each individual murder had been specifically designed and executed. An

251

accident here, natural causes there, nothing that even hinted at out-side hands. Totally unaware of their impending demise, each claim-ant had succumbed to his skill without being given a chance to react in any way.

Bentson had been different. He'd had the time to see it coming and had chosen, late as it was, to strike back. That was what Norman expected of Luther. The claimsman's background spoke well of past capabilities, old but possibly not forgotten. Rusty as he probably is, he may be more of a challenge than the others, Norman thought, anticipating his plan. Since he will be my last victim, a challenge could be fitting. One on one, *mano a mano,* all that.

It'll pump some life into the last act, he mused, turning his atten-tion back to the movie. Not that he was bored with the game, far from it. But now he knew what had been missing—the lack of a direct challenge to his considerable talents. So I'll let Sitasy get close, play with him a bit, then kill him. There wouldn't be a problem, he knew. Norman knew the extent of his limitations. He had none.

MAY 3, THREE HUNDRED MILES WEST OF ANCHORAGE, ALASKA

While Norman chased the sun half a world behind him, Deacon Drachman was already eight hours into his trip to Singapore and the headquarters of Kallang, Ltd. He had persuaded John to let him go, explaining that the rest of the crew, under Gil Epstein's direction, could carry on without him for a few days. A feeling had been nagging him almost from the beginning in spite of all the other evidence they were finding, that personal gain lay at the root of the murders.

John had reluctantly released him, admonishing Deacon that he would be pretty much on his own, but that was understood. He had wasted no time in arranging his flight.

As he neared the international dateline, and prepared to lose a day in transition, the young investigator thought back on his discus-sion with the team of agents regarding their suspicions about Kallang.

The brokerage firm seemed to be intricately linked to the investment department at Trans Patriot. But Kallang itself appeared legitimate, as evidenced by its track record in the marketplace. For a fairly small company with a new reputation, it was doing quite well for its investors.

"That could be part of the cover," John had said, "to avoid attracting attention."

"It's a fair assumption," Deacon agreed, "but the connection to TPI is the key. To my way of thinking, Kallang is as crooked as the people running it. Once again, coincidence works against it. Despite the other real business of this brokerage firm, the fact is that twenty-three deaths have contributed to its assets."

"Possibly more than twenty-three," John said. "The final tally's going to be higher."

"I was giving it the benefit of the doubt," Deacon replied. "But there's a lot of doubt here. On paper it checks out. I think a personal look is in order. If there is sufficient cause, we'll have to ask the State Department to request the Brits to get the warrants we'll need."

Deacon relaxed into his seat, appreciative of the relative comfort of the British Airways 747. His return ticket remained open. There was no telling what lay ahead for him in the heat and humidity of the old former English colony. In fourteen hours he would land in Singapore.

MAY 4, DALLAS–FORT WORTH AIRPORT, TEXAS

The Southwest Airlines 757 touched down at 3:23 P.M., eight minutes late. The minor delay, caused by a thunderstorm, irritated Dana Quinn, but she shrugged it off and stared out the window at the leaden skies over the airport as the jet rumbled toward the terminal gate.

Anyone who knew her would have a hard time recognizing her now. Her auburn hair was hidden under a dark chin-length wig. Contact lenses had once again changed her violet eyes to a deep brown. Her more subdued makeup enhanced her thin nose and high cheekbones. She appeared younger than she was, the look bolstered by jeans and a bargain-store blouse.

So far so good, she thought, on this, the second leg of her great escape from Norman. She was nervously pleased at how smoothly her carefully orchestrated plan was going. Even her supposed trip on behalf of Trans Patriot to Atlanta had been genuine, as she had stated in her computer message. She had set it up herself and had even booked her hotel reservation at the Old Colony Inn in downtown Atlanta in case Norman grew curious enough to check. As far as the company was concerned she was meeting with real clients.

She was excited by her cloak-and-dagger adventure. In all the years she and Norman had played the game, she had always been a distant spectator when it came to carrying out the executions. It was always Norman who ventured out into the field. Now it was her turn, and she was enjoying the turnabout.

Rain began to strike the plastic window in heavy fat drops as the aircraft nosed into the docking collar. Dreary weather, she mused, unbuckling her seat belt and beginning to collect her carry-on things. Then with a wry smile on her full lips, she thought, What perfect weather to set the mood for dear Allen. She needed him in the Caymans, but only temporarily. She had plans for him, too. Dana intended to burn all of her bridges behind her. Norman was the first. Allen Parkman, poor man, would be the second.

MAY 4, PHOENIX, ARIZONA

Seven o'clock Friday morning found Norman parked two blocks down the street from Gordon Hatton's home. The killer sat upright in the rental pickup, a white Chevy S-10. He had decided that his Porsche was a bit too flashy for this kind of work. Better to drive something less noticeable and more in keeping with the neighborhood.

He was dressed in high-top black Nikes, jeans, and a short-sleeved gray uniform shirt with a name embroidered over the left pocket. To a passerby, he would look like a man from the utility company, out to read the meter.

In the quiet interior of the truck, Norman's features were immobile as he waited for his target to leave the house. He perked up when the garage door rose and he saw Gordon's big charcoal-and-silver 1982 Cadillac Seville backing out.

"Off to another day at TPI," Norman said under his breath as Gordon backed the car into the street. Norman had all day to do what he had to do, so time wasn't his primary concern. His target would be gone for a good eight hours or more. That meant there would be no interruptions, which was critical.

Norman watched the Caddy drive away from him until it was out of sight around the far corner at the end of the block. He checked the contents of the navy blue canvas bag beside him on the passenger seat, making sure the flat pry bar was on top. He zipped the bag shut and got out of the truck.

He walked casually up the street, keeping an eye out for traffic and movement on the sidewalks and driveways of the neighborhood. Seeing no one as he approached the house, Norman turned up the cement drive, and took the walkway that branched off it to cut around the corner of the house. He approached the five-foot-high wooden gate set into the cement wall. The gate was hidden from the street by two tall, bushy pampas grass plants.

Norman looked over the top of the gate at its other side. The ovoid padlock answered the question of easy access. He took a quick look behind him, saw no one, and swiftly hoisted himself over the gate.

The killer crossed onto the small covered patio, went straight to the sliding glass Arcadian door, and knelt down. From out of the bag he withdrew a thick bath towel and the pry bar. Norman fitted the tip of the bar into the aluminum frame near the lock, padded it with the towel, and levered the bar back smoothly. The lock snapped with a flat click, muffled by the cloth. He allowed himself a quick grin, slid the door open, and stepped into the cool interior.

"Thirty minutes will be more than enough," he said aloud, and set to work.

Twenty-four minutes later he returned to the truck. Settling into the driver's seat, he glanced at his watch.

255

"One down, one to go," he muttered, calculating the total effect of the work he had performed inside the house. There was no need to even follow up on it. The results would be spectacular, and terminal. He had no reason to doubt it.

He put the Chevy in gear and glided away from the curb, his business with Gordon Hatton pushed to the back of his mind. Tonight he would eliminate Luther Sitasy.

The office romance between Sheri Moradilo and Gordon had continued in a grand style. Captivated by each other, the couple had gone about the touchy business of making their first tentative meeting blossom into a firmer relationship.

Gordon shared Luther's concern and tightly held anxiety over the FBI investigation. He had taken to looking over his shoulder when working alone, and looking with suspicion at anyone from the investment department. His paranoia was calmed somewhat by Sheri's tender affections as she subtly cultivated the relationship, delighted to see it sprout and grow.

Her mother suggested to Sheri's father that Gordon might be The One, while her father looked on with a skeptical eye on this new interest in his daughter's life, the kind that could become permanent.

Sheri's married sister, Carol, shared their mother's opinion, while Carol's nine-year-old daughter, Nicole, took an immediate and possessive liking to "Uncle Gordon," further cementing the family's approval rating.

It was because of Nicole and Sheri that the end to Gordon's day had been accounted for. May fifth, Saturday, was Cinco de Mayo, Mexican independence day, celebrated by Anglos north of the border as well as by Hispanics in the south. Phoenix always had a variety of events going on throughout the day, and the fact that the holiday fell on a weekend made it all the more special. The festivities, which kicked off on Friday, would include a spectacular fireworks display at Patriot's Park, in downtown Phoenix. Gordon had promised to take Nicole and Sheri out to dinner after work, then to the park. He and Sheri had picked up her niece on the way back from the office.

Gordon drove the big Seville back to his neighborhood. He lifted his wrist to check his watch. "It's coming up on six. We'll just make a quick stop at the house. I have to drop off a few things first. Then we'll get something to eat before dark. Don't worry," he assured Nicole. "We won't miss a thing."

Even though it was early evening, it was still May, and official or not for the rest of the country, Arizona's new summer was in full swing. The sun would be up for another hour almost, extending the daylight substantially, providing a healthy atmosphere for the beginning of the weekend's fun.

Gordon slowed the Cadillac and nosed up onto his driveway. He left the garage door down. There was no need to pull in; they wouldn't be there that long. He braked to a gentle halt, turned off the engine, and pulled the keys from the ignition. He handed them to Nicole. "Would you do the honors?" he asked. "There're some things I have to get out of the backseat."

"Sure," she replied, bounding out of the car behind Sheri, who waited for her at the front of the car.

Gordon got out, opened the rear passenger door, and leaned in. He began stacking his dry cleaning and several packages together, things he had neglected to remove from the car for two days.

Sheri and Nicole walked up the side of the drive and across a path of Mexican paving stones to the front door. The nine-year-old jingled the keys in her hand, anticipating the fireworks to come. They stopped in front of the carved oak door and, after some quiet coaching from her aunt, Nicole found the right key, inserted it into the dead bolt above the handle, and turned it. She removed it, put the second key into the lock on the handle, and turned that one, too.

Gordon made to stand up, dropped two packages, then cursed as half of his dry-cleaned garments in their slippery plastic bags slid off the stack and onto the floor of the car. He surveyed the jumble, stood up, and called across the top of the car. "Hey, could I get a little help here?"

Both women paused, turning to look back. Sheri motioned in Gordon's direction with her chin, and Nicole took the cue. "Men!" she said, in her best exasperated tone, and rolled her eyes.

"Amen," Sheri replied, and watched her niece run back to Gor-

257

don's side of the car. She put her hand back on the doorknob, turned, and pushed.

Gordon leaned back into the car just as Nicole rounded the open rear door. He stacked three boxes and turned to hand them to the girl. She bent a little to accept the load. Then their whole world exploded in a violent purple thunderclap of sound and searing heat.

The instant Sheri pushed open the door, Norman's trap worked exactly as planned. The door moved in two inches, and three blue-tipped wooden matches, screwed to the bottom edge of the door under a piece of roofing shingle, flared across the square of sandpaper taped beneath them, igniting the gas from the four stovetop burners left open by Norman. The gas had had over eight hours to fill up the house.

The front, back, and north side of the structure blew out. The south wall, on the garage side, bulged out grotesquely from the force.

The hammering crack of sound sped toward the Cadillac with the concussive furnace heat of the shock wave, arriving in one awful millisecond of destructive time.

The force blew over, under, around, and against the two-ton weight of the big car, lifting it two feet into the air, pushing it sideways some ten feet off the driveway, to rest upright near what had been an eight-foot-tall saguaro cactus. The blast leveled the spiny plant at ground level. The tires on the Seville were shredded and smoking, melted to the rims.

Gordon's legs were knocked out from under him, clothing and flesh burned as if by a huge blowtorch. The breath was sucked out of his lungs by the ripping hurricane of flame, and the impact of the shock wave hurled the frame of the Cadillac against him, shattering his ribs and both femors. Then, in its lurching sideways hop, the open doorway scooped him inside the car, as if the machine had turned into an animal, eating him alive. But instead of killing him, the movement saved his life.

Nicole faired worse. The explosion pummeled her, the horrendous heat melting her spandex shorts to her legs and lower body, where the bubbling liquid fabric burned itself into the muscle and tissue.

The massive force pushed the car against her, and she took the

full battering crash in her right shoulder and head. The pounding
metal crushed her shoulder and splintered her skull, exposing the
brain. Her breath was pulled out of her slim body, replaced during
her wild, instinctive inhalation by searing heat that ate its way into
her lungs.

Mercifully, that blast of burning pain was all she felt, as unconsciousness claimed her, shutting her off as quickly as a light switch.

In the macrosecond of ignition, the hollow-core wood door of the
house had shivered, rippled, and exploded into a cloud of hyper-
velocity particles, which blew into and through Sheri Moradilo.
Human flesh and bone, up against the terrible thundering violence
of the explosion, stood no chance at all. Sheri disappeared instantly,
dead before her nerve endings could flash the message to her brain.
The largest part found later was a portion of ribs, affixed to a section
of bony spinal column, impaled on the thorns of a sweet acacia tree
187 feet away.

The houses on either side of Gordon's were partly destroyed, then
suffered the fire wave that followed on the tail of the explosion.
Burning debris rained down in a shower of ruin, and glass splinters
were blown into a dozen homes in the neighborhood.

Days later local children continued to make gruesome and sobering discoveries of bits of Gordon's house hundreds of feet from the
blast. Amazed at the distance covered, they occasionally found bits
of something else. They would stand staring until one of the less
adventurous went to find a parent.

In that quiet space of time that always seems to follow sudden
violent destruction, neighbors peered out from ruined windows or
stepped hesitantly down driveways to stand on the front walk staring
uncomprehendingly at the remains of the flaming pyre. But also in
such tragic situations, a few react immediately. Multiple phone calls
summoned fire and rescue help within minutes.

Even as the first distant sirens sounded the approach of what was
going to be a very long night, a small handful of Good Samaritans
approached the conflagration, found the two survivors beside the
ruined, smoldering car, and began to do what they could before the
professional help arrived.

• • •

Miles away, the perpetrator of the burning chaos was oblivious to the results of his sojourn that morning into the palm-lined middle-class neighborhood. Norman had planned correctly around the movements of his first target, with appalling, tragic results. Now he was preparing for the evening's work.

MAY 4, EAST HAMPTON, LONG ISLAND

Allen Parkman was not en route to meet Dana Quinn as the two of them had planned. In fact, for the last four days, since Norman Bloodstone's frightening visit to him, he hadn't set foot outside his home. Phone calls from his secretary had been answered in a voice leaden enough to convince her that he was sick, which was fairly accurate, considering the truth of it.

He had, after all, spent the first twenty-four hours of his self-imposed imprisonment in as drunk a state as forty-year-old brandy could produce. But visions conjured from dead files still filtered through his haze-filled temporary sanctuary.

The lawyer was a shadow of his former self. An amazing transformation had occurred in him in just a few days. But those days had been interminable and chaotic, filled with jagged snatches of terrible nightmares. Sleep, brought on only by total exhaustion, had occupied barely a handful of hours, lasting only as long as his overworked conscience would allow before it tore him to painful wakefulness.

He was far past regrets for his stupidity in trusting Dana. The first day had been spent wallowing in pity brought by what he'd seen on Norman's terrifying diskettes. Allen had cursed himself enough to have served whatever time in purgatory he figured was due him.

That peculiarly vicious mind-set had left him vulnerable for the next round, which delivered in a particularly cruel manner all the legal ramifications of his complicity in the murders. What the courts could not deliver as judgment, he had created on his own. It was a long and singularly horrible, gut-wrenching period, made worse because he knew what the system could really do to him.

But what followed that round was the worst, the hellish bottom, as he replayed the gory, bloody details of the murders so vividly described in Norman's precise narratives. The anguish this caused was finally too much to bear. He had struggled to find a solution, a desperate resolution to this disaster, trying one idea after another, each one failing until he arrived at the only one that offered the one slim hope for him.

Allen sat now in the sunlit study facing virtual obliteration, on a morning when all should have been right with his world. Before him, untouched except for the movements required to open the desk drawer and lift it out, lay a .357 Colt Python with a six-inch barrel, the brightness of the new day reflecting off its glossy blue-black finish.

Suicide was an option he had considered in the beginning and rejected. He didn't think he had the nerve to take such drastic action. Now he wasn't so sure. True, his internal voice agreed, using the weapon would certainly put an end to his problems. But that would leave Dana Quinn free of the torment she had caused, the torment she could not feel, would not feel, unless . . .

"And that, ladies and gentlemen of the jury, is the crucial issue here before you today," Allen suddenly said aloud, his voice harsh and ragged in the empty room. "For where is justice if we fail to punish the guilty?"

He knew that he was guilty—guilty of taking a chance, guilty of placing his lust-driven trust in Dana, guilty of refusing to question her when things seemed too good to be true. Guilty, guilty, guilty.

Fine, then, he agreed, for the hundredth, the thousandth, time. But what of Dana? The love of his life who had turned on him so savagely, tearing his heart to shreds. What would become of her? Why shouldn't she join him in his sentence? He had no response to the jury in his mind. The real question for consideration was this: did Allen Parkman have the fortitude to do what needed to be done?

The answer came back, like a verdict received, a unanimous decision. Shaking a little, Allen picked up the gun, put it back in the drawer, and rose from the desk. His decision had been made.

MAY 4, TPI, THE VILLAGE

At 6:00 A.M. Luther had patted Khanh good-bye and left him to guard the fort, certain that all was well. Mikki was staying with him for a week, but she would be at school most of the day.

The claimsman had set his mind to organizing the work awaiting him as he backed the Mach I out of the garage. He couldn't help thinking how close they were. But as he had explained to Jackie, not being able to control the investigation still caused him some bad moments. He and Gordon were basically along for the ride. He hoped it would be over soon.

He had worked straight through until late in the afternoon without a break. The day had turned into a marathon of management meetings to attend, departmental manpower surveys to complete, and personnel evaluations to review. He glanced at the digital clock on his desk, pausing to sip from a can of Coke. The electric blue numbers silently glowed 5:15 P.M.

Luther surveyed the surface of his desk, covered with stacks of binders and computer printouts, estimating the amount of work remaining. He leaned back, running his fingers through his thick hair. He knew Mikki had a study lab that wouldn't be over until about seven-thirty, so Luther figured he still had a couple of hours before leaving for home. He turned his attention back to the work on his desk. He thought about how he chastised his crew for working late, yet ignored the same rule for himself. One of the perks of the job, he thought ruefully.

Mikki Sitasy turned the nose of her Camaro R/S into the curved brick driveway of Luther's home and touched the garage door opener clipped to her window visor. It had been a long day for her, and she was tired from the three-hour study lab she had just finished after a full day of classes.

She parked the Camaro in the middle bay, climbed out quickly, and turned off the security alarm, using the touch pad near the passageway door to the kitchen. It reset automatically.

She had noted the absence of the ebony Mach I, but wasn't concerned. Luther had told her earlier that he might work late, and she had told him in turn to take his time, since she would be doing the same. They had agreed to order something out when they got together. Considering how beat she felt at that moment, letting someone else cook sounded like a great idea.

She entered the house and was greeted by Khanh, waiting just inside the doorway in his usual spot. The big dog made his affections apparent, and Mikki let him out through the patio doors to roam the grounds behind the house. She admonished him to behave himself while she went upstairs to her room for a quick shower and change of clothes. Khanh huffed once as she closed and locked the French doors behind him, then turned and trotted off into the darkness.

Norman was getting stiff sitting in the shadows of the low-branched mesquite tree. He had been there for a little over an hour, waiting for full dark, a hundred yards from Luther's house, in the best cover he could find without appearing out of place on the street. The homes here were exclusive and private, separated from one another by the meandering two-lane street. Unfortunately, his position blocked his clear view of all of the approaches to the house, and he failed to see Mikki's arrival, although she had driven right past him. Not knowing who she was, he hadn't registered the connection.

At half past eight, with a quarter-moon hidden behind thready high cirrus clouds, Norman was anxious to get started. His Porsche, retrieved earlier in the afternoon after he had returned the rental truck, sat half a mile away, in the parking lot of a small shopping strip off the intersection of Pima and Pinnacle Peak roads. He had parked there at twilight, and casually walked out of the lot, his appearance suggesting to anyone who noticed that he was just another jogger.

He wore low-cut black running shoes and navy sweatpants and shirt. Around his waist was a nylon belt pack, slightly larger than normal, but not out of place. Inside the bag were several other tools and odd bits, and the 9 mm Beretta. Stuck inside his waistband was the flat pry bar, hidden by the sweatshirt. A towel around his neck completed his ensemble.

Norman worked his way out of his concealed position until he was a hundred feet from Luther's property. He studied the house, noting the placement of the few interior lights he could make out. He checked the time again and reached into the belt pack. He withdrew a pair of rubber gloves and tugged them on over his long-fingered hands. His earlier stiffness had disappeared once he was up and moving.

The killer began to skirt the estate, following the high adobe wall until he was away from the inadequate light of the one streetlight nearby. Norman checked the top of the wall for infrared scanners and motion detectors. Finding none, he used a stand of desert pines to mask his actions as he scaled the wall.

He pulled himself up and over and lowered himself to the other side carefully. He checked the lights on the back of the house, noting with satisfaction that only a weak yellow glow emanated from the kitchen, his chosen point of entry.

Norman knew that most homes like this one had security systems. Many of them were hardwired into the phone lines. If the wire was cut, an alarm immediately went out to the monitoring location, and the police would be dispatched in minutes.

He had done his homework years ago and had learned how to circumvent many such systems. Adjusting the belt pack, Norman quietly moved over to the broad patio and up to the French doors. In a few seconds he located the magnetic contact points high on the inside edge of the door. He examined the setup and nodded, recognizing the system.

Aware of the time, he took out a small glass cutter and a two-foot length of insulated electrical wire fitted with alligator clips on either end. He also removed a tube of quick-drying epoxy glue.

Holding the glass cutter like a surgeon, Norman carefully carved a four-inch circle through the windowpane below the top frame of the door. Working quickly but methodically, he attached the wire to each contact point and secured the connection with a glob of epoxy. He put the items back into the belt pack and waited thirty seconds for the glue to set firmly.

Norman removed the flat pry bar from under his sweatshirt and hooked the curved end over his waistband. He pulled the towel from around his neck, balled it up against the serpentine handle, and inserted the flanged tip of the bar into the lock. He levered back slightly and snapped the lock, the towel deadening the crunching crack.

Moving with practiced ease, Norman replaced the bar, draped the towel over his shoulders, and eased the door open slowly, mindful of the limit of travel of the wire spliced to the alarm contacts. He withdrew the Beretta, fitted the suppressor onto the barrel, and checked to be sure a round was chambered. He rotated the safety up to the off position and stepped inside the house.

He surveyed the large kitchen, tuning his ears to the vibrations of the huge home, but heard no one. He hefted the gun and prowled out of the kitchen, hunting his prey. He had to wing this part of the plan because he didn't know exactly where he would come across Luther.

Norman entered the game room and was immediately struck by the furnishings, the quietly bubbling lights from the jukeboxes providing the only light in the large space. He looked up and, with surprise, noted the thirteen-foot airplane propeller suspended from the center of the domed ceiling.

"Jesus," he whispered, truly impressed. Seeing the sheer size of the place underscored Luther's wealth far better than reading about him on a computer record.

He passed deeper into the house, still unchallenged, feeling a nagging suspicion. Though he searched for almost ten precious minutes, Norman found no sign of his target downstairs. He entered the shadowed but deserted opulence of the living room, his senses wired tightly. Glancing up, he saw lights at the top of the sweeping staircase. Staying close to the curved wall, he ascended the gallery steps, pausing every few seconds to listen, straining to hear the slightest sound.

He reached the landing without incident and marked the hallway curving away, several doors visible opening off from it. His frustration at finding no one was building into anger, short-circuiting his caution. This wasn't the way it was supposed to go.

Norman cleared each room as he advanced, crossing from one side of the hall to the other. He found lights and noises at the fourth door. With a slow smile he gently tried the handle, found the door unlocked, and pushed it open. Sliding inside what was obviously a bedroom, he identified the sound of rushing water coming from the bath to his left. His eyes glittered with anticipation as he moved toward the partially open door.

Mikki finished rinsing her hair, turned off the water, and opened the frosted glass door of the shower stall. Her eyes widened in sudden terror at the sight of the tall man in the doorway, holding a gun in his right hand. She froze, then immediately reached toward the towel rack beside her.

"Allow me," Norman said, snapping a towel off the bar and holding it out to her. He let his eyes drag down Mikki's dripping body, lingering on her firm pink-tipped breasts and rounded hips. "Very nice," he said admiringly, then shut off his leer. "Too bad we don't have the time for extracurricular activities."

Mikki ripped the towel from his outstretched hand and hurriedly wrapped it around her shivering form. Her mind was in a whirl, her stomach fluttering in time to her heightened pulse. Thoughts of flight or fight alternated in rapid succession.

"Who are you?" she finally got out, a small part of her mind telling her that by talking she might stall him, buying time.

The stranger smiled again. "Excellent response," he said. "You've answered one question. There's no one else in the house, is there? Had Luther been home, you surely would have screamed for him."

With a sickening feeling she realized he was right and immediately berated herself for her stupidity. "Look, I don't know wh—"

"Out," Norman said, backing away, keeping the Beretta trained on her middle. "Down to the living room. That should do just fine."

The tone of his delivery did it for her. "Oh, God . . . what are you going . . . why are you doing this?"

266

Norman motioned with the muzzle of the pistol. "This way, if you please."

Mikki forced her legs to move, taking hesitant steps past him. She walked ahead of him out of the bath and through her bedroom, both hands gripping the bath towel tightly around her body. She tried desperately to think of a way out, to get away, but the presence of the gun behind her felt as big as a cannon. She walked down the hall and paused at the top of the gallery stairs. Taking a breath, not wanting to go down into the shadows below, she tried again. "Please, what is it you want!?"

"Want?" he replied, amused with her fear. "Your father, of course. He's the one I came for, but he seems to have missed the opportunity. Pity." He was silent for a few seconds, and she shivered again. "Maybe this visit won't be a total waste, though," he said, and tapped the muzzle of the suppressor against the banister. "Down, please."

She started to descend, holding the outside railing with a grip hard enough to turn her fingers white.

"Call it a calling card," he said behind her, far enough back to remain out of reach. But he wasn't worried about that. She didn't appear likely to want to try it. Norman laughed, a dry sound. "That's it," he added, "when you care enough to send only the very best."

They continued down into the muted shadows.

When the tip of the pry bar wrenched open the lock on the French doors, Khanh had been almost to the far back wall of the estate. The undulating acreage behind the mansion had been left in natural desert foliage, which obscured the big dog's line of sight to the patio, while the distance muffled the snap of the lock.

Khanh had gone about doing what dogs do and had gotten caught up in tracking an interesting scent or two among the rock formations and clumps of Pampas grass, following them farther back. His interest in the smells faded once he determined they posed no threat to his territory.

He was returning to the house, padding toward the patio, when the new scent hit him. His night vision was clear, and he saw the open door. All his instincts kicked into full alert.

267

True to his hours of special training with Luther, the dog made no sound as he crept into the kitchen and began tracking the intruder. Instinctively he had one mission: to find the stranger and stop him.

Tuned in to the house, knowing all its sounds, vibrations, and scents, Khanh's nose told him where the intruder had been downstairs. His ears told him the stranger was no longer there. The scent was much stronger toward the living room.

Quartering down the long passageway from the game room, he detected the faint wisp of steps coming down the gallery. He slowed, placing his paws deliberately, nearing the Moorish arch close to the foot of the stairs. His lips rippled silently away from his luminescent teeth. The hair on his withers ruffled, yet the black animal remained silent, his killing instincts moving into chest-thumping high gear. He paused under the arch, locked on to the descending sound of his target.

Mikki reached the bottom step and hesitated in the gloom, wishing she had turned on some of the downstairs lights. She hung back, not wanting to go farther, her little voice screaming its clarion warning.

Norman paused a few steps above her, near the outside railing. He looked around the great room, unable to make out all the details. "There," he said, pointing with the Beretta toward an ottoman. "Sit there." It would be as good a place as any to leave her for Luther.

Mikki walked slowly to it, a premonition blazing into painful clarity. She knew what he was going to do. She turned back to look at him, started to speak, and caught the movement that erupted from the dark. . . .

When Khanh saw them, his instinct and training exploded simultaneously. He took two fast running steps, gathered his great muscles, and launched himself at the intruder on the stairs.

Norman was looking down into the room to his right, watching Mikki. She slowed, began to turn to say something when the black thing came out from nowhere, slamming into his chest, spinning him off balance, knocking him down.

He crashed against the gallery wall, his shout dying in his suddenly constricted throat, surprise and fast reactions forcing him to throw up both hands, instinctively crossed at the wrists in front of his face. Primed to fire, the fingers of his gun hand constricted involuntarily, and the Beretta jumped in recoil, the whump of the shot almost lost.

In the same instant of impact, he heard the thing growl low down, a hideous rumble he felt vibrate against his own chest. Pressure clamped around his left forearm, pressure turning to pain, then to crushing agony as the wild thing lunged again and bit down harder. Reality fought to intrude through his overloaded senses and the pain in his arm, his brain trying to assimilate the startling avalanche of input as Khanh bit harder, wanting the throat of the man pinned beneath him, but needing to destroy the arm to get to it.

The searing pain spiked up a new level, lancing up his nerves, and Norman cried out, then screamed, trying to roll away, struggling and thumping on the stairs. Through the pain flashed the distant memory of the gun, pushing it into the forefront of his agony. Kicking under the weight of the dog, he wrenched his arm down, forcing the gun down, awkward with the length of the suppressor.

Their furious wrestling moved the two of them, Khanh still above, off the stairs and onto the carpeted floor. The movement was enough to allow Norman to twist the long, bulky muzzle around and aim it into the side of the vicious animal fastened to his arm. He started spastically jerking the trigger, the thumping cracks incongruously loud.

Khanh flinched with each one, felt the terrible heat drive deep into his side. Still he held on with murderous force, front legs spread wide, bracing with the effort.

Norman cried out again as the long teeth of the powerful jaws passed between the bones of his forearm and almost met. His whole arm went numb, and his finger jerked the trigger again.

Khanh, in a total killing frenzy, mortally hurt, felt the weakening of the arm, let it go, and drove for the throat, running on blood rage.

Heady with pain, Norman pulled the trigger for the sixth time. The 9 mm bullet crashed into the dog's heavy shoulder joint, shattering bone and splintered off, piercing the dog's pounding heart.

Khanh's desperate lunge brought his blood-glistening teeth into

Norman's neck, and he bit down just as the round went off. The shot convulsed his body, jerking his head back and down, even as his jaws pistoned together, dragging his teeth off, snapping along the soft skin to tear a long superficial gash.

The dog yelped with a high screech and arched away from Norman, who clumsily rolled away, scrambling quickly, pedaling away from Khanh. He propelled himself backwards into the edge of the bottom step, saw where he was, and pulled himself painfully up onto it. He cursed, his breath coming in short, ragged gasps, and stared at the dying throes of the animal.

Khanh, his body on automatic, his senses collapsing, lay twisted, his rear legs splayed out, upper body supported by his front legs. His head snapped around to bite at his left shoulder, trying to stop the hurt, numbing now as the dark veil slid down over his eyes. He slumped down, muzzle thudding onto the carpet. A spasm shook his black, bloody frame, and he was still.

Norman's chest heaved, and pain burned dully up his left arm. He cursed again at himself and at the dead animal. He dropped the Beretta, looked down, and became aware of the blood. Dark red rivulets ran unevenly but freely from the rents on his sleeve from Khanh's teeth. More blood from the dog glistened wetly down the front of his sweats and traced a grisly trail over the whiteness of the carpet to the dark mass of the beast.

A small, strangely calm corner of his overtaxed brain told him the steady flow indicated no artery had been punctured. He wouldn't bleed to death—at least not right away.

Remembering as if from a fog, Norman looked for the girl and saw her still form curled up next to the ottoman. Her towel had come partially undone, but he could see the bloody hole above her right hip, the bunched towel already soaked. He realized the stray round he'd fired when the dog hit him had scored, and he felt a glimmer of satisfaction. The girl's face was obscured by her wet hair, and he couldn't see her breathing. He didn't really care. His own battered body took all his attention. With an effort he began the slow process of damage control.

He managed to shove the gun back into his belt pack, grunting with the effort. Using his good hand, he helped himself up, steadying

270

himself when the room tilted for a few seconds. He held his damaged arm across his stomach, unable to feel his hand. He remembered the towel, found it lying on the steps, and wound it around his damaged arm several times, as tight as he could stand it. The bleeding slowed to a drip.

Norman stared down at the dog, ignoring Mikki. He had never been so frightened in his entire life. The feeling was new, raw, and devastating. It had happened so quickly. Completely shaken, drained of all energy, he walked unsteadily across the long living room to the entrance foyer's high double doors. Blood dripped from his torn arm, marking his passage. The laceration on his neck added to the growing stain on the front of his sweatshirt.

He leaned his back against the doors for a moment, thoughts of escape temporarily overridden by the throbbing pain, confusing him, making him almost forget his reason for being there. Norman no longer cared about anything but the pain. That and the man he had missed.

He rested, gripping the towel tightly around his arm, and tried to flex his hand. The thumb and first two fingers curled inward and then, reluctantly, the last two. He could barely make them out. "Son of a bitch," he mumbled, as he tried it again. At least he could move them. That rational part kept telling him he had somehow avoided nerve damage from the crushing injury, but the information barely registered.

His breathing was slower now, easier, but the fright remained, like the bad taste of an old penny sitting on the back of his dry tongue, and he couldn't swallow the taste away.

Norman held his good hand up before his face, fingers straight, and watched it vibrate. He tried to control it, willing it to stop, but couldn't. Then he felt it in his legs, a jumping twitch above the knees, weakening the joints, and he slid to the floor, his back to the doors.

He had never before experienced adrenaline shock, not once in his entire deadly, emotionless life. He had no way of knowing that what ravaged him now was simple biology, his physical body draining off its reaction to the combat it had just gone through. For the first time he was not in total control of himself, and he knew it. The knowledge scared him as much as his terrible fight with the black dog and the pain coursing through his battered body.

271

Fright flowed into anger as he considered how close the dog had come to taking him out permanently. As Norman felt his legs calming down, he focused on the man he had come to find. He had never botched a plan so badly before . . . never! All the hunts, the victims taken so cleverly, proved his abilities. He didn't miss, knew he shouldn't have here, and knew, with an absolute certainty that cut through the easing pain, who was at fault.

He looked around, nodding his head, understanding becoming clearer. He had come up with the right idea but had chosen the wrong ground. That was the only concession Norman was willing to make to his failure.

Taking on Luther was exactly right, but Norman had picked the wrong killing ground. Neutral ground was called for, a place where they would enter on equal terms. I have an idea about that, he remembered, coming more under control.

Norman flexed his arm and hand again, grimacing at the pain. He would be stiff in the morning, but functional. Good, because another idea had been awakened, one he was more intimately familiar with. Facing Luther was not just a matter of eliminating a road block. No, Luther was in the same category as Dana and Allen Parkman—those who had crossed him.

The word came easily, as it had when he had discovered Dana's treachery to him. Retribution, Norman thought. Retribution and finality. He envisioned a contest between himself and Luther Sitasy. And he would dominate.

This—he gazed around at the bloody scene in the living room— was no good. "Right idea, wrong place," he said aloud. Norman pushed himself up to a standing position. His inner reserves were coming on line, but he paused again while the room steadied. There's a reason for everything, he thought, and considered Luther. "And an end to everything, too," he said. "There'll be another time," he promised through clenched teeth. "Count on it, Luther."

Norman opened the tall door and, without looking back, left the wreckage, and the bodies, behind.

• • •

He emerged out of the tree line into the sodium-lit parking lot, the odd lights casting a purple haze on everything. He unlocked the Porsche and fell into the cockpit gratefully. His arm had settled into a steady throbbing, but there was more feeling in his hand and fingers, and the bleeding seemed to have stopped. But up close, if anyone had happened to see, he was a fright.

One-handed, he started up, got the car into gear, and caught a glimpse of his haggard face in the rearview mirror. He smiled with a grimace of pain, the reflection ghastly. Luther's will look the same, he promised, when we finally meet. He twisted the wheel and guided the car out of the lot onto Pima Road, driving cautiously. The last thing he needed was to be stopped by a cop.

Several miles farther south, Luther was just pulling out of the Village in the Mustang onto the same road. His "couple of hours" had been extended by a few more, but his reports were finally finished. He planned to stop and pick up a pizza on the way home. Later he and Mikki might watch an old movie together.

He was tired—tired of work, the profile, the investigation, and the pressure. As Luther slid the gear selector into drive, his fingers grazed the grip frame of the pistol. "Hell of a way to live," he said, hesitated a moment, and added, "again." Carrying the weapon had become second nature to him, but the reason for its presence in his life, the need for the protection it offered, remained unresolved. It ain't done yet, fella, he reminded himself, but he was surely getting tired of it. Tired of it all.

Luther turned on the FM and pushed the preset for an all-news station. His concentration wasn't up for any music. He just wanted something unobtrusive to fill in the background for him.

He had only half an ear tuned in as the quiet-voiced announcer ran over the headline news of the hour, noting a few local stories concerned with the valley-wide Cinco de Mayo celebration. As the local news continued, Luther picked up something about an explosion and fire at a residence late that afternoon. He was slapped back to sharp reality when he heard Gordon's name mentioned.

Luther's hand shot out, spinning the volume up, and he immediately backed off the gas, frowning as he coasted along. The rest of the story forced him off to a slow stop on the shoulder of the road.

"... Survivors of the huge explosion included the owner of the residence, Gordon Hatton, and Nicole Gilbert, age nine, the niece of Ms. Moradilo. Both are listed in critical condition at John C. Lincoln hospital. Sheri Moradilo, an acquaintance of Hatton's, was killed in the blast. Fire authorities are continuing to investigate at this hour, but have not ruled out the possibility of arson. Damage to the house . . ."

Luther sat stunned, all other concerns evaporating in the face of the shocking news. "Gordon? What the hell . . . Sheri dead? Ahh, damn!" All he knew at that instant was that his people were hurt. He immediately logged the question of how and why in the "to be considered later" column. What mattered was getting to Gordon and the little girl. And then a switch flicked inside him, a cold blade of certainty. He knew why.

"Arson," the announcer had said, and the answer was right there. His hands remained loose around the wheel while the thoughts raced through his brain, clicking into place.

He wondered how badly Gordon and Nicole were hurt. Whoever had done this might try for Jackie and Mikki, too. That was a remote possibility, he tried to tell himself, but he held on to the supposition. He had no choice. Sheri's loss was pushed down gently. He would deal with that later.

Once his people were accounted for and taken care of, he would phone John Paraletto. Something bad had happened, something very, very bad. And he was sure it had happened because someone had been careless. So much for trust, he thought bitterly. The failure hadn't been at this end.

He dropped the selector into gear and punched off the shoulder and back onto the highway, pushing the Mustang hard. Within seconds he was well over twice the national speed limit. In a few more, he was three times it. The coal-black machine rocketed up the road, sending a moaning howl before it. Both the car and its driver were into overdrive.

Luther braked to a halt beside Mikki's Camaro, his heart thudding, and climbed out quickly. He was rushing, feeling the edge, letting it take him along while he crossed to the door.

He turned the handle and opened the door, and the silence of the house rolled over him like a physical wave. There was no real way to describe that absolute absence of sound. But to his inner, more primal self, the effect was the same as that of screaming sirens. Luther froze, and in the space of his next breath, went into full-on, sense-heightened combat mode.

He released the door handle carefully, stepped back, and retreated to the car, continuing to face the doorway which eased closed on its spring-loaded hinges. He leaned into the open car window and drew out the 10 mm pistol.

He straightened, moved the safety off and checked the chamber for a loaded round. Holding the weapon barrel up, he approached the door again, opened it, and slipped into the hall, automatically registering Khanh's absence.

Luther eased toward the kitchen and, as soon as the room was in view, saw the open patio door. Keeping his index finger on the trigger guard, he cocked the hammer even as his eyes rapidly cleared the rest of the empty space. His ears strained for sound, his breathing slowed down to deliberate shallow inhalations, his nostrils flared to cut down even that tiny vibration of his own intake of air. Sweet adrenaline flowed into his system, adding an edge.

It all came back in an instant, the old and dangerous friend. Abilities never forgotten settled softly into place with unsurprising ease.

He left the kitchen, all of his senses probing the house, hunting for the source of his uneasiness. He longed to call out, but didn't want to reveal his presence. He moved silently through the game room, the bubble lights on the jukeboxes painting his impassive features with muted shades of melting color as he passed. Sensing something as he neared the arch to the living room, he paused in the shadows, listening with his entire being. He heard nothing, felt nothing. The house seemed dead to him.

Staying in the splintered patches of darkness, both hands wrapped around the pistol, he surveyed those parts of the domed room that he could see. The staircase was just past the corner. He peered slowly around the arch, and saw Khanh.

His heart leaped at the sight, vision telling the truth even before he detected the smell of blood and the sharper smell of gunfire. Luther took another step and his breath stopped.

"Mikki!" he said harshly, rushing to her, another part of him reporting that the house was safe, the danger had gone. He hushed further exclamations, hit the triple switch near the stairs, flooding the chamber with warm light, and knelt beside her. His civilized brain recoiled at the sight, her half-nude body lying on its side, the ugly dark hole above her right hip, purple-red blood still seeping out of it, soaking the carpet beneath her and the bath towel bunched around her.

The part of him that had been there before continued on, making the first cursory examination, gently moving her damp hair off her face, feeling for the carotid pulse first. He was rewarded with a faint tap back against his fingers, and he saw the slight, oh-so-slow rise of her chest.

"Single entry wound," he said aloud, beyond feeling anything hot, cold, or emotional. He reached under her gently, touching, feeling for the exit hole, and pulled his bloodied hand out when he didn't find one. "No arterial damage," he continued, judging by the dark color of his daughter's blood still oozing from the hole. Brighter, pumping red would have signaled more serious damage.

He reached for the telephone on the table on the other side of the ottoman, pulled it over, and dialed 911. With his other hand he picked up a dry part of the towel and pressed it firmly but gently against the wound. Mikki's breathing modulated for a moment, but that was the only reaction she gave him.

"Yes, this is Luther Sitasy," he began, talking precisely, wasting no time and no words. "I have a gunshot victim, my daughter," and gave his address, then answered the dispatcher's questions, starting the process to try to save Mikki's life.

"I'll be here," he told her, and requested that the police roll a unit as well. "Tell them I'm the homeowner and I do have a weapon." He described himself, what he was wearing, and where he would be in the room when they arrived. He wanted no accidents, no complications to get in the way of the paramedics, but he knew that the police would be there, too.

"I found my daughter, but whoever did it is gone. I don't want the police making any mistakes when they arrive. Just get them out here," he added, and hung up.

He checked the bleeding, then got up and ran up the stairs quickly, returning with a blanket, which he tucked carefully over Mikki and sat down beside her, keeping his hand pressed over the towel and bullet wound. He picked up the phone again with bloodied fingers, refusing to let the emotions come in, and dialed Jackie's number. She picked up on the second ring.

"Jackie? It's me," Luther said, not waiting for her greeting. "Are you okay?"

"Lute? Am I what? . . . Yes, why? What's hap—"

"Listen, babe," he began, using a gentle tone he didn't feel. "Mikki's hurt . . . bad." He cut off her exclamation. "She's here. I just found her. . . . She's been shot." This time he couldn't interrupt her anguished cry, and let her get it out.

"I don't know when, I just got home. She's in the living room. She's hanging in there, but it's ugly. It's on her right side. . . . Yes, I've called the paramedics and the cops."

"Oh, God, Luther," Jackie said, her initial outburst over. She clamped down on the hysteria welling up inside her. "What happened? Are you all right?"

Luther stared down at his daughter, bleeding beside him, then over at Khanh, and saw the matted mess on his side. "I don't know what happened, Jackie, but whoever did it killed Khanh, too." He heard her moan on the other end.

"Luther, what's going on . . ." She stopped. "My God, Lute, do you think this has anything to do with . . . ?"

"The investigation of the limits files?" he finished for her. "Yeah, I do. Somebody screwed up, Jackie, and this is just the beginning." He didn't tell her then about Gordon, Sheri, and her niece. There would be time for that later. But someone had been busy this day.

"Look, the medics are on the way. I don't know where they'll want to take her, but I want St. Joe's." St. Joseph's hospital had the best trauma care center in the city. "You'll never get over here in time. I'll call you when I know where Mikki's going. . . . Yeah, in a few minutes. I'll take the cellular with me. I'm going to have the cops send someone for you. No more chances, babe. Not anymore."

"Lute, is she . . . ?" Jackie didn't know how to ask the question. Personal involvement put an entirely different slant to tragedy.

"I don't know," he replied. "I really don't know. I've seen worse. I'm right here with her, and she's hangin' in there. Ah, Jesus, Jackie, this place's a mess. I'll call, okay? Right now I've got to get hold of Johnny."

The undulating sound of the sirens could be heard approaching. "Yeah, that's them. I'll let you know . . . yeah." And right before they disconnected. "Jackie? . . . I'm sorry. This is my fault."

Saying the words didn't help him. Only one thing would now. Whatever had gone on before, now it was personal. That was all he could concentrate on.

Luther picked up the 10 mm, ejected the magazine, and racked the slide back one-handed, thumb through the trigger guard, fingers curled over the slide, letting the chambered bullet fall out. He put all the parts on the table in clear view, leaving the gun open with the slide locked back, so the police would see them. Efficiency was one of the traits he had learned all those years ago. Then still holding his hand against Mikki, he dialed John's home number.

"John Paraletto," the agent said after the third ring. It was eleven-thirty at night in Virginia, and the call had shaken the agent out of sleep.

Luther took another slow breath, maintaining his concentrated purpose, still denying the emotions entrance. They couldn't help, not at all.

"Hello? This is Paraletto."

"John, Luther. Something's happened." His voice was a flat monotone.

The sound of it brought John fully awake. "Lute? What's happened? Where're you calling from?"

"Home, I'm at home." His gaze never left Mikki. God, she could be sleeping, he started to think, and slammed the thought away. "John, Mikki's been shot. No. Here, in the house. I just found her, Khanh, too. He's dead."

Exclamations were followed rapidly by questions, their delivery methodical, professional, structured to get facts in the face of trauma.

Luther's responses were not those of a man unable to cope with what he had just walked into, and John heard the difference.

"No, no, it's what I said. They've both been shot, Johnny. Yeah, Mikki once. The medics are about to kick down the door . Khanh . . . got hit several times. Looks like the old guy put up a pretty good fight. Christ, there's a blood trail runs clear to the front door. Yeah." The tears came then, but he kept talking. "Someone's walking around with a big piece of 'im missing."

Outside he heard the sound of heavy vehicles, powerful diesel engines shutting down, voices shouting, and doors slamming.

"They're here, John," he said, and shouted across the vast room for them to come on in, noticing for the first time that the tall double doors were already unlocked. He stayed rooted on the floor, holding his daughter. Men came through his door, big men who could have passed as linebackers, dark blue T-shirts with their logo on the upper chest, carrying the tools of their trade. They made straight for him. Behind them a pair of uniformed police stepped through cautiously, and followed, holstering their weapons.

"They've come for Mikki, John. I gotta go." The reality of the mayhem visited upon them this day slowed down his words. He rubbed a hand over his eyes wearily, as one of the medics motioned him gently away and knelt beside Mikki's quiet form. "They tried for Gordon, too. They missed, but Sheri's dead."

"Okay, buddy," John replied, "I know you have to go. Look, I'll get things going from here. You do what you have to, man. Lute, I'm sorry, honest to Christ. I'm coming out there now. We'll find you."

Luther moved farther back and let the medics work on his daughter. He shut out their professional patter and stood up holding the phone, watching them put needles into his little girl, oblivious to her nakedness, her hair still wet from her shower.

"Man, I got to go," he said for the second time. "Someone screwed up, John," Luther continued, unaware of Sheri Moradilo's innocent, and fatal, lunch conversation, "and it damn sure didn't happen here."

John heard the lack of trust and felt the stab go deep. "Okay, Lute, I hear you. We'll work it out, man. I promise you that."

"Yeah," Sitasy replied, "I will, too," and hung up.

279

It was back, that other self. Luther let it shut down the feelings one by one, hiding them behind the wall he had taken so long to break through. But though broken, the wall remained, always there, a part of him from another time. He labeled each emotion as he set it aside and turned it off, all the while answering the questions of the paramedics, then the police, then asking them to send someone over to Jackie's place.

It was better this way. After this was all over, he would take the feelings out, the parts that proved you were human, and start them up again. He knew how; he'd done it before. But the price to be paid for the road back was costly. Problem was the price on that bill never quite got paid in full.

Luther climbed into the back of the big square ambulance and sat as close to Mikki as the medics would allow. He had told them which hospital to take her to and had met no resistance. The pistol rested in the small of his back, inside his waistband. No one had argued over his taking it.

She was covered up now, and he approved of that. No one should see her that way. Now she had lines snaking under the blanket and a plastic mask on her face. A memory cycled past, and his older self noted, We never had all this stuff back then. Two of the medics hovered over her, working, checking, keeping Mikki alive, and Luther gave them room.

The ambulance swayed with speed, the sirens not as loud as he'd thought they would be. "C'mon, baby girl, hang in there," he prayed, his voice lost in the overhead noise. He knew she could hear him, and that was all that mattered. "Just stay with it, Mikki," and he held on to the handle on the enameled wall. "Just stay with us," he corrected, thinking of Jackie.

Norman collapsed on his bed, too exhausted to do anything else after spending the past hour patching himself up from the dog attack. Unable to seek professional treatment at an emergency room for fear of the questions his ravaged appearance would raise, the killer had been forced to attend to his injuries himself.

Luckily, as a result of the pharmacy connections he had made over the years to obtain black market drugs to use on some of his victims, he had also accumulated a respectable sampling of other medical supplies.

He had found some Betadine solution to cleanse the bites, while a few butterfly bandages sealed the holes, which had finally stopped oozing blood. A couple of sterile gauze pads secured with an Ace wrap, awkwardly done one-handed, had left him with a pretty fair approximation of what any hospital could have provided. The neck wound had been easier to clean and patch. Norman had added an injection of tetracycline.

He lay on his back, eyes staring, still clothed in his blood-spattered sweatpants and running shoes, his throbbing arm held across his bare chest. To get his mind off the pain, which was not as bad as it had been when he staggered through the door, he was trying to remember where it was he had seen . . .

"That's it," he said, identifying the source. He forced himself up, painfully favoring his arm, and walked slowly through the empty house to the living room. He sat heavily on the long couch and started pushing through the stack of glossy magazines promoting the fun things to do in the Valley of the Sun.

"Here it is," he said, stopping at the right one, the rest of the stack now strewn haphazardly over the table and the floor. He flipped through the pages, looking for the article, remembering the pictures, and found it.

"Phoenix War Museum Set to Open Memorial Day," the headline said. Four pages of color pictures augmented the article about the project.

It was an ambitious endeavor, this theme park devoted to America's major wars of the century. A parcel of land far out on the west side of the valley, over a mile long, would depict in chronological order scenes of the First and Second World Wars, Korea, and Vietnam. Battlefields would be replicated in detail, as would be authentic villages, with actors depicting civilian life indigenous to each area. The public would be able to stroll or ride through, passing from one era into the next.

It was called a living museum, one of the first of its kind anywhere in the world. It was funded both by grants and by extremely generous

281

private benefactors. It was already being touted as a showplace to rival Gettysburg and the like.

But only one part of it interested Norman. "Vietnam," he said, studying the pictures for some time. "An appropriate place for Luther Sitasy to end up."

He could see it in his mind's eye: two hunters—warriors, actually—playing out the ultimate game. The choice of ground would allow Luther a chance to use what he had once been good at, according to his record. And it would allow Norman to stretch out his own considerable skills.

The outcome was preordained, of course. He would play with Luther for a time, then kill him, eliminating the last obstacle. Gordon was out of the picture, according to the news Norman had heard earlier, all of the money was safely locked up in his personal account in Georgetown, and Dana and Allen were well out of the way.

Luther would be his last piece, the final move in the match, and what a match it would be. Young skill versus older experience, and may the best man win. And he would, Norman thought confidently. He would.

He looked at the clock on the mantel across the room. It was very late, the end of a long, hard day. He needed a few hours' sleep. There was a great amount of work to be done. He pulled himself up, feeling the weight of the day through his entire battered body, thought better of it, and fell back full length on the couch. He was asleep in seconds.

MAY 5, SINGAPORE

Twelve thousand miles away on the other side of the world, it was Saturday morning.

Deacon Drachman, after almost twenty hours in the air, took a taxi to his hotel, the Hilton. The early morning hour brought with it the weighted heat and humidity of the Pacific climate. Anticipating such weather, Deacon had packed accordingly, but he suffered in the taxi ride in his Western suit. The driver, in a clipped British accent, apologized for the breakdown of the car's air conditioning.

Deacon checked in without trouble, went to his room, and settled in quickly. His plan was to check out the offices of Kallang that day, on the off chance they would be open. He took a long shower, washing off the graininess of the flight, called the front desk for a wake-up call two hours hence, and went to bed. He only needed the minimum of sleep to restore his stamina.

Two hours later, refreshed and dressed in a conservative short-sleeve shirt and walking shorts, he left the hotel with a pocket map of the city in his hand. Ambling along the incredibly clean, wide boulevard with their abundance of tropical gardens, he felt like a character from an Ian Fleming novel. His stomach, after enduring five airline meals, was just now coming around to feeling normal. He decided he would eat later. His internal clock was still playing catch-up. Still in all, the day was marvelously bright, with an on-shore breeze that seemed to ease him along the wide streets.

Old-world charm coexisted with angular modernity in the gleaming new architecture of the downtown area. The relaxing atmosphere of the streets made him forget his purpose for a short time. Deacon was abruptly nudged back to awareness when he recognized the office building address before him. His strolling gait had led him to the intersection of Victoria Street and Basah Road, and Kallang's building.

The building was an old brick-and-stone affair, a modest six stories tall, lending an old colonial aspect to its place on the tree-shaded boulevard. He entered the cool, quiet lobby and found Kallang's floor and suite number on the brass plaque set into the wall near the two elevators.

Deacon rode up to the third floor, then stepped out and right, following the discreet brass direction signs toward Kallang's suite. The occasional artificial light in the hallway was augmented by large floor-to-ceiling windows at both ends of the building.

Almost at the end of the corridor he found "Kallang, Ltd." in gold relief on a replaceable placard at eye level on the heavy, satin-oiled mahogany door.

He tried the S-curved door handle and found it locked, as he expected. Through the opaque glass of the transom above the door, he could make out the glow of outside light, but there was no hint of electric bulbs within. He stepped back, looking for some posting of office hours, when a voice interrupted him.

"May I be of assistance?" the voice called out, in proper, educated British tones.

Deacon turned to watch a man, in his early thirties, he guessed, approach from the elevators. He was of medium height, dressed in a short-sleeve tropical-blend white shirt, knotted striped tie, and impeccably tailored dark gray pleated slacks. He carried a well-worn russet briefcase in one hand. In the other was a set of keys.

Receiving no reply to his query, the man slowed, glanced at Deacon, and repeated his question.

Deacon replied with one of his own. "Excuse me, but do you work here? For Kallang, Limited, I mean?"

The man hesitated, not expecting the question. Deacon knew his guard was up by the slight narrowing of his eyes.

"Yes, I should think so." The man set the briefcase down, appraised Deacon once again, and offered his hand. "Graham Aderlan, I'm office manager and chief broker for Kallang. And you are . . . ?"

Deacon took Aderlan's hand. "Emil Drachman," he said, releasing his grip and fishing his wallet out of his back pocket. "I'm with the United States Securities and Exchange Commission, and I've come a long way to see you."

Graham smiled slightly and looked at the proffered identification, satisfying himself that it appeared genuine.

"I suppose you have at that, come a long way, that is. Only I wouldn't have the slightest idea why you would want to." Graham stood his ground, waiting for Deacon to speak.

Following his hunch, Deacon went straight to the point. "The SEC is conducting a joint operation with the Federal Bureau of Investigation into a series of apparent murders, all connected to the financial practices of a company titled Trans Patriot Insurance."

There was a look of confusion on Graham's face. "TPI? That's one of my better clients." He paused for a moment. "Murder? I'm not sure I quite get the connection with Kallang."

"I was hoping we could talk about that," Deacon said, trying to get a feel for the man.

"I'm afraid that's not really possible without a proper warrant. Our records are private, you see, but I suppose you know that. Still, Trans Patriot is a valued client, and I should like to avoid anything that impacts on that relationship. I would need substantially more information than the little you've mentioned. Now, if you will excuse me, I've some work to do."

Graham made to pass by Deacon and unlock the door.

"Look, Mr. Aderlan," Deacon said, touching him lightly on the forearm, "I realize this is very unusual, having a perfect stranger appear out of nowhere and tell you something as far fetched as this must sound. But let me assure you, the United States government didn't see fit to send me halfway around the world to threaten you in the middle of this hallway with some imaginative story."

Graham stopped turning the handle and looked sideways. "Very good, Mr. Drachman, a most impressive speech. The almighty bloody American veiled threat. It must work on those Third World types. Here, however," he said, gesturing at the door with a nod of his head, "it carries little weight. I've been about for a few years, seen quite a bit, actually. You're way out of your jurisdiction."

Deacon began to think his first impression had been wrong, but he gauged the broker's reaction, and it seemed natural enough. He would have acted pretty much the same so far, whether or not he had something to hide. "I didn't come here to argue with you, Mr. Aderlan. If need be, I can arrange to shut this brokerage down in a heartbeat and seize every scrap of paper in it equally as fast. I'd like to avoid that. You must believe there is solid evidence that some of the business transactions brokered by Kallang, involving an American insurance corporation, are directly linked to several murders for profit.

"This is highly irregular, I grant you," Deacon continued, "and as you stated, I'm out of my jurisdiction. These matters have a way of steamrolling, once started. The body count tallied up can be most impressive." He paused to see how his words were being taken. Graham stared back, unmoving, but still listening.

"As it stands right now," Deacon continued, "any direct, deliberate participation of your office is unknown, but I venture to say that the proper authorities would look upon your involvement as highly suspect, given the evidence we have. Now, sir, you can take that as

285

a threat, if you wish, but if I were you, I would choose my next words carefully."

Graham looked at him with open hostility as the rebuke stung him. But he wasn't cowed by Deacon's presence or by his story.

"By rights, I should have representation here, you know that."

"That's entirely up to you, but if you'd rather go inside and let me ask a few questions, we might just get through the unpleasantness without a lawyer, for now." Deacon then gave him his out. "All I want to do is ask my questions. Whether you decide to answer or not is up to you. None of what you tell me is on the record, and none of it will, or can, be used to your detriment. I'd have to testify to that. You have the right to counsel. The decision is yours."

Graham considered the younger man's proposal, still confused over the premise. None of it made sense. None of it, that is, except the seriousness of this fellow, he thought. It was the first glimmer that something might indeed be wrong here.

He pushed open the door and waved Deacon in. "Done," he said in reply. "I believe you Yanks call this cooperating with the authorities. I'll do what I can to help you, Mr. Drachman, subject to restrictions over which I have no control."

"Thank you, sir. I couldn't ask for more than that," Deacon said.

"Really?" Graham replied dryly. "I believe you've done just exactly that. Now come in and tell me the whole story."

Two hours later Deacon returned to his hotel, considerably more informed on the workings of Kallang, Ltd., and just as sure that its manager was not directly involved in the fraud or the killings. Aderlan had been used. That much seemed apparent, Deacon thought, striding across the lobby of his hotel, but that was the extent of it.

He requested a fax form at the front desk and began writing quickly: "John, I believe I have the connection. It's too complicated to explain now. I'll give you details upon my return. I'm on my way home as we speak. We'll have to handle this end by the numbers. Time to rock and roll, folks. Deacon"

He added his flight number and schedule, provided John's number at the Bureau, then returned the form to the desk. In minutes he was handed the confirmation.

Deacon walked to the elevators, thinking about Graham Aderlan, hoping he would be all right after the smoke cleared. It was coming together, finally.

MAY 5, MOON VALLEY, PHOENIX, ARIZONA

Norman awoke with a start in the pre-dawn darkness, sore all over, his position on the long couch virtually unchanged since the night before. He groaned, more from exhaustion than from the ache in his arm. He raised the bandaged arm, tentatively trying it out, expecting the worst. Surprisingly, it didn't feel that bad. Movement was un-restricted, though stiff, and judging from the deep tissue throbbing, he reasoned that he would need a diet of Tylenol, three at a time, for a while.

Norman allowed himself a good stretch, sending the wake-up call down the length of his muscles, feeling each system check in. The sight of his ruined jogging pants, coupled with the stale smell of his body, was almost repugnant. That situation was easily remedied. He struggled up off the couch and headed for the bathroom.

His plan for Luther Sitasy, though, that was something else. He had work to do.

An hour and a half later Norman sat staring at the cellular phone. He had the number, but it had taken a few calls to track Luther down. Hospitals can be so damn closemouthed, he thought. But it would be all right. He looked out the window at the dawn light emerging. The day would be fantastic, in fact.

"Except for Luther Sitasy," he said aloud, and turned his gaze to the sniper rifle. The FAL was a thing of pure beauty, so lean and black and deadly accurate. He had become intimate with it of late during his practice sessions. Today he would show Luther how good that was. He idly tapped a fingertip on the long barrel, wanting to achieve the right psychological impact with his call. "Soon," he mused quietly, alone with his singular thoughts. "A few more minutes."

The Gulfstream II, bearing a small discreet U.S. flag on its white vertical tail, slid in for a landing at Sky Harbor airport thirty seconds in front of a loaded United L-1011 from San Francisco.

It rolled passed the civilian terminals, taxied over the north set of active runways, and came to a stop at the single-story brick executive terminal near the airport entrance off Twenty-fourth Street.

John Paraletto, along with agents Paul Gorley and Dale Reichley, climbed down the short steps, to be met by the special agent in charge of the Bureau's Phoenix office, Steve Drexler, and his second-in-command. The SAC was in his mid-forties, of average height with gray hair, a Bureau veteran with twenty years' experience.

The five of them huddled for a moment or two, making introductions, their heads bowed in discussion to compensate for the jet noises. To the casual observer, they appeared to be average businessmen, discussing some venture. There was the occasional nodding of heads to various questions while Steve spoke occasionally into his small portable tactical radio, giving orders and listening to the responses.

The meeting broke up, and they all climbed into a navy blue Ford Aerostar. A second, similar van followed, carrying their luggage.

Inside the lead van, seated in the front passenger seat, Steve turned sideways to talk with the Washington agents, John in the middle seat, Dale and Paul in the back. All three listened as the SAC continued his explanation of the new situation they were facing.

"We've sealed the scene at Luther's, and they should be about finished up by now. The body of the dog is with the pathology people."

John nodded, looked outside the van, then at his watch, concerned with the amount of light already at six-thirty in the morning. "What's the word on Mikki Sitasy?" he asked.

"She's out of surgery," Steve said, "but otherwise not good. The bullet went through the upper lobe of her liver. She's got a lot of damage. They won't know for a few days yet how bad."

"Will she make it?" Dale asked.

Steve shrugged "She's made it this far, but she's critical. You know how that can go."

"Where's Luther now?" John asked. "At the hospital?"

Steve nodded "All night. His wife, too."

"Ex-wife," John corrected.

"Ex-wife," he acknowledged, and continued. "You know she's a news producer for NBC out here. Her station's had a team working the incident at the Hatton residence."

John nodded. The media had to find out sooner or later, but maybe the information could be controlled, with Jackie's involvement.

"Anyway," Steve continued, "she seems to have the whole story so far. Seems like Luther told her all about it some months ago." It was obvious that he thought that any possible leak about the Bureau's case had come from Jackie.

"I don't think she's the source," John said, answering Steve's unstated supposition. "Still, I think we had better discuss this with her. Keep in mind one thing."

"What's that?"

"That's her daughter lying in that hospital room."

Steve nodded. "Luther, though. He's something else."

"Meaning?" John asked.

Steve shook his head once. "It's like this. I met him when we put the team in the hospital. You expect people to act a certain way when these things happen. Luther's not like that. He's a little wired, but under control, like he's been through this before."

"He has," John said, simply. "What's the status on the house explosion?"

Steve shifted in his seat, disregarding the seat belt for the moment. They were on Central Avenue, heading for St. Joseph's.

"Local fire marshal's office and police have been amazingly cooperative on this one," he said. "Initial report is confirmed so far. Fire and explosion were arson. A set of do-it-yourself incendiary triggers, wired to two different entrance points of the house. Looks like the one on the front door blew. It's all still preliminary, but the perp apparently came in through the back patio doors, set the devices, and turned on all the gas burners on the stove. Crude but effective. The point of entry was similar for Luther's house."

"What's Hatton's medical picture?" Dale asked.

"He's still critical. He's got third-degree burns on his legs and back, fractures to both legs, some internal injuries, and inhalation burns, pretty deep. His chances are fifty-fifty."

"And the little girl?"

Steve paused, looked out the side window, and silently shook his head. "She died an hour ago."

The Aerostar turned onto the hospital's long semicircular drive and braked in the shadows cast by a group of tall date palms near the entrance.

The five agents got out and entered the lobby. Three minutes later they emerged on the seventh floor, the surgical intensive care ward, where two more agents met them.

"Luther's down there," Steve said, leading the others down the hall.

They found him dressed simply in a light gray sweatshirt, sleeves pushed up, faded jeans, and well-worn white sneakers. The change of clothes had been brought by another agent earlier. Luther had refused to leave the hospital since arriving almost seven hours ago.

Steve slowed as the group approached to allow John to move forward. He went straight to his old friend, who was standing outside a closed door. They shook hands slowly. This time there were no brotherly hugs.

"John," Luther said in quiet greeting.

"Lute," the bigger man answered, "I'm sorry . . ." he began, but Luther shook his head.

"No, man, we're past that. I shouldn't have jumped down your throat. Let's just get on with business, okay?"

John nodded, feeling the rift between them, saddened by it. While Luther greeted the others, John's professional eye swept over him. Other than some redness around his eyes, Luther didn't show a hint of the strain he had been under or the tragedy that had been visited upon him. He looked long at his friend and asked, "You get any sleep?"

"Some, while Steve's boys here did their thing. Figured it might be a while before I got any more, the way things are going. Johnny, what the hell happened? Who leaked the investigation?"

"I don't know, Looter. That's what we're here to find out. Where's Jackie?"

Luther hooked a thumb toward the door. "Inside with Mikki." Surprisingly, he spoke with normal inflection in his voice, but John saw the look in his eyes. It was unmistakable, and all too familiar. They had shared it once before.

John looked past Luther at the door to Mikki's room. "Any change with . . . ?"

Luther shook his head. "Not yet, John. She's . . ." He inhaled and held his breath for a few seconds, then let it out slowly. "Mikki's holdin' on, but she's torn up pretty badly inside, I mean . . ."

"Lute, listen, we're putting this together fast now."

Beyond John and Luther, Steve Drexler was conferring with two of the people from his staff. He nodded and then spoke quietly into the handheld radio.

Luther seemed not to have heard John's statement. "I put Mikki in danger," he said. "I should have been there, and I wasn't. So Mikki paid for my actions. So did Khanh, the poor old bastard."

John let him talk. There wasn't much point in interrupting.

"He wanted it this way," Luther said, knowing deep down that the killer was a man. "He didn't find me, so he did that to my daughter." Luther put his hands into his back pockets and stared down at the floor, tapping idly at something on the tile floor with a toe.

All the time he was talking, John was examining his friend, recording the signs. Luther was operating in mode, taking it all in. John thought back to the last time he had seen that look. It had been twenty years.

He had started to reply when the door to Mikki's room opened and Jackie walked out. Her face showed much more clearly the strain of the past hours. Like Luther, she was dressed in simple casual clothes, hastily thrown on. Luther immediately went to her, putting his arm around her shoulders, waiting for her to speak. The way they stood together spoke of other issues resolved.

She shook her head. "She's still out. They say it could be hours before she can respond." She saw John and greeted him.

"John, how are you?" She spoke automatically, with little emotion. Her voice was tired, husky with fatigue. She had stopped crying a while ago. "Lute said you'd be coming out." She paused, and took a breath. "Because of Michelle."

It was the first time she had used her daughter's given name. It sounded strange to Luther, but he knew why she'd used it. A distant voice said sadly, She's just getting ready . . . for the memories, if Mikki doesn't . . . Luther turned his attention back to the living. He wasn't ready to write his daughter off, not nearly.

John hated this part of the job the most, doubly when the victim was someone he knew. And he had known these two people for a long time.

"Jackie, I'm sorry. Saying that is not enough, I know. It never is." They were the expected words, the only ones he had. That angered him, and he said it again. "It's not enough, Jackie . . . you too, Lute. But I promise you both, we will catch this guy. Whatever happens from here on, that's a given."

Jackie held on to her husband, aware that she thought of Luther that way again. She knew that had been coming, without any special prompting from either one of them. It was just the way of things, she supposed, content to let it happen. A part of her was cautious from the memories left from the first failure, but another part of her was curious to see if they could find each other again. Would their relationship be the same? It just felt right, but dear God, what a horrible way for it to happen.

Luther stood quietly beside her. It was so simple, really, he thought, wishing he could feel happier than he did. But his ability to enjoy normal reactions, emotions lit up by the beautiful things in life, had been suppressed. He had an entirely different feeling now. He thought of only one thing, and kept his thoughts to himself. So why now, and why like this? Why did tragedy have to be the motivating force?

John cast a glance over to Steve, who was quietly listening to the radio he held beside his face. Steve gave an imperceptible shake of his head. Not yet, he said silently.

John felt the tension. It was time.

MAY 5, MOON VALLEY, PHOENIX, ARIZONA

Phil Goff, the leader of the hostage rescue team assigned to Phoenix, made his final check, listening to his men confirm on the net that they were in place.

All eleven of them wore full tactical gear, face shields attached to their helmets, double-layered vests, the usual complement of flash-bangs and more serious hardware. Half of them carried CAR-15s, the short-barreled M-16 version, while the others had H&K MP-5s, 9 mm submachine guns, standard-issue items for fast in-and-out work like this. They also carried the new 10 mm pistol developed by the SOARS unit.

None of the neighbors near the big ranch home in the quiet cul-de-sac had been up and about to witness the silent invasion by the heavily armed team. Even so, before first light a dozen uniforms from the Phoenix PD had quietly and efficiently evacuated the small number of confused civilians who might have been in harm's way.

The tall black agent standing with the team leader temporarily wore his CAR-15 across his back while he waited patiently with the .10-gauge Remington pump. It was loaded with special steel-and-copper solid rounds designed to destroy the hinges on almost any door known. The shotgunner was pumped, psyching himself up for action.

The team leader nodded to himself, then pointed to both places on the carved wooden doors and said, "Go!"

The shotgunner fired at the bottom hinge first, obliterating it in a shower of blue smoke and splintered bits. He then racked the slide, riding the recoil up, and blew out the upper hinge, all in five-tenths of a second.

He stepped quickly out of the way as two other agents, carrying a heavy steel four-foot-long ram, six inches in diameter, charged the battered doors, slamming the foot-square end plate of the ram into

293

the wood, pushing the doors off the frame to crash resoundingly into the front entranceway.

Around the sides and back of the rambling ranch house could be heard the sound of shattering glass, the heavy crack of windows and other doors being forcefully violated by concentrated blunt force, and the whump of concussion grenades designed to blind with their blast and deafen with their detonation.

Black-uniformed men raced into the house from half a dozen different points of entry, weapons out, safeties off, selector switches rotated to full auto. They took no chances with this one; their suspect was considered extremely dangerous. They were not to give any quarter, if it went down that way. Steve Drexler's order to the team leader had been simple: if the suspect resisted, shoot to kill.

In seconds it was all over. Agent Goff stood, barely breathing hard, used to the adrenaline rush. The assault had been well planned, though they'd had only a few hours to prepare for it, working quickly in the last hours of the night. He called out to his men once again, clearing them one by one over the radio net, ensuring that all were safe, taking their reports until the news was in and confirmed.

"Damn it!" he said in disgust, snapping his weapon back on safe. He looked around the living room one more time, trying to will the object of their assault to be there. It was no use this time.

"Call it in," he said, pulling off his helmet one-handed. "Tell him we missed the suspect. Norman Bloodstone's not here."

John and Steve were standing together, in that calmness of professionals waiting for information. Luther and Jackie remained a few steps away, caught up in their own waiting and in their own thoughts. Jackie's thoughts were of her daughter, and she remained painfully optimistic. Luther thought of darker things, his ears only half hearing the muted conversations around him and the faint hospital sounds.

The two agents were making small talk about facts uncovered so far. John was recounting to the SAC the peculiarities of the double homicide in Santa Fe.

Luther overheard something about the autopsies, the coroner's

294

opinion, and the killer's hand width. The words slipped inside his thoughts, barely registered, then shot into the forefront of his mind.

"What?" he said suddenly, whipping his head toward them. "What did you say about his hands?"

Both men stopped to stare curiously at him, and John replied, "Hands? Oh, the handprints. The victims both had these bruises from the killer's hands, indicating a long finger span." He saw something stir inside Luther and took a step closer. "We found similar marks on the Pittsburgh victim. . . . What's the matter, Lute?"

The information slipped into place with an almost audible clunk, and he had it. It was so obvious that Luther felt anguish at his blindness—blindness that had killed more people, blindness that had left Gordon, and now Mikki, close to death.

He whirled and slammed his fist against the wall, hammering it in time to his words. "It makes sense," he said through gritted teeth. "He had access! That's why he left." Then the thought flowed into the natural progression of Norman's relationship to Dana as the truth revealed itself to him. "Oh, God, it's Dana, too!"

John instantly caught the name. "What do you know about Dana?" he asked, and felt Steve step up beside him, both of them facing Luther, who began to calm down.

Luther reached over to Jackie, pulling her close, his grip firm around her middle, reinforcing his discovery. He looked at her, at her questioning face, and answered John while looking into her worried eyes.

"Dana Quinn," he began. "It makes perfect sense, so perfect I had myself convinced it couldn't be that close. She works in the investment department . . . *investments!* Where else would you expect to find greed? She had access to the claim files too; it had to start there."

Jackie looked back, not following, but understanding glimmered a little, as she drew strength from the conviction in Luther's face.

He turned to John. "Gordon was right all along. Oh, man, I'm sorry. I got fixated on this whole corporate thing, when it was so much more basic than that. It was pure greed. Blood for money. The killer's a guy named Norman Bloodstone, Dana's lover. Check him out; he's got to be the one. It's the hands, Johnny, don't you see? He has these extraordinary hands."

But instead of showing surprise, John only looked back and said simply, "We know. You're right, Lute."

"God damn it!" Steve swore suddenly, his expletive precise and angry. He held the portable radio to his ear.

John started to ask what was wrong, but Steve interrupted him. "They missed him," he said, still listening to the after-action report from his team leader at Norman and Dana's house. "Norman wasn't there," he said. He continued listening, fingertips touching the tiny earpiece attached to a thin wire coiled into the collar of his suit jacket. "Understood," he said into the radio's mike. "Secure the site. Notify the investigation team to come on in."

Steve brought John up to date. "Looks like the suspect boogied just before the tac team got there. They're itemizing everything now, and they say there's a ton of evidence, especially in Norman's study. Your people are tracking down the financial analyst?"

John nodded. "Deacon has a scheduled stop in Hawaii. I've requested a military courier pick him up and fly him straight here. The navy agreed to pull one of their birds out of Barbers Point." He checked his watch, calculating the time difference. "With luck, they'll have him here by midafternoon."

That information fit with the SAC's plans. "Okay. I'll have them bring Deacon in to Luke AFB. We'll get him to the site from there." He turned back to pass on his information to his people still in the field.

Luther heard their exchange and felt sure they were all on the right track. "All right, John," he said, "what's . . . ?"

John waved his hand. "I'm sorry, Lute. I couldn't tell you until we knew." He took a breath before starting. Things had been happening rapidly over the past few hours. He included Jackie in what he was about to say.

"A lawyer named Allen Parkman walked in off the street to the New York City field office yesterday evening. He was the connection Deacon confirmed in Singapore, the man who filed all the licensing agreements for Kallang, Limited. Basically, he was a third partner in the scheme to rip off the policy limits reserve money."

Luther started to react, but kept silent as John continued.

"Parkman had two partners, Lute, both connected to Trans Patriot,

296

just as Gordon surmised. One was the outside guy, Norman Blood-stone; the other was the inside contact, Dana Quinn."

Luther's face showed no surprise, only failure for not having be-lieved his friend and associate. "I should have listened to Gordon. He had it nailed right from the start."

Jackie looked from Luther back to John, now sure of the signifi-cance of these new names. "You mean the two of them . . . ?"

John paused, remembering the conversation he'd had with the agent who had interrogated Allen Parkman. His description of Park-man's fear of Norman had been balanced by his hatred of Dana Quinn, whom he deemed responsible for dragging him into the mur-der conspiracy.

"That's right, Jackie. She selected the policy limits files at random, and Norman figured out how to kill them. At least, that's what the lawyer told our people. Seems Norman knew nothing about Allen's involvement. It's a bit complicated, but Allen controlled some sort of trust account for Dana, which supplied her the seed money to create Kallang, Limited, with Norman. Kallang's a brokerage that Quinn and Bloodstone created to launder the funds—the policy limits re-serves invested through Trans Patriot."

"It's almost perfect," Luther said, seeing it all clearly now. He had motive and names, but more than that. Now he had a target.

Jackie was following along, seeing the pieces fall into place, but there were still gaps. "If they were all partners, why did Allen go to the FBI?"

John addressed her question. "Dana kept his presence a secret from Norman, for reasons we're still not sure of. Anyway, Norman found out, presumed Allen was a threat of some kind and that Dana had lied to him. So last Wednesday Norman showed up at the law-yer's place on Long Island and confronted him."

Jackie was confused for a moment. "To kill him?" she asked. Obviously it didn't happen. Allen had survived.

John shook his head. "That's what Allen thought, too. But appar-ently Norman figured out that the lawyer didn't know anything about the killings. So he told him the bad news."

John smiled thinly and continued. "He showed Allen computer records he kept of each murder, pretty grisly stuff, Parkman said, almost like trophies. He did it to prove to Parkman how much trouble he was really in, and to prove that Dana had lied to him, too. She knew Allen would never have stood still for the murders. He was greedy, but he wasn't a murderer. Norman also wanted him to know how outclassed he was. Allen said he took some pleasure in grinding him down, and then pointed to Dana as the real villain. I guess the technique worked."

"It was all revenge, then," Jackie said, trying to make some sense of all this.

Luther kept his emotions in check, still dealing with the revelation of who had been responsible for all of this tragedy. "Dana was at TPI all the time. I saw her, passed by her, but never had the slightest idea she was . . ." His anger coiled tighter inside, but he reined it back. Maintain, he cautioned himself. Keep a handle on it. Still, it was obvious that Norman had tried to kill Gordon, had succeeded with Sheri, and now Mikki . . .

"Oh, man," he said, understanding it. His hands went into his back pockets, and he looked up at the ceiling, feeling the guilt come in. He lowered his eyes back to his friend. "They found out, didn't they, John? Somehow, Dana and Norman caught on to the profile and came after us. And I thought your people had leaked it."

John saw the pain in Luther's eyes and offered his hand. "Hey, Lute, forget it, man. I'd have thought the same."

Luther took his hand, ashamed of his lack of faith. "I should have known, John."

The big man waved it off. "As you said, we're past that. Now we have to find Norman."

"What about Dana?" Jackie asked, feeling more settled now that Luther and John were friendly again.

John rubbed his chin. "Long story short, okay? Dana is supposed to meet Allen Parkman tonight. The two of them planned to fly out of the country, leaving Norman high and dry. Only she doesn't know that Norman has already transferred all their millions into his own account in the Cayman Islands. That was his parting shot at Allen. He forced the lawyer to transfer all the funds from Switzerland to Georgetown."

Steve Drexler picked up the story. "New York hustled the lawyer down to Washington a couple of hours ago. He's to meet Dana Quinn exactly as they planned, and they'll bust her right there. An assistant U.S. attorney general is cutting Allen's deal for witness protection, in exchange for his testimony. Allen's pretty shook up about meeting Dana, but this is the best chance we'll have of getting her."

John looked at Luther directly. "We were already on our way out here. We had to move fast on this. There just wasn't any way to tell you and Jackie until we knew. I mean, what with Mikki lying in there . . ."

Luther took a breath, feeling no anger at his friend for withholding information. "I understand, Johnny," he said. "But this isn't quite over yet, is it? Norman's still out there."

"We had him, Lute. We just didn't move fast enough. But we'll find him," he said, certain of it.

"This is a game for him," Jackie suddenly said. "All the deaths, the details so carefully arranged to make them appear to be accidents, the way he's played Dana and Allen against each other. All a game." Her eyes misted with pain as she realized her daughter was near death because of some perverse, horrible game played for money.

John shared her anguish, unable to avoid the if-only's. If only we had been just a little faster on this, he thought, despite the sure knowledge that they had all done the best they could. Their best wasn't enough this time, and he had little else to offer his two friends by way of consolation.

Luther suddenly smiled. "He doesn't know," he said, almost to himself.

"Who doesn't know what?" Jackie replied, catching his look.

"Norman," Luther said, looking up, taking them all in. "None of them do, or did," he corrected, his eyes animated. He had their attention now, and continued. "Look, it's safe to figure that some way, somehow, Dana and Norman found out about the statistical profile, right?" He didn't wait for an answer, for one wasn't needed. "So, presuming that Gordon, Sheri, and I were about to discover their little scam, they decided to take us out so as to eliminate a possible threat to them."

"Yes," Jackie said grimly, "I understand that, but . . ."

299

John caught the gist of Luther's logic. "But they had to feel confident enough to even try such a thing so close to TPI."

Luther nodded. "Right," he said.

"Right," John repeated, then added, "they don't know about us. They don't know we're here, that we've been on this thing for months. That's why Norman's still here. He has no idea the Bureau's breathing down his neck."

One of the floor nurses approached the group, interrupting further discussion. "Mr. Sitasy, you have a phone call from the main switchboard. A man insists on talking to you." She glanced from Luther to John and back, nervous about all the agents on her floor. All the staff knew who they were. "It's against hospital regulations, the call I mean."

"What about it?" Luther asked, his voice calm, getting her past her unease.

"The caller said he knows something about your daughter, about her getting injured."

Something moved inside Luther, a premonition. "Where's the phone?" he replied, starting to lead her down the hall.

"At the nurses' station," she said.

John immediately snapped his fingers at Steve, who hurried over to him. "Can we set up another line and put a trace on it?" John asked the Phoenix agent hurriedly. He had a feeling about the caller, the same feeling Luther had.

"If we're fast," Steve said, and the two of them jogged ahead to the nurses' counter, motioning to the floor supervisor.

She nodded, picked up another phone, and spoke briefly into it. She listened to the reply, said something more, then turned to John. "When he picks up, you both push the buttons for the same line together," she said, indicating another phone.

John thanked her and gave Luther the high sign. Steve, with another agent in tow, jogged down the hall, all the while talking into his tactical radio, trying to set up a fast tracer on the line. The equipment was downstairs.

"Right here," the other nurse said, stopping with Luther at the station. She reached over the counter, picked up the phone, and spoke into it. "This is Marge. You may put the caller through," she said, and punched the hold button. She gave the handset to Luther and stepped back.

John picked up his handset, then silently counted to three on his fingers. They both pushed together.

"Sitasy," Luther said.

"Ah, Mr. Luther Sitasy. I guessed correctly that the hospital would put this call through. I was being most insistent. It took a while to find you, you know." The man's voice was taunting.

Luther knew immediately who it was, but he remained silent, listening passively as the voice continued. Don't give it away, he warned himself. Beside him Jackie's eyes questioned silently.

"I doubt you remember me," the caller continued. "My name is Norman Bloodstone. You and I have something in common. Some months ago you and one of your associates, Gordon Hatton, made up a computer profile on policy limit fatalities."

John gestured to Luther and silently mouthed, "Keep him talking!"

Luther nodded, took a breath, and answered the voice on the other end. "Yes, what about the profile?"

"You should have developed it further. You would have had it—the game—if you had just looked a little further."

"Look, I'm a little busy at the moment. How did you find me, anyway? And what exactly are you talking about, Mr. Bloodstone?"

Norman ignored the first question. "Why, I'd have thought the answer to that was obvious, Mr. Sitasy. I'm talking about murder and mayhem in the insurance business. Murder and mayhem," he repeated.

"I realize that you are probably having difficulty following what I'm saying," Norman gibed. "Allow me to give you a few reminders. Milligan, in Kansas City. That was no accidental fall down the basement stairs. Ricles near Boise, definitely not a heart attack. Sanford, just north of St. Petersburg. Her 'faulty' hair dryer had a little help. Some of them were very interesting and quite challenging, in their own way. Kersten in Pittsburgh was one. An overdose of an anesthetic called Marcaine. The latest was a doubleheader: Bentson Larcalle and his wife in Santa Fe, lawyer and claimant both. Four shots from a twenty-two for him, a broken neck for his wife."

He let that sink in for a few seconds and then continued, his voice lilting. "Understand, please, that these are what you would call my bona fides."

Luther reacted well enough to ask for more information from the unbalanced singsong voice, keeping Norman on the line. "You seem to have some inside information on all this, assuming what you've said is correct."

"Oh, it's more than just correct. It's perfect!" Norman snapped back. "Twenty-five claimants and eleven of their lawyers. I can give you exact details on each and every one of them. I can do that, you see, because I'm the one who killed them. So we can continue to dance around this for a while longer, Luther, or we can get on with it, or are you just trying to be cute?"

Luther's jaw clenched, but he held himself in check. "Go on. What is it you want?"

"What? No curiosity about all of this? Aren't you going to ask me why I killed them?" Norman's voice was quiet, complacent, condescending. "I would think that from your point of view the reason would be terribly important. Let me lay it out for you," he said, "so there are no doubts. After all, I do have an ulterior motive for making this call. All those people were done in for the reserve money on the insurance policies, of course."

Luther started to answer, but Norman cut him off. "Tell you what. I'll make it even easier than that. You're looking into something of mine, so I've done something to you. How's your daughter doing? Pretty little thing. I see she favors her mother. Too bad, there were some real possibilities there. I heard her chances were fifty-fifty."

Luther didn't react to that the way Norman expected, refusing to give him the response he thought he would hear. The line was quiet for several seconds, so quiet Norman thought he had been disconnected. Jackie saw it then, saw Luther reach into another level, one even she had not witnessed before.

"You're out of your league, Norman." Luther's voice came back, absolutely cold. He was stalling for time, to give the trace a chance. But he was also into the other man's mind. Norman had called with something specific in mind, and Luther was beginning to understand what it was. He realized he had two advantages over the killer. One was Norman's ignorance of the feds' involvement. The other was

Luther's own experience with violence. At one time he had been very good at it.

Another silence came from Norman's end. This one was interesting, he thought. "Outstanding, Luther, really. You're very good. Much better than any of the others. Perhaps I was right in my assessment of you. Now let's find out just how good you are. Is it all talk, Luther? Or do you still have it? Your record says that once upon a time you were a dangerous human being. But that was a long, long time ago."

John shoved the receiver into the crook of his neck and shoulder and reached for a pad and pen on the countertop. He scribbled a few words and held the pad up for Luther to see. "Agree to *anything*," the note read.

Luther's brow furrowed, but he acknowledged the message with a nod. John's intent was plain. Aloud, Luther spoke back to the killer. "A lot of things happened a long time ago. What's that got to do with you and me?"

He's being very cool, Norman thought admiringly, ignoring the tiny, sharp warning that tried to intrude. He had the upper hand in this, and it was time to make sure Luther knew it.

"Look, my request is simple. I propose a contest between equals, a one-on-one match to settle things. At this moment I am at the gate of the killing ground—the Phoenix War Museum. I've been here since dawn. Such a lovely day, Luther. What is that old Indian expression? Today is a good day to die."

Norman's voice dropped in pitch and became menacing. "If you think you still have it, look for me in the Vietnam section at the far north end. I'll give you a few hours to get ready. What with your background, this encounter should be easy for you. Call it a trip down memory lane."

So that was it, Luther thought. He wants to really play the game. But John and his men will never let me get close to him. Unless . . .

To Norman he said, "Why should I give a good goddamn what you want or why? What's to stop me from telling the cops about you and letting them blow your head off for me?"

Norman had considered that possibility, but presumed Luther was too vain to ignore the challenge, now that their conflict was personal.

But he decided to underscore the family part further. "Look, you know how to play at war. But you forget something. What I did to your daughter I can easily do to Jackie, too. In fact, I kind of have a fantasy thing for older women. I'm sure she and I would have a fabulous time before I . . . well, I'll let you fill in the blanks."

Luther felt something stir inside him, something primal and cold, but Norman was still talking.

"But I'm digressing," the killer said. "The countdown has begun. I'll wait, but not for long."

Luther stood in silence, knowing everything Norman had claimed responsibility for was true. He looked at Jackie beside him, so near now, and knew Norman would do exactly what he had threatened, if he could. There was only one way to make sure he couldn't kill anyone ever again.

He pushed thoughts of his wife and daughter out of his mind. "You did Gordon, too, didn't you? Gordon and Sheri and Nicole?"

"So I'm told," Norman answered.

Feeling nothing, Luther stared down at the floor.

John was talking to Steve now, quietly, his hand over the mouthpiece. The Phoenix agent had just returned.

"What? No reply? Surely that must anger you," Norman mocked, his voice climbing upward again. "I understand your anger, really I do. I killed that pitiful animal of yours, too. He caused me a bad moment or two there, but in the end . . . a bit messy when I left him. I just wish I'd had more time with the girl. She really is exceptional, you know."

Luther's stare went through the floor, focusing on images only his soul knew. He thought how dangerous this man was and what a pleasure it would be to kill him. But he knew there was no way he could do that. John was setting the trap even now.

The line was silent for a few moments. Norman's breathing could be plainly heard. "Don't cross me on this, Luther. Just get here."

Luther looked across at John, then at Jackie. He knew that John could make the trap work, but he also knew what he had to do, in spite of logic, in spite of friendship. He owed John a debt for saving his life a long time ago. But this went beyond even that blood bond. Norman had forced upon him another bond, and the blood on this

304

one went even deeper. This was Luther's job, and he knew how to do it. Sorry, Johnny, he thought, making his decision. When this is over, maybe you'll understand. I hope to God you do.

Luther grasped Jackie's hand and held on. "All right, Norman, I'll be there. Just you and me. That's what you want, isn't it?"

"That's precisely what I want," Norman said, his voice calmer. "Just keep in mind what I said about those two lovely ladies in your life." He chuckled.

"Go to hell," Luther shot back and dropped the handset onto its cradle.

John hung up and looked at his friend. "I know that wasn't easy, but you did good, Lute," he said.

Steve Drexler spoke into his portable radio and nodded a few times. To the group, he said, "Sorry, John, Luther. We didn't have enough time to track him down precisely by the time we got on the line, but my people have confirmed that he was calling on a cellular phone from the west side of the valley. It's a good bet he's where he says he is."

For Jackie's benefit Luther said, "You guys are going to drop a net over him, aren't you?"

"That's the plan, Lute," John answered. "Norman will be expecting you alone, but we'll go in with a few hundred cops instead, and we'll send in a hostage and rescue team to find him."

"And kill him," Luther added.

"If it comes to that," Steve said. "It's the logical way to handle this situation. This asshole's killed enough. I see no reason to let him do any more. Of course we'll protect your family the entire time."

Luther listened to the SAC's declaration, but his eyes were on John. "You're not going to let me go in, are you, Johnny?"

His friend looked back for a long while. Finally he spoke. "I didn't think it would be necessary to spell that out, Lute."

"Yeah, yeah, I know. You had me play along with the son of a bitch to set him up for you guys."

"C'mon, Luther," Steve said. "You know how it has to go down."

"I understand all that," he replied, "but I've got the right to be there. *I'm* the one who thought up the damn profile, and it's been my people—hell, man, even my own family—who've suffered for it. You said it," he said to Steve. "Norman's killed enough. He's got to be

305

stopped, and stopping him is your province." He turned back to John. "But when it's done, when he's dead, I've got the right to be there, John," he said again. "I have to see the end of this, see the body on the ground. I need to know the bastard's finished." Luther held John's eyes. "Don't deny me this part, man, not now."

The agent felt Luther's plea and weighed it against his professional obligations, sure of what he should do. The decision he made, though, arose from his personal loyalty based on the history between him and Luther. "All right," he said, and immediately cut off the beginning of Steve's objection. "I'll take you in, Lute, much as I by God know I shouldn't. But you're staying in the back, right next to me, all the way. The HRT guys have the edge here. Let them do their jobs."

It was done. The choice had been made. Luther felt it settle inside him. He squeezed Jackie's hand reassuringly while he replied to John. "Thanks, John. That's all I can say." And that's all I needed, too, he added silently.

Jackie touched his cheek, turning his head, her face showing her concern. "Are you sure, Luther? Do you really want to go with them?" Her questions voiced her most obvious concern, but they raised other issues as well. She recognized the danger, and couldn't help but fear that she would lose him. Not now, she thought, not when things are just beginning to open up again, not with Mikki so . . .

Luther saw her fear and love in her blue eyes and was unsurprised to see the latter. He pulled her closer, put his arms around her, and held her close, really close, for the first time in a long while. For a few moments it was just the two of them standing there. He tried to settle her fears and concerns.

"It'll be okay, Jackie. I'll be in the background with John, as he said. But I have to do this. I have to see . . ."

"Norman," she said, finishing for him. "To prove that he's dead." She wanted the same thing, justice for their daughter and an end to the killings. Jackie searched his face, looking for whatever it was that she had seen in him when Norman first called. But it was gone, now. Maybe it had never been there at all.

"This is the only way, babe," he said.

Jackie kissed him then, gently, but with passion, wanting him to know by the intimate touch how things stood between them. "Keep your head down, Lute," she said, using his old expression and meaning it more sincerely than ever before.

"I will," he said simply. It was what he needed from her right then. It was enough.

"Right," John said, bringing them back to the business at hand. "Let's find this guy. What's this Phoenix War Museum place?"

"I saw something about it on TV not long ago," Luther replied, getting his head into the task. "It's way out on the west side, somewhere north of Luke airbase. It's big, I can't recall the actual distance it covers. They've replicated actual scenes from both world wars as well as Korea and Vietnam."

"It's a tourist thing. You're supposed to be able to walk from one scene to another," Steve added, having seen the same television show. "Each section, as I understand it, is a mix of battlefields, villages, farms, things like that. The intent is to present the action as compared to normal civilian life. They'll actually have actors going through their everyday activities and reenacting the battles."

"How long has it been open?" John asked.

"It's not," Luther said. "The grand opening is set for Memorial Day, end of this month, as I recall."

"Either of you actually been out there to see it?" John inquired.

Both men shook their heads. "Only pictures on the tube," Steve said. "It's been under construction for a few years, and it cost several million dollars, all donated by veterans' groups, private funds, and some very wealthy contributors. It's pretty ambitious, kind of like Gettysburg."

"Okay," John said. "We'll need everything you can get on this place ASAP—plans, photos, engineering specs, the whole nine yards. Seal off the whole museum area, Steve, completely. I'd like to contain this bastard until we can get a full hostage rescue team in place."

"I'll alert the county sheriff's office and a half dozen other agencies. We'll need them all," Steve said. "I'll alert the HRT boys at the same time. They're probably still primed from this morning's miss. Shouldn't take too long to get them briefed and reequipped."

"Good," John said, momentum driving his thoughts. "How soon can you put together a full briefing?"

Steve looked at his watch, estimating. It was just after 8:00 A.M.

307

"It'll take an hour to alert all of them. If we can get what we need on the museum in time, we should be ready by, say, nine-thirty, earliest."

John nodded, thinking along the same lines "Make it ten o'clock, just to be sure. Don't forget to put a team in charge of the media," he reminded them all. "They'll be monitoring the whole show once we get rolling. This is going to be a big one, and damn hard to miss. I'd rather control the newsies going in."

"Shouldn't be a problem," Steve said. "We can handle the hot dogs and their cameras."

Jackie had held back, letting Luther take center stage, but now they were into her area. "If you don't mind, this newsie would like to get in on this." She put an arm around Luther. "I can set up some coordination for you. This story is going to turn into a zoo unless you control it now. I can make some calls." She looked at Luther. "I'm sorry, hon, but the other stations will be here asking questions once the calls start going out. There's no way I can prevent that."

She addressed the agents. "I'll use my connections with the other networks and the newspapers, but I'll be at the museum when the raid happens." She looked at Luther, who let her go on. "I need to be in on this, too. If something happens, if Michelle doesn't pull through this, I need to know that this . . . this monster is not going to walk away from what he's done."

Luther slid his arm around her, showing his understanding through his touch. "If you think you can help in this . . ." He nodded to John, getting his okay.

"All right, Jackie, but let's try to limit the media presence," John said. "I don't want the slash and gore crowd getting in the way. This thing's going to escalate big time when we start rolling resources out there—if Norman's really out there," and he stopped for a few seconds. "That's something else, too. We have to confirm that he's there without tipping him off."

"I have a suggestion," Luther said. "Can I steal you for a little while?"

"What do you have in mind?" John asked.

"You're going to need a recon of this museum place. Why can't you and I do that now? I can have Dutch prep the Hughes, and you and I can give the park a once-over while Steve's getting the rest of this going. The Hughes is configured like a standard military bird, so it shouldn't attract any attention going over. The museum's close to Luke air base, after all. It ought to be okay."

John looked at Steve, who nodded back. "That's not a bad idea, John. You guys can take the chopper back to the federal building. There's a helipad on the roof."

"Let's do it," John said.

One of the many phone calls being made, this one by Luther, got the director of personnel for Trans Patriot, a fellow named Glenn Canon, away from his breakfast and on his way to the Village to meet with Dale Reichley. He was to pull out all of the records available on a former employee named Norman Bloodstone, including pictures. He was curious about this odd request from the claims manager until Luther mentioned the FBI.

Luther then called Dutch Oderssen's office at Falcon Field, requesting that he prepare the Hughes 500 for a run to the west valley. Oderssen assured him the bird would be ready.

Luther saw things were picking up now. He motioned to John, "I guess we'd better get going, then."

"I'll have a car brought around for you," Steve said.

Jackie took a breath. "Go on, hon. I'll stay here with Mikki for a while yet." She felt better about her daughter now, for some reason.

Luther didn't miss Jackie's use of their daughter's nickname this time. "She's going to make it," he said.

"I know," Jackie said. She noticed John off to the side. "They're waiting for you."

Luther acknowledged John, started to move, then hesitated. "Jackie, I . . . "

"Not now," she said, pressing her fingertips to his lips. "Tell me later, Lute, when this is over."

Their eyes danced back and forth while a thousand words were spoken in silence. Luther exhaled quickly, nodded once, and turned to John. "Let's go," he said.

As they stepped into the elevator, Luther tried to catch a last glimpse of Jackie, but she had gone back into their daughter's room. He turned his thoughts inward, and toward his new mission.

"We're here," Luther said, looking up ahead toward the entrance to Falcon Field and told the driver where to turn.

The Hughes 500-D had been rolled out, and they were met by Dutch and two of his crew. Introductions were quickly made, and Luther went with Dutch to do a visual pre-flight while John went with another crewman to get suited up.

Minutes later the two of them were settled in the cockpit, John watching as Luther ran down the checklist, his movements flicking memory switches in the agent's mind.

Luther looked out, cleared the space around the Hughes, and acknowledged Dutch's hand signals for engine start.

Two-handed, he engaged the switches. The electric generator whine presaged the low rumbling whoosh of the turbine, and he engaged the rotors. The five-bladed hub above them cranked up slowly, quickly moving into a translucent blur, the engine and blades taking on the characteristic hornetlike buzz of the 500-D.

"Brings back a lot," John said into the intercom as Luther lifted the ship into a low hover and moved out past the hangar toward the runway. "Jesus, the smells are day-tripping me back in time."

Luther spoke to the tower and received clearance. He advanced the throttle grip, raised the collective, light on the controls, and canted the machine over, climbing in a sweeping arc to the left, heading west.

As he set a course across the valley, he told John, "We'll be there in about ten minutes. I figure to take a few passes over the entire place first, then check each area. If we stay high enough, Norman should think we're just more traffic out of Luke."

He glanced over at John, "I don't suppose you want to try it?" he asked, indicating the controls.

John looked down at the stick, then at the rest of the instruments, and shook his head. " 'Fraid not, Lute. It's been too long. I haven't been in a cockpit for twenty years." He sighed, though, remembering. "Maybe another time."

"You got it," Luther replied, turning his attention ahead, "just call me. You've got the number."

310

John nodded and settled into his seat. He looked over at Luther's helmeted face hidden behind the dark green visor. We've been here before, old friend, he thought, feeling the vibrations of the ship, the sights and smells sweetly familiar. It was a strangely comfortable feeling. He settled in for the ride.

MAY 5, HONOLULU INTERNATIONAL AIRPORT, HAWAII

The JAL Boeing 747 settled lightly on the long runway, the pilot kissing the wheels down in the prescribed manner, right wing, center-nose, left wing, so nervous passengers could count each contact.

Deacon Drachman, seated halfway back on the left side of the huge cabin, reset his watch to local time, 7:04 A.M. He was bound for Chicago, then on to Washington, D.C. The layover in Honolulu would last forty minutes.

The big Boeing snubbed its nose into the dock, stopping with a slight bounce. Deacon sat in his assigned seat, hands folded in his lap, eyes closed. He intended to remain on board during the layover.

"Mr. Drachman?" A man's voice interrupted his thoughts. Deacon opened one eye to see a young man in a light tropical suit and white shirt leaning over him. A gorgeous almond-eyed Japanese stewardess stood behind him.

"Are you Emil Drachman?" the man asked again, reaching into his inside breast pocket.

"Yes . . . yes, I am," Deacon answered hesitantly, imagining a gun appearing in the stranger's hand. Jet lag, he thought, shaking the notion off.

The man produced his identification, and Deacon read it while he introduced himself.

"Sir, I'm special agent Tom More, Honolulu field office. May I see your identification?"

"Certainly." Deacon handed his opened wallet to Agent More. "What's this all about, Mr. More?"

Satisfied that Deacon was the man he had come for, More an-

311

swered, "Sir, I've been instructed to meet your aircraft and transport you to Barbers Point NAS, where a U.S. Navy courier is standing by to expedite the rest of your itinerary."

Confused now, Deacon spoke up. "Expedite what? I'm going to D.C."

"No, sir, that's been changed. You're going to Phoenix. Highest priority, fastest means available, and that means military courier."

"On whose authority?"

"A Special Agent J. Paraletto, I believe. He seemed real anxious to find you, Mr. Drachman."

Twenty-three minutes later, still amazed at the haste around him, Deacon arrived on the flight line before a two-tone gray-camouflaged twin-tailed Grumman F-14D. He had been suited up and briefed, and now was introduced to his pilot. Navy Lieutenant S. T. Nowicky was short, five-seven or so, with blond hair and green eyes. He explained to Deacon the ejection procedures and told him what he could touch and not touch in the rear cockpit. The discussion was one-sided as Deacon quietly absorbed everything, nervous flutters jostling with the excitement of the upcoming ride.

He was ushered up a metal rung ladder onto a platform, then into the second seat under the long canopy behind the pilot. A flight-suited crew chief helped strap, hook, and plug him into the Tomcat's cockpit. He showed Deacon where the intercom switch was, went over the bailout procedures again, then patted the top of his helmet and disappeared.

The engines came on and spooled up quickly. The pilot released the brakes, and the plane rolled out of the flight line at the direction of a baton-waving figure before them, then headed down the taxiway. Nowicky turned the aircraft and stopped, centering the plane in the middle of the long concrete runway. Deacon could hear the brief tinny-sounding discussion between the pilot and the tower.

The engines went from their rumbling idle to a rapid boom, and the Tomcat lunged forward, pushing Deacon strongly into the seat. There was a second push when the afterburners lit off, and then the nose seemed to pivot sharply and they shot almost straight up.

The speed of the aircraft pushed them ahead of their own sound, and over his shoulder Deacon watched the green island fall away.

The noise faded to a soft hiss, and they leveled off, seemingly only seconds later.

"Where are we?" he asked the pilot.

"Just past thirty thousand, heading for forty-seven. We'll hold there a bit, then let down to tank with a KC-135 in about five minutes. Then we'll go back upstairs to forty-seven thou and put the pedal to the metal."

Deacon was impressed, and noticed the speed on the instruments. "How fast will this go?"

The pilot looked up in the rearview mirrors while he answered, his eyes smiling mischievously above his oxygen mask. "Fast enough to get you there, Mr. Drachman. We'll have another pit stop before arrival. Orders are to burn the taxpayers' money on this one. They must want you real bad. You like fast living, Mr. Drachman?"

"Yeah, but this is something else," he replied, awed by the flight.

"Ah, roger that," came the nonchalant reply.

MAY 5, WEST VALLEY, PHOENIX, ARIZONA

"That's it up ahead," Luther called a few minutes later, pointing. At two thousand feet they were following Union Hills Road, a palm-lined five-lane road that intersected 114th Avenue on the south edge of the museum property.

Luther tilted the craft left, heading farther south. "I'll make the first approach from the direction of Luke air base, up the west boundary of the park," he said. "I'd like to see how big this place is first."

John nodded and looked out his window. From this approach angle, neither man could see clearly the single-story administration building on the east side of the park, located halfway up the mile-long length of the museum grounds, nor the two vehicles parked nose in to it.

The Hughes 500, its dull olive drab skin dark against the brightness of the morning sky, cruised along the western length of the war museum. It overflew trenchworks, a shelled and cratered no-man's-land, and ruined houses. Beyond the mock destruction they saw orchards, grape arbors, a small village, hedgerows, patches of woodland forests, and terraced rice paddies, their bright green shoots pushing up from the glimmering water. Nearby was another village, the small square houses fitted with tiled roofs.

"Where's our section?" John asked, looking ahead, feeling a weird sensation. The terrain was beginning to look too familiar.

"The Vietnam scenes are supposed to be on the far north end," Luther said, slowing the bird down as they came near that area. The sections of the museum park melted one into another, with pathways and a few narrow roadways connecting the different areas. They crossed over into the Vietnam section, and the change in terrain was immediate, and unsettling for them both.

"If I didn't know better . . . "

"Man, you got that right," Luther agreed, fascinated by what he saw. "Jesus," he said softly.

The terrain chosen to represent South Vietnam was modeled after the Central Highlands, which most closely resembled the Arizona landscape. The builders had done their work well.

The two former combat pilots saw below them their Kodacolor memories, replicated to the smallest detail, containing the same red, broken plateaus, the stands of thick, tall bamboo, and the triple-canopy jungle.

Two villages were represented. The first was rural Vietnamese. It consisted of one-and two-room shacks with corrugated steel roofs interspersed with a few wood-frame structures. A dozen or so buildings lined both sides of a narrow tarmac road, complete with vendor's stalls and gaudily lettered banners strung across the road. A large plastered and whitewashed church anchored the northwest end of the village.

The other village, located some distance off the road, was hill country Montagnard. Its focal point was a large swaybacked longhouse mounted on pilings with a Polynesian-style thatched roof. Grouped around the longhouse were smaller hooches, capped with similar roofs, elevated about six feet off the ground on thick beams. The huts were barely visible through the double-and triple-canopy forest. The effect was beyond a mere reconstruction. It was real.

314

"Damn, they really got it right," John said, amazed at the accuracy of the scene.

"Maybe this is too good, man. If Norman's serious about making us go in there after him, this hunt could get real messy."

"I suppose that's why he chose this park," John remarked. "Have you seen anything moving?"

"Negative. Let's go back for another pass."

They took another circuit over the grounds and saw no movement. Luther cut diagonally over the eastern edge and passed over the parking lot and administration building. "Got two vehicles down there," he said, pointing.

"Circle back. Let's get the plate numbers," John replied. "You have any binoculars in this thing?"

Luther motioned back over his shoulder. "Bag on the floor there. I'll try not to be too obvious."

He overflew the parking lot while John read the license numbers and wrote them down. Then he got on the radio to the Bureau's field office and relayed the numbers for them to check.

The reply came back in less than a minute. "Hotel Uniform zero seven five," the operator said, using the Hughes's call sign.

"This is seven five. Go ahead," Luther said, piloting the bird toward the city.

"Roger, seven five. We have identification on those numbers. One vehicle belongs to a William Mecklenberg, the other to a Norman Bloodstone."

"Damn!" John cursed, listening in. "He's there." He cut in on the net. "This is seven five bravo. Advise Drexler the suspect is in place and that there might be a hostage situation down there. Get an identity check on Mecklenberg soonest."

"Roger, seven five."

"What's our ETA?" John asked, unfamiliar with the distances involved.

"Five, six minutes," Luther answered, pointing straight ahead, beyond the bubble front of the Hughes. "That second set of skyscrapers there, what the newcomers call 'uptown.' "

The two men fell silent for the remainder of the short flight, accompanied along the way by their individual dark thoughts.

315

At a quarter past eight o'clock that morning, William Mecklenberg had been sitting in his office chair, tied to it with telephone cord, staring at the business end of the fat black suppressor fixed to the muzzle of the Beretta that Norman had left casually lying on the desktop between them.

Bill Mecklenberg thought the armed stranger looked like one of the exhibits, dressed as he was in camouflage fatigues and a nylon mesh vest that contained several box magazines for the long-barreled rifle the man had propped up against the desk. His face had been streaked with camouflage sticks, shades of dark and light green alternating with brown and black. He had tied an olive drab scarf around his head, lending him a pirate-like look. Only his gold eyes shone out of the muddled colors, and they were bright, much too bright.

While Norman perused a pile of detailed maps and engineering plans of the museum grounds, Bill calculated the odds on ever again seeing Claire, his wife of thirty-seven years. A gambler at heart, he didn't think the odds were very good.

Bill was retired from the air force and had taken the job as museum director to stay active. He happened to be in the office that Saturday morning preparing for the opening. His unexpected visitor had simply walked through the door, which Bill had neglected to lock. With a curious smile, the man had quietly asked for all the plans and blueprints for the museum. His request was reinforced by the appearance of the pistol.

Norman, who hadn't spoken more than ten words to him since tying him to the chair, studied the maps and plans strewn all over the desktop. He chuckled once. "This is very good . . . very, very good."

Bill listened to the tone of the man's voice and to his choice of words. He decided, without using much imagination, that the stranger was extremely dangerous. He was right.

Abruptly Norman straightened up and rolled up several of the maps into a tube, all the while humming a nonsensical tune. He picked up the Beretta and stepped over to Bill, who remained rigidly quiet, watching him approach. Norman raised the weapon and traced

316

the edge of the suppressor down his captive's cheek. He was humming again as he moved the weapon up and down, up and down.

This is it, Bill thought. I love you, Claire, he thought, and he closed his eyes tight.

Seconds ticked by so slowly that Bill had time to review his life, astounded that it actually happened as it always did in the movies. He saw everything, but heard only the sound of his own heart, pumping his blood at high speed through his veins.

After several more seconds—hours, so it seemed—Bill realized his rushing pulse was the only thing he heard. No humming, no giggling. Slowly he opened up his eyes to find himself alone in the room. The stranger had left without a sound.

Norman had left the administration building through a rear entrance four minutes before the county sheriff's advance units arrived and disappeared into the park. By sheer chance, he never saw them begin to set up their perimeter, sealing the museum grounds.

Luther lowered the Hughes into a perfect landing on the helipad on the roof of the local FBI headquarters on Central Avenue. An agent met both men and waited while they peeled off their flight suits and helmets, leaving them behind in the cockpit. They followed their guide down a short flight of stairs into the building, then into an elevator to the tenth floor, where a group had assembled for a briefing.

They walked into a large room filled with navy blue, tan, and brown uniforms, representing the various law enforcement agencies called to the hastily convened meeting.

A U-shaped grouping of cloth-covered tables opened toward the front of the paneled room, facing a burnished maple lectern to the right, a movie screen, and two chairs back against the wall near the lectern.

Seated on one of the chairs was a white-haired gentleman dressed in a salmon-pink golf shirt, rose-colored slacks, and pink-and-white wing-tip golf shoes complete with hard rubber cleats. His presence lent a jarring note to the bustle and noisy talk in the room.

Steve Drexler stepped behind the lectern and quickly called the room to order. All of the seats were filled, and people were standing along the side and back walls.

"Each of you already has one of these," he began, holding up a thick packet. "As most of you know, the situation has taken an immediate turn for the worse. This briefing will, consequently, be short and to the point." He read from the pages before him.

"The suspect is Norman Kearney Bloodstone, age twenty-eight. There are photos of him in your kits. He is currently suspected in the murders of thirty-six people across the country committed over the last two years. Additional charges of arson, securities fraud, a dozen violations under RICO, and a laundry list of SEC and IRS violations are pending." He let that information sink in as he gazed around the room. He received only concentrated stares in return.

"We believe Bloodstone has been working with at least one accomplice, Dana Quinn, an investment counselor employed at Trans Patriot Insurance, a Scottsdale-based company. This information comes primarily from the third partner, Allen Parkman, a New York law firm senior partner, who turned himself in late yesterday evening."

He motioned toward the elderly man in the chair. "I'd like to introduce to you retired Brigadier General James L. Dormet. General Dormet is the CEO of the Phoenix War Museum. He has graciously agreed to describe the park for us and explain any problems we might encounter. General Dormet?"

The man stood up, unfolding his gangly six-foot-six-inch frame off the chair. He stepped to the lectern to address the officers. His voice filled the room, the microphone on its flexible stalk before him unneeded. "Agent Drexler's description of how I came to be here is most diplomatic, if you can count being kidnapped from the second hole at The Boulders, and flown here by helicopter, gracious. Still in all, gentlemen, I will do what I can. I realize how serious this situation is.

"You will find area maps, topographical and scale, in your handouts, along with some overhead color pictures of the site. The museum grounds measure roughly four hundred meters by fifteen hundred meters, oriented north-south.

"As noted, each of the four sections replicates battlefields and civilian dioramas of our last four major armed conflicts. The intent of the park was to allow the visitor a unique opportunity to observe both sides of these conflicts." The general softened his voice and glanced down at his papers. "We never suspected it would be used in this manner."

On the movie screen in the middle of the front wall, still pictures appeared, showing the details of the grounds. The general led them through the construction, foliage, access roads, pathways, and maintenance roads of the complex.

"In addition to all that you see here," he continued, "the grounds are accessible by way of a series of four tunnels that run parallel to the long axis of the park and are interconnected by branch tunnels. The main tunnels route and protect the substantial power, utility, and water lines involved in the project and are large enough to accommodate the electric golf carts used by the maintenance staff.

"Your suspect is supposed to be somewhere in the northern part of the park, probably in the Vietnam section. If he chooses to avail himself of any of these tunnels, he can travel fairly rapidly from one end to the other, or change from one to the other using one of the connecting branches. Please note also the manholes scattered about the grounds," he went on. "There are forty-seven of them, and most of them are camouflaged from normal view, so as not to detract from the aesthetics of the park."

The officers took the warning for what it was. The general finished up and fixed all of them with his ages-old eyes. "It appears that my director, Bill Mecklenberg, is on the grounds somewhere. I have a pretty good idea how you are feeling. I have attended a few meetings like this myself. Find my man, gentlemen, and get him out, if you can. I wish all of you the best of luck." He gave them a wave that was closer to a salute, and stepped aside.

Steve leaned into the mike and introduced John, who was standing with another man a step or two back. "Overall command and control of this operation will be with Supervisor Agent John Paraletto from D.C. This has been his investigation since day one. John?"

"We have two missions here," John said, getting right to it. "The first is to secure the administration building and recon it. If Mr. Mecklenberg is located within, an extraction will be attempted. The sole maneuvering element will be the hostage rescue team under Phil Goff." Paraletto turned to the team leader standing with him.

319

"The other agencies and departments we've brought in will establish a perimeter two hundred meters beyond the northern portion of the park's boundaries. Maricopa County Sheriff's Department units will seal off the dividing line between the Vietnam section and the rest of the park, completing that side of the 'Nam perimeter.

"All available SWAT units from the six departments who have them will be set up on the perimeter to augment the hostage unit inside the park. Once we have accounted for Mr. Mecklenberg, we'll go after the suspect."

John referred to the list handed to him by one of Steve's subordinates. "Air support will come from the Phoenix, Glendale, and Maricopa County departments, plus two UH-1s from the 189th Tactical Air Wing of the Arizona National Guard. At least two of the police aircraft have infrared imaging capability. Unfortunately, the forecast for today calls for temperatures in the low hundreds by noon and a high of one-oh-seven. It's ninety-two degrees at the moment. All that reflected heat will pretty well nullify the infrared equipment, so the air surveillance will have to be visual only."

"What about the news media?" a voice from the back of the room spoke out.

John looked in that direction and acknowledged the speaker. "I was coming to that," he said, addressing the reporter, who stood with a dozen or so others from the three networks, two privately owned television stations, several Phoenix radio stations, and the newspapers. Cameras had been banned from the briefing. He saw Jackie Sitasy and nodded slightly to acknowledge her wave to him.

"The reason you are here," Paraletto said, "is that we acknowledge media's right to the story. We also understand that trying to exclude all of you would be impossible. It's my understanding that some coordination is being put together for you people to set up an information conduit between Bureau command and the media. That will all be tied into this operation through Agent Drexler's office."

John leaned forward slightly, underscoring his next statement. "I will not tolerate any interference, intentional or accidental, from any unauthorized source which might compromise this operation." He held up his hand to still any objections.

"These are the ground rules. Minicam units will be permitted at

320

the perimeter, and information will be distributed once it has been screened and cleared"—he ignored the collective groans—"to all news agencies at the same time. That includes interviews with any officers, agents, what have you. Agent Drexler will provide a list of contact people for you prior to leaving this building. I understand most of these gentlemen are familiar to you."

Steve stepped up and whispered in John's ear for several moments. John nodded once, then spoke into the mike again. "As most of the broadcast stations have some form of aerial capability, I must insist that there be no flyovers of the museum grounds. Things are going to be difficult enough as it is. Violation of this directive will result in immediate suspension of the license of the pilot by the FAA and probable criminal prosecution of the station involved."

He looked about the room. "Unit leaders have specific assignments. See your appropriate commands. If there are no questions . . ."

An immediate low level of talk sprung up, but no hands were raised. The grousing from the media reps was a bit louder, but all of them had caught the hint. Jackie's efforts were already under way.

John waited a few seconds longer, then announced, "That's it." He signaled to Luther to join him up front, and the two of them followed the HRT leader, Phil Goff, out of the briefing room by another exit.

Down in the basement of the building, in the well lighted and equipped locker room, Phil and his team were getting suited up. John introduced him to Luther.

"I understand we have you to thank for initiating this party," Phil said to Luther, as he exchanged his suit coat and shirt for camouflage fatigues.

"I guess you could say that," Luther replied, feeling like a fifth wheel, standing there doing nothing. "I take it you're the guys who tried to grab Norman this morning?"

"We're the guys," Phil confirmed, continuing to suit up. "Hopefully we'll get him this time."

"That's what I wanted to bring up with you, Phil," John said. "Luther's going in with us."

Phil finished buttoning his shirt, as if he hadn't heard. He raised his head and looked at John, then at Luther. Their physical differences were apparent, but their eyes were the same. The team leader had been getting vibes off the civilian, one of them pretty obvious. Who did he know to allow him to be escorted by the chief honcho from D.C., unless he was part and parcel of the scenario? And there was something else in the shorter man's face, a similarity Phil recognized.

"I hate to sound like Michael Corleone at a time like this," he said, sizing Luther up, "but is this business or personal?"

Luther started to answer, but was interrupted by John. "A bit of both, I suppose. Just say he's earned the right, and whatever happens out there today, the responsibility is mine alone."

Phil considered that and replied, "You got that right. And you can have it."

He saw the look in Luther's eyes again and turned to him. "Can you shoot?" he asked abruptly.

Luther smiled quickly. "I get by."

"What are you carrying?"

Luther pointed down at the long bench in front of the row of brown enameled lockers, at the weapon resting among the other equipment piled on the seat.

"One of those," he replied, indicating the 10 mm pistol, now issued on trial to various hostage units around the county.

His knowledge of the new weapon spoke volumes about Luther's relationship to John. That was enough for the team leader. "He stays with you, all the time," he said to John. "And I hope to God you know what you're doing."

"Don't we all," John answered.

Phil returned to their business. "How do we do this, John?"

John studied the team leader, the apparent detachment in his gray eyes, which the agent knew to be false. Goff's record was exemplary. The thirty-two-year-old had been with the hostage rescue unit for eight years. When he or his men had had to kill a suspect, there had been no hesitation. Phil knew the rules of the game.

"In a nutshell, I'm not sacrificing any more people for this bastard to up his body count," he said. "He's taken credit for a lot that's happened. I see no reason to doubt him. So be it. Leave him where you find him."

"No options?"

"None," John confirmed. "You have a total green light going in."

"You're the man," Phil said, and called over to one of the two snipers on his team.

"J.D., get Mr. Sitasy and Agent Paraletto suited up."

"Yo, boss," the short, somewhat stocky shooter said. He shot a questioning glance at the leader.

Phil's eyebrows went up, and he cocked his head at John, then drew up his right hand and made the sign of the cross in the air. "It's sanctioned," he said lightly.

"Gentlemen?" J.D. gestured for them to follow as he preceded them to another row of lockers.

Luther took a slow breath and fell in behind them. "Here we go," he said softly.

"Amen," John answered.

MAY 5, WEST VALLEY, PHOENIX, ARIZONA

They rode in silence inside the armored bus, a pale gray vehicle built by the Mattman Company, specialists in such conversions. Few windows were uncovered, which left the men inside to their own thoughts.

The hostage rescue team numbered eleven all together, two sniper teams, each consisting of a shooter and a spotter, and two three-man assault teams, with Phil Goff as HRT leader.

The snipers were armed with weapons that had married some of the finest precision work of Germany and America: Heckler and Koch PSG-1s, heavy barreled semiautomatic 7.62 mm rifles mounted with 4 × 12 variable auto ranging scopes.

The assault team members all carried the same complement used in this morning's raid: MP-5s and the ASP/SOARS-developed 10 mm pistol. One man on each team also carried a .10-gauge Remington pump shotgun. All of the men had wireless radios and tiny boom-mounted headsets, full web gear, ammunition, and other equipment.

John, as overall site commander, and Luther were dressed the same as the hostage rescue team, in camouflage fatigues that were a variation on the older pattern first issued to the marines in Vietnam. The coloring was predominantly shades of greens, chosen to match the terrain of the museum. The color scheme had worked in Southeast Asia, and would work here.

Each man prepared for the mission in silence, balancing repetitions of their operations orders against their personal anxieties.

Luther sat next to John in an aisle seat near the front of the cruising vehicle. Ahead of them ran a phalanx of police cruisers, blue and red lights flashing. Behind them, he knew, stretched more vehicles, including a couple of emergency medical teams and the press vans with their satellite dishes and video cameras.

Luther's only gear was the 10 mm pistol in a horizontal nylon camouflage holster. Two spare magazines in a Velcro-closed pouch hung off the other side. Underneath his fatigue shirt he wore a bullet-proof body vest as did all of the team members. He was sweating already from its confinement, despite the air conditioning in the bus.

He felt ready, in the groove, calmly at ease. He realized he had been psyching himself up from the first. Things were happening, and he was a part of them, much more than just an observer, despite John's orders to the contrary. The clincher was the feeling, the deep certainty, that he and Norman were going to meet. Their paths, set in motion toward each other months ago, it seemed, were about to collide.

He'd had to renew old acquaintances to get here. And he'd gotten back into the intense level of concentration that had enabled him to survive two tours in Vietnam. "The Nam," he said to himself, recalling the phrase they had used. And here he was again, having come full circle back to that pivotal moment from his past. Luther sighed heavily, tilted his head against the swaying headrest, and looked up at the metal ceiling. Can I really do this? More importantly, can I come back from it? The answers were out there, waiting.

John rocked along in his own silence, feeding off the presence of the professionals around him, including Luther. His friend had a calmness under the surface tension.

Lute's holding up great, he thought, not surprised by the observation. He'll do fine. Then John sobered, thinking of the worst-case possibilities. Yeah, he'll do just fine, if I don't get him killed today. He glanced over at Luther, who sat with head back, eyes hidden by the curved bill of the marine-style camouflage hat. The blood bond between them felt heavy as he thought about what his longtime friend meant to him, and the resolve tightened inside.

Not today, he said firmly. Whatever happens will happen. But not to him. It's just a job, man, just another job. We'll find this guy, and that will be the end of that. Norman's a part of the equation, but we have most of it, now, anyway. It's his choice how this encounter goes down.

John looked past the driver, out the wide windshield, at their rolling escort headed west. "Just another job," he whispered. No one else heard.

It was just 11:00 A.M. Tall cumulus clouds reflected the midmorning sun downward in the manner tourists had come to call "dry heat." The effect promised that the day would be even hotter than the ninety-two degrees already registered.

The bus slowed, made several turns, then gunned its way up the hundred-yard-long four-lane entrance road to the museum. Just inside the parking lot, the vehicle turned right and stopped. They were inside a perimeter of dozens of police cruisers, vans, and four-wheel-drive trucks, which stretched away to their left and right, a wavering line of vehicles seemingly joined by the flashing red and blue lights rippling along the tops of the vehicles.

Clustered behind and between the vehicles were officers and deputies, with enough firepower for a small war. Several Bell Jet Rangers and Hughes 500s circled overhead, bearing the markings of their respective agencies. Thumping underneath the din was the heavy pulsing throb of the National Guard Hueys, out of sight at the moment somewhere over the park grounds.

Seventy yards across the sun-baked parking lot was the pale sand-colored administration building. Parked nearby were the Porsche and the tan Ford. The building appeared silent.

325

Phil Goff stood up from his seat behind the driver and called out, unnecessarily, "This is it."

The rest of the team was in motion, smoothly exiting the coach, falling into their assigned teams behind the safety of the vehicle.

Luther stepped down, John behind him, and looked around. The heat washed over them, replacing the coolness of the air-conditioned bus. Beneath the stiff-crowned fatigue cap, Luther felt his scalp tingle and his temples dampen.

Phil Goff and his team leaders were conferring with several uniformed and plainclothes lawmen. It was clear they were the hierarchy of the perimeter force. There were occasional gestures at the administration building. The tension of the senior officers was plainly felt.

Since the arrival of the first backup units, the scene had remained quiet. There was no sign of the suspect or of the museum director.

Phil squatted down for a few minutes with his team and went over the detailed floor plan of the building and the area surrounding it one more time. "The choppers will fly a counterclockwise race pattern," Phil explained, "the PD birds at a thousand feet, the Hueys down lower at five hundred. The National Guard jocks are better at this kind of thing. All the crews are geared to cover the same track at fifteen-second intervals. If the suspect is aboveground, they should spot him, and their presence will keep him occupied."

Luther and John looked on. They were baggage at the moment, even though John was the overall task force commander. This immediate business was left to the pros.

Phil remained crouched as he went on. "We'll be the only ones inside the grounds. Keep colors in mind, and make damn sure to identify your target. The sniper teams will visually scan the terrain in standard quarter sweeps once we get into the park. If you see the suspect, call the information in. Let me know if you have a clear shot"—he looked at each of the long gun carriers in turn—"and I mean *clear*. I'll confirm the green light. This one is too dicey to fool around with."

"All right, we're moving on the building," Phil said into his tiny boom mike as the team rose. All of their transmissions would be picked up along the line, and by the flight crews monitoring overhead on their FM bands.

326

There was a general shifting and rattling as the men checked and loaded their weapons. Luther pulled out the 10 mm, ejected the magazine, tapped it against the bumper of the coach to seat all of the rounds, and slid it back into the butt of the gun. He jacked the slide back and let it go, chambering a round, and verified that the safety was on. Then he repeated an old trick learned his first tour. He ejected the mag again, took a single cartridge out of his pocket, and reloaded the magazine, which he returned to the pistol.

Phil had caught the routine, and smiled inwardly. Whatever Luther's motivation was for being there, he knew his stuff.

One sniper team took up a covering position facing the admin building, using a shielded spot on the roof of the Mattman bus, designed for such a purpose. J. D. Winslow, the shooter on the other sniper team, would maneuver with the two assault teams until he and his spotter found a spot from which to safely cover the side and back of the building.

John and Luther attached themselves to Phil Goff, the team leader, who gave the command to move. It took five minutes of leapfrog maneuvering to reach the front of the building.

The two assault teams began a careful sweep of the structure, moving down the front of the building using a small handheld five-inch dark gray disk, which they pressed against the lower edge of windows or flat against the wall. The disk was a parabolic booster, a military ANPLR-53 listening device, known as a bionic ear. It amplified sound thirty-seven times over the normal human range, allowing the smallest movement, even an exhalation of breath, to be detected inside. The two teams worked independently, searching the structure room by room, space by space.

The southern half had been cleared, with no discernible sounds heard. The operator of the bionic ear on the other team then placed the disk up against a shuttered window at the northwest corner of the building and held up his right index finger. The sound of hard, irregular breathing and the muffled thump of something heavy, signaled the presence of at least one person. Moving around the north face of the building, he confirmed that the corner room contained the only movement, which appeared to be only one person.

This information was relayed to the team leader, who instructed the snipers to relocate to more strategic positions. Once they were set, Phil told the first assault team to gain entry through the main entrance while the second prepared to go through the office windows, tossing in a couple of stun grenades as prelude.

Covering each other, team one slid quickly and silently through the open doors, sweeping the small lobby with their weapons. They crossed quickly to the short hallway leading back to the office, from which sounds continued to emanate.

Morris "Boomer" Tanner, the man with the .10-gauge shotgun, cautiously peered around the corner and through the open door into the corner office. Something caught his eye, a small movement, and he took a second look. Quietly he spoke into his mike.

From his position behind the county sheriff's department vehicle in front of the building, Phil Goff listened and nodded to himself. He spoke to the outside team, set to go in through the windows, and ordered them to stand down, but on alert. Then he told Tanner and his team to take the office.

Bill Mecklenberg had almost had it. Since the tall stranger left, the director of the museum had been working on loosening the phone cord that bound his wrists and ankles to the chair. He had almost freed his left arm and was twisting, turning, and tilting the gray metal chair, when it abruptly tipped too far. Unable to correct it with a vain lurch of his body in the other direction, Bill cursed loudly and cringed when the chair toppled sideways.

The side of his head slammed against the edge of the desk as he went over, and the impact flashed red across his vision. Then he hit the carpet sideways, the weight of the chair pinning his arm tight beneath him. He held his eyes shut for a moment or two while the room whirled around, and the colors subsided. When he opened them, he was staring into the biggest, blackest gun barrel he had ever seen. A part of his exhausted mind finally cried, Enough already!

"I'm sorry," he managed to say, trying to speak louder, "but I've seen quite enough of those things for one day."

The next thing he knew he was lifted, chair and all, back into an upright position, and the cord was being cut away. The muzzle of the shotgun was removed, replaced by a big black face obscured by camouflage.

"Mr. Mecklenberg?" Boomer asked, as the cord dropped away. "We're here to get you out, sir."

Bill was too astonished by the politeness of the giant to react before he was again lifted quickly and half carried, half propelled on his own legs, out of the office and down the hall toward the front door. As he was hustled along, Mecklenberg heard other voices murmuring, and slowly his vision cleared. By the time they got to the main entrance, he was able to grasp what was going on. "You're the good guys," he declared, looking at the three men around him.

"That's right," Boomer said, touching the bill of his cap, "but usually we wear white hats."

One of the other members was talking on his tiny headset microphone, and Bill became aware of movement outside the doors. He was prevented from looking out by Boomer.

"Just a few minutes, Mr. Mecklenberg, and we'll have you out of here."

Unseen by the director, Phil, upon hearing the civilian had been rescued and the building secured, had called up an armored police van from the perimeter to pick Mecklenberg up.

Boomer and his team kept the director inside while the van approached, the big agent asking Bill to describe Norman in as much detail as possible, including his clothing, weapons, and such. Mecklenberg told them as much as he could remember, although the shock of his ordeal had still not subsided. Boomer passed along his description of the suspect.

"He's totally camouflaged?" John repeated. "He could be mistaken for one of us."

"He's really into the role," Luther cautioned.

"I agree," Phil said.

The white police van arrived, driving up over the curb, and stopped at the foot of the low entrance concrete steps.

Bill was about to ask a question when he was propelled out the door, held between two agents, just as the sliding side door of the van opened. He was hustled inside, though gently, and the door was slammed shut behind him. The team remained behind while the van pulled quickly away.

Frustrated, confused, and frightened by the rapid chain of events, Bill called out to the driver, "Who the hell is this guy, anyway? What's he supposed to have done?"

The driver, a uniformed Phoenix PD officer, looked over his shoulder at his lone passenger lying on the floor of the armored van, and replied, "No one you'll ever have to see again, Mr. Mecklenberg. Count yourself lucky you're still here," and turned back to his driving.

The van stopped, and the sliding door was opened by someone on the outside. What seemed like a dozen hands reached in to assist Bill out. He recognized the navy blue uniforms of the Phoenix PD and wondered what they were doing this far out on the west side of the valley. Then he saw the massed vehicles and dozens more officers, and intimidation set in. Things were getting even more complicated.

Norman, incensed by Luther's treachery, was almost beside himself as he watched the entire scene from amid a stand of low trees above and behind the administration building. His location was on a low ridge that encircled the entire park, marking the boundary of the museum.

"That son of a bitch," he growled through gritted teeth. He must have gone running to the police right after I called. Look at all this shit! God *damn* you, Luther! This was a complication he didn't need, forcing him to change his plan on the run.

His hands twisted around the stock of the FAL, his mind whirling. He had counted on killing Luther immediately and then simply driving away, leaving his body behind. Now it was all changed. There had to be five hundred police out there, and the goddamn helicopters!

"I wasted too much time," he railed against himself, but it was too late for regrets now. Since leaving the director tied to his office chair, Norman had gone on a short orientation trip of the grounds to get his bearings. Using the maps he had found in the office, he had located one of the manhole entrances to the maintenance tunnels, up on the ridge line. He had lifted the heavy hatch, noticing the excellent cover the heavy foliage provided overhead, and slid inside. After exploring the tunnels, he had retraced his steps, and emerged through the same manhole. What he saw below had surprised and shocked him. Luther had obviously betrayed him. His assessment of the man had been all wrong. That was the only explanation for the massed vehicles and uniforms facing him.

The sheer numbers impressed him, though, and he started to calm down. Maybe there was a way to take advantage of all of this. He saw the arrival of the big Mattman coach and watched the men get out of it. These were the real professionals, probably Bureau people. He had read about them. The hostage rescue team, the FBI's tactical team, he seemed to recall. They weren't to be underestimated. This is really going to screw things up, he thought. How the hell am I going to get out of here? He put part of his mind to work on that task while he continued to study the action going on below.

As angry and concerned as he was, a part of his mind was fascinated by the workings of the men below. He watched the rescue of Bill Mecklenberg through the rifle's scope, the magnification set on 9X power. Heat haze rippled up in his vibrating image while he observed the white police van return to the perimeter of vehicles.

The presence of all the uniforms and guns had given him an idea. That large a force was going to be a nightmare to control. Why not give them something to shoot at? The confusion might help him.

He settled the butt of the weapon into his shoulder, steadying it on the bipod, and tracked the officers helping Bill out of the van. He bracketed the chest of one man, rotating the cammed ring to allow for the bullet drop over that range. The officer turned his broad back toward Norman as he held one of the director's arms. Norman rotated the safety off with his right thumb, let out half his breath, and settled the crosshairs in the center of the officer's back. "Now it begins," he whispered, and squeezed the trigger.

That Norman was a killer was without question. Still, all things considered, his expertise in the art was not perfect, especially when it came to killing a man at distance with a scope-sighted rifle. Lack of experience accounted for his failure to take into consideration any obstacles between him and his target, in this case, the whip antenna on the trunk of a police cruiser, over which he had taken his shot.

In the magnified, light-enhanced picture through the scope, Norman could not have seen the antenna even if he had been looking for it.

The velocity of the round had dropped 500 feet per second when the 168-grain projectile encountered the narrow wire, turning an intended fatal strike into a wounding miss. He had also failed to consider that all of the officers present would be wearing body armor under their uniforms.

The bullet glanced off to the left and struck the officer in the back of his left arm, a half inch above his elbow, fracturing the humerus and blowing right out the other side, punching a two-inch hole in the process.

Bill heard the officer grunt, covering the sound of the round hitting, and the man's body reaction jerked him into the director, knocking both of them off balance. His ears registered the flat crack a millisecond later, but his brain washed it out, as people all around him threw themselves down. Bill had time to utter, "What the hell . . ." before his legs were swept out from under him and a tense, angry voice snarled in his ear, "Stay down, idiot!"

Luther heard the shot, the familiar whipcrack snapping reality and memory together into the same fraction of a second. He was in motion before he knew it, diving flat, reaching for his weapon, his eyes searching for the source of the shot before he stopped moving. Instinct had triggered his reaction. Now his conscious mind calculated, ranging out for a target, the realization that he could see nothing ringing another old, familiar bell. Damn, he thought, it never does go away.

The bulk of the administration building blocked his view of the slope behind it, and he had no idea where the shot had come from. He looked behind him and saw the wounded officer stumbling behind the cover of the Mattman coach.

Voices were shouting all over, guns were cocked and trained in the general direction of the slope above the building. Headsets came alive with the overlaid radio calls.

Up on the ridge, the shooter had seen the non-fatal strike of his first shot. He scanned the available targets through the scope and found one that was almost perfect, an officer hunched over a cruiser's trunk, most of his upper body exposed. Norman settled the crosshairs right over the man's hands clasped around his service pistol, and fired.

Thirty yards to Luther's left, he saw the officer jerk in response to the incoming high-velocity crack. The man fell flat on his back on the hot tarmac, arms outspread. Luther couldn't see the bullet's impact from that angle. It had entered right over the officer's hands, tearing through the base of his throat, half an inch above the protective edge of the bulletproof vest.

That was enough for the men on the line. Guns opened up, beginning with the first ripple of a dozen or so, quickly swelling in two quick waves to include almost every weapon there. Some raked the hillside and ridge line with every round in their first load. Others, without a target to zero in on, simply got caught up in the popping, ripping fusillade and added their noise and bullets to the volley.

John waited for the first drop in volume as men frantically reloaded, then shouted into his mike, identified himself on the net, and commanded silence. "Don't these idiots know anything about fire discipline?" he said to no one in particular.

Luther merely remained behind cover, eyeballing the ridge line. He hadn't fired with the rest. There hadn't been anything to fire at. And after those few seconds of destruction, he doubted if Norman was up there anymore.

Once the shouting and questions had quieted, John touched Phil on the arm. "Anything?" he asked the team leader, looking out toward Goff's people. Phil called his team to report.

"This is J.D., nothing here. From the sound, I'd guess the shooter used a suppressor. Maybe straight out."

"Roger that. Williams, whatcha got?" Phil called to the other sniper.

"This is Williams. Same-same, boss. Can't track it without getting farther along."

"Great," Phil muttered. "Hell of a way to confirm that Bloodstone's using the rifle," he added darkly. No one liked to lose people, and

333

he felt for the downed officers. But now the others were sensitized, and that could cause mistakes. "Hope these guys get some semblance of control," he said to John. "I don't need any of my people getting whacked by friendly fire."

John had just finished chewing out the task force leaders on that exact subject. When Phil signaled, he ran with Luther and the rest of the hostage rescue team to the corner of the building, joining up with Boomer's assault team. In the parking lot, medical personnel attended to the men hit.

Phil surveyed the area beyond the building, taking in the sloping ground. "He's probably on the ridgeline somewhere," he rightly guessed.

"Two hundred yards out, maybe more," Luther estimated. "Not a bad shot, for an amateur."

"Let's see if the choppers can pick him up. Whiskey three-eight, this is blue team Alpha," Phil called to one of the National Guard helicopters.

"Ah, blue team Alpha, this is Whiskey three-eight," came the reply from the UH-1H pilot, his voice broken by the characteristic warbling of the Huey.

"Roger three-eight, did you copy that last? We have two friendlies down. The suspect may be on the ridgeline west of the admin building."

"Ah, roger, Alpha. I have you in sight. We're coming around now and will let you know what we see."

"Roger, three-eight."

They watched the National Guard Huey bank in from the south and begin its pass. John called back to the perimeter and got the condition on the wounded officer, which was not serious, although the second officer down was a fatality. The director was fine. John ordered them to be taken out of the area and watched as one of the ambulances prowled its way passed the phalanx of vehicles and onto the long entrance road.

The Huey pilot came up and announced that they hadn't seen anything moving on the ground. Phil advised all the choppers to maintain their racetrack-pattern sweeps. "Probably went to ground in the maintenance tunnels," he guessed, and called in the warning on the radio net. "We'll send in a team to flush him, if that's where he's gone," he advised. "All other units, maintain position."

Norman had indeed done exactly that, dropping down the manhole tube after he fired the shots. He knew he had scored well. He had seen the first officer stagger to the side, evidence enough that he had been wounded, at least. The result of the second shot had been much more satisfactory.

Once he was down far enough, though he had some difficulty with the length of the FAL and the suppressor on its long barrel, he paused to pull the lid closed over him. He was hidden before the Huey crew made their pass.

On the northern perimeter, Sheriff's Deputies Jill Harrell and Leif Hommen heard Phil Goff's warning. Their position was a blocking force, in case the suspect went north, as expected. The Vietnam section was immediately in front of them. But for now they were one of the farthest units from the action.

"He's gone down into the maintenance tunnels," Jill said. She was new to the Maricopa County Sheriff's Department, only halfway through her first year.

"Let me have your packet," Leif said. He was a three-year veteran, up for sergeant on the next board exams. He dug through her folder to find the plans of the underground system.

She watched him while he unfolded the diagram and spread it over the hood of their Chevy Caprice cruiser. "What are you thinking?" she asked, sure she was thinking the same thing.

"I'm thinking we could drop in right about here," Leif said. "If he is underground, how else are we supposed to stop him from getting past us?"

"My thought exactly," she answered. She liked the way her partner worked, and they were a good match, especially since she was almost his size and could outshoot him on the qualifying range.

As for her partner, he thought Jill had plenty of potential, though she had a long way to go. Something like this, taking on a job on their own, was one of those times when a do-it-by-the-book attitude could screw things up. Jill wasn't like that, luckily for him.

Leif opened up the passenger side door of the Chevy and unlocked the Ithaca pump .12-gauge from the dash. He jacked in a round, set the safety on, and pointed ahead toward the thick trees fifty yards away.

"Let's do it, partner," he said.

"Right with you," she said, taking the map with her. They did not call in on their radio. They had heard the shooting off in the distance and the excited calls on the radio net. No one would miss them. Procedure was procedure, but they were street cops. They knew what they were doing. They approached the tree line, their tan uniforms contrasting starkly against the shadowed greenery.

Norman stepped off the last rung of the ladder into the expanse of the maintenance tunnel. The tunnel was a well-lit tube eight feet in diameter, its sides covered with pale yellow ceramic tiles, the concrete floor flat, seeming to rise off in either direction. Overhead were myriad metal, insulated, and plastic PVC pipes, different labels and signs designating their purposes. Conduit pipe in a rainbow of colors and different sizes coursed along the walls, carrying the electric power required above. The low-key sounds of mechanisms resonated the length of the tunnel, muting Norman's footsteps.

He noted the number on the wall near the hole he had come through, matched it to the blueprints taken from his bag, and oriented himself. "Got to go west and north a bit," he said aloud, his voice echoing, and started walking. He hoped to surface at the end of the park, and slip through the cordon.

Phil recalculated the situation rapidly and discussed it with John. Both agreed that immediate movement against Norman was imperative. The suspect had gone on the offensive. To counter that advantage, the hostage rescue team had to stay in motion, hunting him, driving him into a predetermined area where he could be contained.

Norman's long-distance shots had told them that he was effectively dangerous with his weapon. That could complicate the equation, but wouldn't prevent the team from completing its mission.

336

The team leader called up the county sheriff and told him to take his units south of the dividing line between the Korea and Vietnam sections. He wanted them to link up with both sides of the perimeter now, while the hostage team maneuvered onto the grounds, keeping the suspect busy.

Unknown to Norman, law enforcement teams were already belowground in the maintenance system, to the south, east, and west, clearing the tunnels. They coordinated their progress with the aboveground troops, squeezing Norman toward the north, into a pocket.

On the perimeter men began to stir, and engines turned over. Several tan four-wheel-drive trucks, light bars flashing on the cabs, detached themselves and rolled around the parking lot, then climbed the curb on the far southern end and, in a small convoy, entered the park. They separated, leaving forty yards between vehicles, and drove west in a ragged line.

Phil looked back at Luther and John and said, "Let's go . . . and keep well behind me and the others." Running in short spurts, hedgehopping from point to point, they covered the ground up the slope to the ridgeline.

The two sniper teams had already gone over the ridge and set up secure positions, covering the others as they came over one at a time, keeping their silhouettes low.

Luther went over behind John, and moved into a changed world of dappled shadow and light. The replicated double-canopy forest began immediately, and the HRT members in their woodland camouflage melted in.

Luther felt the familiarity of the scene wash over him, tripped by the landscape, the midday heat, the feel of the fabric rubbing against his skin, the sight of camouflaged figures moving cautiously in the bush. Overhead, the choppers wheeled in great circles, their crews straining for anything indicating the suspect's location. Luther glanced over at John, huffing from the effort of moving his overweight body up the incline, sweat rivulets running down his face and the back of his neck, his bare forearms glistening.

He saw Luther looking at him, and motioned around with his eyes, "We got to get out of this place . . ."

"If it's the last thing we ever do," Luther ended. But not before we take care of some unfinished business, he added silently.

Phil knelt down next to a large tree and asked his people for a situation report. Waiting for an answer, he noticed that the bark of the tree wasn't bark at all but a clever covering of fiberglass. Weird, he thought, just as the reports came in.

"Negative," came the unanimous reply. "No sign of the suspect."

One hundred yards away, Norman's head and shoulders appeared out of another manhole. He had surfaced to check his progress against that of the police pursuers. The opening was screened from above by a rocky overhang, which also hid him from the approaching hostage team. He stood on a rung inside the concrete tube, and his view was restricted to the south only. He was unable to see to the east, in the direction of the approaching HRT team.

His limited view did enable him to see the convoy of vehicles bumping across the park, skirting a series of rice paddies that rose behind them gently. The trucks were downhill from him, almost three hundred yards away. It didn't take him long to guess what the men inside were doing.

"Waste of time," he said derisively. "I'm not down there." He hauled the FAL up, rotated the legs of the bipod, and set the weapon down. He shouldered the rifle, traversing sideways until he picked up the prowling machines in the scope. He watched a tan Ford Bronco roll to a stop, its side door emblazoned with the badge of the Maricopa County Sheriff's Department.

Three uniformed deputies climbed out, their shotguns easily distinguished in the magnified view. Norman checked the range on the scope by bracketing one of the figures between the stadia wires, moving the camming ring.

"Just like the first one," he murmured, settling on the shoulder of the man crouched beside the vehicle in profile to him. The crosshairs held on the man, his image shimmering in the heat waves rippling up. Norman began a slow trigger squeeze.

One of the Bell Jet Rangers passed by, and the deputy raised his arm to wave. The unexpected movement exposed his underarm, an area not fully protected by the bulletproof vest.

Norman's concentration was thrown off by the sudden movement, and he jerked the trigger. The movement tipped the end of the suppressed barrel a fraction. It didn't matter.

The boat-tailed hollow-point cracked across the distance, thudding into the exposed space above the curve of the vest. The impact punched the breath out of the deputy as the bullet tore through his right lung and two chambers of the heart and blew a three-inch piece of rib out through his chest.

The deputy pitched forward, dead before his forehead thumped against the ground, legs twitching. The other two men threw themselves flat, reacting in stunned disbelief. The radio exploded once again, while everyone within hearing distance hit the ground.

"Christ!" John shouted. "He did it again!"

Over the radio din, Phil received a shouted call. "This is Williams. The shot came from in front of us, a hundred meters out!"

"See anything?"

"Negative! He's definitely using a suppressor. There's a covered spot up ahead. Wait one." The sniper was glassing the area through his rifle's scope, run up to $12 \times$ power. His partner was doing the same, using the more powerful $50 \times$ handheld spotting scope.

"This is Williams. I got him. It's the only possible place. We have good cover between here and there."

"Roger," Phil replied, "let's get the air in for cover, and move on it." The team leader was deliberately ignoring the scene to the south. The commotion around the fallen man attested to the fact that help was on the way. It was a situation that would have to be handled by someone else, sorry as he was that it had happened.

"Blue team Alpha, this is Whiskey three-nine. Roger that last, we just went over the sierra delta people. Looks like they got one down hard."

"Roger three-nine. What can you see?"

"We're coming around now," the second Huey pilot answered, having overflown the shooter's suspected position. The chopper cranked around in a tight turn, its rotor blades whapping in a thumping rhythm. The ship dropped down to five hundred feet, but kept up its speed. The pilot raised its nose high in a gentle climb, one hundred yards out in front of them. Downrange to their left, more vehicles, red and blue lights flashing, converged on the site of the stricken deputy.

"Alpha, we got movement," the chopper pilot called. "Man in the rocks . . . one zero zero meters to your front."

"Roger, three-nine," Phil replied, in motion with the assault teams. "Is he up?"

"Negative, Alpha. We caught a piece of him going down one of those holes. Cover appears to be still open."

"He sure as hell ain't going south," John said grimly, splitting his attention between the immediate scene and that to his left. This assault was his responsibility, and so far it had all been going one way.

"He's playing with us," Luther said matter-of-factly, "and he's going north next. It's what he said he'd do."

Phil looked at the smaller man. It struck him that, with all the excitement, Luther looked, not relaxed really, but more used to all of this. The more he saw, the more he respected the bearded civilian. What's more, he agreed with Luther's logic. "I think you're right," he said. He turned to look downrange in time to see the arrival of the other Huey, call sign Whiskey three-eight, preparing to land and pick up the body near the stationary Bronco.

The rotors kicked up clouds of red dust that obliterated the scene but couldn't cover up the anxiety and hatred radiating from the uniforms. Phil could feel it clearly over the distance. It was time to do something about it.

Referring to the schematic diagram of the park he carried, he called up the other UH-1 pilot. "Whiskey three-nine, plot the location of the next four access points along tunnel line forty-one, running north."

"Roger, Alpha, I have those."

"Set up a tight pattern over all four of them. Odds are the suspect's going to show out of one of them pretty quick."

"Roger, Alpha, will do. Three-eight's got the downed man. We're real sorry, Alpha."

The team leader looked sideways and caught John's eye. Both men felt the same way. John keyed his headset twice.

The flight crew in the Huey heard the double click, acknowledging the message. "Now let's find the bastard," the pilot said over the intercom, and hauled the chopper around onto their new course.

"He's definitely in the tunnels," Jill Harrell said to her partner. They were inside the tunnels themselves and had advanced only a short distance when the news came in about the latest officer down.

"This is getting out of hand, Jill," Leif Hommen replied. "That was one of ours he just tagged."

"I know," she said, checking the safety on her Smith & Wesson model 645. The big stainless .45 fit her like a glove, and she loved it. "He's coming our way, too. Maybe we should set up for him. Let the rest of them drive him right into us."

"That sounds like a good plan," Leif said, checking their progress on the detailed map. The tunnels were well lit, without too many shadowed places. They could see for some distance ahead before the tunnel curved upward gently.

"Let's get a little closer to the action first," he said. "I don't want to miss this guy."

They continued on ahead, looking for the right spot to set the trap.

Norman pushed up carefully on the forty-pound metal manhole cover, and the hinged lid opened several inches. His map showed that this exit was near some kind of tree grove. Far behind him he heard the commotion of the advancing police, and smiled, slightly out of breath. He had run the entire distance down the tunnel. He looked around and saw shiny green tubes wavering subtly in the mild breeze. Their trunks clacked as they swayed and danced together. Bamboo, he thought, good enough, and pressed the heavy lid up fully, then eased it down on its hinge.

His rapid breathing underscored his excitement, while the physical exertion had sharpened the dull ache of the dog bites in his left arm. He could feel each pulse beat as a faintly burning throb, causing him to check the thick bandages for any fresh blood. He didn't see any, and flexed his arm a few times, rotating it. The heavy foliage trapped the sun's heat, and he felt it wash over him, sweat dampening his shirt and waist. He pushed thoughts of his injuries out of his mind.

He was four hundred feet north of the cautiously advancing HRT teams and, according to the plans he carried, had just entered the edge of the South Vietnamese village. The stand of bamboo he had come up in was on the west side of the village amid the shacks and small buildings.

A few yards away stood a two-story church, its plaster walls showing the ravages of neglect and gunfire. Norman gauged the distance to the building, figuring that the darkened interior would give him a vantage point from which to watch his opposition approach. Maybe they would pass him by, thinking he was still using the tunnels exclusively. It was worth a try.

He waited for one of the smaller helicopters to finish making its pass. He let the FAL dangle from the shoulder strap held in his hand as he watched the chopper pass north of him, the popping sound of its rotors fading.

He looked through the bamboo, their stalks gently scissoring in the slight breeze, checking the area, but could see little. He knew he was ahead of his pursuers, but had a lead of only minutes at best.

As Norman started to climb out of the hole, the long-barreled rifle, unwieldy with the suppressor's added length, jammed between the lip of the hole and the metal rungs of the ladder. He yanked on the strap, lost his grip, and jerked again, wedging the weapon deeper into the hole. The sudden pull sent a stab of pain through his wounded left arm. He cursed as he managed to crawl all the way out while maintaining his hold on the strap. Then he knelt at the edge of the hole, working on freeing the gun.

The whapping sound of a Huey passing several hundred yards away masked the approach of the second UH-1 returning from airlifting the body of Norman's latest victim to the perimeter. The pounding of the chopper seemed suddenly to thunder overhead, catching him in the open above the manhole. The bamboo trunks stilled between breezes, letting in space and light. Norman's head snapped up at the sound just as the rifle jerked free, surprise registered on his upturned face.

Leaning out of the right side of the cargo hatch, scanning the ground, the crew chief caught the movement, the way it stood out from the symmetry of the colors flashing underneath the racing bird. Then he saw the face, and the image was gone.

"Got 'im, Major!" he called out in surprise.

The pilot's reaction was immediate. He banked hard over, standing the craft on its side, and called out at the same time, "Where?"

"That stand of bamboo near the church back there, west side of the village. Plain as day, Major. He was kneeling on the ground among the trees."

"Roger," the pilot replied, turning the ship around and flicking his transmission switch. "Blue team Alpha, this is Whiskey three-eight, we have a sighting on your suspect, stand by one."

The chopper came back around as Phil acknowledged, and hundreds of ears pressed into radio handsets all over the park. The ship returned to a normal attitude and decreased speed, then added altitude.

The crew chief sang out. "He's moving, sir, out in the open, clear of the trees."

"I have him," the pilot replied, watching the figure run toward the church and disappear inside. The Huey passed over the building and banked to come around again.

"Three-eight, this is Alpha. What's the situation?"

"Ah, this is three-eight. Suspect's aboveground. Appears to have taken refuge in a church in the Vietnamese village, west side."

"Roger, three-eight, we can see you," Phil replied. He made quick decisions. "He may have just stepped on it," he said to John. Then he instructed his teams.

Luther's senses began to intensify, fine-tuning into the mission. Twenty years is a millisecond in memory. His thumb touched the safety on the 10 mm, making sure it was still on. A touch would take it off.

John saw him, and his eyes asked the question.

"Just in case, Johnny. Lead on, man. I'll be right behind you."

John held back for a few seconds while the team leader got his people moving toward the village. "Okay, Lute, let's go." They got up and ran together, following the team.

Inside the church, Norman stopped for breath, his headlong race for the building forgotten. The surprise generated by the sudden appearance of the helicopter was fading away. He realized he had made a mistake by running here, and this time he couldn't shake the shiver of fear that ran through him. His mind raced, taking in the data, discarding ideas as fast as his fevered brain created them.

"Must do something," he said, recognizing the trap he had set for himself. "Yes, they'll be coming soon . . . too soon." He looked around at the simple wooden pews and the scattered straw on the compacted dirt floor of the deserted interior.

"Nothing here, nothing here . . ." he chanted, feeling the pressure. He spun back toward the door.

Whiskey three-eight saw him first. "He's out and moving!" the pilot reported from his orbit over the site.

"What? He's done what?" Phil asked, almost in position half a football field away.

"This is three-eight. I say again, the suspect's moving. He's left the church, and disappeared into the woods. He's heading away from you, through the woods. Double-canopy trees . . . can't see him anymore. Out."

"Damn, the guy's uncanny," John said. They were forty yards from the church and could see it clearly now.

"Yeah, I know," Goff said. "Clever bastard. We're not completely set yet. Maybe he's slipping. That was a mistake, stopping there."

"Uh, Alpha, this is three-eight. Suspect's heading north-northeast, straight as an arrow. Should break out in the open and cross the blacktop a hundred fifty, a hundred seventy-five meters from the village. Over."

"J.D., can you move on him?"

"Negative, Alpha. Too much between us. If the bird can track him, keep them on him. We'll try to play catch-up."

Phil and the others set off, too. Now it was a footrace.

Whiskey three-eight reported that Norman had crossed the narrow road toward the Montagnard village. Ground cover was not as heavy until the village, when the thick trees would once again hide the suspect from them. The chopper crew stayed high enough to track him but remain out of effective firing distance.

On the perimeter, a caravan of news trucks and vans lay scattered down the length of the entrance road, their parabolic antennas bouncing live reports off satellites from the scene of the manhunt. Minicams hovered over the wounded and dead, adding the gory touches to their reports. They fed their reports to the studios, breaking into golf matches and Saturday afternoon movies to broadcast this latest story of mayhem in the Valley of the Sun.

In the NBC studio van, Jackie Sitasy monitored the feed going out from her reporters. She had two working the line, getting footage, taping interviews, fighting for the same information the other stations were trying for.

What they didn't know, and what she was having an increasingly hard time handling, was the fact that Luther was out there, amid the gunfire they had heard. She had no idea where he was or how the hunt for the killer was going. She kept her attention on the bank of television screens filling the wall of the van, taking reports and issuing orders over the headset she wore. It was bad enough that she had left her daughter in ICU to be here. But she had no choice. Her future, like Mikki's, was here. "Maybe it always was," she whispered to no one but herself.

"Did you say something, boss?" one of the technicians asked, rolling back from the control board on his chair.

"No," she said, turning back to her job, "just thinking out loud."

Norman paused under the deep shade, safe once again from the helicopters. His run from the Vietnamese village had winded him, but he had managed to put some distance between the pursuers and himself. He pulled the maps out of the deep pocket of the fatigues

345

and studied it, trying to orient himself. He checked his compass, matching terrain features, and looked back sharply.

"Damn!" he said. "I'm too far north!" His run had taken him several hundred yards, almost to the edge of the museum grounds. The cops were bound to have units guarding the perimeter to keep him from escaping. He studied the maps again, looking for an out, looking for options. Absently he wiped sweat off his forehead with his sleeve, smearing the camouflaged streaks. The weight of the vest with the extra loaded magazines was beginning to cut into his shoulders, and it seemed to trap his body heat despite its mesh design.

The need to decide had turned into its own voice, harping at him, pushing, rushing his thoughts. "Should I take to the tunnels again? They'll have sealed them off by now . . . probably running teams down through them."

He took a few calming breaths, getting his wind back, shoving it back into his pocket. He dropped the compass in with it and unslung the rifle from off his shoulder, wincing at the throbbing from his left arm. It was getting worse, and a few bright spots of blood had soaked through the tight bandage, sending a rivulet down his wrist into his palm. The pain channeled his thoughts for him. He had an idea. Maybe they weren't expecting him to use the tunnels again. There was another manhole entrance a few meters ahead, just inside the tree line. He could use it to backtrack, then take one of the branch lines off in a completely new direction. It might work, if he was quick enough.

He took off, staying deep enough inside the thick underbrush and trees to remain hidden from anyone watching from the perimeter a scant fifty yards away.

In two minutes he found the manhole, opened the cover, and dropped inside. He failed to notice the empty sheriff's department cruiser just visible through the trees. Once down below, he started moving quickly, pausing every few seconds to listen.

Sound traveled strangely in the tunnels, as he had discovered earlier. At first Norman almost missed it, his own boots masking the noise. He slowed down, then stopped, ears straining, and heard it again.

Police radio! he thought, alarmed. They were down there with him and, from the sound of it, were fast approaching. Norman panicked, his eyes flitting rapidly back and forth, an animal caught. Stop it! he commanded, hands gripping the rifle tightly, pain lancing into his injured arm. He gained control with an effort. Look around, idiot! he chastised himself. Find a way. He checked quickly above, behind, left, right, and saw the oval entrance to a side tunnel branching off just a few yards ahead.

He had time, barely, if he could just get to it without being seen. The sound of the radio was punctuated by pounding feet. They were coming faster.

The two deputies, hearing that the suspect had been spotted and lost by the chopper crew, had done some rough calculations of their own. Referring to the markers and signs on the walls of the main tunnel they were in, they compared the report of the suspect's sighting, and realized it had happened just yards from where they had gotten to.

"I'll bet the bastard's run past us by now!" Leif half shouted.

Jill ignored his outburst. But now they had another problem. If Norman kept going the way he was last reported, he would emerge from the museum grounds perilously close to their assigned position, now abandoned. If he got away . . .

"We have to go back," she said, seeing no other option. "If he gets by us—"

"Bad move, Jill," her partner said, cutting her off. Both realized the dangerous stupidity of their error. Their calculated gamble had just folded. "Let's move," he said, and broke into a run, heading back the way they had come.

"Right with you," she replied, and fell in beside him. Neither said anything further. There was no need. And there was no time.

As they neared the spot where they had entered the tunnel, they slowed to a walk, listening to the radio chatter. People above them were looking for the suspect, but had lost him for the moment. Jill and Leif both had a bad feeling about the lack of a sighting. Anxiety, pumped up enough, could be a killer. For the two deputies, it suddenly took on human form.

"Stop right there," a voice said from behind them, and they froze. "Just like that," Norman said, the FAL leveled at them. The two officers had run right past him, though he was barely hidden inside the branch tunnel. But he was quick to capitalize on his good fortune, and their mistake. "How stupid can you two be?" he asked, turning on the sarcasm.

"Stupid enough," Leif replied, staring straight ahead, forcing a bravado he didn't feel.

"Right, sports fans," Norman said, and calmly shot him through the back of the head.

In the Montagnard village, sunlight changed to dappled shadow, which held the heat of the day like a thick weight over the elevated huts that replicated those of a typical B'nai tribal village in the Central Highlands.

The hostage team advanced on the village in alternate groups, using the broken ground for cover. No one had seen Norman for almost a quarter of an hour, but his last line of travel had been in this direction. They had to check it.

The trees and foliage grew thicker as they got closer to the village, and each man tried to make sure there was always something between him and the hamlet. No one cared to test the killer's capabilities one more time.

Off to their right, across a few yards of broken, red-tinted ground, a stand of bamboo curved away from the edge of the village. John pointed to it and said, "You know what it is?"

Luther looked, and shivered at the brightness of the memory.

"Yeah, the landing zone," he added quietly, referring to the one they had been shot down on years before, the story Luther had related to Gordon. Now he and John seemingly stood on the same ground where they had lost half of their crew, the one where they had formed their blood bond. They looked at each other, saying nothing, yet knowing the truth. They were back. Again.

In a reflection of events from the twenty-year-old war, the imitation village found itself the target of a search-and-destroy mission conducted by armed soldiers. Camouflaged men cautiously moved from

348

one raised hooch to another, probing, peering, clearing the way, hunting for a single killer.

They advanced a third of the way into the village, challenged only by the breeze slipping by them. They came to a circular clearing that opened to one side of the hamlet near the large swaybacked long-house, the centerpiece of the village. Several small trails in the beaten red earth wound deeper into the village. The plaza was shaded by a group of tall, wide-branched trees, while more low vegetation grew on the broken terrain of the open side of the village.

Several elevated huts stood on the edge of the clearing, and more were visible farther in. Phil split the teams up, motioning to John and Luther to hang back and cover as the HRT people checked each hut.

They took a position near the wide trunk of one of the trees, watching while the team continued their sweep. They had reached the second hut when the distinctive high-pitched crack of incoming high-velocity rifle fire tore through the plaza.

Everyone hit the ground, turning to face the source of the shots, each wondering who had been hit. A quick radio check discovered that none had, even as a second long burst raked the area.

"H and I fire," Luther called out to John, who was several feet away, and both men hunkered down behind a low rise in the ground. "Bursts are too long. He's just throwing it out."

"Yeah," John said, "like he's playing again. I don't think he wants to hit anyone."

"He's picked his time," Luther murmured.

"This is Alpha," Phil cut in on the radio. "We have him spotted. He's in one of those elevated hooches about sixty yards farther in. We caught his muzzle flash." A third burst, shorter than the first two, cracked out, and then another.

"We're going to pin him down," Goff continued, calling in instructions. "John, you stay put, and keep Luther with you. Break . . . Williams, pull your team in, and flank the shooter's position from the west."

"Roger that, Alpha. On the way," the sniper acknowledged.

"J.D., move up on your side, and anchor the east side."

"Roger, Alpha, we're moving."

349

More rounds cracked overhead, fired in quick doubles.

"He's getting more selective, Johnny," Luther said, crawling a few feet closer. He felt it coming, the opening he had hoped would materialize. He was ready.

"That's probably because he's got our attention so well," John replied wryly. "Man, I'm getting too old for this shit." His last remark was punctuated by two single shots, both of which struck the dirt just inches from his body.

"Damn!" he exclaimed, and he and Luther rapidly crawled toward a couple of mounds that provided better cover.

Luther's senses slowed time down. His hearing became acute, his concentration finite, his visual perceptions heightened. He felt the certainty of his impending confrontation with the killer.

The incoming shots were suddenly drowned out by full automatic bursts from several MP-5s. Luther chanced a quick look to see Phil's people maneuvering toward the pinpointed hut, covering each other as they alternated.

The leader shouted over the radio, "John, you guys okay?"

"Yeah, so far," John answered. "You?"

"About the same. We're keeping him busy."

Another long burst rang out, singing over their heads, but fired high, blindly. The two snipers called in then, confirming their positions. Phil looked over the situation and saw that to take the hut Norman was in, they would have to get past a natural depression that ran diagonally through the village. Maneuvering down and out of it would take them out of sight of the hooch.

He kept a man up on the near side, watching, laying down covering fire, and sent the rest of the team down.

Norman, lying prone on the floor of the hut, observed the whole thing through the six-power setting on his scope and saw his advantage. He fired off the remaining six rounds, ejected the magazine, and snapped in his last one. Using three- and four-shot bursts, aiming deliberately, he emptied the twenty-round magazine at the moving figures, then let the weapon drop down on its bipod.

Rolling carefully to his left, he made a last appraisal of the scene

350

he had constructed, and judged it effective enough. Norman grasped Deputy Hommen's shotgun and pushed out the back of the small hut just as the assault team dropped out of sight into the depression. He hit the ground in a crouch and sprinted toward the outside of the village. No one had seen him move.

Luther felt the weight of the 10 mm in his hand and remarked, "I wish I had the fourteen," referring to the M-14, predecessor to the M-16. The M-14 had been his main weapon on his first tour.

John heard him, and they both looked in the direction of the assault as the HRT teams worked their way toward the hut. They heard the renewed bursts of fire from the MP-5s as they began the assault.

"No return fire," John observed, listening for the higher-pitched crack of Norman's rifle. "Maybe they got him."

"He's not there," Luther said in a rush, feeling it, knowing the moment had come. "They're gonna lose him," he said, and pushed up. "Charlie used to do the same thing."

"What?" John said, turning to his friend, but Luther was up and running behind him, crossing over toward the edge of the village, heading deeper into the jungle.

"Lute!" he shouted, rolling up to follow and stop him, but he was too far ahead. "Alpha, we're moving!" John said rapidly into his mike. "Eastward . . . heading eastward." He pounded after his friend, fearing for him, angered by Luther's rash move.

Phil Goff was too busy to answer. His people were maneuvering toward the hut, putting out suppressing fire, keeping the suspect occupied, unaware their target was gone. There had been no return fire for a while. But something was in the hut, evidenced by the silhouette of the suspect's long-barreled rifle. Maybe we got 'im, the leader thought.

Norman stopped suddenly near a tree, looked to his right, and caught a glimpse of mottled color cutting toward him on an intercept. He swore under his breath, fear openly pushing him now, each direction he chose to run suddenly cut off. He was breathing hard, bent over, looking for a way out. He had all but forgotten about Luther now. All he wanted to do was disappear, but that simply wasn't happening.

He struck the tree beside him with his fist, hammering the solid trunk. This was not the way it was supposed to happen! He threw another glance back the way he had come, but lost the trail. God-damn trees all look the same, he thought. He flipped a mental coin, and pushed off.

John stopped, out of breath, controlling his rising anger, and more than a little afraid. He'd lost Luther in the gloom, unable to keep up with his infiltration into the trees. He had to keep looking. "This is Paraletto," he called in to Phil. "Luther's off to the east. I've lost him in the woods."

"What!" the leader shot back. Sounds of the assault carried over his radio. "Well, find him, John. We're a little busy right at the moment!"

"This is just what the hell I need," John replied, and started forward again, searching with his eyes, the safety off on his pistol.

One hundred sixty yards outside the village on the east side, J.D. caught movement in his scope. "Oh, man," he said, under his breath.

"Yeah, I see him, too," his spotter said beside him.

"Alpha, this is J.D.," he called in. "We have a county mountie walking around out here."

Phil listened to his sniper's call, just as his lead team reached the hooch. The sniper's announcement was unexpected. "Wait one, J.D." he replied. "Perfect," he said to himself. He looked over at the hut and saw Boomer Tanner waving at him, pumping his arm in the hurry-up signal. The shooting had stopped.

Boomer motioned quickly as Phil trotted up, noticing his men had redeployed, facing out from the hut. Something wasn't right.

"Couldn't say over the radio, boss," Boomer said. "You'd better look inside the hooch."

Phil walked around to the back of the elevated structure, its sap-

352

ling sides showing the damage from dozens of bullet strikes from the assault teams. The hut was ten by ten feet, its floor made of lashed-together poles on a level with his chin. The back of the structure was nothing more than a large floor-to-roof opening roughly five feet wide. Norman had been firing at them through the much narrower front entry.

Inside, two of Phil's men were crouched down, hovering over a camouflaged body turned up full length on its side. He could see numerous bullet strikes in the blood-soaked clothing.

"We have a problem, boss," one of them said, working on wiping the blood off the lower half of the corpse's face with a handkerchief. Phil could see most of the forehead was gone, an obvious high-velocity exit wound.

"This isn't Norman Bloodstone," Boomer said.

"Who the hell is he?" Phil demanded, a sudden very bad feeling descending over him.

"Got no way of knowing, but we didn't kill 'im. This poor bastard was dead before we got here. Look here, at the back of his head."

Phil leaned in closer and saw the entrance hole at the base of the skull. The realization came to him in a flash. "J.D.!" he all but shouted into his mike. "Describe this other cop!"

The sniper was still tracking the figure passing into and out of the mottle shade on the edge of the tree line, skirting the village, working his way south.

"Tan uniform, about six feet, carrying a shotgun," he said, then stopped. The man's face, partially blocked by heavy foliage, still was large enough in the magnified view of the scope sight. "Wait one . . . Something's not right there," and he saw the smudges along the chin line and down the side of the man's neck.

"Alpha, this guy looks like he had on camo paint . . . and tried to wipe it off."

"The son of a bitch suckered us," Phil said. Then to the sniper, he said, "That's Norman Bloodstone. The guy killed a local and switched clothes. You have the shot?"

J.D. held the crosshairs steady, smoothly traversing slowly, barely moving. It wasn't much, only square inches of open space at a time through the trees, but it was enough. "Roger that," he replied.

"Take it."

The sniper let out part of his breath slowly, held it, and touched the trigger.

The shot hit Bloodstone like a solid blow from a four-by-ten-inch board, slamming in through the intercostal space between the seventh and eighth ribs under his left arm and out the far side of his chest so fast it felt as if he had been hammered on both sides simultaneously.

It punched the breath out of him, and Norman tried to gasp, but all he felt was a peculiar numbness. His legs quivered, and he stumbled, a question forming, and then he was down on all fours, his chest heaving, trying to drag in air. He was hit and hurt, and he knew it all at once, and it was a revealing experience. A small corner of his brain disassociated itself from the situation and tried to explain it to him.

He didn't know it, but the shot had been one in a million. The 168-grain-match bullet exited the barrel at 2800 feet per second. It had entered between the ribs at a slight back-to-front angle, not fracturing anything. But that's when the physics of wound ballistics took over. A high-velocity .308 caliber projectile will yaw left or right within ten to fourteen inches once it strikes the target. This tumbling effect causes a large, temporary wound channel that can devastate surrounding soft tissue and incapacitate the target. Often the round exits the body backwards. But it didn't happen here.

The bullet itself had a tiny hollow cavity at its tip, the result of the construction process. When it struck Norman, the tip bent slightly, changing the line of travel. Spinning at over three thousand times per second and with a deformed nose, the bullet corkscrewed over the solid bone, following the curve of the rib, spiraling across Norman's chest in a millisecond to erupt from the front of his chest in front of his right arm. The bullet hadn't shed its velocity into the surrounding tissues to make a temporary wound channel, and the permanent track cut by the rapidly rotating bullet was confined to the surface of the chest cavity. Even the exit wound was no larger than an inch.

Under other circumstances he would have survived. Right at the moment, there was no pain, only the oddly centralized numbness. He remained on all fours and managed to suck in a breath, then another, and another . . .

Luther heard the solid boom of the sniper's shot and waited, weapon out, pausing in his hunt for the man. He listened to his radio earpiece for the follow-up, feeling how close he was to his target.

"Suspect's down," J.D. reported, "but I lost him in the brush. It was a good hit."

"Got it!" Phil replied. "We'll sweep the area. Start coming in on the position." He ordered his assault teams to reassemble and got them moving tactically again. They would report the body in the hut as soon as Norman was located and identified. "John, did you copy that last?" he called.

"Roger, Alpha," John answered, pausing in his own search. "I still can't raise Luther."

"Keep looking," the team leader said, more than irritated at the stupid move the civilian had made.

Norman managed to pull himself up to his feet, and gingerly touched the bullet holes, odd rips in the fabric, fascinated by the welling stains, unable to realize the import of the wounds. That part of his mind wasn't working too well. It's not so bad, he thought, finding that he could stand. He didn't know that his body was operating automatically, his central nervous system going into shock, priming itself for the pain to come. His brain attempted some damage control before the systems started to shut down on their own. The shock would only last a brief time, and that fact he did recognize.

Got to move, he told himself, and took a few steps, finding he could walk fairly well. He pressed his free hand against the larger wound on his front, feeling the blood spreading over the shirt to form rivulets that slid along his once elegant fingers. His beleaguered brain was fascinated by the feel of it, oblivious of the serious peril it represented to him.

Norman had left the shotgun behind, but he did take out Deputy Harrell's .45 pistol. He had taken it after donning her uniform. The other deputy's shirt had been too bloody to use. He turned the stainless-steel S&W in his hand, unfamiliar with the weapon, and flashed for an instant on her seminude body, lying back there on the tunnel floor. He found the rotating safety and thumbed it back and forth until he saw the small red dot exposed. "Must be off," he mumbled, and continued his slow steps.

John had worked his way far enough to see he was near the tree line, with open fields showing through. He was more relaxed, now that he knew Norman had been hit, but he wouldn't drop his guard until the body was identified. In the meantime he had to find Luther.

He stepped around the tree, and saw a man in a tan uniform standing there, not twenty feet away, hand clasped to his side, big-bore pistol pointed at him. Instinct older than training almost won as nerves fired off the message not to fire on the friendly target, but his conscious mind overrode that order, synapses leaping with the new command, knowing the uniformed man was not what he seemed to be. It all happened as fast as a blink, John's weapon snapping down, his finger squeezing the trigger. It took two one-hundredths of a second. It should have been quicker.

"Hi there," Norman said, his own weapon already leveled, the last word drowned out by the double blast from his .45, beating John's single shot, which burned past his left shoulder so close he heard the peculiar spinning burr of the bullet. Both of the killer's rounds hit the agent right of center, smashing blows, knocking him back and down into blackness even before he felt the pain.

Norman stood for a few seconds, not believing his luck. They had almost walked right into each other. "Stupid, stupid," he chanted, and started toward the fallen figure. "Better make sure with this one," he said.

• • •

They all heard the shots, the flat double pop of the .45, the sharper crack of the 10 mm. Phil silently gave his commands, and his people fanned out. The team leader's bad feeling had just gotten worse.

Luther heard the shots too. For him they were sharp and loud, a little to his left, not far. He worked his way cautiously but quickly toward the sound. He knew who it was.

He kept to cover, and saw the two figures, John lying on the ground, Norman approaching him slowly, hand outstretched, pointing the big pistol down. . . .

There is a difference between those who have done it for real and those who only play the game. In reality there is no posturing, no game-playing, no warning line uttered just as the bad guy turns around, no snapping of fingers, no sound. That sort of fantasy is left to the movie heroes, who always win. In the real world, for those who have actually done it, not for some wanna-be, the routine is aim, fire, and kill him, just as quickly as you can. That is the reality.

Luther brought up the pistol, both hands wrapped around it, steadying it, and tightened his grip a fraction, keying the laser sight. The red beam centered on Norman's chest, a fraction above the third button of the uniform shirt, going for center mass. He fired twice, double-tapping his shots. Both rounds hit solid, the 200-grain hollow-points tearing into Norman's chest two inches apart.

The first did the major damage. It blasted between the killer's lungs, was deflected by the shattered sternum, angled upward over the heart, and clipped through his spine at the eighth cervical vertebra. The second shot ripped a one-inch hole in the edge of his left lung, missed the descending curve of the aorta by a tenth of an inch, and punched out his back, mushrooming exactly as the manufacturer said it would, blowing out a ragged three-inch exit hole.

Norman's mind had a millisecond to register the overwhelming cascade of pain that flash-burned through him before everything went completely and totally black. His forward momentum sent him tumbling into a jumbled heap. His legs were gone, useless, numb, unable to support the body that lay twisted and bleeding in the dirt.

Luther saw the two bullet strikes, saw Norman pitch down in the sudden relaxed way that signified a hard hit, and then ignored him. He whirled instead toward the fallen form of his friend in time to hear John curse, cutting off his cry.

"God-*damn*, that hurts!" the big man said, biting his lower lip, rolling slowly into a sitting position, clutching a hand to his right side. He levered himself up, sucking in deep breaths, fighting against the roundhouse-punch effect of the two bullets. Luther looked on, astonished, until he realized why his friend was still alive.

"Son of a bitch if I didn't break some ribs!" John muttered angrily, then realized he was alive. He looked up at Luther in sheepish surprise, and managed a bleak smile. He started to unbutton his fatigue shirt, revealing the Second Chance vest beneath it. He looked in wonder at the rents from the impact of the two rounds from Norman's pistol, and shook his head. "Damn if this vest didn't work," he said slowly, his breathing returning to normal.

Luther, sure seconds ago that his friend was dead, offered his hand, and asked the obvious, "You all right?"

John took his hand, and struggled to his feet with some difficulty. He held on to his side, gingerly exploring up and down, wincing with each new discovery. "Yeah," he finally announced, "I think so, but my ribs are definitely broken."

The agent gazed back at Luther with the full knowledge of how close he had come to the edge once again. Then he turned and saw the crumpled form. The radio was alive with calls from Phil, then other voices as more questions were shouted over the net.

John said simply into the tiny mike, "Suspect's down," then to Luther, "That's it, man." Recriminations over his friend's sudden fade into the bush would wait, and maybe never be voiced. His anger suddenly carried little importance.

Luther stared at Norman's body while John bent over slowly to retrieve his weapon from the ground where he had dropped it. Without further word, they walked slowly up to the quiet form.

Norman lay on his right side, pinning that arm beneath him. His left arm was thrown awkwardly backwards, the long fingers splayed, touching the red ground. Both legs were twisted oddly, one foot toe up, the other parallel to the dirt.

Dark wine-red blood had spray-patterned itself down his right side and back, soaking the stolen uniform shirt. It ran and pooled around his waist, edging out from beneath his pinned arm.

Slow rivulets flowed from the entrance wounds in his chest, one dark and welling up slowly, the other pumping freely but spasmodically, the small bubbles indicative of a lung shot. In the back, the exit wound of the second shot pushed a white shard of bone through the large rip in the fabric, more dark red blood oozing through. A trace of pink crystalline bubbles, laced with threads of bright red, trickled out of the killer's slack mouth.

Luther squatted down near the figure's head as John holstered his own weapon, and picked up the .45 from where it had fallen, several feet beyond Norman's body. He immediately cleared it, palming the magazine and the round from the breech.

Luther looked dispassionately at Norman's closed eyes, then reached out with his left hand, placing his fingertips along the jugular on the side of the neck. He felt a faint, erratic pulse, almost subliminal, but there nevertheless. He looked closer at the bruised and dirty face, and saw the hesitant intake of shallow breath.

Luther made no sound, no utterance, no expression at all. Without even thinking about it, he pressed the muzzle of his pistol behind Norman's left ear. A hand touched his shoulder, and he heard John say, "Let it go, Lute."

He stopped the trigger squeeze, turning his face up to look at John, who shook his head back and forth. Luther held the slight tension on the trigger, never wavering, and turned back to Norman. "No prisoners, Johnny," he said softly, yet still held it back.

They heard a quiet step, and J.D. and his spotter appeared, the sniper covering the scene with his weapon. When they saw the setup, J.D. lifted the rifle, cradling it in his arms. His spotter dropped the MP-5 muzzle down, safety on. They were out of this part of it.

"It's your call, man," John said to Luther. "Can you live with it?"

Their eyes met, and Luther's decision passed between them.

"Yes," he said, "I can," and pulled the trigger.

The shot cracked loudly in the enclosed space, but Norman's head never moved. The copper-jacketed projectile drilled clean through the lower half of his brain, exiting out the frontal lobe, and exploded through his right orbital cavity, destroying the deformed cat's eye. That too, was reality.

John, the man in charge, looked over at the HRT sniper team. "May as well put it on the record," he said. "J.D., what did you see?"

The long gunner passed a look at his partner, who nodded, then at the body on the ground, and back. "The suspect died in a hail of gunfire, sir, resisting arrest."

"Done," John said, closing the issue. "Report it."

MAY 5, DULLES INTERNATIONAL AIRPORT, WASHINGTON, D.C.

Allen Parkman sat in the booth in the terminal lounge, wondering when Dana would arrive, trying not to look anxiously around at imagined, or real, police. He felt distinctly uncomfortable, slightly disoriented from too many hours on his feet. Now he was exposed, out in the open, but it was necessary, he knew. He needed to be here, where she would see him, where they had agreed to rendezvous.

He wore an off-the-rack Haggar suit with enough of his former self-esteem to disdain the feel of it, the cheapness, but this, too, was part of the plan. It was important to him, looking around for the hundredth time, for this meeting to proceed according to plan. When Dana appeared, he figured, things were going to get out of hand immediately. He hoped no one else would get hurt in the melee that was sure to follow. His stomach churned, surprising him despite the queasy aftertaste, considering the minimal amount of decent food he had managed to get down into it in the last few days.

Allen tried to appear normal, but gave up the effort in nervous disgust. Dana's appearance out of the crowd almost caused him to cry out. "God, Dana, don't sneak up on me like that!" he whispered hoarsely. He scooted farther into his side of the booth as she slid in across from him.

"Allen," she said, alarm in her voice, "are you all right?" He looked terrible, she thought, his eyes haunting from a face that was gray with fatigue. He had aged ten years since she had last seen him.

Her question amused him, and he almost laughed, but was afraid of what strange noise might actually burst out of his mouth. He studied her, amazed at her own transformation, deliberately done, of course. She wore expensive high-top running shoes, stone-washed jeans, and a bulky ivory cotton sweater. She had retained the short wig and had added clear glasses with small round rims. The disguise made her look younger; she could have passed herself off as a college student.

Not as a murderess, Allen reminded himself. He shook it off. To business, Counselor, he said silently, forgetting her question. "Are we set?" he asked, striving for calmness. "Passports, shot records, luggage?" It was as if he were reciting dialogue from a script. In a way he was, he realized.

"Yes, love, I'm ready," she replied, curiosity pinching her fine brows together. His voice sounded too tight, on edge. "And you?" she added.

"Ready as I can be," he said, and she saw it again, the furtiveness slipping out.

He's really going to hell, she thought, beginning to feel uncomfortable this close to him. He kept darting looks around, and she was sure his behavior would give them away. Dana considered what lay ahead for them, wishing he would snap out of it, but it was too late to be rid of him now, and she still needed him. A few more hours, dear girl, that's all. Just keep him together that long. Then . . .

"I've been careful to look for tails," Allen said, much too quickly, and now she felt uneasy again. She shifted in her seat, wondering what was wrong with him, already rethinking her options.

"There don't appear to be any, but you never know," he finished, looking about.

"Look," she said, wanting to get started. "We're just a few minutes away from the first boarding call. I'll proceed down to the gate and get checked in. It's easy now, my darling," she said reassuringly, hoping her words and sincerity would help.

Allen reached across the table suddenly and grasped her wrist. He let go quickly, but not before she had felt the power in his grip, the strength. His eyes were bright, shiny, and sad, all at the same time. Then he withdrew his hand, glancing around as if the touch had burned him. No one seemed at all interested in the two of them.

"Can't be too careful," he admonished, almost mumbling, his eyes downcast.

Dana stood up to leave. "I'll see you aboard, Allen," she said, her instincts telling her to run from him, all but shouting it in her ear. Instead, she forced herself to turn casually and walk away.

Don't look back, she told herself, but of course she had to. He remained sitting there, watching her, hands below the table. She turned around, and stumbled straight into a gentleman in a dark suit. Dana started to apologize, waiting for the man to move aside, as expected. But he stepped closer, and his hand came up, holding something before her face.

"Dana Quinn," he said. It sounded like a statement, and her mind shouted against the image her eyes took in, the laminated card with the picture, and the words on it.

"Gerald Pierce, FBI," he said, and reality slammed into her, shattering her fabled control, smashing into her with a brightness that hurt. Dana's stomach lurched upward once, then contracted coldly into a painful knot. She turned to find her way blocked by two more men—big men, incredibly tall and solid, their faces impassive even as they clamped their hands around her arms. While Pierce was still reading her her rights, she started to turn toward Allen. Yes, Allen would help her, she told herself, forcing down the rising panic.

But they threw her face down on the floor in a controlled, painful lock of hands and legs and arms, roughly forcing her hands behind her back, cuffing them together. She twisted her head, searching for Allen. He would help her, he would fight them off, he would save her . . .

And he was there, standing now. Another man was beside him, the two of them watching silently, letting it go on, and he wasn't coming to her aid, wasn't moving at all. She saw his face clearly, and his deception was suddenly obvious. Then she screamed, the name ripping out of her as she was lifted off of the floor: "Allen!" Her glasses were thrown off, her wig was askew, the men were holding her unnecessarily tight. She couldn't run, couldn't fight them, the shock had drained her, numbing any desire to even move.

Passengers stood fascinated, some in fear, small children suddenly turned away by their parents from the sight of the poor woman. Staring eyes followed her, wondering what . . . why . . . ?

She was dragged right past Allen, but still he did nothing but look back at her. And his eyes . . . There was something about his eyes, and it became of immense importance that she figure out that look he gave her, but in a cold stab of terrible insight she realized she would have plenty of time to wonder about that look. Forever, in fact.

"Testifying should be fairly straightforward," the agent said to Allen, who turned away from the sight of Dana, not wanting to see any more of her. But he heard her, or imagined he did. And then even the sound of her voice was gone.

The other agent, Gerald Pierce, stopped near Allen. "Are you all right?" he asked, only because it seemed appropriate. What he knew about Allen Parkman's involvement didn't warrant any particular compassion. Guilt was guilt.

Allen took a deep breath, one part of the ordeal over. "I suppose," he said, feeling only emptiness. How had it all gone so wrong? Did it matter now? It wasn't important anymore. It was over, for him.

"Look at it this way, Allen," the other agent said, unable to resist the black humor of the situation. "You're going to enjoy Idaho. By the way, do you fish?"

Allen stood mesmerized, depleted by what he had witnessed, what he had done, and the agent's question took a few seconds to register. "Wha . . . what did you say?" he responded absently.

"You know, fly fishing?" the agent said, motioning with a flick of his wrist. "I hear the steelhead go crazy this time of the year."

He and Pierce fell in beside Allen, and walked with him out of the terminal.

EPILOGUE

The Bell Jet Ranger lifted off with Steve Drexler and two of his agents on board. The rotors' downwash created small dust clouds to whirl up from the tarmac. The noise of the departing helo temporarily masked the heavier whomping of the two inbound National Guard Hueys. The Jet Ranger tilted its nose down as it accelerated up in a curving line toward the final site of the manhunt.

The UH-1s descended and settled behind the phalanx of police vehicles still forming the perimeter. Roving minicams and reporters waited impatiently, thoughts of deadlines ticking away, each team wanting to be the first to speak to the man who had killed the killer.

Camouflaged figures climbed out from the craft, ducking away from the spinning rotor blades, Phil Goff and his people forming into groups of two and three men, shepherding John and Luther between them, protecting them without any deliberate thought. Behind them, the helicopters lifted off and pounded away. They had more work to do.

Luther and the rest trooped across the parking lot while other professionals started the final procedures to wrap up the incident. Word had gone out over the net, and they all knew now. They had suffered casualties, and that hurt, and procedures would be redefined to avoid it next time. Still, some of them took the time to wave at the man with the beard as he passed with the others.

Luther acknowledged them when he could, but made no show of it. It was over. He saw Jackie waiting beside the white news truck, and one of her reporters politely stepped away as the group approached.

John stopped and gestured toward some uniformed officers. Immediately they cleared a spot around the couple, keeping the others at bay. They all knew who Luther was, too.

Jackie started to say something, but forgot about it in a tumble of thoughts. Emotions swirled deep in her eyes, and he saw them. Questions, anger, fear, and concern all flickered past in the space of a few heartbeats. Finally she resolved her predicament in the natural way. "Oh, Lute," she said, opening her arms and stepping toward him.

The center of his chest tightened as his arms encircled her. Her forehead burrowed into his shoulder, prompting him to pull her closer. "Hey, babe," he started to say, gently, and felt her arms tighten. "Hey," he said again, frustrated that that was all that came out, wanting to say more.

"Please," she said, "talk to me, Lute. I need to know . . ."

Her tone triggered his response, almost by instinct, remembered from distant times, other confrontations, and his guard went up immediately. And almost as quickly, he regretted the way it came out: "Who wants the story?" he said, and pulled away from her. "You or them?" He pointed down the line, where groups of reporters had gathered, eager to get on with their work.

His remark stung, but she chose not to play that old game. The way he said it and the look in his eyes hurt her. She had expected to see one thing but saw something else instead. Understanding dawned slowly, and it made perfect sense, as she knew it would. "No," she began, "they can get their own story tonight. This one's for me only." Her blue eyes picked up a smile, and she stared back at him, teasing him with her sudden understanding.

Her response made him uncomfortable, but he didn't look away. He challenged her instead, needing to hear her say it. "Why?" The question, simply put, didn't have a simple answer, and they both knew it.

She firmly took hold of his hands, but remained at arm's length. " 'Why' can ask a lot of things. It can also get a lot of answers. I've got a few answers, but I think you already know what they are."

She pressed on, going by feel, trusting in what was stirring inside her, way back in that special place reserved for the best things.

"Look, I don't know how all this came about, but I think we should just let it go, and trust in it. I think it's worth trying again." It all sounded like rambling gibberish to her, even as she said it. *And if I think that's what it is, what must he think?* But she let it go, because it felt right, and the dam cracked open a little more.

She shook her red hair, and her eyes searched his. "You asked why," Jackie began again, slower this time. "The only thing that I can say, standing here, is that I'm supposed to be here just now. I don't know why it should be this way for us, but it feels right. Something's changed."

His eyes reflected his answer, and his smile confirmed it. "And I thought it was just me, Jackie." He wondered if she could see what he was feeling, the sense of returning. He reached out a hand, and touched her cheek. "It's all right. We've both been changing. If things hadn't been so crazy around here, maybe I'd have seen it sooner with you. Lord knows, I've been dealing with all of it for a long time." He took a deep breath, let it out slowly.

"And after today, after all this"—he jerked a thumb toward the controlled mayhem going on around them—"I really think it's come full circle, me and the old demons, and I've broken it. It's over, Jackie," and his arms went around her waist and tightened, just a little, and his eyes smiled back. "But not us. We're just starting, aren't we? There's something here, isn't there?" He let the question hang out there, waiting for her reply, because that was the way it was going to be.

She looked back at him, and saw it. Not the desperation and the anger she expected, but the resolution, and that other thing. His gaze was steady, not furtive. The wall was gone. There were remnants of whatever he had gone through today, and she realized she wanted to hear about it, about all of it. But that could wait. First she had to answer him, and her answer was the only issue remaining between them.

"I don't know," she said back, the apprehension tinting her reply. "Do you want something to happen?"

He studied her for a long moment before answering. "The last time, things didn't work out so hot, you know."

"That was before the new you."

366

"Not so new, not after today."

"Look, Lute," she said, needling him a little. "You're not the only one who can change," realizing the truth of it the instant she said it.

"This could be very dangerous," he said.

She leaned back a little and tilted her head to one side in the old, familiar way. "I don't think so," she said, her eyes smiling, "not this time." Her voice softened with concern. "Besides, you look like you could use a shoulder right about now."

She let the pause run just long enough. "What do you think?"

Luther slowly and deliberately looked her up and down, letting the feelings continue to swirl around, scared, yet sure at the same time. "Great boobs," he said, finally, harking back to their first meeting, another lifetime ago.

"Old line," she responded, yet pleased that he remembered it.

"It's a start," he said, pulling her closer.

"Uh-uh," she said, shaking her head. Her eyes held his. "New start."

He flushed, embarrassed, and looked over her shoulder for John. The space behind her was empty. John had eyes, too.

"God, I could use a drink," he sighed.

Startled, she pulled back, the brightness in her eyes dimming. "I thought that you didn't . . ." she began before his fingers quieted her lips.

"I don't anymore, not for a long time. Which is not to say I don't think about it, but that, too, is part of the deal. But I could spring for a couple of Cokes."

Jackie relaxed a little. "Where do you want to go?"

"Someplace where there aren't people with guns and badges, and the smell of"—he looked around—"all this. First, though, I want to see Mikki, check on her, you know."

She knew, and squeezed his hand. "I do, too."

Luther looked around at all of the cameras and reporters still jockeying for position. "We may have to fight our way out first," he added.

"No more fighting today," Jackie replied. "But leave the reporters to me. I can handle this situation. This is my turf," she said, taking his arm and turning him to leave.

Luther slid his arm around her waist. "Okay, and after that, maybe I can get in to see Gordon. Bring him up to date, let him know it's all over."

Still taking care of his people, she thought. "Of course," she answered. "We have time." All the time we need, again, she thought, as they headed into the crowd.

NE   1/02